Honor Versus Lies

Also by Judy McGonagill

The Widow Jane Parker

The River Rider

The Twelve Mile School

Honor Versus Lies

Honor Versus Lies

HEARTS OF TEXAS,
BOOK FOUR

JUDY MCGONAGILL

EDITED BY
PHYLLIS ROSALEZ

Dedicated to my longtime friend and superb editor, Phyllis Ann Heath Rosalez.

The word *honorable* has to do with people and actions that are honest, fair, and worthy of respect.

The word *liar* is someone who tells lies. So, a liar is someone who often tells falsehoods, especially if it works to his or her advantage.

Chapter One

Clink, scrape, clink, scrape! The sound floated in the hot wind but had not yet reached the man in the buggy.

The early October sun beat down on the man, causing sweat to trickle from under his wide-brimmed straw hat. Droplets of sweat ran down his broad back in small rivulets, staining his white shirt. Trenton Zachery Sanderson, Trent to family and friends, drove his sleek, black buggy in a southwesterly direction out of Amarillo, Texas, toward the ranch headquarters. A trip of about eight miles as the crow flies. In this flat, open country, a buggy or horseman could take more or less the same path. Trent was normally a man of good nature, but today, he felt a bit downcast, as once again, he had failed to find a housekeeper and cook.

"Damn it anyway, Helen! Accounts of your cantankerous behavior have spread far and wide. No woman within a hundred miles is willing to come out here and put up with your sharp tongue," he grumbled aloud as he permitted the team of horses to plod along.

Yes, Helen was becoming a rock around his neck in many ways, but he loved her despite her ill-tempered ways and tongue as sharp as a two-edged sword. If he faced the life she faced, he might be a bit on the cranky side himself, Trent lamented. Damn shame what happened to her in the accident, but sometimes, a person just needed to pick up the pieces and go on with life as best as they could. He knew Helen didn't really mean half of the hateful things she flung at him or anyone within earshot. Her voice had always been harsh in nature. One of those voices, a bit loud for a lady. It just naturally carried a piercing sharpness.

Most folks misunderstood the tone of Helen's voice, but her irritable disposition was her own doing. He had tried time and again to explain to her that folks just didn't like being talked to in a degrading manner and didn't have to put up with her hatefulness. Helen would just give him one of her piercing stares. If she said anything in response to his lectures, it was not fit to be repeated in public.

What am I going to do now? he wondered. Helen needed a certain amount of help with her personal body care. He had to run the ranch as well as cook, clean the house, do a little laundry, and on and on. It was just too much for one man to handle for the long haul. It was hard enough between help that came and went faster than tumbleweeds blowing across the open plains.

Some folks had suggested he put Helen away in a home and get on with his own life. He had thought about it but just couldn't bring himself to do it. Somehow, he had to manage, he told himself for the hundredth time.

He pulled back on the reins to halt the horses. Trent stepped down from the buggy and stretched to relieve the tension in his muscles. Just thinking about the situation that waited for him at home made his muscles ache. Then he heard an odd sound that diverted his attention.

Clink, scrape, clink, scrape!

Trent cocked his head in the direction he had heard the curious noise and listened intently. Then it came again.

Clink, scrape, clink, scrape!

Trent stood perfectly still. His eyes scanned the distance to where heaven and earth met. In this flat country, there was little of nothing to interrupt his view except for the small stand of scrubby mesquite trees to his left, blocking his view of what might be causing the peculiar sound.

Trent stood a bit over six feet, lean but muscular, and had a thick head of dark brown hair streaked with flaxen highlights from not always wearing a hat while working out in the sun. His piercing golden-brown eyes sometimes gave the impression he could look into a person's soul. Women found him quite handsome. Trent spent little time dwelling on his looks. He maintained a clean-cut appearance, and that was all that concerned him.

He took long, quiet strides, leading the horses to the nearest tree where he tethered them. He walked softly through the small clump of trees, not wanting his presence to be detected until he reached a vantage point where he could see what was making the curious sound. He halted, listened, and then spotted a lad with a shovel trying to dig a hole. A lump wrapped in a faded, threadbare blanket lay on the ground nearby. Trent supposed it held the remains of a dead person.

The boy looked to be in his middle teens. He also looked as though he had missed a few meals. Dirty blondish hair hung limply from beneath his hat, and his filthy, baggy clothes looked much the worse for wear. Trent knew he would still be digging three days from now to get a grave dug in this particular spot. It was just a rocky hill with some of the hardest dirt on the entire ranch.

Clink, scrape, clink, scrape! The sound continued, yielding little results. Each dip of the shovel produced scarcely more than a cupful of dirt and rocks.

Trent supposed the dilapidated wagon he could see down the hill near the creek belonged to the lad and his family. He watched the activity beside the old wagon. There appeared to be four children, but he didn't see any adults. Maybe someone was inside the wagon, he hoped. From what he could see, they were a disheveled-looking bunch. The two scrawny horses looked like they might drop in their tracks instead of making a trip to God knows where, Trent thought.

He had an uneasy feeling in his gut. He should get back in his buggy and head on home. It would likely be wise to leave this bunch to their own doings. In his gut, he also knew he was not the kind of man to leave such a pathetic-looking bunch to fate, especially on his ranch.

Trent stepped out of the clump of trees.

"Son, you're still going to be digging that grave three days from now in this spot," he said in a normal tone, trying not to frighten the lad.

The boy whirled around and drew back the shovel as he took a defensive stance. The lad stared at Trent with huge blue eyes that carried a distrustful look.

"No need for that," Trent nodded toward the shovel. "I'm Trent Sanderson, owner of this ranch, the Flatland Ranch."

The boy still held his defensive position as he stared at Trent.

"I reckon you're intending to dig a grave, but I'm telling you, this isn't the best place. In fact, this is about the rockiest hill and the hardest dirt on the entire ranch. There's a small cemetery near headquarters where we can bury your—?" He left the sentence unfinished, hoping the boy would tell him who was wrapped in the old blanket.

The boy still stared at Trent as though deciding whether to believe him or not. Finally, he spoke in a subdued voice. "It's our pa."

"I'm mighty sorry for your loss," Trent said sympathetically.

The boy snorted. "'Tweren't much of a loss even if he was our pa."

That bold statement certainly took Trent by surprise. "What do you mean by that?" he asked out of curiosity.

"I mean, about all he was good fur was causin' our ma and us young'uns trouble and givin' Ma another baby about every year. She was so wore out from havin' babies it finally kilt her too."

Trent was startled at that news but felt compelled to ask, "How long ago did your mother pass?"

"'Tweren't too long after we started to Texas. I guess about three, maybe four weeks ago. The baby died, too. Two or three died bein' born, and two more died of the flu," he said, with a trace of sadness in his voice. "Now 'tis just the five of us left. We're goin' to Mason County to some of Pa's kinfolk."

Trent removed his hat and ran his fingers through his sweaty hair. He looked at the remains wrapped in the blanket. He replaced his hat and looked at the boy once more. "What happened to your pa?"

The boy shrugged slightly. "Don't rightly know. He got an awful hurtin' in his side about three days ago and just lay in the wagon moanin'. Wouldn't eat nothin' and hardly drank anything. I wanted to take him to Amarillo to a doctor, but he wouldn't have it." The boy paused and shrugged again. "Just after noon, he just let out a loud moan, and that was the last we heard. He was gone," he finished in a somber tone.

"So, you mean to tell me both of your parents are dead, and it's just you and those other four kids left on your own," Trent said, not hiding his dismay at their pathetic circumstances. It was several hundred miles to Mason County. This bunch would never make it in that old wagon with that broken-down team of horses. He would also bet they didn't have two nickels to rub together.

"Yeah, that's about the size of it," the kid said with little emotion.

Trent stood staring at the boy, thinking the kid had not fully grasped the enormity of their situation. He cleared his throat. "I believe we better load your pa's body in the wagon, and you follow me to the ranch headquarters. I'll have a couple of the ranch hands dig a grave first thing tomorrow."

Before he could say anything else, the kid interrupted. "Me and Timothy'll dig the grave for Pa."

Trent saw the proud look on the lad's face. That was fine with him. Let them dig the grave and bury their dead. What worried him was what came after that. Where would they go in a wagon that looked as though it might not even make it the next few miles to headquarters? From this distance, he could plainly see the other children looked as skinny and as unkempt as this one; how would they survive?

"Go bring the wagon up here, and I'll get my buggy. The younger kids can ride with me, so they don't have to be in the wagon with your pa's body."

The boy did not answer. He simply took his shovel and headed down the hill.

Trent walked through the mesquites to retrieve his team of horses and buggy. What was he going to do? If Helen weren't enough of a problem, now he had five orphans dumped on him to boot.

Trent was not a particularly religious man, but on occasion, he found calling on the Lord for help somehow seemed to ease matters, even if it wasn't always in the manner he had hoped.

When they loaded the dead man into the old wagon, it was the next oldest boy who climbed into the driver's seat. The older boy helped the three younger kids into Trent's buggy. Rather, he tried to help them, but his little sister clung to his neck and wouldn't let go until he threatened to smack her if she didn't get in beside her brothers.

"By the way," Trent finally asked, "what are your names?"

All eyes turned to the older boy.

"I'm Sam. Timothy is next; he's twelve." Sam nodded to the wagon driver. "This is Nathan; he'll be ten next month. Daniel, he's seven. Our little sister, Martha, is four."

"How old are you, Sam?"

Sam lifted his chin slightly, "I'm almost seventeen."

"How close to seventeen?" Trent asked.

Sam never wavered. "In two months."

Trent just nodded his head, thinking what a responsibility had been dumped on a sixteen-year-old kid.

"Just one girl out of the bunch, huh," Trent commented, more for something to say.

Martha opened her mouth to say something but was quickly hushed by Sam. "Martha, just mind your talkin' and don't cause no trouble. I'll be right behind you, and if I see any misbehavin', I'll tan your backside good," Sam scolded his little sister.

Trent assumed the children were accustomed to their older brother acting as a parent since their ma had passed.

They plodded along toward headquarters at a slow pace so the wagon could keep up.

When they pulled up in front of the house, Trent saw Helen looking out through the front window. Just as they reached the porch, the door flew open, and Helen yelled at the top of her voice.

"Gosh all mighty, Trent, it was bad enough when you brought wounded animals and that mangy, limp-legged dog home. But look what you've come dragging in here this time!" Her anger was all too apparent from the red flush on her face, emphasizing her fury.

Trent felt his temper rise. "That's enough, Helen! These youngsters need some help, and we're giving it to them! Their pa is lying dead out in their wagon, and their ma died about a month ago." He hoped that bit of information would soften Helen's attitude.

"Don't count me in on any helping! They aren't anything to us," she spat back in her hateful tone.

She looked toward the empty buggy. "Where's the help you went after?"

"I couldn't find anyone fool enough to come out here to put up with your ill temper!" he answered in exasperation.

Helen looked at the five wide-eyed children listening to their exchange. The little girl was half hiding behind her older brother and clinging to his leg as though for protection from her. Good, she hoped they were all scared to death and would be on their way first thing in the morning. She scowled in disgust.

Trent saw the look of fright on each of the children's faces. He would likely be scared, too, listening to Helen rant. Her unkempt look didn't help either. He noticed her scraggly hair didn't look as though it had been brushed lately, and the pallor of her skin gave her a ghostlike appearance. The old dress she was wearing just hung on her gaunt frame, and it had seen better days. He had tried to interest her in getting some new clothes, but to no avail.

"Just go back to your room because they're coming in and spending the night right here in the house," Trent informed her with a firmness he rarely used with Helen. He hated to be harsh with her, but sometimes, she pushed him to his limit of patience, and this was one of those times.

The five children stood stark still, looking wide-eyed from one adult to the other.

Helen whirled her wheelchair around and pushed it as fast as possible to her room. She slammed the door with such vehemence the windows rattled. For several moments, there was silence throughout the house.

Finally, Sam spoke. "Mister, we can sleep in the barn just as good as in the house if you want."

Trent looked at the five pathetic, scared children. "No, you can sleep upstairs," he said in a calm manner as he nodded toward the house.

Once inside, Trent pointed out the stairs leading up to what he called the loft, but it actually led to two big bedrooms over the center of the house. Downstairs, you entered the west-facing house into a wide central hallway. A large door on the left led to an enormous living room with grand furniture. Two large sofas and several high-backed plush chairs covered in elegant royal blue and gold-patterned fabric were arranged near the huge rock fireplace that dominated the front wall with large windows on either side. A piano sat against the far wall, flanked by more large windows. Double doors led to a formal dining room with a table that could easily seat a dozen or more people. An elegant hutch with glass doors on the upper half dominated one wall. Inside the glass doors were beautiful dishes trimmed in gold and gleaming stemmed glasses. In the hallway, Helen's room was on the right. Trent's office was near the stairs, and the last door on the right led to the room Trent now used. A door led out of the hallway into the dining room, with another door leading into the large kitchen where they took their meals. Beyond the kitchen were a sizeable pantry and the bathing room. There were covered porches extending across the front and back of the house. It was the biggest and most grand house Sam and the other kids had ever seen.

The children looked curiously at everything but did not touch a thing. Sam was keeping a close watch on what they were doing, and they all knew Sam would sternly reprimand anyone who dared touch anything.

"We have a room just for bathing and a big tin tub. We'll put a couple of buckets of cold water and one bucket of hot water in it, and when everyone is finished bathing, we just pull the stopper, and the dirty bath water runs out through a long hose to the garden," Trent explained.

The five children looked at one another as though they hadn't quite understood what the man had just said.

Trent read their questioning expressions.

Sam was the first to speak. "We ain't ever seen a room just for bathin' or a tin tub either. We just bathe in a number three washtub about twice a month."

Trent didn't find that hard to believe from the looks of them or their smell, now that they were in a more confined space. "Well, you'll feel better once you've had a good bath. Do you have a change of clothes so those can be washed tomorrow?"

"Yes sir, but they is about as dirty as these," Timothy answered.

Trent rubbed his forehead to ease the tension that was beginning to take hold. "Well, put back on your dirty underwear, and we'll try to wash everything else tomorrow."

"I'll see what I can rustle up for supper, and then you can each take a bath before turning in."

"Mister, I know how to scramble eggs and make biscuits if that sounds all right for supper?" Sam offered.

Trent smiled. "That sounds just fine." He directed the five to the back porch to wash their hands and arms in the pan of water kept on the washstand with the bar of lye soap lying nearby.

Much to Trent's surprise, the biscuits were flaky and delicious. The eggs were cooked just the way he liked them. He poured milk for the children and took a tray to Helen's room. When he entered, she neither looked at nor spoke to him as he sat the tray on a small table near the window. Trent left without saying anything, either.

When they finished eating, Sam looked at Trent. "Excuse me, sir, what did you say the name of your ranch is?"

"Flatland," Trent answered as he swallowed his last spoonful of eggs.

Sam let out a snorting chuckle. "You sure picked the right name for this place. This is the flattest country I've ever seen."

The three younger boys laughed at Sam's remark. Martha joined in, her sky-blue eyes sparkling, although it was doubtful she really knew why they were laughing.

Trent chuckled, too. "Actually, it was my father who named the ranch. He and one of my uncles came here from the hills of Tennessee to settle and build the ranch. I think he must have felt about the same way you do, considering the name."

"Reckon why he picked here?" Sam ventured.

"That is a rather long story," Trent answered. "I think it'll have to wait for another day," he said as he left the table.

He showed Sam how to work the water pump and put a big pan of water on the stove to warm. Once the bath water was ready, Trent found three towels for the five to share.

He then found five clean quilts in his mother's old trunk for the children to use. After stacking the quilts at the bottom of the stairs, Trent retreated to his office to contemplate writing a letter to the newspaper in Lubbock and another to the newspaper in Wichita Falls, advertising for a housekeeper and cook. He poured himself a generous glass of whiskey to help soothe his lingering headache and calm his nerves from worrying about what to do with five orphans. He had heard there were homes for orphans, but he didn't know where any were. Maybe he should write to the sheriff at the county seat of Mason County to locate their family. He smiled to himself. *I don't even know their last name. Guess it would be a good start to find out who to contact,* he decided as he started the first letter to the newspaper.

After he finished the letters, he rose to go ask Sam their last name, when he realized the house was quiet. He decided to go check to see what kind of mess might have been left in the kitchen and bathing room. Much to his surprise, the kitchen was spotless, and the damp dishtowel hung neatly over the edge of the sink. The door to the bathing room was left open. He entered, holding the lamp high so he could survey the room. Once again, he was pleased to see no water on the floor, the tub was clean, and two of the three towels were hung neatly over the edge of the tub. The third towel, still clean, remained on the chair.

Trent walked to his own room, undressed except for his underdrawers, and quickly fell asleep. His last thought was a reminder to ask Sam about their last name tomorrow.

All the children slept soundly except Sam. How would they make it all the way to Mason County in that dilapidated old wagon with those two old, worn-out horses? Pa's pockets had only yielded two dollars and three nickels. Sam tried to hold back the tears, but they burst forth from sorrow and weariness as worry consumed the sixteen-year-old.

Trent rousted the children out before daylight. He had cooked breakfast and told Sam and Timothy he would let Biggun, his longtime friend and trustworthy ranch hand, know they were going to help around the barn and barnyard after they buried their pa. "You'll have to keep the three younger kids with you and make sure they don't get into trouble," he warned Sam.

Much to the children's relief, that mean, cantankerous Helen had not reappeared since closing herself in her room the night before. They each hoped to make it outside without seeing her this morning.

Sam assured Trent there would be no trouble with the younger kids, and they would help Biggun do whatever he told them needed doing.

"Is he big?" nine-year-old Nathan asked as he crammed his mouth full of eggs.

"He's a bit taller than me and bigger around, too," Trent answered with a smile.

Daniel and Nathan looked at one another with big eyes. "He must be a giant, like Goliath in the Bible," Daniel remarked in awe.

"Is he mean like Goliath?" Nathan asked as he swiped his mouth with his arm to remove the extra eggs that clung to the outside of his mouth and chin.

"No," Trent shook his head. "He's not mean, but he does expect you to follow his orders, and so do I."

The two younger boys exchanged another look of doubt. Before either could ask anything else, Sam put in, "Don't worry. They'll mind, or I'll whop their backside with Pa's old belt."

Trent studied Sam for a few seconds before pushing away from the table. "I'm sure they'll be fine. Do you think you can clean up the kitchen real good, like last night, before going out to the barn?"

"Yes, sir," Sam and Timothy answered in unison.

Trent smiled at Martha, who had sat quietly, looking from one brother to the other and listening during their meal. "How are you this morning, Miss Martha?" he asked with a teasing grin.

Martha looked at him with her sparkling blue eyes and then put her small hands over her pretty little mouth to suppress a giggle. "I fine," she managed, as she continued to snigger.

It seemed Martha had taken a shine to Trent. She had nudged Daniel over so she could sit next to him. That might have been her way of protecting herself in case the mean lady appeared at breakfast. Sam knew he would have to keep an eye on her to make certain she didn't make a nuisance of herself.

Trent wondered why Helen couldn't take a liking to these kids. At only age four, Martha must miss her ma and could be a lot of company to Helen while the others worked. This pretty little girl should be able to wrap herself around anyone's heart. Well, likely anyone but Helen, he thought resignedly.

What was he thinking? He was making it sound like they would be around for a long time, which was out of the question. Tonight, he would talk to Sam and try to find out about their family in Mason County. Maybe the boys could earn enough to get a better team of horses, and they could fix up the old wagon enough to make the trip. It must be close to three hundred miles to Mason County, and winter would be coming on soon. Trent felt the tension building in his head again. They might be here longer than he had planned after all, he thought, as he put on his hat and headed toward the barn to tell Biggun about his new helpers.

The big man agreed to show the children where to dig their pa's grave and said he would read a Scripture. He was indeed a gentle giant but could become a Goliath, if necessary. He was held in high regard by the ranch hands. Every man knew not to cross the line, or he would likely find himself on the receiving end of Biggun's wrath, not a place anyone cared to wind up.

The news of the five orphans underfoot didn't seem to bother Biggun as it might have many of the other ranch hands. He was an even-tempered man and rarely questioned his boss's decisions, even though they were near the same age and had practically grown up together.

Biggun did just as Trent expected. He not only showed Sam and Timothy where to dig the grave but helped as well. Then he pulled a small, worn Bible from his shirt pocket and read a few Scriptures. He led the children in saying *The Lord's Prayer*.

Then it was time to get on with the chores waiting to be done by the living.

They cleaned stalls in the barn, gathered eggs, hoed weeds in the fall garden, and helped feed the animals in the barn and barnyard. By late afternoon, Biggun suggested Sam go to the cellar to get potatoes, onion, garlic, and some carrots for a stew. He brought some meat from the smokehouse.

By the time Trent stepped up on the back porch to wash up before going into the house, the aroma of the simmering stew filled the air.

Just as he entered the kitchen, Sam was pulling a big pan of cornbread from the oven.

Trent greeted the group with a smile of approval. "My! Now, this is a fine surprise to come home to."

"I believe you got yourself a hardworking crew here, Trent, and Sam has the makings of a pretty good cook," Biggun told Trent with his own wide grin of approval.

"Fine, fine," Trent agreed. "Has Helen come out of her room yet, or is she still sulking?" he asked with a slight trace of dread.

"No, sir," Sam answered. "We ain't seen nothing of her since we come in to make supper."

Trent walked through the other part of the deserted-feeling house. There was no sound except for the clomping of his boots on the wood floor. He knocked on the door to Helen's room. She did not answer. He knocked a bit louder. "Helen, supper's ready. You better come to the table tonight if you intend to eat." He turned and retraced his steps to the kitchen without waiting for a reply.

Sam ladled the steaming stew into bowls. Timothy carefully carried a bowl and a big piece of cornbread to each person seated at the long table. There was a chair at one end, occupied by Trent, with benches stretching along each side. The other end was left empty for Helen's wheelchair. Just as Sam started to the table with the last bowl, Helen wheeled into her place without greeting anyone. Sam served her and returned for another bowl of stew and cornbread.

Biggun filled Trent in on what all the children had done that day and bragged about what a fine job they had done.

Nathan and Daniel sat up a bit straighter with a slight smile on their faces. Trent guessed they weren't used to hearing somebody brag about them. Martha took several bites and leaned her head on the table as though she were about to fall asleep.

"Now, Miss Martha there is real good with the chickens and the barn cats," Biggun said a bit louder to be sure Martha heard him.

She lifted her head and smiled at the man seated across the table.

"De kitties like me, but de chickens chase me when I get de eggs," she said, and yawned.

"Hurry up and finish your supper, Martha, and I'll put you to bed," Sam told her.

Helen ate her stew and cornbread but did not speak. Nor did she make eye contact with anyone at the table during the entire meal. She pushed her wheelchair away from the table and started to leave. Then she paused. She looked directly at Sam. "That's the best damn stew I've tasted in many a day!" Then she wheeled herself out of the room.

When she was out of earshot, Trent turned to Sam. "Well, now, it seems you've done at least one thing to please Helen. When you're finished in here and get the children settled, would you come to my office?"

Sam nodded.

"I just need to get a little information so we can locate your family in Mason County," Trent explained when he saw the worried look on Sam's face.

Sam felt a dread set in, thinking about having to answer questions about their family. Pa's secret may have to be told if Mr. Trent was going to look for their family. Now that Pa was dead, the secret shouldn't matter anyway, but Mr. Trent might think less of them than he probably already did when he learned the truth. Most folks that lived in grand houses didn't usually take much to poor folks, Sam thought sadly.

Trent sat at his big walnut desk, going over the expense account for the past month and entering the figures in the ranch ledger. He didn't understand why Helen couldn't at least do this much to help out, but she didn't and wouldn't. He wondered if anyone would answer the advertisement he sent to the Lubbock and the Wichita Falls newspapers. Maybe that was far enough away they hadn't heard of the notorious ill-tempered Helen Sanderson. He rested his head on his folded hands and thought, *Oh, Helen, if only, if only—what? If only you would soften your attitude and learn to accept what life has handed you. All the rebellion in the world isn't going to change a dad-blasted thing.* He lifted his head to continue his work.

Sam and the others were proving to be helpful. Trent doubted they would be much use at housekeeping or laundry and would probably resent being asked to do much in that area. He had forgotten to see if they had washed their dirty clothes today. He'd have to ask Sam about it.

Trent contemplated talking to one of the ministers in Amarillo and asking if they knew of any orphans' homes where he could take the children until matters could be settled with their family in Mason County. That would give him time to find their family and determine if any of them were willing to take on five more children or maybe split them up between several families. Sam was old enough to stay at the ranch and work if he was willing to let go of his siblings. Yes, after he talked to Sam, that is what he would do while in town tomorrow getting supplies. Or, he could just give them a decent wagon and team of horses, a little money, and send them on their way. But Trent knew he could not do that. The likelihood of all them surviving that long journey in the winter was unlikely. Then there was the chance they might run across some low-down jackass that might do them harm. No, his conscience just wouldn't let him be that hard-hearted.

Although the door was open, Sam tapped lightly before entering Trent's office. Sam had never seen a room like this one either. Trent sat at a big, shiny desk, and behind him was a large rock fireplace. Over the center hung a huge rack of deer horns, and on either side were more big horns, but not as big as the ones in the middle. To the left of the desk was an entire wall of bookshelves from floor to ceiling filled with all kinds of reading books. He must be a real smart man, Sam thought, considering the number of books that lined the complete wall. To the right was a liquor cabinet, and Sam noticed a glass of amber liquid sitting on the desk. The glass of whiskey was still almost full.

"Have a seat," Trent gestured toward a large chair covered with cowhide.

Sam sat, waiting for the questions.

"I failed to ask your last name yesterday when we met," Trent began.

Sam squirmed a bit and wouldn't look Trent in the eyes.

"Well, what is your last name?" Trent prompted.

"I—I ain't rightly sure, sir," Sam said, scarcely above a whisper.

"What do you mean you're not rightly sure? Everybody should know their last name," Trent said, a bit annoyed to think the boy would be that ignorant.

Then Sam looked at Trent. "We go by McCoy, but I don't think that's our real name."

"Why not?"

"Well," Sam hesitated, and then the story poured out in a waterfall of words. "'Afore I was borned, well, my ma was already carryin' me. Pa got into an argument with another man over who was supposed to water their livestock at a certain spring. Ma said Pa was always hotheaded. The man wouldn't move his livestock, and Pa wouldn't move his either. They got into a bad fight, and the man came at Pa with his quirt and hit him hard several times. Then, Pa pulled his gun and shot the man in self-defense. Some of the other man's hands rode up about that time. One picked up the quirt while the other held his gun on Pa. They said it didn't look like no self-defense to them, and that's what they was gonna tell the sheriff, that Pa just got mad and shot their boss. Pa was scared the other fellow's kinfolk would come after him. He was afraid they would shoot him or hang him with no chance to tell what really happened. So, he got Ma, and they lit out for Kansas. Ma said he drove that team nearly day and night, getting as far away from there as he could. She said it's a wonder she ever had me after ridin' for hours over bumpy old cow trails. They didn't tell nobody where they was a-goin' 'cause Pa was afraid of what that man's family or the sheriff might do if they ever found him. He said most folks headed west, so he fooled 'em by headin' north. They finally stopped in a little town in Ness County, Kansas. Pa figured nobody would ever find them there."

"If he was afraid all these years to even keep in contact with his kinfolks, why were you going back to Mason County?"

"Pa went out drinkin' sometimes. One night, he met a man from Mason County in the saloon. At first, Pa was really scared. He thought sure the man had come to kill him. The man just laughed and told Pa the man he shot was alive and doing fine. Then Pa brung the man from Mason County home with him so he could tell Ma for sure the feller was still alive. She didn't believe him either till he told her to fetch her Bible, and he put his hand right on it and swore on it he was tellin' the truth. After that, all Pa could talk about was goin' back to Texas. Ma didn't much want to take the chance even though the fellow had swore on her Bible, but finally, Pa won out. We ain't never had much money. Pa didn't work too steady, but he finally scraped enough money together for that old wagon and them two wore-out horses. We hadn't been travelin' but about seven days when Ma lost another baby and just kept on bleedin' till all the life went out of her. I did everything she said to try to help her, but nothin' helped. I think she was just wore out."

Trent could hear the sadness in Sam's voice when he talked about his ma dying. Mercy, what an ordeal for a sixteen-year-old boy to go through, Trent thought as he looked at the sad expression on Sam's face.

"Pa said we needed more than ever to get back with his family so they could help take care of us young'uns." Sam paused with a distant look of uncertainty reflected in his somber-looking eyes. "I reckon it's up to me now to get us back to his kinfolks," he said a bit doubtfully.

Trent stared at the boy as he listened to his dismal story. "So, you think your pa changed his name, and now you don't actually know what his name really was. Is that what you're telling me?"

"Well, I heard Ma say somethin' about some McRoys being kinfolk, so that might have been our real name, but I ain't for sure."

"That does sound likely, but what about your ma's kinfolks? What was her name before she married your pa?"

Sam thought for several moments. "I ain't never heard her say."

"So, you don't know any of your ma's folks?"

"No, I reckon not."

"She never talked about where she grew up or if she had brothers or sisters?" Trent asked in dismay.

"No, sir," Sam answered with a shake of his head. "The only thing I ever heard her say was her ma didn't want her to marry Pa, and if she did, she would be disowned. I guess that's why she never talked about her folks."

Trent took a generous swallow of the whiskey sitting on his desk. "Well, I am going to write to the sheriff at the county seat in Mason County and see if he knows anything about your family. I'm sure folks will remember the shooting that happened before your pa and ma left."

Sam looked at the floor, ashamed of the blemish on the family name his pa had caused. "Yes, sir, I expect they would," was all Sam could think to say.

Trent felt sorry for the boy. He looked so dejected and ashamed of his family. It certainly wasn't his fault his pa hadn't been a very upstanding man.

"Sam, don't feel so bad about what happened years ago before you were even born. All of us have skeletons in our closets, so to speak."

Sam looked at Trent with a puzzled expression. "What does skeletons in a closet mean?"

"It means we all have some kinfolks that don't always do the right thing. We aren't responsible for the things they do, and it shouldn't reflect ill on us. What your pa did doesn't mean you are a bad person, or your brothers or sister. Each of you is your own person and has to answer for the things you do, not what your pa did. Do you understand what I'm trying to tell you?" Trent asked, honestly hoping the boy did understand he wasn't responsible for his pa's actions. That was too much of a burden for a boy to carry. Sam had enough to worry about with four younger siblings to care for. Damn, but life dealt some people a piss-poor hand, Trent thought as he watched the boy.

Sam finally looked at Trent. "Yes, sir, I think I do." There was a pause in their conversation, each just looking at the other. "I sure don't want to be like my pa. He really weren't much good. He didn't cotton much to work, and poor Ma just had to scrape by as best she could."

"Don't judge him too hard; maybe he couldn't help the way he was. Just remember, you can do better if you really try. I think you have it in you to really try," Trent said with an encouraging smile.

"Yes, sir, I want to do lots better and take care of my brothers and sister. I ain't got much education, so I don't know what kind of work I can do to give 'em a better life."

Trent was at a loss for any suggestions. About all the boy could do was ranch work, livery stable work, or clean up a store or saloon. Unfortunately, none of those jobs were going to put much extra in the boy's pocket to help his family. It was sad to think about the plight of these children, now dependent on a sixteen-year-old to take care of them. Trent became more convinced an orphans' home might be the best place for the children. They would get an education and a decent place to live. Sam was likely too old for the home, and maybe Timothy, but the others would have a better chance at life. If there happened to be a home in Amarillo or Wichita Falls, he would gladly keep Sam and Timothy on at the ranch. They were good workers, and he could look out for them until they were old enough to really be on their own. Of course, he couldn't say anything about this plan until he found out more information.

"I'll write a letter to the sheriff in Mason County and mail it when I go to town tomorrow for supplies. It will take two or three weeks before we hear back from him. Meanwhile, you all can stay here and help Biggun and do a little cooking and so on." He didn't mention his intent to talk to the town minister about an orphanage. "You better get on to bed now," Trent said as he reached for his pen and paper. "By the way, did your dirty clothes get washed today?"

"Yes, sir, they did. Good night." Sam turned at the doorway. "I thank you fur all your help, sir."

Before Trent could answer, Sam disappeared into the darkness.

Trent wondered if Sam would consent to his younger siblings going to an orphans' home if there was no family in Mason County to take them in.

Just as Trent turned his attention to writing the letter, he heard the squeak of Helen's wheelchair. Apparently, she was on her way to the kitchen for a drink of water before bedtime. Then he realized she had stopped in front of the open door. Trent glanced up, "Do you need something, Helen?"

"Yes, I need to ask you something."

"Okay."

"Do you know what's wrong with you, Trent?"

Trent gave his shoulders a slight shrug, knowing it wouldn't matter to Helen whatever he said. "I expect there are several things wrong with me," he answered.

Helen stared at Trent and then pointed her finger. "You are an honorable man. You take on the problems of the world and try to fix everything. But I'm telling you, Trent, even you can't fix everything." Then she rolled her chair down the hall.

Trent sat for several minutes, mulling over what Helen had said, and mumbled to himself, "Honorable...honorable...huh."

27

Chapter Two

Trent had found there was an orphanage in Wichita Falls. He promptly wrote a letter of inquiry and, twelve days later, received a lengthy letter saying there was room for the four younger children. The age limit for acceptance was twelve years of age or younger. That came as a relief to Trent as that meant all the children except Sam could be placed there, and Sam could work at the ranch for as long as he liked. He could even make a trip to Wichita Falls occasionally to see his brothers and sister. Now, all he had to do was wait for word from the sheriff in Mason County to see if there really was family willing to take them in.

Trent also received a letter of inquiry about the housekeeping and cooking position from a Flossy Tatum, age twenty-three and single. Previous work experience was a bit sketchy. Trent had a strong feeling Flossy might have been in a profession with less status than a housekeeper and cook. Well, maybe she was just trying to better herself, and there was nothing wrong with that except being on a ranch full of single men. If no other reply came within a week or so, he would send her the ticket to Amarillo. He could only hope she would be as ugly as homemade soap and have the temperament to put up with Helen.

Sam continued to cook breakfast and something for supper. The meals were plain but very tasty. He and the children proved helpful in the barn and barnyard. Biggun had taken a real liking to all the boys and adored little Martha. He often joined them for the evening meal and teased Martha just to hear her giggle. Helen also joined them for meals after being summoned by Trent, but she remained sullen. The children were not quite as afraid of her as they had been at first, but they made no effort to interact with her or Helen with them.

Trent was grateful that things were moving in a more peaceful mode.

No other reply came concerning his advertisement. So, he wrote to Flossy Tatum and enclosed the train ticket to Amarillo, where he would pick her up the following week.

The day he went to pick Flossy up, he was pleased to see a reply from the sheriff of Mason County, Texas.

Dear Mr. Sanderson,

I recall the shooting incident you described in your letter and it is true, the man is indeed alive. He says if Henry (McCoy) McRoy, being his actual name, were alive, he would press attempted murder charges against him, but that appears immaterial at this point.

Two McRoy brothers and their families still live in Mason County, but neither is of a mind to take on their brother's five orphaned children. They were both sorry to hear about the passing of their brother and his wife, but both have large families of their own to care for. It appears best they remain with you or be put in an orphans' home.

Sincerely,

Joseph Clanton, Sheriff, Mason County, Texas

Trent folded the letter and stuck it in his shirt pocket. Well, now, he would have to break the news to Sam and explain about putting the four younger children in an orphans' home. He was going to have to be very persuasive. It had become apparent they were a close-knit bunch. Maybe that was because of them losing their parents so young and Sam taking their place.

∾

30

As he stood on the train platform, contemplating how to approach the subject of an orphans' home with Sam, he heard the distant whistle of the 12:15 p.m. train. On time for a change, he thought. He watched the passengers disembark and wondered which lady might be Miss Flossy Tatum.

The last two women to get off were exact opposites of one another. One was tall, slim, and nice-looking. The other was short, plump, with rosy cheeks like two red apples and a half-toothless grin. He certainly liked the looks of the tall, thin woman but hoped, for his peace of mind, the short, plump one was Miss Flossy Tatum.

Trent removed his hat and nodded to the two women.

"Excuse me, ladies, I'm Trent Sanderson, and I'm supposed to meet a Miss Flossy Tatum. She applied for a job as a housekeeper and cook at the Flatland Ranch."

Both women stared at him, but neither spoke.

"I'm Flossy Tatum," Trent heard a pleasing voice say from behind him. He turned and almost forgot to breathe.

Standing before him was a beautiful redhead with eyes as green as the spring meadow, a perfectly shaped mouth made for kissing, and a stunning figure. She didn't exactly look like a woman of the evening or a housekeeper or cook either. She looked like every man's dream of a woman to please him in every way possible. *Oh boy! This woman might mean more trouble than having Helen and five orphans combined,* he thought as he smiled and introduced himself again.

The nine-mile ride back to the ranch seemed to fly by as they talked and laughed as though they had known one another for years. He did notice she was a bit evasive when he asked questions of a more personal nature. As they pulled into the yard, he realized he had learned virtually nothing about the woman.

He also realized all the single men would be ogling her, wanting to take her to the nearest barn dance, or Lord only knows what. Yes, this beauty might lead to a whole peck of trouble. Maybe he should warn her about being the only single woman, except for Helen, for miles around on a ranch full of hot-blooded men, young and old.

She smiled and nodded her head but appeared a bit indignant at his feeble attempt at explaining the situation about the men.

Trent had prepared her as best he could about Helen and the five children that resided in the big house. Flossy would live in the other upstairs room since all the children shared one room. She seemed agreeable to almost anything he told her. His hopes soared, thinking that, at last, he had found a woman who, with any luck, could handle Helen. She even seemed impressed that he had taken on five orphans. For some reason, he wanted to impress her enough to make her want to stay. Besides, he had to admit she was easy on the eyes.

To his relief, they found stew and cornbread still warm on the stove. Everyone else seemed to have retired for the evening. Trent showed Flossy the bathing room and offered to draw her water for a bath. It would make her feel better after her long journey, he suggested. She graciously accepted his hospitality.

As he lay in bed that night mulling over the day's events, his thoughts rambled back and forth between the redheaded beauty upstairs and telling Sam about the circumstances in Mason County and the orphanage in Wichita Falls.

Much to Trent's surprise, when he arrived in the kitchen, he found Flossy humming softly as she finished preparing the breakfast. Sam stood beside the stove in silence, waiting with the stack of plates to be filled. The other children were seated at the table.

"Good morning," Trent greeted everyone in a cheerful mood.

"Mornin'," came several replies.

"Please sit," Flossy replied. "Breakfast is ready to be served." She heaped the first plate full of eggs, bacon, and two biscuits. Sam carried the plate to Trent.

"Did anyone wake Helen?" he asked, although he knew they had not. They all still avoided Helen as much as possible, as though she had chicken pox or worse.

Trent rose and walked through the quiet house to Helen's room. He knocked firmly on her door. "Breakfast is ready; come to the table."

He was getting a bit tired of this daily ritual. He needed to speak to Helen about having to be summoned for every meal. This was the last trip he or anyone would be making to her room, he decided. She knew when meals were served, he thought as he returned to the kitchen.

When Helen appeared, she took her place and scarcely acknowledged the new woman when she was introduced. The children said little during most morning meals, often yawning as though wishing for more sleep. Much to Trent's relief, Flossy took everyone's behavior in stride.

Trent looked at the plate filled with runny scrambled eggs and half-burned bacon. When he tried to split the biscuit to add butter and jelly, it was like cutting a raw potato. He hoped her housekeeping skills were considerably better than her cooking. Maybe Sam should continue cooking, and Flossy could find something besides housekeeping and helping Helen occasionally to earn her wages, he thought.

"Sam, when breakfast is done, I need to speak to you in my office before you go out for chores. The others can go on without you."

Sam nodded and continued to eat the unpleasant meal.

The children snuck looks at one another as they too tried to down the unsavory food, but no one verbalized a complaint. Not even Helen.

"Helen, when I'm done speaking to Sam, I need to see you in my office."

Helen gave him an icy stare and turned to Sam. "Trent's ultimatums make it sound as though you and I have done something naughty and are about to get forty lashes with his quirt," she snipped.

At the sound of the word *quirt*, Sam's head snapped up, and his huge blue eyes stared at Trent.

Trent saw the reaction and calmly answered, "Helen, I don't recall ever taking a quirt to anyone, so you have no reason to make such a remark."

Helen gave a sneering laugh. "I'm sure something we've done isn't pleasing to you, or you'd just say it aloud for everyone to hear."

"This is a private matter, and that's that."

After breakfast, Sam knocked on the door to Trent's office.

"Come in, Sam. Close the door, and take a seat."

Sam did as instructed. He looked with dread at the man seated behind the huge desk. In this room filled with books and important-looking ledgers strewn across the desk, Trent looked different than he did anywhere else Sam saw him. Perhaps it was a reminder that he was the boss, and his word was law on the ranch.

From the look of unease on Sam's face, Trent was sure the boy was worried the boss had bad news for him. "Sam, I got a letter from the sheriff in Mason County, and the news is not good. Your pa still has two brothers there, but neither of them can take in any more children." He paused to gauge Sam's reaction to this news.

The boy's shoulders slumped, and his gaze fell toward the floor.

Trent waited, but Sam said nothing. He couldn't help but wonder how he would be feeling if he were in Sam's shoes. The arduous burden placed squarely on his young shoulders must be getting heavier by the day. No family was willing to help. Now, he and his siblings were dependent on strangers for food and shelter. What a bleak, uncertain future the boy must see ahead.

It was impossible for Trent to fully imagine how Sam must be feeling since he was a young man before he lost his parents; his circumstances were far different. He had grown up with the love and support of his caring parents. Money had never been a bothersome issue, Trent reflected.

Maybe the idea of an orphans' home would look better to Sam under these circumstances, Trent reasoned.

"I also wrote to the director of an orphans' home in Wichita Falls to inquire about a place for the other children, just in case there wasn't anyone in Mason County to take you in."

Sam continued to sit with shoulders slumped and head downcast.

"They do have a home there and can take all the children twelve years of age and under."

Sam lifted his gaze, "No! I ain't lettin' my kin go to no orphans' home. I promised Pa I'd get them to Mason County."

"Sam, there is no one in Mason County to help you. What would you do once you got there? How could you make enough money to support the five of you?" Trent repeated with patience. "I know this isn't the news you had hoped for, but you have to think about what's best for your brothers and sister. You can stay on here and work." Trent gave Sam a little time to really think about their situation. "I promise you, once a month, I'll buy you a round-trip train ticket to Wichita Falls so you can go see them. I'll pay you regular wages on top of that."

Trent waited for some reaction from Sam, but he still sat looking down at his worn pants and ragged shoes.

"Now, Sam, you need to think it over and talk to your brothers and sister. You have to explain to them that there isn't anyone in Mason County to take care of them. This is the best for them and you. They will get an education and be cared for too." Trent knew he had to convince Sam this was the best plan.

"Why can't they stay here like we are now?"

"They won't come near the house without you, and winter is coming on pretty soon. It won't do for them to be out in the cold barn all day. What would you do when one or more of them got sick? They need to be where they can go to school and have proper care." Trent paused again to give Sam time to take in all he was saying.

After several long minutes, Sam looked at Trent and asked, "Will I go live in the bunkhouse?"

"No, I think it best you stay in the house for another year or so. Sometimes, the men get a little rowdy and pick on the younger hands. You'd be better off here. Besides, I think you better keep on cooking," Trent said with a slight grimace, remembering the awful breakfast they had been served by Flossy.

Sam finally smiled at that suggestion. "Miss Flossy ain't much of a cook, is she?"

"No, but hopefully, she can get along with Helen and keep house."

Sam rose to leave and then paused. "Mr. Trent, I guess this ain't none of my business, but why did a nice man like you ever marry such an ill-tempered woman like Mrs. Helen?"

Trent looked stunned when he heard Sam's question. Then he threw back his head and roared with laughter. "Where in the world did you get the idea we were married? Helen's my sister!"

It was Sam's turn to look stunned, but he managed to croak, "Sister?"

Trent laughed even harder. "Lord a mercy, it never occurred to me you would think Helen was my wife. I guess I better start making sure people know the truth of things," he said, still chuckling.

35

"Sorry, sir, I didn't mean to talk bad about your sister, but she can sure be uh, uh—" Sam trailed off since he couldn't seem to manage to come up with the proper word.

"How about a pain in the ass?" Trent finished for him, still grinning.

"I guess that's as good a way to put it as any," Sam smiled, still looking embarrassed. Then he grew serious. "I'll tell my brothers and little sister about what you said. They know they have to mind me now, so there won't be no trouble. Do you know how soon we'll be goin' to Wichita Falls?"

"The director sent me the information about the orphans' home, so I'll write a letter and send it to be posted today. As soon as we hear back, which will probably be a week or so, we'll make our plans. Just enjoy being together and reassure them this is for the best. Be sure to tell them you'll be coming to see them every month," Trent said with genuine compassion in his voice. He had grown to genuinely like the children and wished it were possible for them to stay. However, he had a ranch to run and knew there would be lots of problems coming up. Besides, there was no school near enough for them to attend. Two of the families, with seven school-age children between them, rented a small house in town, and the two women with school children spent the week in town. He knew it wasn't an ideal situation, but people did what they had to do. Trent paid their rent, as their husbands were top hands with cattle and horses, so it was worth the extra expense to keep them employed.

"Tell Helen I'm ready to see her on your way out."

"Yes, sir," Sam answered in a subdued manner as he left the room.

In a few minutes, Helen wheeled into the austere office. Well, that was the way it had always seemed to her, she thought as she looked at her brother seated behind the huge desk that had belonged to their father. She remembered being called into Papa's office when she was in trouble, which was quite often throughout the years of her childhood and adolescence.

She would be the first to admit she had always been a hell-raiser for as long as she could remember, although she couldn't exactly account for such behavior. She certainly wasn't a neglected child, but she demanded more attention, more privileges, and always wanted to be the center of attention. She thought this mindset started after Trent was born. Even at an early age, she understood that someday he would take their father's place behind the big desk. Trent would be the chosen one to run the ranch. It didn't matter that she was older and could learn just as much about ranching as her brother if given the chance. She wasn't given the chance, so she became more demanding and overbearing. Maybe that was her way of ensuring her own place in the family, even if it hadn't turned out to be the best solution.

There had been a boy born before Trent, but he had only lived a few hours. The loss of his first son had crushed their father. A year later, Trent was born healthy and continued so and was their father's pride and joy. Two years later, another girl was born but died when she was about six months old from some mysterious fever. There were no more babies, so that left her and Trent for many years until the change-of-life baby girl was born. They had named her Angel. Her birth had taken a toll on their delicate mother. Now, they only saw the girl for a brief visit in the summer, and, truth be told, that suited Helen just fine.

The strange part was she had always loved her little brother and didn't resent him for being the favored one by their father. Now, she often wondered why she couldn't let go of the bitterness and hurt that had put her in this damn wheelchair and be more help to Trent. For some reason, her resentment and self-pity just wouldn't let go of her. The saddest part was none of it was Trent's doing, but he was the one paying the ultimate price.

"Well, dear brother, give me my comeuppance so we can get on with the day," Helen said in her normally loud, tart voice.

Trent looked at his sister for a long moment. He took a deep breath and leaned back in his big leather chair. "Helen, you will not be summoned by me or anyone else for another meal. You get there on time or do without until the next meal. Next, you treat the new housekeeper with respect and cooperate, as she came all the way from Fort Worth for this job. We've already run through all the local help within a hundred miles. Your surly attitude and behavior have to stop," he paused and leaned forward, looking her straight in the eyes. "Now!"

Helen stared back at Trent for a few seconds. "I may never show up for another meal if breakfast is any indication of her cooking skills."

Trent couldn't suppress a smile. "I told Sam to keep cooking, and Flossy can do the housework, help you with your personal needs, do all the laundry, and tend to what's left of the garden. If there's anything else domestic, she can take care of that, too."

"From the looks of her, I doubt she even knows how to sew on a button," Helen commented. "I'm glad to hear Sam's going to cook. I suspect that boy had to learn to be mama and papa quite a while before their parents died," Helen said thoughtfully.

"Yes, I expect you're right. I'm making arrangements for the four younger children to go to an orphans' home in Wichita Falls. The sheriff of Mason County wrote that none of their kinfolks are willing to take them in, so there isn't much other choice."

Helen looked rather astonished at that bit of information. "Sam agreed to that?"

"It took some persuading, but he finally agreed. I promised him a round-trip train ticket once a month and regular wages to get him to consent."

Helen looked thoughtfully at her brother for several seconds. "Trent, you really are a good man. You deserve a better sister than me." She said with a trace of humility. She let out a deep sigh. "I promise I'll try really hard to get along with Flossy," she said with more contrition than Trent had heard in many years.

Helen started to back toward the door, then stopped.

"You're not going to put Sam out in that bunkhouse with all those raucous cowboys, are you?" she asked with genuine concern.

"No, he'll stay upstairs. Do you want to hear something funny?"

Helen looked at her brother, a bit surprised, as they hadn't shared much camaraderie in a long time.

"Sure."

"Sam thought we were married."

Helen looked shocked, but then she started to laugh. "Good Lord, I certainly hope you straightened that out!"

"I did," Trent answered with a grin.

"I'm going to find Flossy and get her to help me bathe. Don't forget to tell her she isn't the cook, and I'll tell her you're not my husband," Helen said over her shoulder as she wheeled herself out of the office, still chuckling.

Chapter Three

Everyone was amazed and greatly relieved to see Helen was making a real effort to be more congenial. Within a few days, even Timothy, Nathan, and Daniel would enter the house without Sam's protection, but not little Martha. She still clung to Sam as always. Martha made sure she sat next to Trent at meals and as far away from Helen as she could possibly manage.

Sam continued the cooking, and Flossy seemed to find enough to do to at least make it appear she was busy most of the time.

Sam noticed she lingered in the fading garden longer than necessary. It was near the barns, cattle pens, and horse arena, where a number of the men worked daily. Sam also noticed most of the single men's wistful stares in her direction. It was true; she was a beauty, so it wasn't any wonder she grabbed their attention when she went to the garden.

On Saturday, Flossy offered to trim Helen's hair after her bath.

"Yes, I know it's a mess," Helen responded. "Do you really know how to cut hair, or is it going to look worse than it already does when you've finished?" she asked, a bit suspicious.

"I do know how to cut hair very well. Would you like for me to demonstrate my skills on someone else first?" Flossy responded sweetly.

"Who?"

Flossy thought for a minute. "How about Sam and the other children. They all look so bedraggled. A good haircut would do wonders for them all."

"Okay," Helen agreed. "You go find Sam and tell him I said he and all the kids are getting haircuts today."

Helen sat in her wheelchair on the back porch, waiting as Flossy and the children rounded the corner of the house.

Flossy smiled at Helen. "Sam said he would be first, so the others won't be scared. He usually cuts their hair, but their only pair of scissors got lost somewhere."

"Go get that stool out of the kitchen and the dirty apron," Helen told Sam.

In a few minutes, Flossy was fast at work as Sam's blond locks fell to the porch and blew away in the wind. Each child climbed up on the stool when it was their turn until Flossy had finished them all.

She turned and looked at Helen. "Well, Miss Helen, did I pass your test?"

"Yes, in fact, you surprised me. Were you a hairdresser before you came here?"

"No, I just learned to cut hair on my two sisters and some friends when I was growing up."

"Oh, and where was that?" Helen asked casually.

"Here and there, we moved around a lot."

"Where are your sisters now?"

"I believe one lives in St. Louis, and the other went somewhere out west. We've kind of lost contact over the years," Flossy replied nonchalantly.

Trent walked around the corner of the house and stopped short to take another look at the sight on the porch. He almost didn't recognize the children with their fresh haircuts, and, more astounding, Helen was sitting there calm as you please, getting her hair cut, too. Amazing, he thought as he walked up the steps. He smiled at Martha as he reached out to ruffle her freshly cut hair. "You sure look pretty, Miss Martha, with that new haircut," he teased.

Martha giggled as her blue eyes twinkled.

"Trent, you're just in time for a haircut, too. Goodness knows you need one. Look what a fine job Flossy does." Helen smiled with approval as she said the words.

Trent grinned. "If she can make me look half as handsome as this bunch, I'm all for it."

Flossy gave him a pleasant smile. "Sit right down, sir," she almost cooed as she draped the dirty hair-covered apron around his broad shoulders. She'd barely made the first snip when the others went into the house to prepare for supper.

As Flossy moved around to reach various parts of his head, her full bosom brushed against his upper arms more than once. The first time, he thought it was an accident; the second time, he began to wonder; and the third time, he was quite certain it was no accident. This was turning out to be the most alluring haircut Trent had ever experienced. It took all of his willpower to not move his arms a bit when they came in contact with Flossy's ample bosom. He'd caught her gazing in his direction several times since the revelation that Helen was not his wife. He knew in his position, he had to maintain the decorum of employer and employee with Flossy, no matter how tempting she might be. Just as he finished that thought, he realized she was standing directly in front of him. His head had been bowed slightly forward while she worked on the back of his neck, but now she had moved to the front. He saw her hand reach out. She lightly placed two fingers under his chin to gently lift his head.

"Now, let me be sure I have both sides even," she said sweetly as she bobbed her head back and forth, checking her handiwork. She leaned slightly forward, allowing the neck of her blouse to fall forward just enough so Trent had a grand view of her well-rounded twin buttes.

"Yes, I believe that's just about perfect," she cooed again.

Yeah, Trent thought, and I have a perfect view of your wares from where I'm sitting. He had no doubt Flossy was fully aware of what she was doing. He reminded himself that as her boss, he would have to use great restraint, a challenge for any man, but it was especially necessary because he was her boss.

The tranquility of everyone getting a fresh haircut didn't last long.

That evening at supper, it was nine-year-old Nathan who arrived last at the dinner table and was forced to sit on Helen's right. The only other empty place was to Helen's left, so there was no escape for the boy.

Nathan felt his stomach rumble and breathed in the delicious smelling aroma of one of Sam's stews and cornbread. In his eagerness to ease the hunger pains, he crammed his mouth so full he had to chew with his mouth open, making rather unpleasant smacking noises.

Helen looked up and shrieked, "For heaven's sake, stop cramming so much food in your mouth and chew with it closed. I ought to smack you to teach you some proper manners!"

Nathan's eyes grew larger. He dodged just in case she made good on her threat. His quick movement caused him to suck in his breath, making bad matters worse. He choked and spewed food from his mouth, part of which landed on Helen.

Helen yelped and drew back her hand as though to strike the lad.

Sam jumped up, motioning to Nathan to go outside, which he did with great haste.

Sam followed close behind while glaring at Helen. "If there's any smackin' done, I'll be the one doin' it, not you," he flung at Helen. "And I ain't smackin' my brother for bein' hungry!" he shouted at Helen just as the back door slammed.

Helen looked stunned. "Trent!" she bellowed. "Did you hear what that ungrateful brat yelled at me?"

"I heard."

"Well, what do you intend to do about it?"

"Nothing."

"Nothing?" she half shouted.

Trent banged his fist on the table, rattling dishes and making everyone, including Helen, jump. "I said I'm not doing anything to Sam for telling you what he did! He's right! It's not your place to be smacking anyone."

Helen opened her mouth to protest, but before the words came out, she was again interrupted by Trent.

"I don't want any more talking during the rest of this meal!" He looked at each person seated at the table, and then his gaze landed on Helen. "That certainly includes you, Helen. Not one more word."

When Trent saw the anxious look on little Martha's face, he felt a stab of guilt for frightening the sweet child.

Sam and Nathan returned to the unusually quiet room.

"Sir," Sam began.

Before Sam could go on, Martha put her finger to her lips and whispered, "Shhhh, Mr. Trent say no talkin'."

All was quiet.

At the end of what became a very long meal, Trent entered his office and poured himself a shot glass of whiskey. He sat at his desk for a long while, staring into space while massaging his temples to relieve the tension.

Trent pondered the life that had been handed to him. He had inherited a huge ranch and a huge responsibility to go with it. Men with families depended on him, men with no families depended on him, Helen depended on him, and now five orphan children were depending on him to make the right decisions that would affect each of their lives. One mistake could have far-reaching consequences.

Trent felt as though he were constantly in a battle. He battled the stock prices and had to know when to sell and when to hold on. He battled the ever-changing whelms of the weather. The winters were cold, with the relentless north wind pouring down across the great plains, often bringing snow and ice to pound at the men and livestock until the humans felt they could take no more. The rains came in torrents all at once or in sparse sprinkles that did little good. The relentless heat of summer could be as daunting as the cold of their winters. He fought fires sparked by lightning storms that burned acres and acres of grassland and that often stampeded the cattle. Then, it took days to rectify the resulting destruction.

Trent had come to believe that ranching was a gamble and only a fool would embrace it with his entire being. He supposed he was a fool gambler because he could not imagine any other life, no matter how grueling, how frustrating, or how exhausting ranching could be. It was the rewards that kept him going. The rebirth of nature each spring, the sunsets that could not be captured on any canvas, a swim in the cool creek at the end of a long, hot day in the saddle, the big sale that fattened his bank account so he could continue another season.

Finally, he swallowed the amber liquid and savored its familiar sting in his throat. As he reached for the ranch account books, he couldn't help but mutter, "But what the hell have I gotten myself into this time?"

Chapter Four

The letter from the orphans' home arrived ten days after Trent had reluctantly persuaded Sam to place the younger children in the home.

Much to everyone's surprise, Helen volunteered herself and Flossy to accompany Sam and the children to Wichita Falls. This trip would be Helen's first outing away from the ranch in three years.

Trent wondered if Helen's motive was to be certain the children were accepted and didn't return to the ranch.

After the accident at the creek, she had gone to several doctors in Fort Worth, San Antonio, Houston, and even Chicago, but each trip ended in disappointment. There was nothing that could be done to repair the damage done to Helen's lower body. She would be confined to a wheelchair for the remainder of her life. After the last journey, she refused to go anywhere except for a few outings to Amarillo for a little shopping. After several years, she stopped seeing longtime friends. When they tried to maintain their friendship, she rejected their attempts until they finally gave up.

Helen had, so to speak, locked herself away at the ranch and thrived on her bitterness and self-pity. Trent couldn't help but wonder what had happened to make her suddenly want to make this trip to Wichita Falls, but he certainly wasn't going to discourage it. He was grateful for her help and encouraged that she had at long last shown some interest in something other than herself. He hoped the plight of these children had bothered Helen in much the same way it had concerned him. Perhaps the sadness of the children's situation had touched something deep within Helen to unchain some of her self-pity and make her want to reach out to help someone else. Whatever the reason, he was grateful for the remarkable change he was, at long last, beginning to see in his sister. He genuinely cared about the orphans' well-being and certainly wished for Sam's sake they could stay at the ranch, but it just wasn't the place for them. They needed education and care that even Sam couldn't manage.

Trent had to give his sister credit. After his ultimatum about her behavior and trying to get along with Flossy, she had indeed made a vast improvement. There were still times when her old self came to the surface, but she seemed in far better control of her behavior, and lately, she had managed to calm the beast within before he had to take a stand.

Friday, November 30, 1900, Sam turned seventeen. They had celebrated Sam's birthday the night before at supper with a cake Sam had baked, as they were leery of what might have happened if Flossy had attempted to bake a cake. Sam had made a valiant effort to be cheerful, but it was obvious to the adults he was putting on a good act for his siblings.

On Sunday morning, Trent drove the wagon to Amarillo, loaded with five children, Helen and Flossy. A brisk north wind made the nine-mile trip miserable, although they were wrapped in blankets. The chill still seeped through clear to their bones. He hoped this trip wouldn't make Helen sick since she had been so confined to the house.

Trent saw the group off on the afternoon train that should arrive in Wichita Falls in the wee hours of the next morning. He had sent a telegram to a nice hotel near the train station, making them a reservation. The hotel would provide transportation from the train station to the hotel.

Trent found a room at one of the nicer hotels in Amarillo for himself. He entered the spacious dining room, where he dined at a table laid with a white tablecloth, gleaming silverware, china plates, and crystal glasses. He enjoyed a large T-bone steak, cooked medium rare, and downed two beers with his meal.

Then, he ambled down the street to one of the better saloons, where he gambled until 11:00 p.m. As he walked back to his hotel in the late hours of the cold night, he reminded himself it was time to settle down and start looking for a wife. One thing he knew for sure was it wouldn't be Flossy's finger he would place a wedding ring on, regardless of her eye-catching ways. There was something devious about her. She was far too secretive about her past, and that he didn't trust.

The next day, the wagon Helen had hired pulled to a stop in front of a large red brick building flanked by two other three-story red brick build-ings. It looked pleasant enough. Evergreen shrubs covered in red berries adorned the front of the center building. The huge front door was deco-rated with a large Christmas wreath. A red brick fence, about four feet tall, surrounded the entire complex with its large open lawns. A nice place for the children to play, Helen thought, as the driver unloaded the children and their few belongings. Then, he placed her wheelchair next to the wagon and, with strong arms, lifted her and gently sat her in the chair.

"You are welcome to come inside out of the cold to wait for us if you like," Helen told him.

"Thank you, Miss. I'll wait here. I'm used to the cold, and the horses might get spooked if I'm not here."

Flossy pushed Helen's chair up the long sidewalk while Sam and the other four children followed slowly behind as though dreading what was about to take place. Flossy and Sam lifted Helen's chair up the three steps leading to a wide covered porch adorned with five archways across the front.

The door was opened before they could knock. They were greeted by a short, round-faced woman with graying hair pulled up on top of her head in a bun. She had a pleasant demeanor as she surveyed the children to be left in their charge.

"Come in," she greeted them in a cheerful voice. "This must be the McCoy children," she stated as she looked from one child to the next. "My, my, what a handsome group, and look at this little angel," she beamed as she turned her gaze to Martha.

"Yes, they are and well-behaved, too," Helen spoke up. "I am Helen Sanderson. My brother, Trent, is the one you have been corresponding with about the children. This is Sam, their older brother who works for my brother, and this is Flossy Tatum, my housekeeper and personal attendant."

"So pleased to meet all of you. I'm Miss Jolene Martin, head of this orphans' home for twenty-two years. As a young woman, I felt the calling to help those less fortunate than myself, and this is where I wound up," she gestured at her surroundings; a broad smile crossed her comely face. "It is a fine home for our children. I assure you they will be educated and well cared for."

"That is what we expect," Helen said a bit sternly. "Sam will be coming once a month to visit his siblings. If we hear of any problems, my brother will come to get it straightened out pronto." Helen continued in her unyielding manner to let Miss Martin know it would be in their best interest to see that the children had proper treatment.

Jolene Martin stared at Helen for a few seconds. "I don't think you will find anything to complain about," she stated in her own strict manner.

Miss Martin turned to Sam. "Would you like to look around while we fill out the paperwork?"

Sam nodded politely to the lady in charge. He had not joined in the conversation as Miss Helen seemed to know what needed to be said. Maybe Mr. Trent had told her what to say and ask, he surmised.

Jolene stepped to the door and summoned John Carter, the man in charge of the boys' dormitories.

"These are the McCoy children that will be joining us, and this is Sam, their older brother. Please, show the boys to their dormitory and then take Sam and Martha to the girls' quarters, where Mrs. Caroline Foster is expecting her," she said with a pleasant expression.

The boys soon joined their new dorm mates in various games. Even the two younger ones seemed pleased with their new home and getting to know lots of other boys for playmates. After Sam saw they were readily settling into their new home, he gave each one a quick hug, reminding them not to cause any trouble, before he left with Martha.

It was a different story with Martha. She clung to Sam and screamed, "Please, don't go! Please, don't leave me!" she begged. Sam could feel her trembling as she clung desperately to him, as though she were about to drown. Two of the women literally pried her tiny arms from around Sam's neck and shooed him outside. Mrs. Foster soon followed and reassured Sam that Martha would adjust to her new surroundings in no time. Sam wasn't convinced, but he hoped it was true. Sam longed to grab Martha and run far away, but where would they go? He knew this was for the best, but it hurt deeply to hear Martha's screams and pleading for him to not leave her here with strangers.

It took all of Sam's courage to trudge back to the main building where Helen waited. Tears threatened to spill over, but Sam held a tight grip on those emotions. There would be time for crying when it was dark, and no one could see the tears. Somehow, tears seemed to signal a weakness, and Sam certainly didn't want to be perceived as being weak.

By the time Sam returned to the main building, the papers were filled out, and he was asked to sign consent for the four children to be committed to the orphans' home.

Sam felt a small tremor in his hands as he picked up the pen and scrawled his name on each paper.

"Have you said your goodbyes?" Helen asked, seeing Sam's troubled expression and noticing his hand tremble as he signed the papers.

Sam nodded. Speaking would surely bring forth the torrent of tears he was working so hard to hold back.

It did look like a nice place, but it wasn't home and never would be, Sam thought as they returned to the waiting wagon.

That night, as Sam lay in the luxurious bed at the hotel, tears were finally released and rolled silently from eyes that soon became red and swollen. The fluffy pillow was soon soaked. The tears weren't just for what had happened today but for a combination of events: the passing of their ma and the stillborn child, Pa, and now the loss of three brothers and sweet little Martha. Sam felt alone, adrift on the endless plains with no family.

Chapter Five

The trip back to the ranch seemed like an unending journey to Sam. The north wind blew constantly. About three miles from the ranch house, they were pelted with sleet. When they finally arrived, the blazing fireplace in the huge living room was a welcome sight. It was hard for Sam to leave it long enough to go stoke the wood stove in the kitchen to start the evening meal, but soon, the kitchen was warm enough for the heat to seep into Sam's almost frozen body.

The evening meal seemed unusually quiet without the four younger children. Although they hadn't been rowdy, they had kept up a constant chatter about what they had done during the day. Now, those remaining sat in silence as they consumed the meal.

Trent finally broke the silence. "What did you think of the orphans' home?" he asked no one in particular.

After a long pause Helen finally answered. "Trent, the home you picked out seems very nice and well run. There are two dormitories, one for boys and one for girls. Sam said the boys took to it right away, but little Martha wasn't very happy when Sam had to leave her," Helen said with unusual sympathy for the child and Sam. "I must admit I miss the little ones, but, as we all know, it's the best place for them," she said with as much compassion as she could muster as she looked toward Sam.

Trent could tell the ordeal had been particularly hard on Sam. He was surprised that it had actually seemed to affect Helen. It was hard to judge if Flossy cared one way or the other if the children were gone.

Trent cleared his throat. "I'm glad to hear you approve." He turned to Sam. "What did you think of the home?"

Sam hesitated a few seconds and then met Trent's gaze. "It's the nicest place they've ever lived besides here. Like Miss Helen said, my brothers took right to it, but Martha—" he hesitated. "I expect she'll need a little time to get to know folks. The lady in charge of the girls said most little girls don't want to stay at first, but they get to like it pretty quick. I hope Martha will like it, but it was sure hard to leave her crying," Sam finished with evident sadness.

"I'm sure the lady's right. She's taken care of lots of children," Flossy attempted to soothe Sam's feelings in her off-handed manner.

The four lapsed into silence once more as they finished their meal.

As Sam cleared the table and the others were about to leave, he asked, "Does anyone want to use the bathing room tonight?"

"No," Trent answered.

"Me neither," Helen and Flossy answered in unison.

Sam put hardly enough warm water to cover the bottom of the tub and knelt in it to wash off. Realizing there was no towel in the room, Sam called out to someone still rattling around in the kitchen.

"Please bring me a towel. There isn't one in here. Just lay it by the door," Sam called out.

A few seconds later, the door opened, and Trent started to toss the towel onto the chair.

Trent was met with the piercing scream Sam let out that could have been heard halfway to Amarillo. "Get out, get out!" Sam yelled. One hand tried in vain to cover budding breasts while the other hand covered private parts obviously not belonging to a male. Besides, a male wouldn't care if another male had opened the door.

Trent stood like a statue, still holding the towel in his outstretched hand. He could hardly believe what he was seeing. Sam did not have the flat chest of a seventeen-year-old boy but the well-rounded breasts of a young woman. The other parts Sam was trying to hide most definitely were not that of a boy either. Then he saw the pink stain in the water. Stunned at the sight of the young woman in his bathing tub, he jerked back through the door as if the devil himself were after him.

"What the devil is this? Why have you lied to us all this time?" he thundered in a fuming voice that also could be heard halfway to Amarillo.

"Get out, get out!" Sam continued to scream.

"I ought to yank you out of that tub and whop your backside for lying to us." Trent roared in obvious anger as he slammed the door.

Helen and Flossy heard the uproar from the living room and were almost in a race to see what in the world all the screaming and yelling was about when they heard the door to the bathing room slam.

"You get dressed and come straight to the living room!" Trent yelled through the closed door.

He turned to see Helen and Flossy in the kitchen doorway, staring at him.

"What in the world is all this ruckus about?" Helen asked when she saw the livid expression on her brother's face.

Trent raked his fingers through his hair and shook his head as though he were trying to clear his thoughts. "Just go back to the living room and wait a few minutes. You'll find out," he said, still in shock.

Helen and Flossy exchanged a worried look but did as they were told.

Trent walked past them to his office, where he filled a glass full of whiskey. He carried the glass with him, taking several swallows, as he walked to the living room and sank into one of the plush armchairs.

Helen started to speak, but Trent held up his hand, motioning her to remain quiet.

Although it was rare for Helen, for once, she followed his unspoken request.

The three sat in silence for several minutes. Just waiting.

Flossy and Helen exchanged another look, obviously wondering what in the world had caused such an uproar in the bathing room a few minutes earlier.

Sam walked slowly through the door and stopped as though afraid to come any further into the room.

Trent looked up and motioned for Sam to sit on the settee beside Flossy.

Sam slowly advanced and perched on the edge as though ready to run if necessary.

Trent cleared his throat and looked directly at Sam. "Now," he paused. "Tell Helen and Flossy the secret you've been keeping from us," he said in a quiet, scarcely controlled, irate manner.

Sam stared at him for several seconds, her huge blue eyes meeting his stern, brown-eyed gaze that seemed to bore a hole right through her. Sam's chin rose slightly and, in a clear voice, stated, "I'm a girl!"

Helen and Flossy both let out a gasp of shock at Sam's announcement. They stared at her as if they were trying to see some evidence of what she said to be true.

"A girl!" Flossy almost scoffed as she scrutinized Sam.

"Well, I'll be damned!" Helen responded and started to laugh.

Trent glared at his sister. "Just what do you find so damn funny about her deceiving us all this time by pretending to be a boy?"

"I think it's so damned funny because she got away with it for this long, Mr. Trent Sanderson. You've always prided yourself on knowing all about people. You hire men just on a first look or a few words because you think you are such a good judge of people. Well, everyone makes a mistake now and then, even you. I don't suppose it helps your male ego to know what a drastic mistake you made this time," Helen finished and laughed even louder.

Trent didn't try to argue with Helen but opted for a few sips of whiskey instead. It burned less than his sister's sharp tongue.

He turned his attention back to Sam. "Surely, you have some other name than Sam," he inquired.

"Evangeline is my given name."

"Good heavens, I hope your parents called you Eva," Trent said in response to such an atrocious name.

Sam shook her head no.

"Vange," Trent ventured.

"No."

"Maybe they called you by your middle name; what is it?"

"No, they didn't call me Serafeni either," Sam answered.

"Well, what the devil did they call you? Surely not Sam!" Trent repeated, as he raised his voice in exasperation.

"They called me Sassy, and that is what you can call me from now on," she answered, as her intense gaze shifted from Trent to Helen and finally to Flossy.

"Sassy!" Trent said, as though he may have thought it wasn't much of an improvement.

"Why did they call you Sassy?" Helen asked.

"I've always took up for myself and my brothers and sister. Mama said I was sassy even before I could really talk."

"Well, it suits you quite well. I remember the night you sassed me for threatening to smack your brother for his bad table manners," Helen commented.

"Yes'um and I meant what I said," Sassy answered without hesitation.

Then she turned her attention back to Trent. "You were the one that called me a boy the day you found us when I was trying to dig Pa's grave. Ma warned me about what some men want to do to girls, so I thought it best to just let you think I was a boy. How was I to know if you were or weren't that kind of man?" she asked, never taking her eyes from Trent's face.

Trent let out a long breath. "You didn't at first, but surely, after you were here a while, you should have known better. Why didn't you speak up?"

"I was 'bout to, but then I found out Miss Helen wasn't your wife. I still weren't sure about what you might do, so I jus' kept quiet." Sassy lowered her gaze and spoke softly. "I'll pack my things and be on my way in the morning. I know you don't tolerate liars or people who don't follow your orders," she said in a humble but proud voice as she rose to leave the room.

"Sit down," Trent ordered.

Sassy looked startled, but she sat down again.

"How do you know what I do or don't tolerate?" he asked curiously.

"I heard you tell Miss Helen you fired a man just the other day for lying to you," she answered.

Trent merely nodded his head as he remembered the incident. "Just where do you think you would go? How in the devil would you support yourself? You'd probably wind up in some brothel, and all kinds of men—."

"Trent, that's enough!" Helen spoke sternly.

Helen turned her attention to Sassy. "You aren't going anywhere, young lady. I want you to take care of me, and we need a good cook."

Flossy sat up straighter and pouted. "So, you don't think I take good care of you?"

"You are tolerable at best, but I think Sassy will do much better," Helen answered in her straightforward manner.

"How do you know?" Flossy asked.

"I've seen the way she looked after her siblings, and I believe she can look after me just fine," Helen answered tersely.

"Well, I guess you want me to pack my things and leave," Flossy continued to pout, her mouth puckered with her bottom lip protruding slightly. She turned to Trent with a pleading expression on her pretty face as though in hopes he would take her side in the matter. There was no doubt she knew how to wind a man around her finger.

Trent ignored Flossy's attempt to get him to side with her against Helen. "There's enough work for both of you," Trent stated as he rose and started toward his office. He stopped at the door and turned toward the three women.

"Helen, you take to running this house and assign Sassy and Flossy as you see fit. I've spent too much time trying to solve everyone else's problems, and now I intend to spend my time running this ranch. Whatever happens in this house is up to you, Helen," he stressed. When Trent entered his office, he closed the door with a loud bang.

The three women stared in the direction of the unusually loud noise.

"Well, it seems the master has spoken," Helen said with a slight grin.

He might think he's the master, Sassy thought, but it might turn out that Helen is the one who rules the roost.

Helen looked questioningly at Sassy. "I'm curious; how did you get the children to not give you away?"

"While we were getting ready to follow Mr. Trent to the house, I told them if they said one word about me not being Sam, I'd take Pa's belt to them, and they knew I meant it!"

"Really!" Helen replied.

"Yes, ma'am. I had to make 'um mind."

"Well, they minded because I certainly didn't suspect you weren't a boy."

"If I had known you were a girl, I wouldn't have cut your hair so short," Flossy put in as she gave Sassy another once-over look.

Trent sat at his desk with his head resting in his hands. He massaged his temples in hopes it would relieve some of the tension he was feeling. What in the devil did he do to deserve having three females under his roof, he wondered as he contemplated the most recent revelation about Sam, no Sassy.

Now that it was obvious Sassy was a young woman, Trent felt obligated to keep a close watch over her, especially on his ranch full of often lonely men. No man here better ever try to take advantage of her, or he would have to answer to him, Trent thought, feeling very protective of the young woman. Woman! Yes, she was a woman. She might be wise to the ways of the world in some respects, but he'd bet his last nickel that she was innocent as a lamb. What worried him most was just why he was suddenly feeling so protective toward her.

The image of her silky young body with rounded breasts, trim waist, flat stomach, and shapely thighs he had a full view of in the bathing tub ran through his mind, and he felt a stir of desire he hadn't felt in quite some time.

That's crazy, he thought as he downed the remainder of his glass of whiskey. *She's hardly seventeen, and I'm twenty-six, nine years older and a hundred years wiser and far more experienced. Besides, I'm her employer. I have to maintain the same decorum with her as I would with Flossy or any other woman who has ever worked here, and there have been several, like Flossy, who were more attractive and willing,* he lectured himself.

"Get your head on straight and tend to running this ranch," he muttered as he headed to bed.

Chapter Six

Helen followed Trent's orders and took hold of running the house, a task which seemed to improve her disposition, probably because she had less time to dwell on her own self. Flossy and Sassy, under Helen's directions, each worked out their domain, managing to stay out of the other's way and keep down dissension.

Helen was also a good judge of people. Just as Helen had suspected, Sassy was far more suited to helping her with her personal needs than Flossy had been. Sassy had already proved she was the queen of the kitchen. When she told Helen she knew how to sew and could easily make her some new dresses and new curtains for all the windows if she had a sewing machine, Helen was delighted. They did have a sewing machine that had been tucked away in a corner of one of the barns, where unused furniture resided, collecting dust and critters. It was brought out of storage, oiled, and cleaned to perfection by Sassy. Helen planned a trip to town soon so they could buy materials and do some Christmas shopping.

Flossy contented herself with a dust rag that was swiped willy-nilly over the furniture and a broom and dustpan when necessary or a dust mop to keep the floors in passable condition. She did manage to clean all the windows on the inside, which took three times as long as it would have taken Sassy, but Helen didn't interfere with her cleaning. That way, she didn't have to think of something else for her to do to earn her keep. Helen wanted the china cleaned before Christmas and the silver polished. She wasn't sure about trusting Flossy with the china, so she delegated Flossy the task of polishing the silver, which seemed to irritate Flossy after an hour or so. She would say she had to stretch her legs and back and would put on her coat and go out for a stroll to relieve the tension. Helen and Sassy noticed her strolls usually led toward where the men were working, but that was Trent's domain if she caused any trouble.

As Christmas drew nearer, Helen often noticed the forlorn look in Sassy's eyes and knew she was missing her siblings. Her unhappiness tugged at Helen's heart, and she considered offering to buy her a train ticket to go see them for Christmas, but that wasn't the agreement Trent had made. Helen thought it best not to overstep those bounds.

Helen sat looking at her own reflection in the mirror as Sassy brushed her hair before bedtime. She found she liked herself better of late. All of this uproar with the children and now having two women to visit with, although she was their boss, had given her a purpose besides wallowing in self-pity. After all, it had been ten years since the accident that put her in that damned wheelchair, but that wasn't going to change. Now, it was time to get on with living, such as it was.

One more thing she was going to do was help Trent with the ranch. There was no earthly reason why she couldn't keep the books as well as he could, and that would give him more time to do the other things he needed to do. She smiled slightly at the thought of the look on his face when she gave him that news.

She caught a glimpse of Sassy watching her in the mirror. Sassy gave her a slight smile.

"Why are you smiling, Helen?" Sassy asked with evident amusement and curiosity. "Your impish little smile reminds me of Martha when she was about to get into some mischief."

"You don't miss much, do you?" Helen asked.

"Not much. I always had to keep an eye on the young'uns since Ma always seemed so poorly," Sassy answered with a faraway look reflecting into the past.

"Since I have you and Flossy to keep the house running with less direction from me, I've decided to help Trent with the ranch bookkeeping. I was just imagining the astonished look on his face when I give him that news," Helen chuckled as she put one arm around Sassy's neck. Sassy gently lifted Helen and then turned her so she could sit on the side of the bed. She lifted Helen's feet and covered her as though she were tucking Martha in for the night.

Sassy's smile broadened. "I'm sure Trent will appreciate your help. Sometimes, at night, I get thirsty and come down for a drink of water. Most nights, I see the light still burning in his office at midnight or later. Then, he's up by five in the morning. I know he don't get enough rest."

Helen fluffed her pillow and managed to roll to her side as she watched Sassy clean her hairbrush and straighten her dressing table. "These past ten years, I haven't been a very good sister. In fact, I've been pretty much of a burden. All I wanted to do was feel sorry for myself. I didn't even try to get along with the many housekeepers and cooks he hired." Helen paused. "But you, Sassy, and your brothers and sister started me to thinking about what a good life I have compared to all you've been through. I think that has given me a different outlook on life," she finished as Sassy turned to stare at her in astonishment.

Sassy hardly knew what to say in response to Helen's revelation. "We had some good times, too," Sassy said softly. "Ma used to gather us all around her during a thunderstorm and sing so we wouldn't be so scared. We never had much and sometimes went to bed hungry, but Ma said we was rich because we had each other."

"Your mother sounds like a wise woman," Helen agreed. "I had the love of my family, too. I thought I had the love of a man, but—well, that's something I don't talk about and try damn hard to not think about." Helen closed her eyes as though trying to shut out that part of her past.

Sassy stood beside the dressing table, just looking at the woman lying in the ornate four-poster bed. It was obvious she had once been a striking young woman, and she could still be exceptionally pretty; that is if she would fix herself up a bit. That man must have truly broken her heart, Sassy thought as she blew out the lamp and picked up her candle to leave the room.

Sassy had only taken a few steps when she heard Helen's voice fill the darkness. "Jack Thornton was the most handsome man I've ever laid eyes on, and he had a personality to match. His hair was flaxen blond with just a hint of a curl where it touched his collar. He had the bluest eyes I have ever seen, as blue as the bluebonnets in spring. He stood six feet two inches tall with broad shoulders, a manly man in every sense of the word. In the summer, his skin became bronze, making his hair look even blonder. When he walked into a room, it seemed to light up, and he encompassed everyone with that brilliant smile. All the young women were head-over-heels in love with him, but he chose me. Goodness knows I wanted him with all my heart."

The last few words came out in a choked whisper, and Sassy knew that was all Helen was able to say that night. She slipped from the room, closing the door softly. She stood in the silence outside the door for a few moments, listening to Helen's soft sobs.

Sassy was in a quandary. Should she go back to Helen or leave her to deal with her emotions alone? Somehow, she thought Helen would prefer to be alone, as she would likely feel restrained if anyone were there to witness her sadness.

As Sassy turned to move toward the stairs, she suddenly realized she was not alone. Startled, she opened her mouth to let out a shriek, but before a sound came out, in the soft glow of a candle, she saw Trent put one finger to his lips, signaling her to remain silent.

He had apparently just come from the bathing room as his hair was damp, and his shirt was unbuttoned, exposing his broad chest. The fine, damp hairs that covered his chest were shimmering in the faint glow from her candle. Sassy knew she shouldn't be staring at a man's bare chest, but it was hard to pull her gaze away. Finally, she managed to look up at his face and was met with just a hint of a smile. She knew the flickering flame of the candle revealed her cheeks turning pink under his scrutiny.

He motioned for her to follow him.

They walked quietly to his office, and he closed the door. He lit the lamp and turned to Sassy. "Did I hear Helen crying?" he asked a bit gruffly but with concern.

Sassy nodded her head. "She started telling me about Jack Thornton. It did seem to upset her to talk about him. Just as I closed the door, I heard her weeping, but I wasn't sure if I should go back to her or leave her be to cry alone. Sometimes, a person needs to cry but don't necessarily want anyone to see them. I think Helen is like that," she explained with a note of sadness and understanding.

Trent suspected Sassy had shed many tears over all the misfortune she had experienced. He had never seen her cry but suspected she, too, cried under the cloak of darkness, where no one would see her either.

Sassy saw Trent's expression harden. His fist clenched as though he were about to hit someone or something. She took a step backward, thinking he might think she had caused Helen to become upset.

Trent stared at Sassy's movement and realized what she was thinking. "Don't be afraid of me. I'm not mad at you," he said as he reached for the whiskey bottle and poured himself a generous glass full. "It's just when I hear that sorry son of—" He didn't finish what he was about to say. "Well, when I hear that sorry snake's name, I still want to beat him into the ground and stomp that handsome face until no woman would ever want to look at him again for what he did to my sister." He raised the glass and drank liberally.

Sassy stood rooted to the floor, not knowing what she should do next. Finally, she decided it wouldn't hurt to ask, and maybe it would be good for Trent to vent his pent-up anger.

She steeled herself. "What did he do to Helen?"

Trent met her gaze and motioned for her to sit down. He sank into his big leather chair behind the desk and folded his hands with the tips of his fingers touching, almost as though he were about to pray.

Maybe he was about to pray he wouldn't lose his temper again, Sassy thought as she waited for him to speak. He raised his eyes, but his gaze was peering into the distant past.

"Jack Thornton came to Amarillo about eleven years ago. He said he was from Philadelphia and had come to invest in land for some big shots back east. He made his acquaintance with all the right people: the bankers, the businessmen of substance, lawyers, and some of the big ranchers, and so on. Soon, he was on everyone's guest list for any social event or business transaction that might benefit his investors. We met him at the Felts family's annual spring picnic. The Felts are one of the richest and most influential families in Amarillo. They live in that sprawling mansion on Main Street with the white rock fence and manicured gardens. You've probably noticed it when you went to town." He looked at Sassy to confirm she knew which house he was talking about.

She nodded. It was a sprawling three-story house with rounded turrets at each corner. Long porches with numerous archways surrounded the entire house. The grounds were covered with gorgeous flowers of all colors, even this late in the year, and lots of evergreen shrubs. It would be hard to miss that place, she thought, as he continued talking.

"It happens they have a daughter, Caroline, the same age as Helen. Helen and Caroline were never friends. Caroline went back east to finishing school, and Helen, of course, grew up here on the ranch and never cared a twit for that sort of thing. That evening, it became obvious they had each set out to capture Jack Thornton's attention.

"Jack was a very savvy man, and you would have expected him to choose Caroline with her polished manners and plenty of money, but, instead, he turned his attention to Helen. Helen, of course, was well-mannered when necessary." He chuckled. "She comes from a well-off family, too."

Sassy noticed he did not use the word *rich*, but she suspected they were as rich or perhaps richer than the Felts family. They didn't live in luxury like the Felts, but most people probably realized their worth anyway.

Sassy noticed Trent's grip on the glass he held in one hand. The other was often balled into a fist as he talked. Then, it was as though he realized what he was doing and forced himself to relax.

"Within a few months, Jack was here constantly, courting Helen. All she could see were the stars in her eyes, but he was slowly assessing this place and subtly learning more about our cash flow and investments. Our father caught on rather quickly, and then it became obvious to me as well."

Trent stood, and half turned to refill his glass. This time, he sat it on the mantle and started pacing back and forth across the room, much like a caged animal.

"I knew Helen wouldn't listen to our father, so I tried to reason with her. Mother never tried to intervene in whatever Helen set her mind on, so she wasn't any help. Helen and I had a big row, and she threatened to run away with Jack. I knew that would kill our father. I told her I would run Jack off if she didn't settle down and take a good, long look at the kind of man we thought he was. She informed me they planned to marry at Christmas, but if we, Father and I, didn't back off, she wouldn't wait. She even threatened to get pregnant so we wouldn't try to stop her from marrying him."

Sassy saw Trent's irritation growing, and his pacing increased. So did his sips from the glass of the amber liquid. It disturbed her to see him becoming so upset due to speaking of this very personal matter. It made her uneasy when men drank too much. She remembered what it was like when her pa and his friends drank too much.

"Sir," she spoke softly.

Trent paused and turned to look at her. "Sir," he repeated with a small laugh. "You haven't called me *sir* in quite some time."

Sassy felt a blush burning her cheeks. "I mean Trent," she corrected herself. "I think it's too hurtful for you to go on talking about what happened to Helen. It can wait. Besides, I suppose it ain't really none of my business what happened to her, although I must admit I've wondered, but it can wait for another time," she said quietly, with empathy for the hurt this topic evidently caused.

Trent continued to stare at the young woman. She has a good head on her shoulders, he thought, and she was right. He was working himself up over something long past that should stay in the past.

Sassy dropped her head slightly to avoid his unwavering gaze. She felt vulnerable when he looked at her in such an intense manner.

"It's getting late," he finally answered. "You're right, it's hard to talk about what happened to Helen without me losing control of my senses." He could see the apprehensive expression in Sassy's huge blue eyes and noticed her hands clasp tightly together in her lap. He was making her uneasy, and he certainly never intended to do that. "Maybe Helen should be the one to tell you when she's ready," he concluded as he finished the last of the whiskey in his glass.

~

The next morning at breakfast, Helen announced they would be making an overnight trip to town to shop for the Christmas dinner supplies and a few gifts.

Helen turned to Trent. "You did send money to Aunt Lilly to get Angel's presents, didn't you?"

"Yes, about three weeks ago, so she'd have plenty of time for shopping. I included enough extra money for Aunt Lilly to help Angel shop for her best friends and teachers," he remarked.

"Well, Aunt Lilly better take charge of that, or Angel will spend it on herself," Helen replied with a slight snort.

"Now, Helen, that's not fair. I know Angel is spoiled, but she's not quite that bad. Besides, she has everything she could possibly want," Trent returned.

Sassy was looking from one to the other, wondering just who they were talking about.

Helen noticed the questioning look on her face and began to tell her about their younger sister.

"Angel is our younger sister. She was a change of life baby that broke our mother's delicate health. I wasn't interested in taking care of a child, and Trent had to help run the ranch. After Papa and Mama passed, it really became hard to care for her here at the ranch. I was in this wheelchair and only cared about myself. When she turned seven years old, we sent her to town with two of the families with school-age children, but she wouldn't mind either of the women and was always in trouble at school. Finally, Trent wrote to Aunt Lilly, our mother's only sister, who lives in Philadelphia, and asked her to take Angel. She wrote back that she could not take her into her home; she's one of those social butterflies, but there was a fine girls' boarding school nearby. Trent took Angel there, and now she and Aunt Lilly come for a visit in the summer. Winter's too hard for traveling. When they get here, after three or four days, Angel is bored and raises holy he—heck, so they usually go back after a couple of weeks."

Sassy gave Trent a questioning look. "I thought you told me there was only you and Helen."

Trent gave a sheepish grin. "I likely did. I must admit, I often forget that Angel really doesn't belong to Aunt Lilly."

"Oh, Trent, you men are so—so thoughtless sometimes," Helen said, a bit vexed.

"I'd think she would be happy to have summers off to come stay at the ranch with her sister and brother since you are her closest family," Sassy ventured.

"Not Angel. She's a spoiled, self-centered brat!" Helen stated with a mocking laugh.

"Now, Helen, don't be so hard on her. After all, she really hasn't been around us all that much, and it's very different here than what she is accustomed to," Trent stated mildly in defense of his youngest sister, now that he remembered he had one.

"Well, anyway, you won't meet her until next summer and will likely be glad to see the backside of her when she goes," Helen got in the last word.

Chapter Seven

Sassy felt excited about the shopping trip but sad at the same time, thinking about not being with her brothers and her own little sister for Christmas. This was their first Christmas without either parent or her, and she worried how they would be feeling.

Helen noticed her expression and suggested she buy each one a small gift, and they could mail them while in town so the package would reach the orphans' home in time for Christmas. The thought of sending them a gift seemed to lift Sassy's spirits. She had saved most of her wages and could afford to spend a little money on Christmas gifts.

Every day as she worked, she contemplated what she would buy for each one. Timothy liked to whittle, and his old knife constantly needed to be sharpened. Nathan loved music, so she thought a harmonica would please him. She wasn't sure how much the other boys would enjoy his playing, but he played pretty well for a ten-year-old. Daniel liked to build things even if they didn't turn out to look like much. She wondered if the home would mind if he had a hammer and some nails. Surely, they had some old boards he could use to make something. Little Martha loved that old rag doll their ma had made, but she didn't have time to make her a new one. Her birthday was in February, so maybe she could make a doll for her birthday, but what could she get her for Christmas? Her thoughts rambled as she started making supper. Maybe she would see something once they got to town, she finally decided.

The next morning was overcast with heavy gray clouds that threatened rain or maybe snow. Trent told Helen for them to not take any chances getting back the next day if the weather turned too bad. He had given Lester Hollis, one of the older ranch hands, enough money for the livery and a room for himself for a few days if need be. Lester was still a strong man and could handle getting Helen in and out of the wagon.

"Where is Flossy?" Helen asked, a bit irritated as they waited for her to come downstairs. "She didn't even come to breakfast. Go see what's taking her so long and tell her to come on," Helen told Sassy.

Sassy climbed the stairs and knocked on Flossy's door.

"Come in," Sassy heard her weak voice.

Sassy was surprised to see Flossy still snug under the covers when she opened the door. "What's the matter? We're waiting for you to go to town."

"I have a sore throat and don't feel a bit well. You and Helen will have to go without me. I'll be fine here by myself. I just need to rest," she spoke hardly above a whisper.

"I'll tell Helen, but I don't think she's going to like you staying here with just you and Trent in the house," Sassy said as she started to pull the door shut.

"You just tell her I'm too sick to care a twit about Trent, so she shouldn't get her bloomers all in a wad," Flossy fretted with a bit more vigor.

When Helen heard what Flossy had said, she wasn't one bit happy about the situation. "Sick!" Helen spat. "I'll believe that when I start believing in Santa Claus again!"

Sassy was afraid Helen would change her mind about going to town. After a few minutes of fuming, Helen finally said they were going. "After all, Trent's big enough to take care of his own self," she fumed. "If he's fool enough to be messing around with the likes of Flossy, so be it, and he'll get what he deserves."

~

About mid-day, an old wagon pulled up to the first barn carrying the Schwab brothers, Garvin and Adolph. The two men looked ancient, although they were likely in their early sixties. Worn and weathered from years spent working their ranch, time had taken its toll on the two men. Both widowers, each had sired only one daughter.

"Howdy, Biggun," Garvin called as he pulled the team to a stop alongside the spot where Biggun was working some horses.

"Garvin, Adolph, what brings you two old buzzards this far from home?" Biggun asked with a grin.

"Who you callin' old buzzards?" Adolph quipped, but his dark eyes twinkled, knowing Biggun was just having fun.

The three men laughed.

"Come to have a word with Trent. He around?" Garvin asked.

"He rode out a couple of hours ago but should be back any time. Get down, and we'll see if the cook has some left-over coffee."

The two men followed Biggun to the mess hall, where they did find some left-over coffee. Biggun noticed Garvin's limp seemed worse than the last time he had seen the two men, and Adolph kept blinking his eyes, trying to adjust to the change in lighting.

Before Biggun could feel out the intent of the men's visit, Trent joined them.

"Good seeing you two old buzzards," Biggun said with a grin as he rose to leave.

"You too, you scrawny little rat," Garvin chuckled.

"Trent, we've come on some important business," Adolph said.

"What kind of business?" Trent asked. You never knew what the brothers might have thought up.

"We've come to talk about sellin' the ranch," Garvin answered. His downcast look told Trent they were serious.

"Selling the ranch?" Trent asked in shock. He had imagined someday, someone would find the brothers passed away on their own land. He never thought they would ever live anywhere else.

"Yep, sad business, but we're gettin' on in years, and neither of our girls cares a tinker's damn about the ranch. We figure it's time to move on

JUDY MCGONAGILL

into town and settle in for the long haul to the graveyard," Adolph said a bit sadly.

Trent let out a short snort of laughter, "You boys aren't anywhere near ready for the graveyard."

"Well, we ain't much fit for ranchin' any longer, so it's time to call it quits," Adolph answered.

Trent studied the two men for several moments before he spoke. "A shame when a man don't have children that want what their folks worked so hard for. Yes, I know, it's time I started thinking about settling down and raising a family of my own," Trent admitted.

"Yeah, you need to be doing just that and pray to God for at least one boy. It's for dang sure girls don't want nothin' to do with ranchin'," Adolph agreed.

The three men sat in companionable silence for several moments.

"What price you got in mind?" Trent finally asked.

"You likely know our spread is 170,000 acres with two good flowing creeks and a fine little lake. The house ain't much, three rooms and a porch on the south that we've been intendin' turning into a sleepin' porch." Garvin said.

Trent nodded. "How big is that lake?"

"Oh, I'd guess it covers about twelve to fifteen acres."

Trent nodded again. "That's a real selling point since water's a constant worry. Does it stay pretty level during the summer?"

"Most summers. Just depends on how much spring rain the good Lord sends us," Gavin answered.

The three men went on to discuss the proposition, reached an agreeable price, and shook hands to seal the deal.

Trent stood watching the two men as they departed and realized that could be him in the future. The thought of not passing the Flatland Ranch on to his offspring was disquieting. Yes, it was time to seriously start looking for a proper wife, he contemplated as he headed toward one of the corrals.

Chapter Eight

T rent ate supper at the bunkhouse with the men. Then he sat in on a few hands of poker before heading to the house. He dreaded entering the cold house but decided he would only light the fire in his office, work for a bit, and go to bed early.

As he crossed the threshold into the dark kitchen, he could see the dim glow of light coming down the central hallway from the living room. He made his way quietly toward the light, wondering why a lamp would be lit with no one home. He stepped through the doorway with his hand resting lightly on the handle of the pistol he still wore. The sight of Flossy lounging on the settee came as a shock. She was scantily clad in a rose-colored, silky-looking robe with large lace ruffles around the low-cut neck that revealed another grand view of her voluptuous breasts. The lower skirt hung open, offering a tantalizing view of her shapely legs. The fire in the fireplace was burning bright, filling the room with warmth, and the rose lamp that cast a pinkish glow over the room was sitting on the table beside the settee, where she comfortably reclined on several pillows. Trent stared, speechless, at the alluring scene before him. An array of jumbled thoughts ran swiftly through his mind. Some said run, but more seemed to say stay, enjoy, just once, what is being offered.

~

Flossy felt as though she had been waiting for hours for Trent to come to the house, and, in a way, she had. She had been waiting all day and several hours after dark while planning this little welcome home surprise for her handsome boss, who was standing in the doorway gawking at her. His brown eyes glistened in the firelight, and it was obvious she was making quite an impression on him.

Flossy wanted to laugh. It was obvious Trent was so taken aback by the scene before him that all he could do was just stare at her without uttering a single word.

"Good evening, Trent," Flossy greeted him in a sultry voice. "I was about to think you were going to stay in the bunkhouse tonight."

Trent finally gained his wits. "I don't normally spend the night in the bunkhouse. I thought everyone had gone to Amarillo shopping."

Flossy gave a little wave of her hand. "Oh, it was so cold out. I had a bit of a sore throat and didn't want to take a chance on it getting worse. I decided to forego the shopping trip. I know they're having so much fun, and I truly hated to miss it," she said with a little pout, as though she felt sorry for herself for missing all the exciting shopping.

Trent had seen her use that same pouting expression on several occasions when she was vying for sympathy.

"Well, it seems you've made a quick recovery, as your voice sounds fine now," he commented as he started to turn toward his office.

Flossy thought fast. She didn't want to lose his attention so quickly to those old ranch books he seemed to work on nightly.

"I could use just a bit of whiskey to soothe my throat," she moaned, "so it doesn't get all scratchy again if you don't mind," she said, giving him a charming smile and a few flutters of her eyelashes.

"Of course," he answered in what sounded like a husky voice to Flossy.

Trent returned in a few minutes with two glasses filled with some of his best whiskey.

Flossy gave him an enticing smile. "Oh my, if I drink that much whiskey, you may have to help me ..." She gave a little giggle. "Oh my, I'm embarrassing myself," she said coyly.

Trent stopped in front of Flossy. He had to admit she was a real looker, with flawless skin and striking features. She wore her thick red hair down, tempting a man to run his fingers through it and watch her moods change in those riveting green eyes. What man wouldn't like to come home at the end of a hard day's work to such an enticing woman, he wondered, as he extended the glass toward her.

She glanced up at him demurely and leaned slightly forward to take the glass he offered. Her lips were slightly parted as their eyes met. Trent had another perfect view of her twin buttes like he had been treated to on the day she had given him a haircut.

Trent leaned toward her and said in a low, husky voice. "Flossy, our mystery woman. You certainly know how to tempt a man to sample what you're offering," he murmured hardly above a whisper as he leaned closer and closer.

Flossy gently covered his fingers with hers as she took the glass from his rough hand. She smiled sweetly. "Just what do you think I'm offering?"

Trent hesitated a moment, then answered softly but clearly, "Yourself."

"My, my, I'm flattered to know I tempt the great Trent Sanderson."

"Just what makes you think I'm above temptation?"

Flossy adjusted her position slightly and motioned for him to sit beside her, which he did without hesitation. "I've heard about your reputation as being one of the most successful ranchers in this part of Texas," she said as she took a delicate sip of the whiskey. She turned her gaze to him and continued. "I've also heard you are the most desirable bachelor around and considered the prize catch for any man's daughter, but—yet, you're still single."

"For someone who seldom leaves the ranch, you seem to have heard quite a lot about me, whether it's true or not."

Flossy leaned closer once again, giving him another tantalizing view of her enticing breasts. "Oh, I believe it's all true," she whispered as she leaned even closer, and their lips met.

She brushed her lips lightly across his, and her breasts teasingly pressed seductively against his hard chest.

Trent knew this was the moment for a decision. He knew he should pull away, politely refuse her offer, retreat to his office, and lock the door.

He knew Flossy was not the kind of woman he would ever settle down with. She would only be a fleeting pleasure. Trent admitted he was lonely and had thought more and more as of late about finding a wife and settling down, but this was definitely not leading in that direction.

Flossy increased the kiss by slowly running her tongue across his lips and adding just a bit of pressure. The slight movement, as her body pressed enticingly against his, provoked immense temptation.

What would one night of pleasure hurt? Trent reasoned. Flossy was wise to the ways of the world. Surely, she wouldn't be foolish enough to expect more or hope to win his affections. No one would ever know but the two of them, he decided, as he gave in to Flossy's ardent kisses.

They sampled not only the potent whiskey, but their compelling desires flamed as they enjoyed the tantalizing pleasures of the flesh each brought to the other.

The two became consumed in the powerful allure of each other's bodies and drank their fill of the compelling pleasures their lovemaking produced. In the late hours of the night, when their passion was spent, they succumbed to an exhausted sleep.

Trent's sleep was filled with dreams of passion and fulfillment, but when he opened his eyes to gaze at his lover's face, it wasn't Flossy's face he saw. He moaned as Sassy's sweet face came into focus. Sassy smiled shyly and pushed him away. Then she fled into the swirling, dark mist and was lost from him in its thickening darkness. He could feel his heart race as he searched wildly for her through the dense fog. Constantly seeking, running, calling, *Sassy—Sassy!*

Trent awoke with a start. The first light of dawn was creeping above the horizon. His rumpled bed was empty. He lay looking at the early morning shadows that filled his room. The reality of what had happened the night before came to him in a rush. An uneasy feeling consumed him. Damn! What a fool he'd been for one night of pleasure to satisfy his male lust. Damn, damn!

Trent dressed quickly. As he opened the door to leave his room, he could hear Flossy humming in the kitchen. The smell of bacon cooking filled the air. He walked to the kitchen but said nothing to Flossy as he headed toward the back door.

Flossy, with her hair still in disarray and wearing the silky gown from the evening before, turned and gave him a charming smile. "Good morning," she greeted him cheerfully. "Breakfast is almost ready," she said sweetly.

Trent reached for his coat hanging by the back door. "You can eat it. I'll eat at the bunkhouse."

Flossy gave him a sulking look. "Don't tell me you'd rather eat breakfast with that bunch of stinking cowboys than with me after what we shared last night."

Trent stared at her without any hint of pleasure in his expression. He gave no indication he was pleased with her reference to the night they had just spent together. "Last night will never be repeated between you and me, so don't get any romantic ideas about us," he stated emphatically.

Flossy put her hands on her hips and glared at him. "So, you just used me, and now you're ready to throw me away like an old worn-out boot. Is that all it meant to you?" she asked, letting him know she was insulted by this statement.

"That's about it," Trent answered as he put on his hat and opened the door.

Flossy shouted at his retreating back, her green eyes blazing in anger. "That's what you may think, but we'll see, Mr. Trent Sanderson!" she screeched.

The door slammed behind Trent, and he heard the spatula Flossy had been holding hit the door with a loud thud.

Flossy's temper flared as she glared at the closed door. She picked up the spatula that had bounced off the door, landing near her foot, and hurled it into the sink.

Trent rode to the western side of the ranch to check on the cowboys and ranch operations. As he topped a small hill, he reined in his horse so he could fully take in the expansive vista that stretched as far as he could see and miles beyond. It all belonged to his family. It was an awing thought.

Trent had realized at an early age that he had been born to a life of privilege for which his parents had taught him to be grateful. Now, he was the caretaker of this magnificent ranch and everyone who worked and lived on it.

Those thoughts brought to mind what had happened with Flossy. He was fully aware he had crossed the line in several ways. Trent gazed at the azure-blue sky dotted with a few white clouds. He did not speak aloud. *Lord, I ask for your forgiveness for my weaknesses as a man. I ask you to grant me strength and guidance.*

Chapter Nine

Helen and Sassy got home late in the afternoon, their arms full of parcels that Lester unloaded for them. Flossy was nowhere in sight, but that was not unusual. They thought she was probably out for one of her strolls or napping in her room.

Sassy hurried to the kitchen to start supper. She was a bit puzzled when she saw a glob of something stuck to the back door. It was obvious Flossy had made some attempt at cooking from the looks of the stove and dirty pan and spatula left in the sink.

When Flossy came in for dinner, she didn't say anything about the mess she left in the kitchen. Nor did she ask about the shopping trip she had missed.

Helen and Sassy exchanged a quick glance. "Are you still sick?" Helen finally asked.

Flossy stared at Helen as though puzzled by her question, then nodded as Helen's question sank in. "I feel a bit better," she answered in a surly voice.

Trent joined the three women for dinner; Helen and Sassy's talk centered on their trip to town and the purchases of material for new curtains and dresses for Helen, the gifts they had mailed to the children, and special foods purchased for Christmas lunch.

Flossy sat in sullen silence. She excused herself as soon as she had finished her meal, saying she had a headache. The others remained at the table, discussing the upcoming Christmas celebration.

"Now, let's see," Helen said. "We'll have Sonny Tate and his family, that's seven. Biggun makes eight. The four of us will make twelve for Christmas lunch."

Sassy knew Sonny was the ranch foreman. His wife and children spent the week in town so the older children could attend school, and they came back to the ranch on the weekend. The school was dismissed for two weeks so the ranch families could go home to celebrate the holidays.

Biggun had worked at the ranch for twelve years since he was thirteen. He had been a young drifter with no family. Trent's father had hired him and quickly saw Biggun had promising potential to make a top-notch hand. The family had taken him in and always included him in family celebrations.

"I'd like to include the new horse buyer I hired a few days ago, too," Trent told Helen.

"Oh, I didn't know we had a new horse buyer. Who is he?"

"Ely Murry is his name. He's from Oklahoma originally. Last worked for the Caprock Ranch. He's probably about forty. His wife died several years ago. They didn't have any children. He sure seems to know horses," Trent finished.

"That's fine, one more won't matter. That is if it's all right with Sassy. Do you think you can cook for that many people?" Helen asked Sassy.

"Oh, yes, ma'am. You just tell me what to fix, and I can do it."

"I wish you'd teach her how to make Mama's pumpkin pie," Trent suggested with a wistful little grin.

Sassy looked at Helen. "If you can write it down and help me with the measuring a bit, I'll sure give it a try," Sassy answered excitedly.

Helen smiled. "I'll write it down and how Mama made her dressing, too. That lazy Flossy is going to help, too. She can at least cut up celery and onion for the dressing and fruit for the salad, if nothing else," Helen said, obviously a bit put out at Flossy's lackadaisical attitude.

"I wouldn't be so sure about that," Trent mumbled as he got up from the table.

~

Christmas fell on a Tuesday, and the few days before were a buzz of activity. Sassy thought about her brothers and Martha occasionally but said a little prayer they would have a good Christmas and not miss her or their folks too much.

Just after breakfast, Helen announced everyone was to come to the living room. Trent had a fire going and had lit several lamps since it was not quite daylight. Helen told Sassy to pass out the gifts that had been placed under the most elaborately decorated tree Sassy had ever seen. Each present was wrapped with pretty paper and tied with colorful red or green ribbons. It seemed more gifts were there this morning than the night before.

Each person took turns unwrapping his or her gifts, and much to Sassy's surprise, she found a pretty, new, store-bought dress in her package from Helen and Trent. It was emerald green with beige lace around the collar and cuffs. Tiny buttons lined the front of the bodice, and the skirt flared to a graceful fullness. "Oh! It's beautiful," Sassy exclaimed. "I ain't never had such a pretty dress 'afore, and it's ready-made." Then she glanced at Helen with a questioning look. "Where will I wear such a fine dress?"

Helen chuckled. "Well, for starters, you'll wear it to lunch today."

When Flossy opened her package from Helen and Trent, she tried to look appreciative at the practical pair of brown low-heeled walking shoes, but it was obvious they were not to her taste and she felt slighted.

Helen read her look but had known ahead of time the gift wouldn't be to her liking. In defense of her choice, she said, "I've been afraid you were going to take a fall on one of your walks, wearing those shoes with heels. They aren't very suited for walking over this rough ground. These will make it much easier and safer." Helen tried to sound concerned for Flossy's safety.

Flossy didn't respond but gave Helen an indulgent smile.

When Flossy and Sassy left the room, Trent turned to Helen. "You didn't have to make it quite so obvious that you don't care for Flossy."

"I certainly didn't intend to give her a false impression that I think of her in equal terms as Sassy. After all, Sassy does three times as much work and doesn't pout and sulk about the least little thing. In fact, she never complains about anything I ask her to do," Helen defended herself. "If you're unhappy with my choice, maybe you can think of some way to make it up to her, dear brother." The old insolent Helen emerged.

Trent didn't meet his sister's gaze but stood to leave. "What's done is done. I certainly don't intend to try to rectify anything."

As he headed toward the barn, he thought to himself how doing any favor for Flossy would create more problems than it would solve. He wished she would just leave. But why should she? She had a nice room, three meals a day, and a small salary in exchange for little effort on her part. No, it wasn't likely she'd be going anywhere soon unless she got bored and started chasing some of the other men. Maybe that would be the key to getting rid of her. He'd just have to be patient because, after the night they had spent together, he felt quite certain the enticing Flossy was the kind of woman who didn't like to be without the pleasures of a man's company for very long.

Mid-morning, Trent returned to the house. As he opened the door to the kitchen, he was assailed with a variety of delicious smells. His eyes fastened on the three pumpkin pies, three pecan pies, and a fruitcake sitting on the kitchen table.

"Umm! It sure smells good in here," he commented appreciatively as he neared the table. He leaned over and took a deep sniff of the pumpkin pie. "That sure smells like the ones Mama used to make," his expression was wistful.

Sassy was standing at the stove stirring the giblet gravy. "Would you like to sample a piece to be sure it's worthy to serve the guests?" she asked with an impish grin.

"I'll sure take you up on that," Trent answered as he headed for the cabinet to get a plate and knife to cut the pie.

"How about a cup of fresh brewed coffee, too?"

"Yes, thanks. How about you take a break and join me in sampling this pie and have a cup of coffee, too," he suggested as he cut himself an ample slice.

When Sassy saw the size of the slice of pie he had just cut, she hoped he wouldn't be disappointed.

"I'll have a small piece, about a third that size," she said with a slight smile.

Trent took his usual chair at the end of the table, and Sassy sat on the side next to him.

She watched his face closely to gauge his expression when he took the first huge bite from his fork. He chewed slowly, savoring the various flavors of the spices mixed with the pumpkin and tasting the crisp crust. Then, he looked at Sassy and smiled just before he swallowed his mouthful of the apparently delicious pie.

"Well?" she asked, still wanting to hear his verbal approval.

"Well, that's the best darn pie I've had since Mama passed."

Sassy laughed as she took her first bite and had to agree it had turned out mighty fine.

Trent had finished his pie while she was still eating. He took several sips of the steaming coffee. His gaze wandered to the pecan pies. "Maybe I should sample a bit of the pecan pie to see if it is worthy to serve to company," he said with a big grin.

His actions reminded her of something one of her brothers would have done. Men were just big boys in lots of ways, she decided.

"Help yourself, but if you eat much more, you won't have room for lunch."

"You're probably right. Guess I'll wait. I'm fairly certain they're just as delicious as the pumpkin pie."

Then, to Sassy's utter surprise, he leaned over and gave her a quick kiss on the cheek. "You really do a wonderful job around here, and Helen seems so content now. I just wanted to tell you how much I appreciate everything you do."

Sassy felt a slight blush climb to her cheeks at his praise but even more so at his unexpected kiss. When she dared look at him to tell him how much she appreciated what all he had done to help her and the children, she found herself staring into the depths of his golden-brown eyes. He seemed to be studying her in an unusual manner. There was a look in his eyes she didn't quite recognize.

She started to speak but was interrupted by Trent leaning forward and lightly brushing her lips with his. No man had ever kissed her on the lips. His action set a swarm of butterflies loose in her stomach. The kiss was brief. Trent instantly pulled back. His own startled expression indicated he was likely surprised at his own actions.

Trent stood abruptly. "Excuse me," was all he said as he made a hasty retreat from the kitchen.

What had come over him to make him be so forward with Sassy? Just because she was looking more like a woman every day, which certainly had not escaped his notice now that her rounded breasts and the curve of her hips were obvious, didn't give him leave to be forward with her. When he first discovered she was a girl and heard about how her papa's friend had tried to take advantage of her, he had vowed to protect her if any man tried that again. Of course, it had just been a quick kiss. But he would have to make certain to keep his desires and actions in close check from now on, he lectured himself silently as he walked toward the barn. He had made a mistake by yielding to Flossy's enticing charms. He couldn't afford to make the same mistake with Sassy. And Sassy was a different story altogether. He believed Sassy was still innocent, whereas Flossy, he was quite certain, had been down the road and back more than a few times.

Sassy sat for several minutes, sipping the now lukewarm coffee, wondering what to expect from Trent Sanderson. Was he going to turn out like Pa's friend and try to take liberties with her, or was it just a spur-of-the-moment gesture? What if she had to leave here? Now wasn't the time to think about such possibilities. She had to finish Christmas lunch before the guests arrived. As she stood and walked back to the stove, she said a quick prayer that he wouldn't turn out to be a man with no honor. Although inexperienced as she was, she couldn't help but wonder what it would be like to have a real kiss, like a man and woman would share, from Trent.

Special occasions were the only time the formal dining room was used. Sassy stood in the doorway admiring the finery displayed in the room. It was hard to imagine that she would be one of the people seated at the elegant table. The table was stretched to accommodate the crowd and laid with a white tablecloth embroidered with large red poinsettias around the entire edge. Five silver candleholders, each holding a tall red candle, lined the center of the table. The china, silverware, and crystal goblets glistened in the lamplight, and candlelight added a cheerful glow to the room.

The food was placed on the sideboard so people could go back for refills at will. Helen knew all about the ravenous appetites of ranch hands. Trent invited Sonny to say a prayer before the meal.

Then, Helen placed her wheelchair at the end of the sideboard and played hostess, pointing out where each guest was to be seated. Much to Trent's relief, on his left, was Sonny, his three youngest children, his wife, Mary, and their oldest daughter; Helen was seated at the far end of the table; and on Trent's right side were Biggun, Flossy, fifteen-year-old Freddy Tate, Sassy, and Ely next to Helen. The table conversation flowed easily among the guests, except for Flossy, as they consumed the delicious meal mostly prepared by Sassy. Trent noticed while they enjoyed the savory desserts, Flossy had begun to take an interest in Biggun. She had always been casually friendly with Biggun, but this seemed like more, something he couldn't quite grasp. Fine with him.

After what had happened in the kitchen earlier, Sassy was glad she wasn't seated too close to Trent. Her mind kept wandering back to the alluring touch of his lips on hers. He possessed an appealing charm that attracted people and plenty of women, she would bet.

Trent noticed how pretty Sassy looked in her new dress, and her hair had grown enough to curl up slightly at the base of her neck, so she looked more like a young woman instead of a boy. The emerald-green dress fit her well and accented her womanly figure. The color seemed to enhance the blue of her lovely eyes. For some reason, her perfectly shaped lips seemed to have escaped his notice before this morning. *Don't go to thinking about how those lips would taste in a more passionate kiss. Keep your mind on other matters; she's too young for you, and you are her boss,* he chided himself again. However, he did feel compelled to let her know what a good job she had done on the fine meal they were all enjoying.

Trent raised his voice slightly to be heard. "Sassy, this is the most delicious Christmas meal we've enjoyed in a number of years," Trent complimented her.

When everyone heard his comment, they heartily agreed the meal was delicious, bringing a slight blush to Sassy's cheeks.

Flossy had sat quietly, thinking what a dull gathering, a boy of fifteen on one side and Biggun on the other. Biggun had been talking and laughing with Trent and Sonny throughout the meal. So, that left her all alone in the crowd, she lamented. Then an idea struck her. It might prove helpful to show more than a casual interest in Biggun. He wasn't the rich boss, but he might become useful in a number of ways. Biggun was an attractive man. He wore his black wavy hair short, and the dark color enhanced his grey eyes. His strong facial features made him almost handsome, and he was a congenial man.

Helen found Ely Murry to be a most pleasant table companion and noticed he was nice looking to boot. A few silver streaks near his temples shone in his black hair. At first, she thought his eyes were almost black but discovered, when they caught the lamplight just right, they were a deep blue. He had a pleasant smile and a deep, manly voice. Naturally, they talked about horses, one of her passions before her accident. He had the good grace to not ask if she still rode. It also surprised her that he paid little attention to Flossy, only a polite comment occasionally.

Ely had been observing those gathered around the table, assessing the kind of folks that lived in the house and a few that lived on the ranch. During the past few days, he had keenly observed how Trent ran this ranch that stretched almost forty miles north to south and nearly thirty miles east to west. It was the biggest ranch he'd ever worked on. He had decided he approved of the way the young rancher handled the ranching business as well as his employees. The foreman was a decent man as well, and Ely felt certain they would get along fine. He hadn't quite figured out how the big man they called Biggun figured into the family.

Ely had heard about Trent's sister, Helen, but only sketchy details about what had happened to put her in a wheelchair. Biggun had mentioned there had been an accident at the creek but didn't go into any details. Apparently, Helen had become very bitter for a long time but seemed to be doing better lately. To his surprise, he had found Helen to be pleasant company and could tell she had once been much prettier than she was now. She was still a nice-looking woman for thirty or so, he guessed.

Ely knew two more women lived in the main house and wondered if one was Trent's woman. He hadn't asked, as he didn't know anyone well enough to ask such a question. If he were a betting man, he would place his money on Flossy trying to catch the boss and would rule Sassy out. But in the end, although she wasn't as striking as Flossy and was considerably younger than Trent, she might just be the winner. It was more likely neither woman would capture the young man, Ely decided.

By the end of the meal, Ely knew beyond a doubt he had found a place he intended to stay for a long while. He also knew just how he intended to accomplish that fate.

Chapter Ten

Finally, the second weekend in January arrived, and Sassy could hardly wait for the train that would take her to Wichita Falls to leave. As she stood beside the depot waiting to board the train, she smiled, thinking about all the warnings Helen had given her about traveling alone. *Sit by a mature woman. Don't talk to any men. If they persist in trying to talk to you, just act like you are deaf,* Helen had advised, sounding more like her mother than her employer.

It was amazing how much Helen had changed during the short time Sassy had been at the ranch. It made Sassy feel good to think perhaps she had helped Helen regain her desire to live and not stay locked away in the house and inside herself.

The subject of Jack Thornton had never come up again, and that was all right with Sassy. She didn't want to see Helen upset over the past. Sassy had also noticed that Ely Murry found occasions to drop by for a cup of coffee when Trent wasn't home. Sassy strongly suspected he was coming to see Helen. She wasn't sure if Helen had caught on to his ploy just yet, but it wouldn't take long before she realized the man was interested in her. It would be wonderful for Helen to find some good man to love and to love her in return. Sassy sensed that Ely appeared to be such a man from what little she had been around him.

"All aboard!" the conductor finally called.

Sassy entered the train car and looked for a woman to sit beside, just as Helen had instructed. She saw an older woman seated near the middle of the car and asked if she could join her. The woman smiled pleasantly. Even before the train pulled out of the station, the woman started talking and didn't hush until everyone else in the car had dozed off. Sassy was thankful to have found such a pleasant traveling companion, but she had to admit she was glad when the woman yawned several times, adjusted her coat to make a pillow, and fell asleep. Sassy felt sleepy, too, but was far too excited about seeing her brothers and Martha to fall asleep.

At long last, the lights of Wichita Falls came into view. The train started to slow as the whistle announced their arrival. Passengers getting off at this stop began gathering their belongings. Sassy's traveling companion snoozed through their departure.

On their previous trip, Helen had arranged for a room at the home of two maiden sisters, Thelma and Evelyn Jones, who let clean rooms at a reasonable rate, and that included breakfast and dinner. The two women were in their forties, short, with round figures and rosy cheeks, and they loved to talk and laugh. They laughed about most anything. They made every stranger feel right at home, and Sassy liked that feeling. She was to go straight there in a cart provided for delivering passengers to their lodgings. She would have time to freshen up and then go visit the orphanage after breakfast.

Early Monday morning, she would catch the train back to Amarillo, hopefully arriving by early afternoon. She would go straight to the livery and drive the wagon already loaded with supplies back to the ranch and arrive by dusk. If the train was late, Trent had told her to go spend the night with Mary and the other ranch hands' wives and come home the next morning.

Trent had given her a pistol to carry with her, and he'd made sure she knew how to use it. When he had taken her out to prove her skills, he was quite taken aback when she hit each target dead center. She smiled, remembering how amazed he looked at the end of their practice session. She felt sure he had doubts about her taking care of herself if she ran into trouble, but her ability with the pistol seemed to relieve his anxiety concerning that matter. She supposed shooting a pistol was one good thing her pa had taught her.

Sassy arrived at the orphans' home shortly after the children had finished their breakfast. After a few minutes of confusion as to who she actually was and why they had the name Sam McCoy on all the children's papers, Sassy received a stern comeuppance from Miss Jolene Martin, head of the orphans' home. Miss Martin harshly pointed out that she had falsified documents, which could be a serious offense. For a few minutes, Sassy thought Miss Martin was going to refuse to let her see the children. Finally, after her stern lecture, Sassy was permitted to see her brothers and Martha.

At first, the children seemed confused about her appearance as a girl. She wasn't about to tell them how the Sandersons had found her out but just said she didn't need to dress like a boy anymore since she worked in the house and was taking care of Helen.

The boys exchanged a worried look.

"Does she treat you mean?" Timothy asked.

"No. She's really a nice person once you get to know her," Sassy assured them.

They were each excited to see her, and all tried to talk at the same time to tell her about their experiences at the home. Martha clung to her, smiling but saying little, which concerned Sassy. Normally, Martha was a chatterbox.

Timothy had made several good friends and was learning to play baseball. He was getting to be one of the best pitchers for their team. Nathan had joined the school rhythm band and was learning to play the drums. He demonstrated his new skills with his newly acquired drumsticks. Daniel took them to the workshop, where he introduced Sassy to Jacob Smyth, the head repairman. Jacob had a kind face and a gentle manner. It was obvious he and Daniel had developed a close relationship. Jacob fixed the broken furniture and refinished furniture and was patiently teaching Daniel to be his assistant when he wasn't in class.

Sassy could see how excited Daniel was to get to work with tools. She was surprised when he proudly presented her with a prettily wrapped package. The children watched as Sassy gently removed the single ribbon, tied in a neat bow, and the pretty paper.

"Oh, Daniel! It's beautiful," she exclaimed as she held the small wooden box with a simple butterfly carved on the top.

Daniel was grinning from ear to ear, his blue eyes shining, showing his obvious pride.

"Open it, open it," the other three chimed in unison.

Sassy lifted the lid and saw a pretty pair of gold earbobs with tiny green stones that happened to match her Christmas dress.

"Oh, oh!" she was speechless, as tears of joy filled her eyes.

"Them's from me and Nathan and Martha," Timothy said, seeing how pleased she was with the gifts.

"We put our 'lounces together and bought them for you at the five and dime store in town," Nathan informed her.

Martha just smiled shyly as she watched her older sister put on the shiny earrings. Sassy grabbed them all in one big hug as tears of joy filled her eyes.

She glanced up at Mr. Smyth, who stood nearby watching the children and their older sister.

Jacob could see the love they shared, but he knew he would have to speak to her soon about what might happen.

Sassy smiled at Mr. Smyth. "Thank you for being so kind to Daniel. He's always loved to play with a hammer and nails, and now, he is really learning what to do with them."

"He is indeed, and with age, he will become a real craftsman," Smyth replied as he reached out and tousled Daniel's blond hair.

"My wife and our three daughters live only a few blocks away, and we'd like for Daniel to come spend some time with us on the weekends if that's all right with you," he asked as he gently patted Daniel on the shoulder.

"Please, please," Daniel begged with pleading eyes as he looked up at his sister.

"I think that would be mighty fine. I'll tell Miss Martin before I leave that he has my permission to go with you."

Sassy stopped by the office before leaving to return to the boarding house for the night. When she told Miss Martin about Mr. Smyth's request, Miss Martin smiled but had a sad look on her face.

"That's kind of you to let Daniel go visit the Smyth family. You see, their only son died of the flu last winter. He was about the same age as Daniel. I'm sure it will be a great comfort to them, and especially Mr. Smyth, to have Daniel come visit."

"That's good. Daniel seems very fond of Mr. Smyth and loves working with him in the workshop."

Miss Martin cleared her throat. "When you come for your next visit, I'll have all the children's papers ready for your real signature. As I told you before, what you did by signing a false name could be a serious offense, but I'll let it pass this time. What is your real name?" she asked in a firm voice.

"My given name is Evangeline," then she hesitated. "Well, our real last name was McRoy, but when my pa got into some trouble in Texas and fled to Kansas, he changed it to McCoy, so I ain't exactly sure which name we should use."

Miss Martin looked totally exasperated at the young woman. "Do you or any of your siblings have birth records?"

Sassy thought for a moment. "I ain't exactly sure. We was all born at home."

"Was a doctor there or just some neighbor lady?"

"I think just some neighbor lady," Sassy answered, trying to remember if she had ever seen a doctor in their house for any reason.

Miss Martin let out a frustrated sigh. "When you get back to the ranch, have someone there help you write to the state capitol in Topeka and tell them where you and the others were born and see if they have any records of your births. You need to get one for each of you. I think, in this case, you can choose the name your family was going by at the time of your births. Do it immediately, and bring the papers back with you next month," she instructed in a dismissive manner.

As soon as Sassy got back to the ranch, she told Helen, Trent, and Flossy about getting into trouble with the orphans' home for signing the wrong name on the children's admission papers. She explained that she also needed help in getting birth records for herself and the children.

"Don't you worry," Helen told her. "I'll write a letter to Topeka and find out if there are records of your births. If not, I'll tell them to let us know just what we need to do to get the birth records. If that Miss Martin gives you any more trouble, you tell her I'll be coming to straighten things out," Helen declared, indicating she didn't intend to put up with any guff from Miss Martin or anyone else.

A few days later, on an unusually warm afternoon for January, Ely pulled up to the front porch in the buggy. His boots clunked on the wooden front steps and porch as he approached the door.

Sassy had seen him coming and opened the door before he could knock.

Ely tipped his hat politely. "I'd like a word with Helen if she's available."

Before Sassy could answer, Helen rolled her chair into the room. "I'm available. Come on in," she called out to Ely.

"I've come to take you for a buggy ride," he said with a broad grin.

Helen looked taken aback at his statement. "A buggy ride?" she questioned.

"Yes, ma'am. We have a herd of young horses running loose in the near south pasture, and I thought you'd enjoy seeing them. They're real beauties," he emphasized, still smiling.

Small lines crinkled at the corners of Ely's deep blue eyes. He was a fine-looking man, Sassy thought as she watched him. She wondered if he was smiling at the sight of Helen or at the thought of the young horses.

Before Helen could refuse his invitation, Sassy quickly moved toward her room. "I'll get your shawl, and you'll be ready to go."

Sassy watched as Ely easily lifted Helen from her wheelchair, carried her down the steps, and gently set her in the buggy. She stood on the porch, watching as the buggy finally disappeared over a slight hill and out of sight.

Ely got out to open the gate, and Helen drove the buggy through the gate. When he climbed back into the buggy, she handed him the reins again. They drove on, carrying on a light conversation. Suddenly, Ely stopped the buggy and pointed across the pasture toward the creek.

"Just look at that," he said with awe in his voice.

Helen quickly saw the herd of horses running along the creek, their manes flying as they went. The sunlight glistened on their shiny coats of many colors. Even from this distance, she could see their fine shapes and the ripples of their bodies as they moved in a graceful motion.

"Oh, they are indeed beauties," Helen agreed as she turned to look at Ely.

Their eyes met, and they sat just staring at one another. Ely leaned forward and put one arm around Helen's shoulder, pulling her gently to him. Their lips met in a tender kiss. Ely lifted his head momentarily. "They don't hold a candle to you, Helen," he murmured as his lips met hers again in a more passionate kiss. Helen did not pull away.

Ten days after Helen sent the letter of inquiry to Topeka, a reply arrived. There were no records of any births for the McCoy or McRoy children. Some official-looking papers were included in the parcel. Helen and Sassy spent the better part of the afternoon filling out several papers on Sassy and each of the children. They wanted to complete as much information as possible so the papers could be sent to town with Biggun to mail back the next day when he went for supplies.

Sassy reflected on the information the state requested as she cooked their evening meal. She remembered how embarrassed she had felt when she had to tell Helen and Trent she didn't know her own mother's maiden name, and now it was on all of those papers. Helen said if you didn't know something, you wrote *unknown*. By the time they had finished filling out the papers, Sassy realized there were a lot of *unknowns* about her family. She just hoped the birth records would arrive before it was time for her next visit. If she came without them, she felt certain Miss Martin would give her a real comeuppance and maybe even call the law.

Tonight, she was cooking a big pot of chili, pinto beans, and cornbread for six people. She made two mincemeat pies for dessert, as she knew they were one of Biggun's favorites. He came for supper two or three nights a week, and lately, Ely had been coming just about as often, too.

It was rather obvious Ely was courting Helen, and she glowed with her newfound interest in a man. Sassy prayed every night that he wouldn't turn out to be another Jack Thornton. He seemed like a nice man, but he hadn't been at the ranch very long. They really didn't know much about him, only what little he had told them about his past.

Sassy had also noticed Flossy coyly flirting with Biggun. She knew Flossy wanted Trent to like her in the way Ely liked Helen, and she thought Flossy's attention to Biggun was a ploy to make Trent jealous. However, she had also noticed that Trent seemed to pay little attention to anything Flossy did.

It was nice when the two men came for supper. She enjoyed listening to their lively talk about the ranching business. Through their conversation, she was learning about different breeds of cattle and horses. She was still amazed at the vastness of the Flatland Ranch. Her ears perked up when she heard Trent mention buying the Schwab Ranch.

"How many acres does it cover?" Ely asked.

Trent thought for a few seconds. "The surveyor is going over the property again before the final sale, but it looks to be about 170,000 acres with two good springs. One of the springs fills a natural twelve- to fifteen-acre lake."

Biggun let out a low whistle. "Sounds like a good deal."

"Doesn't it lie along your west boundary?" Ely inquired.

"Yes, it does."

"So, the Flatland is growing," Biggun commented as he shook his head and smiled. "If you keep going, you'll outdo some of the old-timers," Biggun laughed.

That must cover half of Texas, Sassy thought as the conversation continued.

"Isn't there a fairly good house on it?" Helen asked.

Trent nodded his head as he took a big bite of cornbread. "It has three rooms and needs some fixing up a bit, but it'll house several hands. I figure I'll need several men to cover that part of the ranch. I'll keep on the cowboys they have and see how it goes. I could make a room out of the back porch and put more beds out there if needed."

"When will you know for sure if it's a deal?" Helen asked.

"Probably by next Friday," Trent said as he reached for another piece of cornbread.

Helen knew she would have to speak to Trent about not sending Ely over there to live. He wouldn't be able to come calling as often, and she didn't intend to lose this man. It had taken her too long to get over Jack, and she wasn't getting any younger. Lately, she had been fixing herself up more. Ely often commented on how pretty she looked. Looks didn't last forever, so she couldn't wait another five or ten years to catch a husband. Besides, she had developed a true affection for Ely and hoped it would lead to the kind of love that would make for a lifetime of happiness. Yes, she had made up her mind. She intended to lasso Ely and marry him. She had the distinct feeling he wouldn't be running too fast to get away.

It was strange to think how quickly her life was changing. It all seemed to have started the day she looked out the front window and saw Trent bringing those five bedraggled-looking orphans home with him. Sassy had turned out to be the best find he had ever made for a housekeeper and cook and to help her.

Flossy actually helped Sassy serve the dessert, and when she seated herself again, Helen noticed she was sitting very close to Biggun. Of course, he seemed pleased to have such a beauty paying attention to him instead of Trent.

Biggun welcomed Flossy's unexpected interest. As long as he had lived here, it had always been a given that the ladies preferred Trent. Trent was a nice-looking man and well-mannered around the fairer sex but could be hard as nails with the men when necessary. The women seemed to pick up on his masculine traits and find them plenty appealing. Besides, he was quite wealthy in land, cattle, horses, and cold hard cash. What more could any woman want? Biggun realized he was just another hired hand, and that was all he would ever be. He made a decent wage but lived in two rooms at one end of a barn. He didn't envy Trent. They had been friends since he had come here at age thirteen. The Sandersons had always treated him well, and for that, he was grateful.

Trent went to bed at about ten o'clock but was still wide awake when he heard the mantle clock strike eleven. He turned on his side and closed his eyes, hoping sleep would come soon. Just as he started to doze off, he heard the creak of his bedroom door. His eyes flew open, and he automatically reached for the loaded pistol he kept on a small table beside his bed. Moonlight filtered through the windows, and he immediately saw what had made the door creak. Flossy stood just inside the door, clad in that silky nightgown she had worn to entice him the night they had spent together. At first, he wondered if she was a spirit trying to tempt him again. No doubt about it, she was an alluring woman. Most men would not hesitate to take her to their bed. But he had tasted her nectar and found it lacking. He desired no further entanglement with her.

"Flossy, if you take one more step into this room, I promise I'll shoot you. I told you before there would never be a repeat of that night we spent together. Now, get out and stay out!" he said in a quiet, rigid voice.

"But, Trent," she uttered sweetly.

"I said get out!" he snarled through clenched teeth. He felt his body on edge as though preparing for a fight. If necessary, he would bodily remove her from his room if he didn't lose his temper and shoot her first.

She slowly opened the door, backed out of his room, and gently closed the door.

She stood outside his room for several minutes, seething at his blatant refusal. *You'll pay for this, Trent Sanderson. Yes, you'll pay dearly for treating me like I was a common floozy,* she fumed as she tiptoed back up the stairs to her own room.

Trent felt the tension in his entire body as he sat on the side of his bed after Flossy's departure. He had to figure out a way to get rid of that woman. He had felt it in his gut the day he picked her up at the train station. When he'd looked into those captivating green eyes and sensed her allure, he'd known she would only bring trouble. Maybe he should just offer her a tempting amount of money to leave. Yes, maybe that would work. How much money would it take to convince her it would be to her advantage to go elsewhere, he wondered. Probably not all that much, he'd bet. Besides, he could well afford to meet a hefty demand if necessary. He needed to work out a plan to make her think it was her idea. If she thought it was his idea, she might turn on him and cause more trouble. He needed to get her to tell him of some business she had perhaps dreamed of owning. Then, he could offer to assist her financially, with the ruse that he, too, would profit from her business. Yes, something along those lines might work, but he needed to think it through carefully.

Chapter Eleven

Thursday morning, Pete Kennedy rode in looking for Trent.

Pete was one of those men who always looked about half mad, and his disposition matched his looks. His pensive look didn't surprise Trent. Pete must have heard about the deal he was offered by the Schwab brothers, Trent thought, as Pete rarely came to the Flatland.

Trent invited him for a cup of coffee at the mess hall. They sat in the same places he had sat with the Schwab brothers.

"I'll come straight to the point for my visit," Pete said as he took a swallow of the bitter coffee. "I heard the Schwab brothers struck a deal with you to buy their ranch."

"That's true," Trent answered.

"I don't know why they didn't give me a chance at it first. We've been neighbors for years, just like your family. Well, anyway, I just wanted you to know I'm going over there to up your offer."

Trent studied the man for several moments. Pete had some bad habits as a rancher. Trent felt certain that was why the Schwab brothers hadn't approached Pete with a deal. He overgrazed his grass and often poached off his neighbors for grass and water. Everyone knew about Pete's less-than-honest methods.

"Actually, I didn't make an offer. They came to me, and we struck a deal. You can do that, Pete, but I'd bet my best horse they turn you down."

Pete let out a disgusted snort. "You're likely right. Those two stubborn mules likely shook hands with you on it and won't likely renege on the deal. If they won't, then I want to make a deal with you for watering rights. I'll make it well worth your while."

"Well, Pete, I'll have to assess the situation a little further before I can strike a deal for water. You know as well as I do we're all limited to scarce sources of dependable water. I plan to expand my herds and just don't know yet if I can spare extra water."

It was obvious by Pete's expression that it was not what he had hoped to hear.

"Remember, I asked first if you could spare any water," Pete said, a bit disgruntled.

"If we get good spring rains, it might be possible. But, there again, we never know what to expect."

"True enough," Pete agreed.

The two men shook hands. Trent didn't want any trouble with his neighbors, but he knew his men would have to keep a close watch on Pete's outfit, or he'd keep on doing the same with the water and grazing. It was likely Pete had already been poaching both off the Schwab Ranch. The Schwab brothers had told Trent several times they had seen signs of Pete's outfit poaching grass and water. They had thought about putting up fences between the two ranches but decided they were too old to tackle such a big job. Besides, it would cost more than they wanted to spend.

The birth records arrived three days before Sassy's next visit to Wichita Falls in February. When she arrived at the orphans' home, she was told Miss Martin had come down with the flu and wouldn't be back for several days. Her assistant told Sassy to bring the birth records back in March. The woman wasn't aware of any new papers for Sassy to sign but assured her Miss Martin would take care of everything when she came back for her visit in March.

Sassy and the children had a wonderful visit. Mr. and Mrs. Smyth invited them for Saturday lunch. They spent most of the afternoon with them and their three girls. Martha was delighted there were girls to play with instead of just her brothers. It was obvious to Sassy how much the Smyths had taken to Daniel.

When Sassy returned to Amarillo on Monday, the trip back to the ranch went smoothly. The afternoon was pleasant for the drive back to the ranch from town. But, about three miles from headquarters, one of the horses seemed to be going lame. Sassy was in a quandary as to what to do. She didn't want to injure the poor animal further. Should she just leave the wagon and walk the rest of the way? Yes, she decided that would be the best thing. She unhitched the two horses, feeling reasonably certain they wouldn't wander far.

Trent stood on the front porch, peering into the distance as the sun sank nearer the horizon. He had begun to worry since Sassy should have arrived home well before dark.

Just as the sun dipped below the horizon, he walked briskly to the barn, saddled his horse, and took off at as brisk of a pace as he dared at dusk. Maybe the train was late and she had stayed in town, he tried to reason. What if he didn't find her soon? Should he ride all the way to town to search for her? It was foolish, now that he thought about it, to have her drive the supply wagon back to the ranch alone. After a couple of miles and escalating worry, he saw a lone figure moving toward him through the darkness.

"Sassy, Sassy, is that you?" he called out.

"Yes, it's me. One of the horses went lame," she answered as he reined in beside her.

"How far have you walked?"

"Only a mile or so. I unhitched the horses. I don't think they'll go far, do you?" she asked, a bit worried.

"No, they'll be fine," Trent answered as he dismounted. "Here, let me help you up. We can ride double back to the house."

"I'm not exactly dressed for horseback riding. I'll just walk. It can't be too much farther," she replied.

"It's a couple of miles. It's dark, and it's going to get cold fast. There isn't anyone here but me to see you anyway, and I won't look too close," Trent teased. "Just arrange your skirt, and you'll look fine," he suggested as he boosted her up to straddle the saddle.

She fidgeted with her skirt, trying to be as modest as possible.

Trent was about to mount behind her when he caught a glimpse of her shapely leg just above the top of her shoe. Without thinking, he reached out and gave her a playful thump on her exposed calf.

Sassy let out a yelp. "You said you wouldn't look!" she reminded him.

"I lied," he said with a chuckle as he bounded up on the back of the horse and gave it a nudge.

Immediately, Sassy became aware of their closeness. His warmth and masculine smell instantly surrounded her. She tried to sit ramrod straight so their bodies wouldn't touch, but it didn't work.

Trent wondered if this had been such a good idea after all as he breathed in the fresh scent of Sassy's hair and the faint fragrance of some womanly soap. He had to fight the urge to tighten his arms around her and pull her snug against his chest.

He should have let her ride, and he should have walked, but it was too late for that now. He'd just have to endure and resist the temptation Sassy presented. Trent chided himself for becoming attracted to a young woman, likely too young for him. She would never develop into the beauty Flossy was. Suddenly, he realized his interest might not be just a physical attraction, and he knew he had to get a firm grip on his feelings. He couldn't afford to make another mistake like the one he had made with Flossy. It was high time for him to start going to town to find a suitable wife.

They arrived just in time for the supper Biggun had prepared. He was a tolerable fair cook, and Sassy was glad she didn't have to cook after spending hours on the train and the long trip back to the ranch. Her bones seemed to ache, and she was ready for a hot bath and to go to bed early.

She did tell the others about Miss Martin being sick. She would have to take the papers again in March and sign the new ones Miss Martin had talked about. Sassy was proud to think this time, she could sign her actual name, Evangeline McCoy.

Chapter Twelve

They were all glad to see March arrive. Hopefully, the worst of the winter weather had passed. The spring rains should start soon, and the grass would turn a lush green. Warm afternoons should give them a chance to spend more time outside. Sassy was already thinking about the spring garden.

Trent had not sent Ely to the new part of the ranch, and Ely and Helen continued their frequent outings.

One pretty day, Helen asked Sassy to pack them a picnic lunch. They were going to ride to the creek and picnic in the shade of the big willow and pecan trees that lined the banks for several miles. Sassy was thrilled to see Helen in such high spirits. She literally glowed at the mention of Ely's name.

Sassy had noticed another change taking place, but she wasn't sure Trent or Helen were aware of what was going on. She had become aware of Flossy slipping out the back door after supper. One evening, she decided to follow her out of curiosity, or perhaps it was nosiness, she admitted to herself. Flossy made her way straight to the back of the barn where Biggun lived. It appeared he was expecting her, as she didn't even have to knock. He opened the door, drew her into his arms, and pulled her inside as they kissed. Sassy couldn't suppress a slight gasp of surprise at what she had seen. She quickly ducked behind the side of the barn in case they'd heard her, but the door was already closed.

Well, well! Sassy thought. *I wonder just how long this has been going on.* She hadn't noticed any obvious outward signs of their attraction when Biggun came to supper. Why would they keep it a secret if they were sweet on one another? She tried to figure out what the incident she had just seen meant as she walked back to the house. That night, she tried to stay awake to see when Flossy returned to her room. After what seemed like hours, when sleep overtook her, she knew Flossy had not yet returned.

The next morning, Flossy came down to breakfast as usual. No one but Sassy seemed aware of her late-night return to her own bed.

A few days later, Helen came down with a cold and spent most of the day in bed. The next day, she seemed better until late afternoon, when she took a turn for the worse and returned to bed. Sassy made a pot of potato soup along with a steaming mug of hot tea and took it to her room. She instantly noticed Helen's color had changed to a flushed pink. When she touched Helen's forehead, Sassy could tell she felt feverish. Helen tried a few bites of the soup and sipped the tea but could take in no more food.

When Sassy returned to the kitchen to serve Trent and Flossy, she told them about Helen developing a fever.

"Do you think I should send for the doctor?" Trent asked anxiously.

"Not yet. It may not linger. I think I'll make a pallet in her room and stay the night in case she needs something," Sassy said.

"The nights are still too cold to be sleeping on a pallet. You'll get sick too, and then I'll have to tend to the two of you," Flossy fretted, obviously not pleased at the possibility of that happening. Not because she was actually worried about their health.

Trent looked at her in disgust, but she didn't seem to notice his disapproving glare.

"I'm used to sleeping on the floor during the winter. It won't bother me," Sassy assured them.

Sassy awoke when the mantle clock struck two o'clock. She heard Helen moaning and thrashing about in the bed. She lit the lamp on the bedside table and saw Helen was drenched in sweat. When she touched Helen's burning skin, she could tell the fever was worse. Sassy spoke softly to her, but she did not rouse from her fitful sleep. Sassy contemplated waking Trent. She decided it might be best to have him come and see his sister's condition. She hurried to his room and knocked on his door, calling his name.

In seconds, he opened the door. His hair was tousled from sleep, and he was pulling on his shirt. Sassy was given a view of his broad, bare chest, and, for some reason she didn't quite comprehend, she felt a blush reach her cheeks. The memory of his warmth during their recent horseback ride rushed back. She quickly ducked her head to avoid his gaze.

"I think you better come see about Helen," she managed to say before turning to lead the way back to Helen's room.

Once in Helen's room, Trent studied his sister's appearance and gently laid his big hand on her forehead.

"Good heavens, she's burning up with the fever. I'll get one of the men to go for the doctor. Meanwhile, bathe her with cool water but keep her covered so she doesn't get a sudden chill. I'll be back to help you," he said as he took long strides, hurrying out of the room.

Trent entered the bunkhouse and found Ely's bunk. He gently shook the man awake and spoke softly but urgently.

"Helen's very sick, burning with a fever, and she won't wake up. I need you to go get the doctor. There's only a sliver of a moon, so take two horses in case one gets hurt in the darkness. Go as fast as you can, but be careful. We need you to get there and bring the doctor as soon as possible."

"Any doctor in particular?"

"If Doctor Baldwin is available, get him, but if not, just find any doctor who can come now."

"I'm afraid it's my fault she got sick. It was almost dark when we got back from our ride the other afternoon. The wind had picked up, and it was getting cold by the time I got her home," Ely said as he pulled on his boots.

Trent knew the two were becoming very close. He didn't want Ely to feel at fault as these things just happened sometimes.

"Don't be too hard on yourself. It might have happened if she were sitting home by the fire." Trent looked at the man now walking beside him toward the barn. "You've been good for Helen." He paused and pinned his gaze on Ely. "Don't ever lead her on or hurt her, or you and I will have a score to settle. One man has already given her enough grief to last a lifetime. So, I won't tolerate it happening again," Trent said in a tone that left no doubt he meant every word.

Ely met Trent's gaze. "I care very deeply for Helen and would never do anything to hurt her. I'm aware of what happened before, and I'm not that kind of man, so put your mind at ease," he said as he swung into the saddle.

As Ely rode gingerly through the darkness toward Amarillo, the conversation he'd had with Trent ran through his mind. Was he telling the truth that he would never hurt Helen? The first day they met at the Christmas lunch, he had decided she was his ticket to the good life. He found Helen still quite attractive, and her rather harsh manner appealed to him more than Flossy's softer, flirty ways. He knew men no longer came calling in hopes of winning Helen's affection or fortune. He made up his mind to start courting her, with the sole goal in mind to marry her. Of course, he would be good to Helen in every way, but he still had doubts about truly loving her as a husband should. Perhaps all of that kind of love had been spent on his first wife. If Helen ever realized that fact, then he would hurt her, and that would also make him a liar. That thought didn't sit well with him.

Ely arrived back at the ranch just before noon, with Doctor Baldwin following close behind in his buggy. Doctor Baldwin was a tall man with silver hair, a well-groomed mustache, silver-gray eyes, and a pleasant demeanor. He had tended the family since first moving to the small community twenty years ago, while Amarillo was still a small cow town.

After examining Helen, he walked to Trent's office, where he and Ely waited.

"It looks to me like the worst has passed. The young lady, Sassy, I believe she said was her name, has taken excellent care of Helen. Just have her continue. I left a tonic with Sassy to give Helen every four hours as needed. She should be as fit as ever in a few days. Do keep her from getting a chill."

"That's good news, Doctor," Trent answered. Both men smiled with relief, knowing Helen was on her way to recovery. "I believe Sassy has lunch almost ready," Trent said as he rose and led the way to the kitchen.

As the two men followed Trent, Doctor Baldwin commented, "If you ever find you don't need Sassy's services, I'm sure my wife would love to have her come work for us. She could help me in the office and do the cooking at home." He chuckled. "I'm afraid cooking is not among my wife's many talents."

"I can't imagine us getting along without her. She even made all the new curtains for the entire house," Trent bragged a bit. Then his own words struck him, and he realized they were true. At least, he certainly didn't want to get along without her. Once more he found, to his own dismay, he was becoming more attracted to Sassy than he probably should. She was still quite young and had never had a proper date or even a proper kiss from a man. He suspected she knew a great deal about what went on between a man and a woman from growing up in a tiny house with little privacy, but still, her own experiences were limited.

Doctor Baldwin paused and looked around at her handiwork. "It was a lucky day when you found her to work for you," he commented as they entered the kitchen.

Trent smiled and thought, found her was right, and Doctor Baldwin would have a good laugh if he knew they'd thought the pretty young woman serving their lunch had been a boy.

"Who is the young woman you left sitting with Helen while we eat?"

"Her name is Flossy Tatum, and she's the housekeeper," Trent lowered his voice. "She's about as good of a housekeeper as your wife is a cook. Would you like to employ her? In good conscience, I'll have to warn you your wife is probably a better cook than Flossy."

Ely laughed at Trent's remark. He had heard the story about Flossy's attempt at cooking.

Doctor Baldwin smiled. "I think I'll pass on both counts," he said as he took a fluffy, golden-brown biscuit and buttered it.

Ely finished eating first and excused himself from the table. He did not head out the back door but went directly to Helen's room.

"Go eat lunch," he told Flossy. "I'll sit with Helen until Sassy or you are free to come back."

He moved a chair beside Helen's bed and sat, quietly watching her sleep. Whatever the doctor had given her seemed to have quieted her as she was resting peacefully. Ely leaned forward and took Helen's left hand in his much larger hands. He gently ran his fingers over her soft hand and looked at her long, tapered fingers. He imagined the kind of ring he could afford to place on her finger. It wouldn't be anything near what the Sandersons could afford. Maybe he was a fool for thinking about marrying Helen, but as he looked at her, he felt a genuine affection for the woman and even a man's desire. He supposed the matter would rest with Helen. As soon as she was well, he intended to ask her to marry him and see if she could accept just a ranch hand as a husband. He found he truly hoped she could. Not just so he could enjoy that good life he had dreamed about but because he realized he had come to care for her far more than he had expected. Surely, in time, that genuine caring would turn into the kind of love a husband and wife should share. Wasn't that how love began?

He couldn't remember how his feelings had started for Rachel, his first wife. It had been so long ago. They were young when they married. She had just turned eighteen, and he was nineteen. She was a very young widow with a small boy. They had big dreams of owning their own ranch and raising a house full of young'uns. The ranch had done well enough, but her two pregnancies ended in miscarriages, and then there were no more. No children by him had been a great disappointment to both of them. Then, her health began to fail, and she just seemed to waste away. He often wondered if she grieved herself to death over having no more children. Her son had run away from home when Rachel became very sick. He couldn't seem to handle her illness and the possibility of his mother dying. After she passed, he sold the ranch and went from one job to another for ten long years. He still had the money from the sale of his ranch and could start over again. But without a good woman and family, what would be the point? He realized Helen would always need help, and to stay here would be best for her. That would be fine with him. Maybe

Trent would let him invest his money in running a few of his own cattle and horses. Well, all of that depended on Helen's acceptance or rejection of him as a husband, he thought as he continued to caress her hand.

Ely leaned over and placed a tender kiss on Helen's forehead. He could tell the fever was waning and knew that was a good sign.

Ely looked around as he heard a slight noise and saw Sassy standing in the doorway. She gave him a sweet smile. "I'm finished in the kitchen and can sit with Helen unless you'd rather stay a while longer."

"I wouldn't mind but guess I better get to work. I'll be back at supper if that's all right."

"Of course. Maybe Helen will be awake by then. I know she looks forward to your visits," Sassy said, hoping he knew how important he had become in Helen's life.

In a few days, Helen did recover, and Ely came every evening for supper. The two sat by the fireplace in the living room sipping tea, or sometimes, Ely had a brandy as they talked.

Ely would spread a quilt on the floor before the fireplace. He would lift Helen from her wheelchair and sit her on the quilt with her back supported by the sofa. He would lie on the quilt with his head resting in her lap. She delighted in running her fingers through his still thick hair as they talked. This was what they would do on their buggy rides when they stopped for a picnic. Only sometimes, she would lie beside him, and they would enjoy the tender pleasures of serious courting, but they always kept within the boundaries expected of an unmarried couple.

"Ely, there's something I want to tell you," Helen said with slight restraint in her voice.

"What is it?" Ely glanced up and asked, a bit apprehensive at her tone of voice.

Helen glanced down at Ely's face. "I want to tell you what happened to me that put me in this wheelchair." She let out a deep sigh. "It was in the summer after I met Jack Thornton. He and three couples we ran around with came out from town one Sunday afternoon. We all decided to go swimming in the creek. You know how young folks are. We got to horse playing, and I started running along the creek bank away from the group. Jack gave chase and caught me about fifty feet down the creek. He picked me up to fling me into the water. The bank was about four feet above the water level. I grabbed him around the neck and held on. We went tumbling off the creek bank, and I landed flat on my back, his weight on top of me, pushing me under the water. I hit a pointed rock just far enough below the surface of the water that it couldn't be seen. When I hit, I felt an excruciating pain flash through my body, and I knew something was terribly wrong."

Her voice sounded almost emotionless in telling the story, as though it were something that had happened to someone else. It was as though she had relived it so many times it had become mundane. At times, she looked at her useless legs and marveled they were, in fact, still a part of her body.

Ely reached up and gently caressed her cheek. She nuzzled her face against his hand and looked down into the depths of his deep blue eyes.

"It truly was an accident. I didn't blame Jack. I saw the look of absolute terror in his eyes when he realized I was badly hurt. At first, he was here almost constantly. He truly felt sorry for what had happened and tried to be helpful. He went to the doctors with us as often as he could. They all said the same thing. I'd never walk again. It was a hard thing to accept.

"Papa kept dragging me to one doctor after another, even as far away as Chicago, but the answer was still the same. By then, months had passed, and Jack's visits were less frequent. He always had some important business deal that kept him away. Eight months after the accident, he came one evening and finally confessed he could not deal with having an invalid for his wife. In so many words, he said he needed a wife who could accompany him to all kinds of functions and be the belle of the ball. That kind of woman would help promote his career. His words crushed me. It took me months to realize what kind of man he really was. The wedding vow that says 'In sickness and health' apparently didn't mean much to Jack. Then, we heard he had married a rich widow in Oklahoma City five months later," she finished with a touch of bitterness in her voice.

"I let deep resentment and anger rule my life for ten years that seemed endless. Poor Trent, I don't know why he didn't shoot me," she said with a little laugh. "I ran off more housekeepers and cooks than I could count. But I know when things started to change," she said with a soft smile.

"When was that?"

"The day I looked out that front window and saw Trent bringing five of the most pathetic-looking orphans I had ever seen home with him. Right then, I began to realize how fortunate I was and how unappreciative of everything I had been. I had let self-pity and hatred eat me alive. Here stood five children with no parents, no home, no money, nothing but each other. It took a while, but now, I know that is exactly when I began to change."

Ely sat up and scooted so he was sitting beside Helen. "Now, I have a confession to make, too," he said as he slipped one arm around Helen and drew her close to him, taking her other hand in his. "When I came to lunch on Christmas Day and met you, by the end of the meal, I had made up my mind I was going to do my all-fired best to court you and marry you."

Helen looked at him in shock. "You did?"

"Not because I had fallen in love at first sight but because I thought I could have an easy life here, and I did like your straightforwardness," he said with a chuckle. "I never cared for women like Flossy, all flirty and helpless acting. Then something happened to my grand plan." He paused and smiled at Helen.

"What was that?" she whispered, not sure she wanted to hear his answer.

"When we started going on our outings, I found my feelings for you growing. When I rode to get the doctor when you were sick, I knew I wanted to marry you because I had come to care for you far beyond what I had ever imagined possible. So, I'm asking you to become my wife. I believe in all of those wedding vows," he whispered in a husky tone and sealed his declaration with a warm, ardent kiss.

Sassy heard Helen calling her and Trent's names. Sassy went in a full run to the living room, arriving just behind Trent. She feared Helen was feeling ill again.

Helen and Ely were sitting on the floor. Both were grinning from ear to ear.

"Well, folks. This fine man has just asked me to become his wife, and I said yes! Yes! Yes!" Helen exclaimed with evident excitement and love as she gazed tenderly at Ely.

He returned her look and then glanced at Trent. "Do I need to ask your permission to marry your sister since you are the man of the house?" he asked with a teasing grin.

Trent extended his hand to shake Ely's hand. "From the look on my sister's face, I don't think I would dare object. But, as a matter of fact, I am very happy for you both. Just treat her well."

Ely recalled their conversation the night he had gone for the doctor and knew what Trent meant.

Chapter Thirteen

Most evenings, after supper, Flossy continued to slip out the back door. Trent went to his office to read or check on something Helen asked him to take a look at concerning the ranch business. Sassy went to her room to give Helen and Ely some privacy on the evenings he lingered after supper, which occurred quite often. They were planning an April wedding to be held at a shady spot beside the creek about a mile south of the homestead. It was another place they liked to picnic. Helen had commented the grass should be green and filled with wildflowers by then.

The creek would make a pretty setting for a wedding, Sassy thought as she worked in the kitchen. She wondered if she would ever have a pretty wedding or even a wedding at all. She intended the man she married to be like Trent: nice-looking, smart, hard-working, and at least able to make a decent wage so life wouldn't be such a struggle like it had been for her parents. She felt a little sad when she thought about marriage, knowing Trent was not likely to ever want someone like her for his wife. She was uneducated, unsophisticated, had no money, and certainly was not nearly as pretty as Flossy. Yes, it would be hard to find a man like Trent for a husband.

A few days before her March visit to see the children, Sassy was cleaning the kitchen after lunch when she heard Helen's raised voice. Thinking she might be calling her, Sassy hung the dishtowel over the edge of the sink and started toward Helen's room. As she drew nearer, she also heard Flossy's raised voice.

Sassy paused in the hallway near Helen's door, where she could hear their lively conversation, but they could not see her.

"I don't believe you," Helen almost shouted in rage.

"Well, it's true, my dear Helen," Flossy answered in a sneering tone.

"Trent wouldn't lower himself to sleep with the likes of you. You're lying!" Helen bellowed, and Sassy could hear a slight quiver in her fuming voice.

"Oh, no, I'm not lying! It happened when you and Sassy spent the night in town just before Christmas, and now I am carrying his child," Flossy answered in a self-assured, flaunting manner.

"I don't believe one word you're saying. I'll ask Trent myself," Helen shot back. Sassy could hear the fury reflected in Helen's harsh voice.

"I think I should be the one to tell him he's going to be a father. But if you just can't wait, then ask him, dear future sister-in-law, go right ahead!" Flossy gave Helen a self-satisfied retort.

"I don't believe he would ever marry you, even if you were carrying his child!" Helen retorted with obvious indignation.

"Oh, do you think he wants a bastard in the family?" Flossy asked in a smug tone.

Sassy stood, stunned at what she was hearing. Trent and Flossy together! No, no! That just couldn't be true! She felt tears stinging her eyes, and her stomach seemed to be tied in knots. Flossy had been sneaking out to see Biggun. Maybe they were afraid of what Trent might do if he found out since he had apparently laid claim to Flossy first, she thought in confusion about the situation. She turned to slip away, but then she heard Helen clear her throat before she broke the brief silence.

"I'll tell you what I'm going to do," Helen paused.

"And just what's that?" Flossy asked, still in that haughty tone.

"I'm not going to mention this conversation to Trent, and neither are you! I'm going to write a sizeable bank draft for you. Lester will take you to town, cash the draft, and buy you a train ticket. He will give you the money when he puts you on the next train headed as far away from here as you can go. You will never, and I mean never, contact Trent or anyone else connected with this ranch or anyone in Amarillo! You have your bastard child, and you can keep it or give it away. I don't give a damn which!" Helen said emphatically.

"What if I refuse your generous offer?"

"I'll persuade Trent to hold off on marrying you until I can have a thorough investigation done on you. I think you have some deep, dark secrets you wouldn't want him or anyone to know about," Helen said with loathing in her voice.

This time, Flossy hesitated before she spoke. "What if you don't find any deep, dark secrets?"

"I will!"

"You'd have some ugly, despicable things made up about me just to keep Trent from marrying me, wouldn't you, you dried-up old prune!" Flossy flung the hateful words at Helen.

"Take the money or take a chance on what that report will show. It's up to you," Helen said, a bit flippant, knowing she now had the upper hand.

Sassy didn't want to hear anymore. She was afraid she was about to burst into tears. She tiptoed back to the kitchen, put on her shawl, and slipped out the back door. She walked toward the south pasture where the young horses were still being kept. Each step was taken in anger, anger at Flossy, and anger and disappointment in Trent. Could it possibly be true he had spent the night with Flossy? Sassy continued on until she reached the gurgling creek, where she sat on a large rock warmed by the afternoon sun. Then she let the tears of disappointment, jealousy, and uncertainty stream down her face.

The strange part was she wasn't exactly sure why she was crying. Trent was only her employer. He had been kind to help her find a good place for her siblings and often complimented her cooking, but beyond that, he should mean nothing to her. That one kiss he had given her on Christmas had been the only slight sign he might think of her as other than the hired help, and nothing had passed between them after that one time. So why did it hurt so much to think he slept with Flossy, and now she carried his child?

Flossy was a beautiful woman, and Sassy knew the men were attracted to her because of her fetching looks. That shouldn't mean they would all want to sleep with her. Or would they? The more she thought about it, the worse she felt. Her head ached, her stomach felt queasy, and even her hands trembled as she swiped at the tears streaming down her cheeks.

"Hello! What are you doing way out here by the creek?" came an all too familiar voice.

Sassy whirled around to see Trent mounted on his big stallion, not ten feet behind where she sat. She had not heard him ride up. What could she say? she thought in a panic.

Before she could say anything, he dismounted and came to sit beside her.

He looked at her tear-streaked face and swollen, red eyes. "What's the matter? Have you had word something has happened to one of the children?" he asked with genuine concern.

"No, no, nothing has happened. I was just thinking about them and— and wishing it were already Friday so I'd be on my way to see them," she lied. It was the only thing that came to mind to explain why she was so far from the homestead and crying. It certainly wasn't her place to tell him about what she had overheard Helen and Flossy discussing.

Trent put his arm around her and gently pulled her head to rest on his broad shoulder. He patted her arm gently in a concerned gesture to console her.

"I'm sorry we couldn't have found a closer place for the boys and Martha. I know this is hard on you to be so far away and only see them once a month," he said in a soothing tone.

Sassy felt like screaming! She wanted to scream at him for sleeping with Flossy, for being so kind to her, for having to lie to him about why she was really crying. She was sure there must be a whole lot of other things to scream at him about, but nothing else came to mind at that moment.

After a few minutes, he straightened. "Come on, I'll give you a ride back to the house. Does Helen know you're way out here by yourself?"

"No, I didn't want to upset her by saying anything."

"Well, come on before she misses you," he said as he pulled her to her feet.

"I can't ride with you in broad daylight. I'm wearing a dress."

Trent laughed. "Don't worry, you can tuck it around your legs like you did before." He guided her toward the big horse.

"I remember what you did before, and it was dark. I'll just walk fast. Besides, we might be too heavy for this horse," she tried to protest. "I can walk back. It won't take that long," she insisted. No need to take a chance on sitting so close to him and feeling his masculine body so close, especially after what she had just heard.

"Sassy, for heaven's sake, get on the horse." Before she could say another word, he was lifting her into the saddle and then swinging up behind her.

She instantly felt uncomfortable, but the sick feeling in her stomach had changed to a fluttering sensation with him being so near. She couldn't prevent her back from leaning against his solid chest, and his arms encircled her while holding the reins. His legs brushed against hers, and she could feel an awareness of the heat their movement created even through the layers of clothing that separated them. If that wasn't enough, his warm breath brushed lightly against the back of her neck and ears. The low rumble of his voice so near set her heart to racing as they rode leisurely atop the big horse. Her anger of a short time ago when they sat beside the creek seemed to fade as they rode together toward the homestead. His masculine presence overtook her senses and pushed her thoughts of anger far from her mind.

Trent liked the feel of Sassy's body so near to his. It was an almost overpowering temptation to hold the reins with one hand and gently lift her hair that now curled a few inches below her collar and kiss the soft skin on the back of her neck. Then he could nibble her ear and—Hold it right there, cowboy, he told himself firmly! You just keep your mind on getting Sassy back to the house. He knew how leery she was of men, and he certainly didn't want to do anything to reaffirm her belief that most men were up to no good, like her own pa's friend.

How could he approach her to let her know he was becoming more interested in her as a woman but not scare her away? Maybe he should try what Ely had done. Take her for buggy rides and just talk until he felt she was ready to hear about how his feelings were growing for her. And then, as the old saying went, "Let nature take its course." He knew she was nothing like Flossy, and there would be no bedding before marriage, and that was what he wanted in a wife, a woman he could respect and one who respected him. Yes, that seemed like a good plan. Now, finding the time for buggy rides and gradually persuading Sassy to go out with him would be the real trick. The one stumbling block to this grand plan might be Flossy. He had heard it said there was nothing like a jealous woman, and he had the distinct feeling Flossy would be outraged when she discovered he had romantic feelings for Sassy and not her. Or, perhaps, he should forget this altogether and go to town to look for a wife. Yes, maybe that was the best option, but finding the time was a big problem. He mulled the situation over as they reached the homestead.

When Trent, Ely, and Biggun came in for supper, and all were seated, Flossy's place was obviously empty.

"Is Flossy feeling poorly tonight?" Biggun finally asked as he nodded toward her empty place.

Helen paused before she answered. Instead of looking at Biggun, she turned her gaze to Trent. "I fired Flossy today," she stated.

All eyes turned toward Helen.

"Why did you do that?" Trent asked, managing to not give away his relief when he heard what Helen had done.

Sassy saw the stricken look on Biggun's face, but no one else seemed to notice.

"She sassed me and refused to follow my orders. That wasn't the first time, so I fired her," Helen told them with a straight face that gave no indication what she said wasn't the truth.

Trent shrugged his shoulders as though it didn't matter to him one way or the other. Inside, he was breathing a deep sigh of relief to know Flossy was gone, and he silently thanked Helen and the Lord for solving that problem. Then he turned to Sassy. "Do you think you can manage taking care of everything, or do I need to look for another housekeeper?"

Helen gave a snort of laughter. "She took care of just about everything when Flossy was here. More often than not, I've seen her go behind Flossy to really clean. Flossy was about as good at housekeeping as she was at cooking, and we all know how that turned out."

That brought chortles from the men, except Biggun, who only smiled at Helen's remark.

"Oh, I can manage the house and helping Helen just fine, but what will I do about going to see the children?" Sassy asked with real worry. "I can't leave Helen unattended for several days every month."

She saw the lines form between Trent's brows as they did when he was pondering a situation.

Before he could speak, Ely made a suggestion, "Maybe the three women who go to town with the children for school could take turns staying at the ranch with their little ones to tend to Helen."

Trent looked relieved. "That's a good idea. I'll speak to them. It wouldn't be all that often, and they might like a change in the routine. I'll pay them what I was paying Flossy, and I know they can all use a little extra money. I'll increase your salary too, Sassy, for taking on more work. You'll have to delay your trip for a week, though, until we can get everything worked out. I'll send a telegram to the orphanage and the boarding house when I go to town tomorrow. Will that be all right?" he questioned, knowing how upset Sassy had been about waiting to go see the boys and Martha.

"Yes." She nodded her head.

Trent felt sorry to delay her trip further, but it couldn't be avoided. He appreciated knowing she was concerned about Helen and would never consider leaving her alone for a few days, either.

Biggun finished his meal in silence and excused himself before dessert was served. He said it had been a long day, and he thought he'd turn in early. No one seemed suspicious of his excuse except Sassy.

As soon as the supper dishes were done, she slipped out the back door and took the path leading to the back of the barn where Biggun lived. She could see lamplight coming through the window, so she knew he had not gone to bed yet. She knocked lightly on the door, and within seconds, it swung open. The expression on his face told her he was hoping it was Flossy coming to call.

"May I come in?" Sassy asked.

"Yes, of course," he answered as he stepped aside.

"Please, sit down." He gestured to a chair near the fireplace.

Sassy wasn't sure how to begin or just what to say, but she thought he needed to know what had been said between Helen and Flossy.

"Biggun, I followed Flossy one night after supper to see where she was going so often and found she was coming to see you. You greeted her as though you were expecting her."

Biggun leaned forward with his elbows on his knees, lowered his head, and began to massage his temples. "Yes, Flossy and I were very close." He paused. "In fact, I believed we were sweethearts, but now I'm not sure what to think."

Sassy hated to tell him why Flossy really left, but she felt it was the honorable thing to do.

"Well, today, I overheard Flossy and Helen arguing. Helen did not fire her because of her sloppy housekeeping or refusing to follow orders."

Biggun looked up with increased interest. "Why did she fire her?"

Sassy reached out and gently laid her hand on his large hand that now rested on his knee.

"Flossy claimed she and Trent spent a night together when Helen and I went to Amarillo Christmas shopping, and she said she was carrying his child."

Biggun looked as though she had struck him.

Sassy went on. "Helen didn't believe her, and she said even if she was carrying Trent's child, he would never marry her. Helen gave her a sizeable amount of money and told her to catch the next train out of Amarillo. Helen also told her to go as far away as possible, and she better never come back or contact anyone on this ranch. Helen even threatened to have her investigated and said when Trent read the report, he would have nothing to do with her."

"How could Helen know if there would be anything in the report that was bad?"

"I think she meant she would have it look bad, no matter if it was or not. Flossy was rather secretive. When anyone asked her about her family or past, she never really answered their question. I think, because of that, Helen believes she was hiding something."

Sassy looked at Biggun and could tell all she had told him had upset him even more. He looked so forlorn, but he seemed to realize the situation was hopeless. He had apparently cared deeply for Flossy, and now she was gone forever.

"Biggun, I'm sorry to be the one to tell you these things. I felt you had the right to know what really happened," she said kindly, to express her compassion for the man.

Biggun slowly lifted his head and said in a quiet manner, "I loved her. I would have married her even if she was carrying Trent's child, and I'd have raised the baby as my own. Why didn't she come to me?" he asked in agony.

Then he took a deep breath, gazed around his humble living quarters with a miserable expression, and answered his own question. "I suppose marrying just a ranch hand that lives in two rooms behind a barn doesn't quite measure up to marrying the boss, living in a fine house, and being the lady of the ranch."

Sassy had to fight to hold back the tears she felt threatening to spill out for the big man sitting before her. She could feel his pain and knew folks like them were somehow destined to live in lowly quarters and always be the hired help.

"I'm so sorry, Biggun," she whispered. "You must never repeat anything I have told you, in spite of the hurt it has caused."

"I know," Biggun answered as he lowered his head again and continued to rub his temples. "Trent is my friend, and the Sandersons were always good to me."

Sassy saw his big shoulders begin to shake. She gently squeezed his hand and quietly slipped out the door, feeling he would rather be alone.

Chapter Fourteen

Mary Tate was the first to stay to care for Helen while Sassy made the trip to Wichita Falls. She was so excited to see the children after five long weeks she didn't even mind the cold rain that fell all the way from Amarillo to Wichita Falls. She arrived at the orphans' home Saturday morning and proceeded to Miss Martin's office with the birth records, ready to sign the new papers.

When she entered the building, Miss Martin's assistant instructed her to have a seat and assured her Miss Martin would be ready to see her in a few minutes.

Sassy kept glancing at the big clock mounted high on the wall, watching the minutes slowly tick by. She wanted to get this business finished so she could go see her brothers and Martha.

After twenty-eight minutes had passed, Miss Martin opened her door and motioned Sassy inside. Sassy was a bit surprised when Miss Martin's assistant accompanied her into the office.

"Please, sit down," Miss Martin indicated in a rather terse manner. Then she took her seat behind her huge desk littered with stacks of papers. Her rather plain face was expressionless. She picked up her glasses and slowly put them on. They rested on the bridge of her nose as her brown eyes peered over the top rim with a rigid expression.

"There have been some recent changes at the home I need to tell you about," she said in an impassive, monotone voice.

Sassy sat staring at the woman, waiting for her to continue.

Miss Martin took a deep breath and let it out slowly. Sassy noticed her assistant sat with her head slightly downcast. She didn't make eye contact with either of them.

Suddenly, a dread of what Miss Martin was about to say filled Sassy. She sensed something was terribly wrong. Had one of her brothers gotten into trouble? Surely, it couldn't be Martha in trouble, she worried as she waited.

"From time to time, the home becomes overcrowded, and we have to move some of the children. Your two older brothers are among the children we selected to be moved, and Martha has been placed with a very wealthy woman who lost her only daughter two years ago. She is a generous benefactor to the home and has taken a special interest in Martha. Martha will have far more advantages with this lovely lady than we could ever give her here," Miss Martin declared as she continued to look closely at Sassy over the tops of her glasses. She made it sound as though giving Martha to this woman was something Sassy should be happy to hear.

Sassy sat transfixed as she listened to what Miss Martin was saying, but she could hardly take it all in. Two of her brothers and Martha were gone! Before the woman could go on, Sassy interrupted.

"What do you mean Timothy and Nathan are gone? What right do you have to give Martha to anyone? They have a family! Me! Where is Daniel?" she demanded, uncertain and outraged about what had happened to her family. Sassy's insides were shaking, but she kept reminding herself to not let them see how scared she was about what had happened.

Sassy's eyes were snapping with fury at the woman seated behind the big desk, looking so smug in her superior position. A position authorized by the people in charge of the home had apparently given her the authority to do as she pleased.

Miss Martin instantly saw the look of resentment and outrage on Sassy's face. "Now, just calm down, and I'll explain it all to you. Timothy and Nathan were put on the orphans' train."

"Orphans' train! What is an orphans' train?" Sassy asked in astonishment, as she had never heard of such a train.

"Actually, it is a train filled with orphaned children that travels from town to town. The train started back east and then came south out of Chicago. By the time the train got here, most of the children had already been placed, so we were able to send some of our children to be placed. Nice families take the children in and sometimes even adopt them. The boys help on their farms or ranches. We make sure they are placed with fine Christian people," she said in a self-righteous manner.

Sassy stood up and walked to the front of the desk. She placed both hands on the desk and leaned forward so her face was within inches of the woman. "How can you know what kind of people they are if you have the children on a train going from town to town? Who is there to vouch for those people's good character? Don't think I am stupid because I'm young. You just give them to whoever will take them off your hands!" Sassy yelled as her temper flared. She had never felt so helpless and scared in her entire life, not when Ma died or even when Pa died and left them all alone.

Miss Martin pressed her body against the back of her chair in an attempt to put some distance between Sassy and herself. Her expression had suddenly changed from one of self-assurance to one of becoming intimidated due to the young woman's aggressive actions.

"Where is Daniel?" Sassy demanded.

"He's with Mr. Smyth and his family. He was willing to take Daniel since his own little boy died, as I told you before," she said defensively.

"You are the most wicked woman I have ever known and a liar to boot!" Sassy shouted in loathing disgust with the woman seated before her. Miss Martin had seemed so kind when they first came to leave the children. Now, though, she appeared to have changed into a cold-hearted, uncaring witch, Sassy thought as she continued to glare at the woman.

Miss Martin looked desperately toward her assistant. "Will you fetch Mr. Brown to help me calm Miss—Miss?" She paused, not knowing what name to use.

"McCoy," Sassy supplied.

As the other woman started to rise, Sassy turned her attention to her. "Stay right where you are. We don't need Mr. Brown!"

The frightened woman glanced at Miss Martin, who reluctantly signaled for her to stay.

"You told me to get the children's birth records, and I brought them with me last month and have them now. You said I would sign new papers, and I am ready to do that, but you haven't kept your word. When I left my brothers and sister here, you assured us they would be educated and well cared for. Now, you have sent them all away. I want to know exactly where Timothy and Nathan are and who has Martha!" Sassy screeched while scarcely controlling her anger. She wanted to reach across the desk, grab a big handful of Miss Martin's stylishly coiffured hair, and inflict on her just a small portion of the pain she was feeling.

Miss Martin gave a nervous little twitter of laughter. She could see the raging anger in the young woman's face, and a chill of fear ran down her spine.

"I'm afraid I can't give you that information. You need to remember you falsified documents when you signed them into this home. You have broken the law, and I can press charges, and I will press charges if you try to give me any more trouble!" Miss Martin stated, trying to regain the upper hand in the situation.

Sassy leaned a little closer to Miss Martin and almost spat in her face. "You haughty, self-righteous bitch!" Sassy shouted. "You have no idea what trouble means when I tell Helen and Trent Sanderson about what you've done!"

A moment of shocked concern crossed the woman's face, but she quickly regained her composure. "We'll see," was all Jolene Martin could think to say.

When the two women heard Sassy slam the big front door, Miss Martin's assistant anxiously asked, "Aren't you afraid of what the Sandersons might do?"

Jolene Martin sat up a bit straighter. "Not at all. I expect they will be glad they are truly rid of that bunch. I think that is why Miss Sanderson, the woman in the wheelchair, came the first time. She wanted to make sure those kids weren't coming back to the ranch. No, I don't think we'll hear another word about the McCoy children," she said, full of self-assurance.

130

~

Sassy made her way on trembling legs to the Smyths' home, where she found Daniel safe in their care.

Jacob apologized to Sassy for not warning her in time about what the home did from time to time.

"I was going to tell you last week, but then you didn't come. I didn't know how to get a message to you, and I knew those people at the home wouldn't tell me how to find you," he said with evident sadness at the situation.

"It's not your fault," Sassy replied as she hugged Daniel to her.

Jacob looked at his wife and then at Sassy. "Sally and I would like to keep Daniel and raise him as our own if that's agreeable with you. We know you likely wouldn't let us adopt him, but we could raise him just the same. You can see him any time you wish," he finished with a glimmer of hope in his voice.

Sassy looked down at Daniel. "What do you think about living with Jacob and Sally and three girls?" she asked with a slight smile, already knowing what his answer would be.

Daniel smiled from ear to ear. "Yes, yes, I want to stay here. Jacob's teaching me to be a woodworker, and Sally is a good cook, just like you," he said as he gave Sassy a warm hug. "I love you, Sassy, but you live at the ranch. Mr. Trent said we can't stay there, and Miss Helen is mean!"

Sassy hugged him close and nuzzled his warm cheek. "I love you, too, and I'll come to see you as often as I can. I think it's wonderful the Smyths want you to live with them. Daniel, do you think you would like the Smyths to adopt you? They would be your family, too."

"Could I live with them always?" Daniel asked.

Sassy smiled at her sweet brother. "Yes, well, at least until you are all grown up."

Daniel looked at each of the family and back at Sassy. He vigorously nodded his head in the affirmative.

"I think that's a good idea for all of us. I will agree to the adoption. That way, I'll know for sure he has a loving family and will be kept safe," she said with a smile and tears welling up in her eyes.

"Daniel, I do want you to understand that Mr. Trent wasn't being mean by not letting you stay at the ranch. He wanted you to have an education and be taken care of like you are now. Miss Helen has been much nicer lately. I don't think she meant to scare you. She just hadn't been around children much and didn't know how to be nice to you." Sassy paused and thought for several seconds before she released Daniel from her firm hug.

"I know all of this is confusing to you, Daniel, and it is to me, too."

Daniel nodded his head as though he understood.

"What will you do now?" Sally asked.

"The only thing I know to do is go back to the ranch and ask the Sandersons to help me find the boys and Martha. I don't have enough money to hire someone to look for them, and I wouldn't know how to go about it myself."

"I think that's exactly what you should do," Jacob agreed. "Don't you worry about this little fellow. Just write out a paper saying he can stay with us, in case the home tries to make him come back. He'll go to public school with the girls, so he won't even be close to the orphanage."

"Will they fire you for keeping him if they decide they want him back?"

"Just let them try! I know a tough lawyer that will set them straight, and I'll do some work for him to pay his bill."

Sassy could hardly wait for the train to arrive to take her back to Amarillo and then make the long drive to the ranch. When she arrived on Sunday, instead of Monday, she found the wagon empty. She ran to the storekeeper's quarters above the store and told him about her dilemma.

"Didn't Trent tell you to not bother with the wagon but to ride one of his horses back to the ranch?" the storekeeper asked, a bit puzzled.

"No, Trent didn't drive the wagon to town, so I guess Hank forgot to tell me," she explained.

"I'll put on the side saddle for you seein' as how you're wearing a dress."

"Thank you. I know how to ride side saddle," Sassy answered.

"That's okay, Miss. I'll come saddle the horse, and you can be on your way."

The evening was chilly with a blustery north wind, but Sassy hardly noticed as the problem of losing her siblings kept running through her mind. Was it expecting too much to think the Sandersons would help her, and how would they go about it? She knew it would cost a lot of money to hire someone to track them down, and she certainly didn't have that kind of money. How could she ever repay such a huge debt? Thus, she spent the hours it took to ride back to the ranch praying for the Sandersons' help and worrying about where Timothy, Nathan, and Martha might be and the kind of people that had taken them.

At dusk, the homestead came into view, and she nudged the horse to go a bit faster as she was anxious to get home. Home? This wasn't really her home. She just worked here, but right now, all of her hopes of finding her siblings depended on the two people who did belong here.

Helen sat beside the fireplace, watching the fading light outside. The sunset was picturesque, with streaks of orange, yellow, and purple painting the western horizon. She suddenly leaned forward in her wheelchair and squinted to see what she thought she was seeing.

"Trent, Trent!" she called to him in his office. "Sassy's back early and came riding by, toward the back, like a bat out of Hades."

Trent walked into the room and gave Helen a questioning look. "Wonder why she would be back a day early?"

"I can't imagine, but I'm sure we are about to find out," she answered as they heard the back door slam. Within seconds, Sassy came almost running into the living room. She stopped short, seeing Trent standing beside the fireplace and Helen seated in her wheelchair. Both were staring at her as though her presence was a total surprise, and it was.

Trent thought Sassy looked wild-eyed, like a frightened colt, one that has felt a saddle for the first time and wants more than anything to rid itself of its burden. He had witnessed this phenomenon over and over during his years of ranching. He could sense her fear and wondered what could have possibly happened to cause her almost hysterical appearance.

Helen had seen that same look that day at the creek when Jack realized something was terribly wrong. His handsome face revealed it all: fear, confusion, and uncertainty. The difference was she didn't think Sassy would run away from this problem, whatever the cause, as Jack had done. She had what the old timers called *grit*.

"They're gone!" she blurted out in a voice much too loud for the distance between them.

"Who's gone?" Helen and Trent asked almost in unison.

"She, that Miss Martin, put Timothy and Nathan on the orphans' train and gave Martha to some rich woman." She sounded almost breathless as the tears started streaming down her cheeks.

Trent stood rooted to the floor, but he managed to ask. "Where is Daniel?"

"Thank God he's safe with the Smyths."

Helen put her hands over her face and let out a moan that would have been heard at the funeral of a loved one.

Sassy advanced toward Trent, balled her small hands into fists, and brought them up in a fighting position.

Trent saw her movement but was not prepared for what she did next.

"You did this!" she screamed through the tears as she delivered the first fierce blow to his chest, knocking him off balance. He quickly recovered his firm stance and readied himself for what was to follow.

"You said they would be safe!" She landed another blow to his chest.

"You said they would get a good education!" she blurted out as more tears fell. Wham! Her fist hit his broad chest again!

"This is your fault!" she continued to shout in rage. Wham!

"Do you hear me? It's your fault!" she gasped as she delivered another violent blow to his chest.

Trent was truly surprised at her strength and thought he might wind up with a few broken ribs, but he was not about to stop her from venting her anger toward him. The sad truth was she was right. Right now, he felt it was his fault. His intentions had been good, but they had certainly gone awry.

When he looked at Sassy's red, swollen eyes from crying and heard the despair in her voice, he wanted to enfold her in his strong arms and kiss away every tear, assure her they would find her brothers and Martha. He would make everything in her life right again, but he knew it was quite possible he could not fulfill such a promise and would only let her down and hurt her more. He was the man who was going to protect her from other men and more hurt. Now look what he had done. Trent felt about as low as any man could ever feel.

He could see Sassy had about spent her anger and was sobbing now from worry and exhaustion. Her blows to his chest were much weaker as her strength waned.

Although he could not bring himself to avert his eyes away from Sassy, he could hear Helen sitting beside him as she tried to control her own emotions.

With one hand, he reached out and placed it on Helen's shoulder, giving her an affectionate squeeze. With his other arm, he encircled Sassy, drawing her to him. She was so spent she did not resist his gesture of kindness. He bent his head and gently kissed the top of her head as he breathed in the fresh scent of her hair. Her tears were wetting the front of his shirt, but he didn't care about that. He only wanted to soothe the two women who meant the most to him. That thought caught him like a bolt from the blue. Sassy had come to mean more to him than he wanted to admit. And now, he had let her down to the point she might truly hate him for what had happened to her family.

He knew one thing for sure. He would turn Heaven and Earth upside down to find those kids and bring them back to her.

Chapter Fifteen

Biggun reined his horse in and dismounted in front of the small house that showed little evidence it had once been painted white. It was one of those small two-room houses that sat on the edge of Amarillo. The room to the left was the kitchen, and a dog run separated it from the room on the right, used for sitting/bedroom. Through the dog run, he could see a large area spaded up for a garden, and the outhouse sat about thirty feet from the back of the house.

"Hello!" he called as he started toward the house. When no one answered, he shouted again.

"Hello, Two-Toes!"

A man appeared from the backyard and stood at the back of the dog run. He did not speak but motioned Biggun forward.

Two-Toes had been a scout for the Army for some thirty years, starting that career when he was fifteen. At the end of the Civil War, when the Army returned to Texas to clean up the Indian mess, as they called it, Two-Toes had been among their first captives. He was a smart young brave and soon realized the blue coats far outnumbered the Indian tribes, and it would be to his advantage to work with them instead of against them. He had built a reputation known far and wide for his superior tracking skills.

Stories abounded about some of his extraordinary tracking endeavors, which led folks to believe he could find the Devil himself if need be.

Biggun was here to persuade his old friend to come out of retirement to find Sassy's brothers. That should be an easy day's ride for Two-Toes, Biggun thought as he walked toward the man. The main problem seemed to be when Two-Toes retired from the Army, he retired from tracking anybody or anything. Rumor had it he had been offered great sums of money to perform certain jobs and had turned them all down. Biggun certainly wasn't any New York lawyer to try to persuade this man to relent and take this job for Trent Sanderson, but that was exactly what he had been sent to do since he and Two-Toes had developed a friendship over a few card games.

Biggun observed Two-Toes' stature and appearance. He was not a big man, about five feet seven inches tall, with a slender build and a few streaks of gray now glistening in his coal-dark hair. His face still looked younger than his fifty-something years. When he spoke, it was in a quiet manner, and his piercing black eyes never left your face. When he set his gaze on you, you had the feeling that he saw far more than just a face.

Most folks seemed under the impression all Indians were ill-tempered and rarely, if ever, smiled or laughed. Biggun had known several Indians who worked at the ranch and found them to be much like anyone else. Biggun had found through the years he had known Two-Toes that he had a quick wit and often laughed at his own antics.

"You are too early to bargain for vegetables from my garden," Two-Toes said as he gestured toward the freshly turned earth.

"I see that. You should have plants knee high by now," Biggun returned with a grin.

"Too early to plant. The mesquites have no leaves yet, so winter will come again."

Biggun had heard that for years and knew it to be a good sign to go by for planting.

"That's good," Biggun answered.

Two-Toes gave him a questioning look.

"I need your help. Well, not me, but Trent Sanderson. Well, really, not him either, but a young woman who works for him," Biggun tried to explain.

Two-Toes laughed. "Are you sure you know who needs my help?"

Biggun laughed, too. "Her name is Sassy McCoy. She and her family started from Kansas to Mason County, Texas. First her ma died and then her pa died. Trent found her trying to dig a grave over on the hill by the north creek and brought her and her three brothers and little sister to the homestead. I helped them bury their pa, and the girl went to work taking care of Helen and cooking." Biggun didn't want to get into the part about them thinking Sassy was a boy.

Two-Toes raised his eyebrows at the mention of someone taking care of Helen. Even he had heard the notorious rumors about the number of housekeepers and cooks the Sandersons had gone through.

"Anyway, Trent found out the family in Mason County didn't want them, and the younger kids needed to be in school. He found an orphans' home in Wichita Falls that took the four younger ones in, but now it seems the home got overcrowded, so they put the two older boys on the orphans' train and gave the little girl to some rich woman. The younger boy is safe with one of the workers. Trent's willing to pay well if you'll help us find those kids. Their sister is about crazy from worry about what has happened to them." Biggun pulled off his hat and wiped the sweat from his brow, although the afternoon wasn't all that hot.

Two-Toes studied the big man with his keen eyes for several minutes before he spoke. "Where are you staying tonight?"

"I've got a room at the Anson's Boarding House."

"Where's Trent?"

"He and Sassy will be here by dark. They want you, Sassy, and me to leave on the early morning train to Wichita Falls. There, he plans for us to buy horses and supplies for the ride to the towns along the train route and search out the ranches where the boys might have been taken."

"When Trent and the girl get to town, send them to see me," Two-Toes said as he turned and walked back toward where he was digging up the dirt for planting.

Trent and Sassy arrived just as the sun was setting. Biggun told Trent about his conversation with Two-Toes.

"That damned stubborn Indian! Why couldn't he have agreed to this trip when you talked to him?" he fumed as he and Sassy remounted to ride to the edge of town.

"Do you want me to go along, too?"

"No need. Just tell the cook to save us a plate of food. No telling how long I'll have to confab with Two-Toes to get him to go with us," Trent continued to grumble.

Two-Toes sat on the hard-packed earth in the dog run. He saw Trent and the girl ride up and dismount. He reached up and lit a lantern hanging on the wall. There were no chairs in the dog run, so he brought one from the small kitchen for the girl.

Trent extended his hand and gave Two-Toes a gripping handshake, a signal he was ready to conduct business and get things settled.

Two-Toes got the meaning of the crushing handshake but did not let on that it was any different from a friendlier shake. He sat cross-legged and motioned for Sassy to take the chair.

Trent sat on the ground beside her and leaned back against the wall. He pushed the brim of his hat up so the man could clearly see the expression on his face. He didn't waste any time getting straight to the business at hand.

As Trent talked, he noticed Two-Toes kept his eyes glued on Sassy. After a while, this began to wrangle his nerves a bit, as he didn't like other men looking at her so intently.

After Trent had been through the same story Biggun had told Two-Toes earlier, he asked, "Now, what will it cost me to get your help? I've heard you've turned down some pretty big offers since you left the Army, but I'll match or go higher than any of those if that's what it takes," Trent stated, ready to get a definite answer.

Two-Toes did not waver his gaze from the young woman but continued to study her in silence.

Sassy felt uncomfortable under the Indian's intense scrutiny. She couldn't imagine what he expected to see in her as he continued to stare at her for so long. She wondered why he hadn't looked at Trent as he spoke. After all, he was the one offering to pay him a large sum of money for his help.

Two-Toes finally spoke directly to Sassy after several moments of awkward silence. "Why do you not speak to me for help?"

Sassy was taken aback at his question. Then she quickly gathered her thoughts. "I am the one that needs your help, but I have no way to pay you," she spoke softly as she ducked her head, a bit humiliated to have to admit she was totally dependent on Trent's generosity. "I—I wouldn't know how to go about it on my own. They tell me you were the best tracker in the Army, so please help me find my brothers and sister," she pleaded with her voice and her eyes as she implored the Indian with all the sway she could muster.

As they talked, she silently prayed with all of her heart that Two-Toes would relent and help them.

"Why can't the three of you do this job without me?"

"We will if we have to, but it might go much faster with your help. We could go in teams. The three of us all know what my brothers look like, but you know how to find them. If they have been taken away from the town where they were taken off the train, and that is very likely from what the woman at the orphans' home told me, we need you to track them. The woman in charge at the home said farmers and ranchers take the children to work on their property, and some may live miles from town. You might pick up on spoken clues as well as whatever you look for when following someone. We don't know what to look for and would likely waste precious time in finding them." She spoke in a pleading tone.

"The visual trail will likely be cold by the time we get there," he stated and finally broke eye contact with Sassy as he turned toward Trent.

"I will go," he stated. "Not because of your money but for the young one here whose eyes tell me she is in great pain from the many losses she has suffered. I, too, was an orphan boy at age nine. An old woman in our tribe took me in and raised me as her own." He chuckled softly. "She probably was not so old, but past childbearing years, and her own children and two husbands had died."

He stood. "I will meet you at the early train," was all he said as he turned and walked toward the outhouse out back.

Trent signaled to Sassy with a nod of his head toward their horses that it was time for them to go.

She started to speak, but he shook his head and whispered, "Later," as they mounted and rode toward the rooming house.

Once they were well away from Two-Toes' house, Sassy couldn't hold her tongue any longer. "You still don't know how much this is going to cost you," she was quick to point out.

"He'll be fair, and the most important part is he's willing to help. On the train ride tomorrow, we'll talk to him about the best way to go about this. He may say something then about the price, although I doubt it."

"Trent, how will I ever repay you? I'll likely never have the money this is going to cost," Sassy said with evident worry about the cost added to all of her other worries.

Trent looked at her as they started to dismount. He smiled as he reached out and put one finger under her chin to turn her head so she would look at him. "I guess you'll be cooking biscuits for me until you're at least ninety years old," he said with a teasing chuckle.

Sassy smiled back at him, not sure how to answer, but she knew she was plenty willing to do that and far more for Trent Sanderson under the right circumstances. That was not likely to ever happen. He would marry a woman of class someday. She would have no claim on him, but she would gladly serve as his cook and housekeeper forever to try to repay her debt.

As they walked toward the boarding house, she turned to Trent. "Is it true he only has two toes on one foot?"

"So I'm told."

"What happened? Was he born that way?"

"I don't really know. I've heard lots of stories about what happened to his other three toes. Some say he was born that way; others say they were bitten off by a wolf, bear, mountain lion, and so on. I guess you'll have to ask him if you really want to know." Trent smiled, knowing how curious she was about everything.

Sassy looked up at Trent as they paused just outside the door. The moonlight lit his face as he had already removed his hat before going inside. He was indeed a fine-looking man, she reflected. Sassy found it a bit disturbing that she was attracted to him as a woman to a man, regardless of what had happened with Flossy. She must try to fight those feelings. She felt sure he would never see her in the same light. She was simply his hired help, just as Flossy had been. The difference was she would never enter his bed without the benefit of wedlock, so she would never know the pleasures with him that a man and woman share. That thought made her sad. She was afraid a part of her would never be fulfilled, even if she married someone else.

Chapter Sixteen

The train car was crowded and cold. The children sat three to a seat, and when there was no more room on the seats, the boys were told to sit on the cold, filthy floor.

Timothy and Nathan sat in the aisle near the front of the car and huddled together, trying to stay warm, but their efforts were mostly wasted. They clutched their small bundle of one change of clothes. That was all any of them could say they had that belonged to them. Some of the children put their extra clothing on to help keep warm. Timothy told Nathan they would wait until night to do that, as it would be even colder in the drafty old train car after dark. Timothy noticed Mr. Carter and Miss Beasley both wore warm winter coats and hats to ward off the chill and help keep warm.

The children talked in soft whispers in fear of Mr. Carter's harsh tone and free hand with his belt. Caroline Beasley, head of the girls' dormitory, was along to supervise the girls, but she did not cross John Carter in any manner, whether he was disciplining the boys or girls.

The train rocked along at what seemed like a snail's pace. After several hours, it came to a slow halt in a small town with only a few stores and houses. Timothy saw a small one-room school and a white church with a tall steeple not far from the railroad track. There were about a dozen wagons and buggies parked near the church.

Mr. Carter stood up and clapped his hands loudly to get everyone's attention. He was a tall, thin man with round, dark eyes and a pointed nose. He wore a neatly trimmed beard that only covered his chin. He spoke in his normal, callous tone.

"This is our first stop. You will march off the train single file and walk to the church, where you will be seated in the front pews. You do not talk to anyone. Miss Beasley and I will do all the talking that needs to be done. When you are called to the front, stand up straight and put a pleasant look on your face. Try to make as good of an impression as possible, as some of these fine folks will be your future parents or guardians." He let his gaze wander around the mass of children. "Are there any questions?" he asked but gave the impression he didn't expect anyone to speak up.

Timothy raised his hand for recognition as they had been taught.

"Yes, Timothy, what is it?"

"Could me and Nathan stay together since we're brothers? He's feelin' kind of poorly and needs me to look after him."

Mr. Carter gave him a derisive look and answered none too kindly, "I'll see what I can do, but I can't promise you will get to stay together. After all, these folks are taking you out of the goodness of their hearts and may only want to take one of you."

He clapped his hands again and ordered, "Let's go now and not keep these fine folks waiting."

The children did as they had been instructed. Nathan clung to Timothy's arm with a vice-like grip as though that might keep them together. Nathan could feel Timothy shaking, dreading what might happen with every step they took.

Names were called, and a child would walk to the front and stand between Mr. Carter and Miss Beasley. If it were a boy, Mr. Carter would talk with greatly animated gestures, praising the boy and telling of all his virtues. Miss Beasley would do much the same for each girl. She wasn't quite as vigorous with her gestures, but she certainly presented each girl as a treasure anyone would be proud to possess.

Timothy noticed most of the women were dressed in their Sunday clothes, but the men looked as though they had stopped during their day's work to come take a look at the orphans. One tall, gaunt-looking man spoke in a loud, gruff voice and even walked around looking at the children still seated. When he came near Timothy and Nathan, Nathan pressed even closer to Timothy as though that would protect him from the man's grasp. Timothy could feel Nathan's body quiver from fright. Thankfully, the tall man passed them by with scarcely a glance.

This meeting went on for two hours or more because the prospective parents often had a lot of questions about the child. When the last of the local folks had chosen their child, and one family took two girls and departed, there were eleven fewer children to return to the train. Timothy and Nathan, along with about half of the others, had never been called to the front.

They were fed a meager supper of cold meat and bread. Timothy, Nathan, and another boy now shared a seat. They put on their extra clothes and huddled together, seeking warmth against the cold night air. Only one lamp was lit to show the way to the toilet. It cast eerie shadows throughout the train car as it swayed with every clackity-clack of the train, moving on down the tracks, farther and farther away from where Sassy thought they were safe at the orphans' home.

Timothy was still awake through the late hours. He wondered what Sassy would do when she found out they were gone. Would she try to find them? How would she know where to look? What if they didn't let him and Nathan stay together? He knew Daniel was safe with the Smyths, but where had they sent little Martha? He had overheard Miss Beasley say some rich lady had taken Martha. Why were they doing this? They knew they had an older sister to see about them. Question after question swirled through Timothy's tired mind until sleep came at last as he held Nathan close.

The next two stops were much like the first. By then, the train car had taken on the sour odor of unwashed bodies, and several of the children had wet their clothing in fear of what would happen to them. In the afternoon, when the weather warmed, they would open the windows to breathe in the fresh air, but at night, when the windows were closed, the strong stench became sickening.

The food was scarce and often almost made them sick to their stomachs, but the children ate every bite. They knew that was all they would have to fill their hollow bellies for hours.

On the fourth day, a man and his wife wanted Timothy but said they couldn't afford two boys. They said they were sorry to have to separate the brothers but were insistent they could only take one.

"I need some boy old enough and strong enough to help me plow and handle the livestock. That little 'un don't look too healthy," the man said, showing little sympathy for the pair.

"I can't leave my brother," Timothy bravely spoke up and earned a scathing look from John Carter.

Timothy ignored the man and went on talking. "Nathan's a bit puny and needs me to tend to him. We have an older sister, and she's goin' to come looking for us anyway, so you won't have either of us very long," he said with as much courage as he could muster.

Mr. Carter gave a short laugh. "See what a fine lad you have chosen; he cares so much for his brother. I am afraid he is mistaken about his sister coming for him, so he will be with you for as long as you like," he assured the couple.

"No! No! Don't take my brother," Nathan wailed and tried to run to Timothy, only to be intercepted by Mr. Carter, who whispered in a threatening manner for Nathan to sit down and be quiet.

Timothy looked at his brother's crumpled face as the couple led him from the church, leaving Nathan behind. Nathan looked so forlorn. His little shoulders were slumped in a dejected manner, and tears streamed down his dirt-streaked cheeks. He followed Timothy's departure with sad blue eyes that reflected such misery it tore at Timothy's heart.

Timothy wanted to break free, run and grab Nathan, and keep on running. He knew they wouldn't get far, and that would only make it harder when they were separated again.

As they climbed into the wagon, he couldn't stop himself from asking once more. "Please, let my brother come with me. I'll work twice as hard, and we'll share our food," he pleaded.

"Sorry, just you, boy, now hush about it," the man snapped, not even looking at Timothy.

~

There were few children left when the train made its seventh and final stop. The people who came to the school to take the orphans grumbled about the *slim pickens*. Nathan was one of the last chosen. A gray-haired, fat man, who was missing several yellowish-brown teeth, and his two teenage boys said they would take the little tyke and make a man out of him. They were dirty, and all carried that soured sweat smell that clung to their bodies and clothing. Nathan thought they likely hadn't bathed since last summer. It was hard to determine the color of their clothing through the layers of dirt. All three chewed tobacco and spat in whatever direction was convenient. After they left the school, Nathan was shocked to hear the three men use words he had rarely heard and a few he had never heard. He knew the words were something he would have gotten a good smacking for if he had said them.

On their way to the man's ranch, Nathan learned the two older boys had also come on the orphans' train when they were about ten years old. They said there were five more boys at the ranch of various ages. Nathan's spirit lifted slightly, thinking maybe he would have someone to play with when chores were done.

Oh, how he missed Timothy and wished he were here with him. He had cried himself to sleep every night since that couple had taken him away.

As they traveled on and on, farther away from the small town, Nathan wondered how Sassy or anyone would ever find him. It seemed they traveled in circles as they followed what scarcely passed as a trail.

They had left town well before noon and rode on and on until late afternoon when an old ranch house and outbuildings came into view. The house looked as though a strong wind might just blow it away, and the outbuildings didn't look any better. There was a porch across the front that sagged in several places. It had never seen a coat of paint. Two old, skinny dogs lay under the edge of the porch and hardly lifted their heads when they saw the wagon and riders' approach.

He had learned just by listening to the two young men that they were probably in their mid to late teens. Their names were Jesse and Ward. He heard them call the older man Mr. B. Jesse appeared to be the oldest. His long hair was a dirty blond, his face was marked with pockmarks, and he had sneaky brown eyes. Ward was probably fifteen or sixteen. He also had long hair, but it was dark brown and tied back at the nape of his neck. His eyes were black as midnight, and his teeth were already brown from using chewing tobacco.

Nathan didn't see anyone around, and he wondered if the two older boys had been lying to him about there being five other boys here. Just as he jumped down from the wagon, two boys did appear from around the far corner of the house. They didn't speak or even act like they saw him.

"Unload the wagon," the old man barked. He turned to Nathan. "You help 'em," he snarled in his usual gruff voice. Nathan followed the two boys as they led the team and wagon around the house toward the barns. Nathan thought the old man always sounded mad.

Once they were out of sight and hearing distance from the others, one of the boys turned and looked Nathan up and down. "Don't look like you'll last long around here."

Nathan stared at him, not sure what to say. He finally managed to ask, "What do you mean by that?"

"How old are you?" the other boy asked as he continued to size him up.

"I just turned ten," Nathan answered.

The second boy, a bit taller than the first, spat a string of tobacco juice near Nathan's shoes. "The last one about your age only lived about two months after they brung him out here."

Nathan felt his insides start to quiver but didn't want to let the boys see how scared he really was. "Wh—what happened to him?" he stammered.

The first boy shrugged his shoulders. "Got a fever and just died. Want to see his grave?"

Nathan vigorously shook his head to indicate he did not want to see the boy's grave.

"Come on, let's get this wagon unloaded afore one of them comes to see what's takin' so long," the taller boy said as they entered the barn.

By the time the wagon was unloaded, Nathan felt so weak he wasn't sure his legs would carry him to the house. His stomach growled with hunger. Nathan thought he could even eat a snake if that was all they had. He was disappointed to hear it wasn't near time to go to the house. The boys laughed at him for thinking they were done for the day; there were lots more chores to be done. When they finally did enter the house as night fell, he found some strange-smelling stew on his plate, but he ate every bite. After the first few bites, it didn't taste so bad as he got used to the pungent odor. He wanted to ask for more but saw each boy take his plate and wash it in a pan of water as soon as he finished eating. No one asked for more food.

Nathan was surprised to find the dishwater was stone cold. Sassy always washed dishes in water so hot it almost burned your hands. She said you had to use hot water to get the dishes clean.

Another boy motioned Nathan to follow him after the last of the dishes were washed and put on the counter to dry. They entered a long, narrow room that looked to have been a porch turned into a room. It had three dirty mattresses lying on the floor, two cane-bottom chairs that didn't look too sturdy, and a small table made from scrap wood. Apparently, two boys shared a bed.

"I'm Toby," the boy who looked to be about ten said, as he sat on the mattress at the far end of the room, away from the door.

"I'm Nathan McCoy."

"We'll be bedmates," Toby said as he removed his sorry-looking boots to reveal dirty, smelly socks that already had several holes in them.

Toby looked around the room to be sure they were alone.

"I'm gonna tell you how things go around here, so you won't get no beatin's if you do what I tell you," he said, lowering his voice. "You do whatever the old man says and, if not him, then Jesse or Ward. Them's the two that fetched you today. They're all mean as rattlesnakes and don't mind beatin', kickin', or starvin' you if you don't do what they say." The boy's voice held no emotion. Toby had accepted life as it was and felt it only fair to warn the kid before he wound up like the boy who had been his bunkmate for a couple of months. He could see the fear in Nathan's eyes and knew that would serve him well, to stay scared to death of this heartless bunch of thugs.

The other four boys soon filed into the room and undressed for bed. The two oldest, Jesse and Ward, unstrapped their gun belts and laid them on the table. Soon, the room took on the same sour, sickening odor of sweat, unwashed bodies, dirty clothes, and pee, just like the train car. One of the boys blew out the lamp, plunging the room into total darkness.

Nathan lay staring into the blackness, wishing it was Timothy he shared this bed with, although Toby seemed okay. He wondered how Sassy or anyone could ever find him here. Even if she did, that mean old man and the two older boys probably wouldn't let her take him with her. Tears started to sting his eyes, and he gulped, trying to hold them back. Then he heard Toby whisper.

"Don't ever try to run away, or they'll catch you and kill you dead! I seen 'em do it, and they didn't make it easy neither. Just stick as close to me as you can and remember to do whatever they say. Don't never back talk 'em, just do it," he warned and said no more.

Chapter Seventeen

When they reached Wichita Falls, Trent hired the lawyer Jacob Smyth told him about. Trent told him to find Martha and bring her to the Smyths' until they returned since they felt reasonably certain she was likely still in the city. He then purchased horses, saddles, and supplies for their trip.

Two-Toes suggested they follow Biggun's plan to go in pairs, with Sassy and Trent checking ranches on one side of the railroad tracks and he and Biggun on the other. They would meet at the small towns and exchange any information they might have learned and would check with the local folks about who may have taken orphans.

"Preachers and teachers are the best ones to ask since they usually take them to the school or church for the folks to get them," Two-Toes told them.

"The first town where the train stopped is about a half-day's ride, so we should reach it by nightfall," Trent said. They would stay at a boarding house when they could but might have to camp out if their search took them too far from town.

Sassy was nervous about not knowing who might have her brothers. She wondered how far they would have to travel to find them. She knew Trent and Biggun needed to get back to the ranch for spring roundup instead of hunting Timothy and Nathan. The only solace she felt was in praying they would soon find the boys and would return to find Martha safe with the Smyths.

Miss Martin had tried to threaten Trent with pressing charges against Sassy for falsifying the papers when they checked the children into the home, but she soon learned she had more than met her match. She turned pale when he told her the name of the attorney he had hired. Miss Martin instantly became more cooperative and revealed Mr. Carter and Miss Beasley had not returned from their trip, so she had no information as to who took Timothy and Nathan. However, she steadfastly refused to tell them about Martha. Sassy felt sure the lawyer would get far more information out of her when he came calling.

When they left her office, Trent said they would try to check the northbound trains for Carter and Beasley in hopes they would have the names of the people who took Timothy and Nathan. Then he added, "Even if they have names, it doesn't mean it is really their name. People can sign whatever name they want, and they wouldn't know the difference or likely care."

Sassy felt her heart sink, although she had already thought about that as a possibility. As they rode, the men talked, and Sassy prayed they would find them safe and could bring them home.

Before they had left the ranch, Helen had said she felt certain she could make arrangements with a respectable woman in Amarillo to take the children in, and they could hitch a ride to the ranch on the weekend with the other families. Sassy recalled her conversation with Helen shortly before they left on this journey.

"I don't know why I didn't think about Irene Johnson before we took them to the orphans' home. She usually takes only girls, but for the right price I'll bet she would take Timothy, Nathan, and Martha. Her husband died suddenly and left her a lovely two-story house, and that's about all, not much money. She's a sweet woman and good with children. I guess I didn't think about her because I hadn't seen her in years. About all I've done is spend most of my time feeling sorry for myself," she said with regret.

"But how will I pay for their keep on what I make?" Sassy asked, showing her constant state of worry over her lack of money to care for the children.

"Sassy, I have more money than I can ever spend, and this will help salve my conscience for the way I treated those poor little tykes when you all first came here," Helen admitted as she gave Sassy's hand a gentle squeeze. "Now I feel so ashamed for scaring those poor kids half to death. I knew they were afraid to even come to the house without you to protect them. I'd like to believe I was a different person then. Not that that's any excuse for the way I behaved," Helen said with sadness at the painful memory.

Then she looked at Sassy and smiled. "Maybe it's not too late for this old sinner to atone for her past misdeeds."

"I think you have already atoned and been forgiven," Sassy said, grateful for her kindness, and she kissed Helen on the cheek.

As they rode into the first town, Trent spotted a small boarding house where he inquired if they had rooms for them for the night. The woman at the boarding house told them the train had been through a week earlier, and they had taken the children to the church.

Early the next morning, the four walked across the street to the rectory to inquire about the children. The minister had already gone out, and his wife couldn't remember either of the boys. They talked to several other town folks, but their inquiries proved to be fruitless.

They met the northbound train about three miles south of the town and waved it down. Sassy and Trent walked through the passenger cars but did not find John Carter or Caroline Beasley.

They rode on, reaching the next town late that afternoon. They were directed to the schoolmaster's house. The schoolmaster did seem to remember the boys but was quite certain they were not taken by anyone in their community. The third day went much the same. They checked a couple of ranches with houses near the railroad tracks. None of them had taken any orphans and didn't think their neighbors farther out had either.

Trent could see the disappointment on Sassy's face. She said nothing, but he could read her mood of despair. His own guilt in the matter still weighed heavily on his mind. Some protector he'd turned out to be, he reflected each day as they rode on in search of the boys.

On the fourth day, they reached the small town before noon. The sky had become overcast, and a chilly north wind was picking up, threatening rain, but the weather didn't detour Sassy from finding her brothers. Once again, they were directed to the church. The minister did remember Timothy and Nathan quite well.

"It was a sad sight when the Carsons took the older boy, but Charlie refused to take the younger one. The look on that child's face broke my heart," the minister said with genuine sympathy.

"Where do the Carsons live?"

"Take the road west for about six miles. Then it splits, so take the right-hand road and it's only a couple of miles to their place. I don't think Charlie will be too happy about giving up the boy, although I recall the lad telling him his sister would be coming for them."

They thanked the minister for his help and walked outside. Sassy was so excited she could hardly contain her eagerness to get started to the Carsons' ranch.

Trent gazed at the threatening sky and then at Sassy. "Looks like we'll likely get wet. Do you want to wait for this to blow over before we go?" Trent asked, although he was fairly certain he already knew her answer.

Sassy instantly shook her head from side to side. "I don't mind getting wet, do you?"

Trent grinned. "I've been wet more than once," he laughed as he mounted up.

Trent told Biggun and Two-Toes to head on toward the next town since they knew Nathan had gone further before being taken by some family.

As Trent and Sassy rode toward the ranch, he would steal a quick look at her occasionally. The fact that she was growing prettier every day didn't make it any easier for him to keep his feelings in check. Her blonde hair fell in soft waves that now reached her shoulders. Her eyes seemed a deeper blue in the pale morning light, and her skin looked smooth and soft. Her body had filled out even more, and there was no way to mistake her for a boy now, he mused as they rode on.

Oh! What a happy day this will be, she mused, when she could hug Timothy and know he was safe with her. Now, if Helen's plan worked, he would live much closer, and they would see one another often. She thanked God every night for Helen and Trent's generosity and willingness to help her.

Her feelings for Trent ran from hot to cold. At times, her womanly instincts became so overpowering she wanted to tell him about her strong feelings for him. Other times, she almost despised him and strongly resented the fact that he had dallied with Flossy, which must be a sin, and now she carried his child. Was it resentment or jealousy she felt toward him and Flossy? She wondered about her feelings every time she thought about him and Flossy making love. Sassy didn't know how to handle the conflicting feelings that were consuming her. Whatever it was didn't change the fact that her feelings were growing stronger and stronger. It frightened her a bit to think she might let those feelings bubble over and she would reveal them to Trent. What would be his reaction to her? On several occasions, Sassy had caught Trent looking at her as a man looks at a woman, but she didn't let him know she had noticed his look of attraction. At times, she wondered if he expected her to give in to his male desires as Flossy had done because he was her boss. Thus far, he had never done anything to indicate that was what he expected. She prayed he never did because that would mean she would have to leave the ranch. She knew she could never do what Flossy had done. She tried to turn her thoughts elsewhere.

This mess with the orphans' home wasn't really his fault either, she realized. He had been trying to do what was best for the children, but now it had turned out to be the wrong thing. She no longer blamed him for what the folks at the orphans' home had done. Somehow, she needed to let him know she wasn't mad at him anymore. Sassy felt certain Jolene Martin would regret the day she crossed Trent and Helen Sanderson.

When they rode into the yard, two barking dogs met them. Soon, Mr.

Carson appeared from the side of the house, where he just stood staring at them.

Trent lifted his hat slightly in greeting. "Morning, Mr. Carson. I'm Trent Sanderson, and this is Sassy McCoy."

Mr. Carson did not respond but continued to stare at the pair. He was an older man, slightly stooped, and wore a long gray beard.

"We understand you recently took Timothy McCoy from the orphans' train. But as you can see, he has a sister who has been very worried about him."

"If she wuz so worried, why'd she put him in the orphans' home?"

"Our parents both died recently, and I couldn't take care of them and work. They needed schoolin' and, where I work, there ain't no school," Sassy answered.

"Well, now, I took him in good faith, so I'd have me a good farm hand, and now you just expect me to give him up. What am I supposed to do for help to run this place?" He made a wide gesture with his hand.

Sassy looked at Trent to answer the man's question.

"Well, Mr. Carson, I wouldn't want to put you out too much, so I'm willing to give you enough money to hire yourself a good, strong man, instead of a boy, to help run this farm."

"Well, that's right neighborly, but it will have to be a sizeable amount. Not many men want to live way out here, so far away from town, and—" he paused as he seemed to remember a young woman was present.

"I am a fair man," Trent assured him.

"Where is my brother?" Sassy asked anxiously, as she had not seen Timothy anywhere around the outbuildings.

"He's done gone out to check on some cattle."

"We'll ride along with you to find him. Then you and I will settle up," Trent told the man.

Carson nodded and walked to the horse pen to saddle his horse.

Trent and Sassy followed Carson, and before long, they spotted Timothy in a draw near a small stream.

"Boy! Boy!" Carson called out.

Timothy looked in Carson's direction. He stared, frozen, for a few seconds. Then he let out a yelp and spurred his horse into a gallop in their direction.

Sassy leaned forward with her arms outstretched to embrace her brother.

Timothy hugged his sister with his entire might.

"I told 'em you'd come for me, I told 'em," he repeated in excitement. "I tried to get 'em to bring Nathan, too, but they wouldn't do it. I don't know where he is," he said with obvious worry.

"We'll find him, too," Sassy assured Timothy and hugged him again.

As the three rode back toward town, Sassy wanted to ask Trent what that had cost him but wasn't sure how to broach the subject.

They arrived back in town just before dusk. Trent spotted a small rooming house and secured rooms.

The next morning, the three rode on south in hopes of meeting up with Biggun and Two-Toes at the next town. They rode to several ranches along the way. None of the ranchers knew anything about Nathan or any of the orphans.

That evening, they checked into another small boarding house. Just as they sat down to supper, Biggun and Two-Toes arrived. They had not found out anything about the boy but were delighted to see Timothy. All Timothy could tell them was Nathan was still on the train when the Carsons took him.

Chapter Eighteen

The five of them rode on south, checking ranches and asking questions in the small towns they passed. Biggun and Two-Toes reached the town first, where the train had left the last of the orphans. All the remaining children had been taken by a number of families.

The schoolmaster remembered well that B. B. Branson and his two young thugs had taken Nathan. He had wanted to refuse to let him go, but the man and woman from the orphans' home had agreed to it before he could intervene on the child's behalf.

The schoolmaster gave them directions to the Branson place as best he could. "You almost have to be lost to find it," he concluded.

"We'll find it," Biggun assured the man.

"A man by the name of Trent Sanderson should arrive with a young woman and boy, asking about the boy, too. Just tell them we have already gone to get him. Tell them to wait here for us to come back," Biggun told the schoolmaster.

The trail wandered through the rugged country with craggy hills and steep ravines. The schoolmaster spoke the truth about being lost to find the place, Biggun decided as they ambled on toward the Branson Ranch. About mid-afternoon, they finally spotted the ramshackle-looking ranch buildings. They rode slowly toward the rundown house so they could size up the place and see how many people might be there.

Two old, scrawny dogs barked at their arrival but didn't leave the sanctuary of their shade beneath the sagging porch.

As they neared the front porch, a big man in old overalls appeared from inside. He stood sizing the two strangers up and finally walked to the edge of the porch, never taking his gaze from the two men. He let go with a stream of tobacco juice that landed near Biggun's horse.

"Are you fellers lost?" he asked none too friendly.

"No, we're looking for B. B. Branson," Biggun answered.

"You found him," the man said and spat again. His steel blue eyes shifted from Biggun to Two-Toes and back again.

Biggun didn't like the looks of the man or the place. He could well imagine why anyone like Branson would take in orphans. Cheap labor he could rule with an iron fist. What chance would a kid have trying to escape this remote hellhole? He remembered what his life had been like before he happened to land on the Flatland Ranch while running away from a ranch all too similar to the looks of this place.

"What business brings you way out here?" Branson asked in a suspicious tone.

"We're looking for a boy by the name of Nathan McCoy. He's ten years old, and the schoolmaster told us you took him from the orphans' train."

Branson studied the two men a bit longer before answering. "I did for all the good it done me."

Before the conversation went any further, Two-Toes spoke up. "Do you mind if we dismount and water our horses?"

"Sure, take 'em around back to the watering trough by the barn," Branson said as he nodded his head in the direction of the barn.

Biggun hoped Branson would stay put on the porch. That would give Two-Toes a chance to look around, but Branson descended the rickety steps and followed along.

"You said you took Nathan, so could we see him?"

"I'd like to see him myself and give him a good lickin' for runnin' off like he done. Me and Jessie and Ward spent over an hour searchin' all over town for that little scallywag."

162

Biggun walked as slow as possible, trying to keep Branson distracted enough to give Two-Toes a chance to get far enough ahead so he could look around a bit after he left the horses to water.

"You never found him?"

"Naw! No telling where he got off to or who took him. Since nobody local knowed him, they 'twernt no help. Like I said, he just up and took off while we was in the general store gettin' supplies. Bein' Saturday not much tellin' who he took up with or which way they went," Branson was obviously trying to give the impression he was concerned about the welfare of the boy.

Two-Toes ambled over to the entrance to the hay barn as though he was just stretching his legs after riding so long. He had a keen sense someone was hiding in the barn, but his eyes revealed no one. Even he wasn't sure if it had been a slight sound or smell that alerted him, but there had been something.

Nathan lay perfectly still behind one of the haystacks. He had no choice since Jesse lay on top of him with the point of his knife pressing into his throat just hard enough to convince Nathan he better not utter one sound while the two men were here.

Jesse had been lounging in the shade of the house watching Nathan work when the two men rode up asking about him. Not knowing who they were or why they wanted the boy, he took quick action in case they were lawmen.

Nathan remembered what Toby had told him that first night about following any orders Mr. B., Jesse, or Ward gave him. The hay was scratching the back of his neck, and he was afraid he might sneeze at any second, but he forced himself to not move or make a sound. He stared into Jesse's hostile, pockmarked face and taunting brown eyes. Nathan felt sick at his stomach from smelling Jesse's sour breath. He remembered Toby saying they were mean as rattlesnakes. During the short time he had been at the ranch, he had become convinced that was true. He felt certain it would please Jesse if he did disobey. It would give him an excuse, if he thought he needed one, to inflict the pain he threatened.

Nathan could plainly hear the rumble of Biggun's voice asking about him from where he stood just outside the old barn. Oh, how he wished he had the strength to push Jesse off of him and call out for help, but he didn't, and he knew better than to try. He had no doubt Jesse would plunge the knife into his throat and smother any sound he might make.

"Why are you and the Injin lookin' for the boy?" Branson asked as he nodded toward Two-Toes, who stood just inside the barn.

Nathan wondered who else was with Biggun. He didn't know anybody named Injin.

"Well, sir, we work for Trent Sanderson. He owns the Flatland Ranch up near Amarillo. He's the one that wants the boy."

Branson's interest perked up at the mention of Trent Sanderson's name. He had heard about the Flatland Ranch and knew Sanderson must be pretty damn rich. Maybe this was a chance for some easy cash.

"Is this Sanderson's kid?" Before Biggun could answer, Branson went on, a bit suspicious. "What would his kid be doin' in an orphans' home unless he's a bastard?"

Biggun felt his hands ball into a fist but forced himself to remain calm. "No, he ain't Sanderson's kid. He belongs to one of his workers, and we're just helping her find him, that's all. She works for Sanderson as a house-keeper. She couldn't keep her three brothers and little sister at the ranch. They needed schooling, so she put them in the orphans' home, thinking they'd be taken care of and get educated."

Branson's hopes of easy money were dashed, and he lost interest in why they wanted the kid. No housekeeper had enough money to make it worth his time to let 'em have the boy. He was turning out to be a pretty darn good worker for his age. In a few years, he'd likely make him a top-notch ranch hand. Now, he just wanted to be rid of these two men. He didn't like the way that Injin kept snooping around.

"Mighty sorry I can't help you. But like I said 'afore, no tellin' where that kid got off to."

Nathan listened to their retreating steps and knew he would be here for a long, long time. He had hoped with all his heart someone would come for him, but this was not the day he would be freed from this snake pit.

Maybe someday he and Toby would get a chance to run away. He remembered what Toby said about not trying to get away, but if they planned it just right and waited for them to get really drunk some night, they just might make it. If Toby wouldn't go with him, he'd go on his own. That was his only hope of ever escaping this *den of 'niquity*. That was what his ma called some of the places his pa used to go that she didn't like. This had to be one of those *dens of 'niquity*, Nathan thought as Jesse eased the point of his knife away from his throat. Jesse gave Nathan a depraved, leering grin as he rolled off him.

When Biggun and Two-Toes were away from the house, Two-Toes finally spoke about the strong hunch he had. "I sensed someone hiding in the barn. I couldn't see him, but I'm sure someone was there. I'm not sure if it was a sound or a smell that gave me that strong feeling," Two-Toes tried to explain.

"Surely, Nathan wouldn't hide from us! He'd come runnin' out to meet us."

"Maybe he couldn't," Two-Toes said quietly. Two-Toes didn't say anything else for several minutes. "I think I'll wait a few days and go back. I'll scout around to be sure he's really not there. Did you believe Branson's story about him running away while they were in the store?"

Biggun had been thinking about that story, too. "It's hard to say. I expect the kid was scared half to death, thinking about being taken off by Branson and whoever was with him. He might have taken off if he had a chance."

"It's strange we didn't see anybody else working around the ranch."

"Yeah, that does seem a bit strange. I guess they could have been away from the homestead this time of day," Biggun ventured.

"I'll talk to Trent, but I think I'll go back," Two-Toes repeated. "They won't see me, but I'll see them."

Sassy stood with one arm around Timothy's shoulders while she listened to Biggun and Two-Toes tell about their trip to Branson's ranch. She felt heartsick when she heard they had not found Nathan. Could the story about him running away possibly be true? She couldn't help but wonder if Nathan would really be brave enough to just take off. If so, the likelihood of them ever finding him had grown even slimmer.

"I think that's a good idea for you to go take another look around out there just to be sure, but be careful," Trent warned Two-Toes with a slight grin when he remembered who he was telling to be careful.

"Don't worry. They'll never know I was there."

Trent turned his gaze to Sassy and Timothy. "I think we might as well head home," he said gently as he saw the tears filling Sassy's eyes and the disappointed looks on Timothy's and her faces. "I'm so sorry it turned out like this, but if he's at Branson's, Two-Toes will get him," he tried to reassure them.

Trent felt about as downhearted as Sassy and Timothy. He had wanted to find the boys and make everything right for Sassy. Now, there was a big question about that happening. He had let her down again. How could he ever expect her to trust him enough to care for him after all the disappointments he had caused her?

Trent knew his feelings were growing for this strong yet fragile young woman. She possessed a rare inner strength for her young age, but her heart was fragile, and it could be so easily broken again. He knew if they didn't find Nathan, she would really take it hard. She likely wouldn't say much, but he knew she would be grieving inside.

She had lost so much. Both of her parents, the family in Mason County that didn't want them, and now it appeared quite possible she had also lost Nathan. How much more could she endure? He had sworn to protect her when they first met, but he had fallen far short, time and again, in that respect.

Trent began to have second thoughts about pursuing a romantic relationship with Sassy. He would likely end up hurting her more.

Sassy knew what Trent had said was true. There was no need for them to linger any longer. It was time to go back to Wichita Falls to be sure Martha had been found and was waiting for them with the Smyths.

She saw the troubled look in Trent's eyes and wanted to tell him she didn't blame him for what had happened. She would tell him when they could be alone, but not here, not now.

Nathan, oh, Nathan, where are you? Please, God, let him be found and returned to us, Sassy silently prayed.

Trent turned to Biggun. "I think we'll sell these horses and gear. We'll take the train back to Wichita Falls and on to Amarillo. It will be much faster, and we've already covered the territory between here and Wichita Falls."

Sassy had overheard Trent and Biggun talking about spring roundup being delayed and knew they needed to get back to the ranch. They had done all they could do. The rest was up to Two-Toes and God.

Biggun nodded his head in agreement. "While you go get our tickets, Timothy and I'll take care of the horses."

Trent turned to Sassy. "I know the next train won't be here for over an hour, so why don't you go on over to the café and order us a big supper? We'll be along by the time they have the food ready."

The train ride back to Wichita Falls seemed to take forever. Sassy was anxious to be sure Martha was safe. As soon as they arrived, they made their way straight to the Smyths', where they were happy to find Martha playing contentedly with their girls and Daniel.

Jacob greeted the weary travelers with a satisfied smile.

"That lawyer had Martha here before nightfall the day you left. He said the woman who took her was a bit unstable. She had tried to change Martha's name to that of her little girl who died last year. Martha was confused about that and everything that had happened so suddenly but is doing just fine now," he assured them.

Martha clung to Sassy, asking question after question. She couldn't seem to grasp why Nathan was lost, and she cried and cried, wanting to see him. Sassy tried to console her sister. After a while, Sassy realized it was impossible to put Martha's young mind at ease and give her the hope she needed to believe Nathan would be found.

Trent had rented rooms for the night at a small hotel near the train station. Biggun and Timothy shared a room, Sassy and Martha shared another room, and he had a room to himself.

After supper at the hotel, Sassy sat in her room rocking Martha until she fell asleep. She still let out little sobs in her restless sleep.

Sassy hurried down the hall to use the washroom before going to bed. She happened to meet Trent on his way to his own room as she returned. He paused to ask if Martha had settled down.

"She fell asleep still crying. It's just too much for her to take in; so much has happened."

Trent reached out and laid his big hand gently on Sassy's shoulder. He cleared his throat and looked into her eyes. "Sassy, I am so sorry I've failed you again. I'd give anything to find that boy."

Before he could say more, she interrupted him. "Trent, I don't blame you for what has happened. You have always treated us with great kindness and done what you thought was best. None of us can see the future to know if the things we do are really right or wrong. I don't believe for one minute you would ever do anything on purpose to hurt any of us, so please stop blaming yourself," she said as she gazed into his brown eyes. She felt very drawn to him. She wished he would take her in his arms and console her as she had done for Martha.

"What you said is true, but somehow I still feel I've let you down, and you'll never—" he paused, "trust me like I'd like for you to."

Then, to his complete shock, Sassy stepped closer, stretched up on her tiptoes, and gently kissed him on his lips. He savored the taste of her sweet breath and the warmth of her yielding lips.

Before he realized what he was doing, he tightened his arms around her, molding her supple body to the firmness of his own body. The gentle kiss suddenly turned to one of compulsive passion. Desire raced through his body. His thoughts ran wild, and he knew beyond a doubt he wanted this woman's affection one way or another. He wanted to hold her, kiss her with the kind of kisses lovers share, touch her body with flaming caresses, and make love to her with a passion that ran unbridled in his imagination.

It was Sassy's turn to be utterly shocked when Trent pulled her to him and deepened the kiss. Sassy sensed a sudden change in him. The excitement of his kiss sent a wave of heat through her that was unsettling. Although she was not very experienced with men, she recognized what was happening between them. She also realized this was a mere taste of what could happen between a man and a woman. Was this awakened awareness an indication of deeper feelings from Trent and from her, or was it just passion like she believed he had shared with Flossy? Sassy wondered about that and many other things as she took pleasure in her new feelings.

Just as suddenly, Trent pushed her away. They stood staring at one another.

Trent cleared his throat and gave her a quirky little smile. "I'm sorry, I shouldn't have kissed you like that." His expression became more serious. "You have become an attractive young woman, and—and I lost my head. I'll try not to let it happen again."

He chided himself for losing control and letting his desires take over. It was true he had wanted to hold her like a man holds a woman he cares for and kiss her the same way for quite some time, but that was foolish and had to stop.

Sassy just stared at him, letting his words sink in. She had to tell him what not to expect in the event it did happen again.

Trent nodded his head slightly toward her. "Goodnight," he said gently and turned toward his own room.

Before he reached his door, Sassy called his name softly. She realized this was the perfect time to set things straight.

He turned when he heard her calling him.

She looked directly at him and then spoke in a soft but firm manner. "Trent, I liked the kiss probably more than I should have. I know I am indebted to you forever for all you have done for my family and me; but if it should happen again, don't get any notions about me coming to your bed like Flossy did to pay my debt."

The instant those words left her mouth, she knew she had said the wrong thing when she mentioned knowing about him and Flossy. Why, oh why, did she say it that way? She rebuked herself for being so thoughtless.

Trent's expression turned from pensive, as she had spoken, to pure fury when he heard Flossy's name. The eyes that moments before had burned with passion were replaced with a hard stare that suddenly seemed to darken with rage. His mouth was set firmly in a rigid line.

"Just what do you think you know about me and Flossy?" he asked in a livid tone, emphasizing his wrath.

"I-I shouldn't have said that. I-I know it's none of my business what you do. I'm sorry—"

Before she could ramble further, he interrupted. "Just tell me what you think you know!" he repeated as his dark gaze bore into her. There was no doubt he was infuriated.

Sassy ducked her head and started to speak.

"Look at me, not the floor!" Trent demanded.

Sassy lifted her head and fought to hold back the tears she felt forming just below the surface in her eyes. "It was the day Flossy left. I was cleaning the kitchen after lunch when I heard Helen's voice. I thought she was calling me. I started to her room, but just before I got to the door, I heard her and Flossy arguing."

Trent leaned his shoulder against the wall and crossed his arms over his broad chest as he continued to stare at her as she spoke.

"I heard Helen say she didn't believe anything Flossy was saying. Then, Flossy kind of laughed and said the two of you had spent the night together when Helen and I went Christmas shopping and stayed overnight in town. Then Flossy told Helen she was her future sister-in-law. Flossy said you were going to marry her. I knew that would really set Helen off, and I shouldn't be eavesdropping on something that was none of my business, so I went back to the kitchen. The next thing I knew, Flossy was packing to leave, and Helen was in one of her ill-tempered rages."

She felt bad lying to him about when she had gone back to the kitchen, but she certainly wasn't going to be the one to tell him Flossy claimed she was carrying his child. Oh no, that bit of news would have to come from Helen if he ever found out.

"That's all you heard?" he asked again, as though he suspected she wasn't telling him everything.

She felt horrible as she lied again and swore that was all she knew. *Please don't ask me anything else and make me lie to you again,* she pleaded silently, as guilt seemed to engulf her like the darkness of the darkest night. She would likely pay dearly for this sin, she thought, as she looked at his stern face. All traces of the pleasure they had shared moments before were gone.

Trent straightened, turned, and walked to his room, not bothering to say goodnight again.

The jarring bang of his door closing made her flinch.

Sassy entered her own room and leaned heavily against the door. She let the tears flow down her cheeks, soaking the front of her dress. Slowly, she slid to the floor and continued to weep softly so she wouldn't wake Martha, who now seemed to be sleeping peacefully. Sassy wondered if she would ever sleep peacefully again, knowing what she had done to the man who had tried to help her. She still had hopes that someday he would see her as a woman he could love, but how could he ever care for her if he knew she had deliberately lied to him, not once but twice?

Chapter Nineteen

S assy felt anxious when they reached the ranch late the next afternoon. She needed desperately to tell Helen what she had done, so she could be prepared when Trent asked her about why Flossy had really left so suddenly. That was another confession she would have to make about listening in on something that didn't concern her. She wasn't going to lie to Helen about when she had gone back to the kitchen. Living with the two lies she had already told Trent carried enough guilt.

Helen and Mary Tate both expressed their empathy to Sassy for not finding Nathan and offered words of hope that Two-Toes would find him and bring him home.

Mary had the evening meal ready and soon left for her own home. Before she went, she told Sassy that Helen had been very obliging to all the women who had come to care for her while she was away.

"It's amazing how much Helen has changed since you've come," Mary told Sassy with a warm smile.

Sassy blushed slightly at Mary's compliment.

"We got off to a rocky start, but before long, she did start to change," Sassy said. "Helen even told me that after a while, she started thinkin' about what a pitiful situation me and the kids were in, and how much she had to be grateful for, and decided she was ready to change." Sassy looked thoughtful. "It's funny, ain't it, the things that happen to make people want to change."

"Yes, I suppose that's one of the mysteries of life," Mary answered with a slight chuckle.

Thankfully, Trent had gone outside to talk to Sonny Tate before supper. As soon as only she and Helen were left in the house, Sassy seized the opportunity to tell Helen what she had done.

After Sassy's confession about letting it slip about what she had overheard, Helen looked thoughtful. "Oh, Sassy, what tangled webs we weave for ourselves," she said with a deep sigh.

Sassy gave her a puzzled look.

"What I'm saying is we all say things that once said we wish we could take back. Then, we make it even worse by trying to say something to cover up our mistake. I'm an expert on that subject," Helen said with a cynical little laugh.

"Oh, Helen, I'm truly sorry for what I've done by butting in where I had no business and then lying to Trent like I done. How am I ever going to make things right?"

Helen did not immediately answer. She seemed to be considering the best solution to this situation. She finally turned her gaze on Sassy.

Sassy felt relief when she saw Helen did not appear angry with her for what she had let slip.

"I think the less said, the better. If Trent asks me, I will say about the same thing you did. I never want him to find out about the child. Besides, how would we know if it were really his child or if that floozy snuck off and slept with one or even more than one of the ranch hands?" Helen asked in an acrid tone. "I never trusted that woman! There was something not right about her. She was too vague about her past."

Once again, guilt seized Sassy. Should she tell Helen about following Flossy to Biggun's and that they had indeed slept together more than once, or should she, as Helen had indicated, say nothing? If Flossy knew she was already with child and Trent wouldn't have her anymore, she may have turned to Biggun for someone to soothe her wounded feelings. Maybe it would be best to say nothing about that, she decided, although she felt unsure about her decision.

Later that evening, when Sassy finished cleaning the kitchen, she gave herself the luxury of soaking in the big tub until the water turned cool. As she passed through the hallway and started up the stairs to her room, she heard Trent's raised voice coming through the closed door of his office.

Oh no, he and Helen must be having it out over Flossy, she thought with dread of the outcome. She took several steps toward the office door and then abruptly stopped herself. *No, don't do it,* she warned herself. Slowly, she turned, climbed the stairs to her room, and closed the door. She sat on the side of her bed and wondered where to start her bedtime prayer. She had so many recent sins to confess and beg for forgiveness. And she must pray for her brother's safe return. And to thank God for Timothy's and Martha's safe returns and for Daniel's good home. The list seemed to be growing. She must plead for Trent to not be angry with Helen. She sank to her knees, turned toward the bed, positioned her hands for prayer, as her mother had taught her, and commenced, "Our Father Who art in Heaven—"

Helen couldn't remember when she had ever, or if she had ever, seen Trent so mad. His face was beet red. He paced the office like a caged tiger and was roaring like one to boot. As she listened to his tirade about Flossy, it occurred to her that she was getting a good dose of her own bitter medicine. That thought struck her as being funny, and she was finding it hard to suppress a smile. She knew if she dared let it out, Trent would never understand why she was smiling, although it would be at her own past misdeeds. That would only set Trent into a bigger frenzy, so she steeled herself to keep her solemn face intact.

Finally, he paused to take a breath. Helen was ready to jump in before he could continue his livid rant about Flossy.

"You should have known better than to get mixed up with the likes of her. It was obvious to the rest of us her beauty would be her downfall, and she'd use it any way she could to try to trap some rich man. That's exactly why I sent her away. She as good as told me she would go to any lengths to catch you, so be thankful she's gone!"

"I am glad she's gone, but I don't like everyone knowing my business and interfering. I am a grown man, and I can handle my own affairs."

"Affairs, that's just what it was! You could have paid dearly for it for the rest of your life, dear brother!" Helen raised her voice as it took on that old tart tone that was so familiar.

Trent hadn't heard Helen use that tone of voice in quite some time and didn't particularly want to set her into one of her ill-tempered moods. He also had to admit she was likely right about Flossy's character and intent. He had been plotting how to get rid of her and had indeed been happy to see her go. Still, it rankled him to know not only his sister but also Sassy knew what had happened between them.

"What's done is done, and I'm glad to be rid of her kind around here. Besides, Sassy has proven she can handle taking care of me and running this house just fine. Be thankful she's not the kind to lure you or any man to her bed to trap him into marriage," Helen stated emphatically.

Helen watched Trent as his pacing slowed and he poured himself another generous glass of whiskey. He walked slowly to the desk and sank into the big leather chair that he now filled as his father had once done. He looked at Helen and gave her a slow smile.

"Helen, I apologize for taking my anger out on you. I realize you had my best interest at heart," he let out a long, deep sigh.

Helen looked at her brother's face. He wasn't exactly handsome, she thought, but he was certainly a fine-looking man with strong features. His brown eyes twinkled when he smiled, enhancing small lines that angled slightly upward beside his eyes. Just his looks alone would attract most women. Add the fact that he co/owned a large sprawling ranch, plus being quite well-off financially, made him a target for lots of women. That was what he had been for Flossy, and there were plenty more like her just looking for a man like Trent. It was time he married and started a family, but it had to be with the right kind of woman.

Helen cleared her throat slightly, and Trent looked at her.

"Trent, you're twenty-six. A man your age naturally has desires concerning women," Helen stated matter-of-factly. Before she could continue, Trent leaned forward in his chair.

"Helen, you are not my mother, and I don't need a lecture about the needs of men and women."

Helen lifted her right hand as a signal for him to just listen.

"What I was about to say is it's time you got married and started a family. You are a target for every woman in the country, and another one a bit smarter than Flossy just might trap you into a marriage of misery. Look carefully, but find yourself a suitable wife."

"Just when do you think I have time to go wife hunting? I've just spent a week trying to find Sassy's brother; it's time for spring roundup; your wedding is in a few weeks, and on and on. Mark a day or two on the calendar, and I'll see if I can fit in wife hunting!" he finished, obviously irritated at her suggestion.

She gave him a sweet smile. "Maybe Sassy and I could take care of that little chore for you," she suggested, too sweetly for it to be Helen talking.

He should have known he wouldn't outdo Helen. He glared at her. "Not even when hell freezes over would I trust you and Sassy to find me a, what did you say, oh yes, a suitable wife," he snapped as he rose from the chair.

He took several heavy strides toward the door, indicating the conversation had ended when Helen got in one last word.

"What if I suggested you marry Sassy?"

Trent almost tripped as he came to an abrupt halt. He looked at Helen and wondered how on earth she could possibly know his feelings concerning Sassy. He had done nothing or said nothing in her presence to indicate he thought of Sassy as anything more than Helen's caretaker and their housekeeper.

"Mind your own business!" he snarled. Then he was gone.

Chapter Twenty

A rrangements were made for Timothy and Martha to come to the ranch every other weekend when the ranch women with school children came home. They were thriving under the care of Irene Johnson. They had also made friends in town and with the ranch families' children. They were happy at either place now that they had plenty of friends and activities to occupy their time. Most of all, they were grateful to have each other and be near Sassy again.

When Timothy and Martha came for the weekend, Sassy found their presence did not interfere with her duties. She loved hearing about their new school and the people they were meeting in town. She was relieved to learn they were both getting along well with Mrs. Irene. Sassy received a letter almost weekly from Jacob Smyth letting her know how Daniel was doing, and Daniel neatly printed a few words in each letter. She could tell Jacob and his family had totally accepted Daniel as a part of their family. Jacob had set up his own woodworking business on the side, in a small shed behind his house, where he made Daniel his official apprentice.

All was well, except there had been no word from Two-Toes for almost a month, and that concerned her greatly. She now added Two-Toes' safe return to her long list for her bedtime prayer.

Helen and Ely had decided to hold the wedding ceremony beside the creek that ran near the homestead. That had been their favorite courting destination.

Sassy and Helen had made two trips to Amarillo, shopping for material for Helen's wedding dress and a new dress for Sassy. They had purchased everything they would need for the wedding, which was quickly approaching. They planned an extravagant menu and arranged to pay some of the ranch women to help prepare the huge meal. Everything would be carried to the creek where Helen and Ely had gone to see the new horses and started courting. It would be a beautiful setting. The spring grass was turning a rich green, the trees were putting on their new leaves in various shades of green, and wildflowers were beginning to bloom. In another week, the land would be awash with color from the bluebonnets, Indian paintbrush, buttercups, and numerous other wildflowers. The trees along the shoreline were somewhat taller and fuller than the sparse ones growing in the pasture. There would be plenty of shade for the guests to enjoy now that the afternoons were growing quite warm.

On the Saturday before the wedding, Sassy took the two dresses and sat on the front porch swing, putting in their hems. She gently swung and hummed a soft tune as she worked.

Timothy rounded the corner of the house, climbed the four steps, and sat on the edge of the porch. He looked as though he had grown two or three inches since they had come here last fall. Sassy had noticed his pants were getting much too short. She needed to buy materials to make him some new ones the next time she went to town. Martha was growing too, but not as fast as Timothy.

"Sure is a pretty day. Reckon Trent would mind if me and Buddy Tate go fishing?"

"I don't reckon he'd mind. Does Buddy have a cane pole you can use?"

"Yeah, he has plenty of poles. He's asking his ma about going fishing, too."

Timothy stretched as he gazed toward the road. He stood and put one hand over his eyes as though to cut out the glare from the bright sunlight.

"What are you lookin' at?" Sassy asked, curious about his intense gaze.

"I see somebody coming."

"Probably just one of the ranch hands."

"No, I think it's Two-Toes. I can't tell if he has anybody with him. He's still too far away," Timothy answered in a serious tone.

Sassy laid the sewing aside and joined Timothy at the top of the steps. She shaded her eyes with one hand, just as he had done, trying to make out the distant figure on horseback.

"What makes you think that's Two-Toes?"

"I ain't sure, but I'd bet it is. It's just something about the way he's riding." Timothy answered, still in that solemn manner.

The two watched closely as the rider approached and soon, almost in unison, declared, "It's Two-Toes!" Timothy's serious mood took on one of excitement as they anxiously waited for him to come closer so they could see if Nathan was mounted behind him.

"There's no one with him," Sassy finally stated with obvious disappointment. She felt her chin start to quiver and knew tears were about to follow. *No, don't do that,* she cautioned and steeled herself for whatever Two-Toes had to tell them. Try as she might, she could not hold back the feeling of sadness that overtook her entire being. It was like when her mother had passed. There was an ache, a longing to see Nathan's face again, but somehow, she feared it might never happen. She tried to tell herself there was hope as long as he was alive, but how would she know if he was?

Timothy looked at his sister's face. He said nothing, just stepped up on the porch beside her and put his arm around her waist. She, in turn, put her arm around his broadening shoulders. They stood in silence as Two-Toes continued to ride in their direction.

He halted at the bottom of the steps. His dark eyes found theirs, and he gently shook his head.

"I stayed for many days and nights and did not see any boy that looked like this one," he said as he nodded toward Timothy. "I rode for miles over the ranch and saw several boys, but still no boy like this one. On the way back, I stopped at ranches we had already checked to look again but found no boy," he said in a solemn mood. The sadness of his failure was evident in his dark eyes and reflected in the expression on his weathered face. "I am sorry I have failed you," he spoke softly, but they could hear the near grief-stricken regret in his voice.

Sassy fought to hold back the tears that so desperately wanted to flow. She wanted to scream *NO! NO! NO! Give Nathan back to us.* Somehow, she managed to keep her feelings in check as she spoke sympathetically to Two-Toes.

"You've done all you could. We all did. Now, it's in God's hands. I pray every night for Nathan's safe return. I fully believe someday my prayers will be answered." Then she realized she likely had lied again. Did she really believe she would ever see Nathan again? she questioned as soon as she had spoken the words.

"It's too late to ride on to town tonight. Please stay the night and have a good meal before you go home. I know Trent will want to talk to you before you leave."

Two-Toes dismounted, and Timothy quickly rushed forward to lead his horses to the barn.

As Timothy reached the corner of the house, he turned and looked at his sister. "Nathan won't forget us and where to find you. Every day on the train, I'd make him repeat, 'My name is Nathan McCoy. My sister, Sassy McCoy, works for Trent Sanderson on the Flatland Ranch near Amarillo, Texas.' I'd make him say it over and over just in case we got separated." Before Sassy or Two-Toes could speak, he disappeared around the corner of the house.

That night at supper, Two-Toes repeated his story to Trent and the others.

"I have failed three times in all my years of tracking, but this time hurt me more than the others. The others were outlaws who needed to be caught and likely hung, but the boy—the boy, I failed him and his family," he said with a sadness that touched them all.

"Don't blame yourself. We all tried, and we all failed," Trent offered in hopes of easing the Indian's mind, but he strongly suspected his words were of little comfort.

Everyone sat quietly for several minutes as they half-heartedly ate the fine meal Sassy had prepared.

Martha scooted closer to Two-Toes and gently tugged at his sleeve. She almost whispered in her childish innocence, "Why do they call you Two-Toes?"

Two-Toes grinned at Martha.

"I've been wondering just how long it would take you or your brother to ask me that question," he answered as he continued to smile.

"Some people say a bear ate three of my toes; others say a wolf or a coyote attacked me, when I was a small child, and gnawed off my toes. Some even say they rotted off after a snake bit me, but some think I was born without three of my toes. What do you think happened to my toes?" he asked, still grinning at Martha.

She pursed her lips and looked intensely thoughtful. Then she looked at Two-Toes with a serious expression. Martha made a ferocious-looking face. "Maybe some mean Indian took you and cut off your toes so you couldn't run away."

Sassy gasped with embarrassment when she heard Martha's answer.

Two-Toes roared with laughter. "I'll have to add that to my stories of what happened to my toes."

Martha looked shy and ducked her head, sensing she had likely said something wrong.

Two-Toes patted her bowed head and then lifted her chin so he could see her sweet face. "One winter, when I was nine and lived with my second mother, the north winds howled constantly, and the snow fell deeper than usual. I had gone hunting for food in the forest. I crossed a frozen stream in haste while chasing a deer. I stepped on a soft spot in the ice and fell. My foot cracked the ice, and the cold water soaked through a hole in the worn-out right boot I had gotten at the trading post. I continued to track and finally killed the deer. We were very hungry that winter. By the time I returned home, three of my toes were frozen and, in time, rotted off. That was when I got the name Two-Toes."

Martha looked a bit pale by the end of his story. "Did it hurt a lot?"

"Yes, it hurt, but being a strong young brave, I did not give in to the pain. I did not cry or let anyone know how bad it hurt. My mother knew and doctored me as best she could, but she could not save my toes or take away all of my pain."

Martha leaned her head on his arm and looked up at him, her big blue eyes glistening with tears.

"I'm sorry you got hurted," she said sympathetically.

"Thank you, Martha. Now, I am fine, and there is no pain," he assured her and ruffled her pretty, blonde curls with his rough, brown hand.

"How did you get food for the rest of the winter?" Timothy asked.

"My friend, Yellow Moon, hunted harder than ever and brought us as much food as his family could spare. Without his help, we would have never made it through that long winter."

"Are you still friends?" Timothy asked.

Two-Toes' face took on a sad expression. "Yellow Moon took sick the next winter and died. I still miss him after all these years." Two-Toes paused, then he went on. "A true friend is hard to find. If you find a true friend, treasure that friendship forever. It may never come again," he concluded in a somber manner.

Chapter Twenty-One

Sassy was relieved she had seen very little of Trent after their return to the ranch. Spring roundup took him away early and, sometimes, for several days and nights. If at headquarters, he left before she and Helen were up and often returned after they had already gone to bed. Some nights, after she finished her prayers and before she fell asleep, she would hear him moving about the house, but not for long.

A few days after Trent and a crew of cowboys had driven the cattle to the railhead, he and the hands returned to the ranch exhausted. No matter, they had to pitch in to get the chores done before they were done for the day.

The next morning, Skip, one of the cowboys from the Schwab section, rode in looking for Trent.

Skip didn't waste any time. "Trent, we got real trouble brewing with Pete's bunch. You've tole 'um, and so have we, about how often they can water some cattle. They're pretty much doing whatever they want. Some of our boys are getting real fed up and making threats," he said in a somber tone.

Trent ran his fingers through his hair and heaved a heavy sigh. "Damn that Pete. The last time I talked to him about our agreement, he swore he didn't know anything about the men watering cattle more than they should have. He'll look you in the eye and lie through his teeth."

That made Skip chuckle.

"I been thinking, if we had a few extra men to keep a watch along the creek and lake, that might keep 'um in line," Skip suggested.

"I'll try it until I figure out a permanent solution," Trent said thoughtfully.

"Why don't you fence along the boundary between you and Pete? You could put in some gates that we could control," Skip suggested.

"I've thought about that but doubt a locked gate or fence will stop Pete," Trent ventured. "I'll send three men later today to help you out. Just try to keep a lid on things for now," Trent told Skip.

Just after noon, Helen called for Sassy as she finished in the kitchen. When Sassy reached the living room, she saw through the front window a rider approaching. Before he could dismount, Helen sent her to see what the man wanted.

When Sassy stepped out onto the porch, she recognized him as one of the men who worked at the train depot and telegraph office in town.

"Hello, John," she called out.

"Hello, I brought a telegram for Trent," John said as he climbed the steps to the porch.

"A telegram?" She stated in dismay. "It must be important for you to ride all the way out here to deliver just one telegram."

"Yes, ma'am, I expect it is. Mr. Blackwell, the telegraph operator, told me to bring it straight to Trent," the man emphasized.

"Come on in for something to eat and drink. I'll go find Trent," Sassy offered.

When the two of them entered the house, they found Helen sitting just inside the door, listening to their conversation. "Give it to me so I can see what it's about," she said as she held out her hand.

"Sorry, Miss Helen, I have to deliver it to Trent. It has his name on it, and Mr. Blackwell always says it has to go to the person whose name is on it," John explained. It was evident he was a bit leery that Helen might try to overrule him.

Helen looked a bit disgruntled about the situation but managed to smile. "Well, come on in for something to drink and a bite to eat. Could Sassy take the telegram to Trent?" she asked.

"I—I suppose that would be all right. Now, don't you be reading it," John warned Sassy.

"Don't worry. I wouldn't do anything like that," she assured the man.

Sassy walked toward one of the corrals where she thought Trent might be. If not, then one of the men might know where she could find him. She wondered if it might be from Flossy telling him about the baby, no matter what Helen had threatened. She could only imagine the uproar that would cause. Surely not, she tried to reassure herself.

As she approached the second corral, she saw Trent talking to Biggun and Ely as the three men stood with their backs toward her. They appeared to be gazing at one of the horses in the corral. When she drew nearer, she could hear the loud rumble of men's voices. They sounded angry. Suddenly, their words became clearer. She was a bit shocked to hear all the curse words they were letting fly. She considered going back to the house and sending John to find Trent. No, that was silly, she thought as she slowly advanced.

Before they could go on, Sassy spoke. "Excuse me, Trent."

The three startled men whirled at the sound of a feminine voice. They all wore expressions as though they had been caught with their pants down.

"Sassy! What the he—heck are you doing out here?" Trent asked in evident surprise.

She extended the telegram. "A rider from town came with this for you. Helen asked me to bring it to you," she said as she stared at him. She was not about to look away or let any of the men know it had embarrassed her to hear such language.

Trent reached out and took the telegram. Before he opened the telegram, he gave Sassy a stern look. "Do you know how to whistle?" he asked gruffly.

Sassy looked at him questioningly. "Yes, I know how to whistle."

"In the future, if you need to find me, I suggest you start whistling a tune when you leave the back porch," he said as a sly grin escaped his stern expression.

Biggun and Ely burst into bouts of laughter.

Trent turned to the two men. "Well, what the hell would you suggest?" he blurted out in exasperation.

Sassy felt her cheeks grow warm. She could not hold back the blush. She wanted to turn tail and run but was not about to give the three men that satisfaction. Instead, she turned, lifted her chin, and started to whistle as she walked briskly back to the house.

Trent had almost caught up with her by the time she entered the kitchen where John and Helen sat chatting.

"Helen, read this," Trent said as he came through the door.

Helen instantly looked worried. "What's happened?" she asked as she took the telegram. "Oh no, it's Angel. Aunt Lily says you should come immediately," she said as she looked at Trent.

"I can't go off again this soon. I have to run this ranch and trouble is brewing with Pete," he said in frustration, as he pulled off his hat and ran his fingers through his thick hair. "I just can't leave right now."

"But Aunt Lily says she may not make it."

"I know, I know. Helen, I'm sorry, but there's only one of me. I can't be in two or three places at once. This ranch won't keep running without me here to see to it. And now, we have the additional land and have to do something to get Pete to stick to our agreement about the water," he fretted as he paced.

Sassy sat listening to Trent and Helen trying to figure out what could be done. She felt a pang of guilt for having taken him away from the ranch to search for Timothy and Nathan. Then it came to her.

"Would it help if I went?" she blurted out.

Trent stopped in mid-stride; Helen's gaze turned to Sassy.

"What?" Helen almost gasped.

"No, I couldn't leave you," Sassy remembered. "I don't know what I was thinking."

"Maybe the two of you could go," Trent ventured.

"Trent, how do you think just Sassy and I could manage such a trip and me stuck in this chair? It was hard enough when Flossy was along to help. Just the two of us couldn't do it," she said, pleading for Trent's understanding.

Before he could respond, Sassy spoke again. "I think we could, Helen. If you could spare some extra money to tip the porters, I think they'd be happy to help lift you on and off the trains."

"I think she's right," Trent agreed. "You know the old saying, 'money talks.'"

"But Trent, Ely and I are getting married in two weeks. We couldn't possibly be back by then, even if Angel gets better. We can't just go and stick our heads in the door and leave."

"Helen, talk to Ely. I'm sure he would agree that you need to go see about our sister," Trent pleaded.

Helen looked disappointed about putting the wedding on hold, but she gave in. She knew Trent was right about needing to be at the ranch. It wouldn't be an easy trip, but it was necessary. Although neither of them felt that close to their younger sister, she was still their flesh and blood.

Helen wanted to cry when she saw the disappointed look on Ely's face when she told him about the necessary trip she had to take to see about their younger sister. She had a hard time persuading him that she and Sassy could manage the train changes on their long journey. Eventually, he accepted the situation, taking her in his strong arms and promising he would be anxiously awaiting her return.

The next morning, Trent drove the two women to town to catch the afternoon train for their long journey to Philadelphia. He cautioned them about keeping their money out of sight and not being too friendly to strangers. He told Sassy that if anything happened to Helen, she should telegraph him immediately.

Trent stood beside the train as it pulled out of the station. As he waved goodbye to Helen and Sassy, a feeling of loneliness overcame him. It struck him how dull his life would be without those two women. Yes, it was time he found a suitable wife and started his own family. Helen was marrying Ely; and Sassy, well, she might choose to leave the ranch at some point, although he couldn't imagine why she would ever do such a thing unless she got married, too. He didn't want to think about that possibility.

As he drove back to the ranch, he made up his mind to make an all-out effort to find someone else to center his attention on. Surely, there was a woman a bit older, more suitable, more educated, and just as desirable as Sassy. Perhaps his attraction to Sassy had been brought on by the lack of female companionship. Yes, this would be the time to find out for sure if his feelings for Sassy were a mere physical attraction or if they were true feelings leading to a lasting love. After what had happened at the hotel, he had been trying hard to focus his interests elsewhere.

Regardless of his responsibilities at the ranch, he had to make time for some social outings. With that in mind, he let his thoughts wander over the list of possible prospects. Most of the women his age were already married. One woman he had thought quite pretty with a pleasant disposition was now a widow with three children. He wasn't sure how he might feel about taking on that kind of liability. It would be preferable to find a single woman. Then, he remembered Mary Tate had mentioned the new single schoolteacher to him earlier as being a lovely young woman. Maybe it was time to make her acquaintance. Yes, he would ask Mary to introduce them, and he could see how lovely she really was. With that settled, he started to whistle as the horses plodded along toward home.

Mary was delighted when Trent approached her about introducing him to the schoolteacher. The school was dismissed at noon on Fridays so the ranch families would have time to travel for miles back to the ranches before dark.

After the introduction, Trent invited Miss Patricia (Patsy) Greenwell for dinner at the Cattleman dining room at the hotel where he always stayed. He would walk the few blocks to where she rented a room from a widow and escort her to dinner.

Trent was pleasantly impressed with the young woman on their first meeting. Patsy was agreeable and smiled freely. He could tell she was devoted to her duties as a teacher. He was glad to learn that her father was the foreman on a large ranch near Austin, and her mother was also a teacher. Trent was pleased to find Patsy to be an attractive woman, likely in her middle twenties. She wore her long, light brown hair pulled back and tied at the nape of her neck. Her eyes were hazel and shone with delight when talking about her students or all the exciting new things going on in town. Patsy also engaged Trent in easy conversation about his ranch and life revolving around ranch life.

As Trent meandered along the street toward the bank, he felt satisfied that he had made this decision. Perhaps this was the best approach to sorting out his feelings. Being with another woman should occupy his mind. Then, he wouldn't be thinking about Sassy so much.

That evening at dinner, Trent observed Patsy as she perused the menu. A slight smile touched her lips as she quickly read the choices offered.

Then Patsy laid the menu aside and smiled at the waitress. "I think I'll have the sirloin, medium, with potatoes and a salad," she said pleasantly.

"To drink?" the young woman asked.

"Tea, please."

The waitress turned to Trent.

"I'll have the T-bone, medium rare, potatoes, salad, and tea."

"No beer tonight, Mr. Trent?" the waitress inquired with a cocky smile.

Trent couldn't suppress a grin. "No, just tea."

"Feel free to have a beer if that is your usual choice," Patsy encouraged.

"You talked me into it," Trent grinned.

"Trent, I grew up on a ranch around hard-drinking men. I don't approve of drunks, but moderate drinking is fine."

"What brought you from Austin to Amarillo?" Trent asked.

"An advertisement in the Austin newspaper. I had just finished college. I was ready to get to work, but there wasn't anything where my parents live, so here I am," she said with a hint of laughter.

"Do you like it here?"

"Oh, I love teaching and have made many good friends. I've found several activities I enjoy participating in."

"What activities interest you?"

"Oh, I belong to a literary discussion group. We meet once a week at Doctor Baldwin's house. Then, I belong to a ladies' Bible study group. We meet on Wednesday evening before the prayer meeting, and I sing in the church choir. We are considering forming a community choir to put on a few concerts each year. I think that would be a great addition to our growing community, don't you?" Patsy asked with a smile.

Trent lifted an eyebrow. "I never thought about there being much to do here. But I don't spend much time in town. The community choir does sound nice," he agreed.

Patsy looked thoughtful. "I can't say much for the scenery here. The hill country is so pretty with lots of small creeks and several bigger rivers. The Colorado River runs through the ranch we lived on. I spent many happy hours swimming and fishing in that river," she mused.

Trent laughed, too. "No, there's not much water here or much to look at except flat land. You do have a good view of the sunrise and sunset."

"Isn't Flatland the name of your ranch?"

"Yes, when my dad and his brother decided to settle here, my mother turned in a circle viewing the land. Then, she just looked at Dad and said, 'Flatland, that's all there is, just flatland.'"

"Mary told me your parents are both deceased, and you have a sister who lives at the ranch."

"Yes, just Helen and I live at the ranch. We have a younger sister, Angel, who lives in Philadelphia and attends a girls' school. Our aunt also lives there and sees about Angel. Helen was in an accident about ten years ago and is confined to a wheelchair. She and our housekeeper have gone to Philadelphia to see our younger sister. Angel is very sick, and our aunt thought one of us should come."

Patsy frowned slightly. "I hope Angel is much better by the time they arrive. That's a hard trip for anyone, much less someone in a wheelchair."

"Sassy, our housekeeper, seemed to think they could manage and was willing to accompany Helen."

"Sassy? Is she sassy?" Patsy asked with a chuckle.

Instant visions of Sassy filled Trent's mind. First was the night he had discovered she wasn't a boy. She had pointed out that it was he who thought she was a boy until that unexpected revelation. Trent remembered the time she had sassed Helen for threatening to smack her brother for his poor table manners and her whistling when she walked back to the house after overhearing him cursing. The one incident that still bothered him most was the night she had pummeled him with her fists when she found out the children had been sent away from the orphanage. That had hurt him to the core, knowing he had let her down in the worst way.

"Yes, at times, she can be a bit sassy, but she is devoted to my sister and keeps the house running smoothly."

"How old is Sassy?"

"She's seventeen."

"Family?"

"Her family started to Mason County from Kansas, but both parents died on their way. In fact, I found her on my ranch, trying to dig a grave for her father. She has three younger brothers and a five-year-old sister. Timothy and Martha live in town with Irene Johnson. Timothy attends your school." Trent certainly didn't want to go into a lot of details with Patsy. Besides, it was likely she had heard about what happened from Mary or one of the other ranch women.

"Oh, yes, I know Irene. We attend Bible Study together. The children are in a good place. I've seen Timothy at school, although he's not in my class. He seems like a nice boy. It's good you have a job for Sassy, and she and your sister get on well," Patsy said and smiled.

Trent wondered if Patsy had also heard about Helen's infamous temperament and the number of housekeepers and cooks she had managed to run off. He, more than anyone, was glad Helen and Sassy got on well.

Patsy gazed at Trent. "What interests you besides ranching?"

Trent was taken aback by her question. He hadn't given much thought to anything except ranching.

Trent gave a short laugh. "I suppose ranching is about it. I don't have time for anything else and can't imagine what else would interest me."

"No hobbies, like horseracing or even traveling?"

"No. I don't have time to take horses for racing and certainly don't have time to travel for pleasure."

"I see."

They lingered over dessert and several cups of coffee. Conversation came easily. Trent walked Patsy home and ended the evening with plans for the next weekend.

Their second outing was spent at a community street dance. They enjoyed home-cooked bar-b-que with all the trimmings and a variety of delicious pies. Once again, Trent escorted Patsy back to her rented room.

They shared a pleasant goodnight kiss and made plans for the following weekend.

On his way out of town on Sunday morning, the telegraph operator waved Trent down and handed him a wire from Helen. She said Angel was doing well, and they would begin their return trip on Monday. He had just read a letter, while eating breakfast, from the lawyer in Wichita Falls and was pleased to know Joleen Martin, Mr. Carter, and Miss Beasley had all been dismissed from the orphans' home with no reference letters. He couldn't suppress a smile, knowing Sassy and Helen would be happy to hear that news.

Chapter Twenty-Two

The next morning, Trent noticed Ely talking to a stranger, likely a horse trader, he surmised. A few minutes later, Ely approached. Trent noticed his somber expression.

"Trent, I have to go tend to some personal business. I should be back in a couple of weeks. If you can hold my job that long, I'll appreciate it," he said a bit nervously.

"I can do that. Helen will be home Wednesday. What do I tell her about where you've gone?" Trent asked, not liking the edginess he sensed in Ely.

Ely looked off and then back at Trent. "Just tell her I'll be back as soon as I can, and then we'll get married."

"That's it?"

"For now. I'll explain more when I get back. Just trust me," Ely answered in a subdued tone.

Trent narrowed his eyes as he stared at Ely. "I'll do just that, but you better not hurt my sister no matter what kind of business you're going to tend to," Trent stated emphatically.

Ely nodded his head as he walked toward the corral to get his horse.

Trent had an uneasy feeling as he watched Ely ride west with the stranger. He dreaded having to tell Helen that Ely had gone away with no real explanation other than going to tend to some mysterious personal business. Trent knew one thing for certain. If Ely didn't return within a reasonable amount of time, he would hire Two-Toes and the Pinkertons to hunt him down. There was no way in hell he was going to let Helen be hurt all over again if there was any way to avoid it.

Helen's disappointment at Ely's absence was heart-wrenching. She tried to put on a brave front, but Trent and Sassy knew her fear of being hurt again had been rekindled. The most troubling part of Ely's sudden trip was it also meant delaying the wedding. Thankfully, not many people knew the actual date Helen and Ely had chosen, so maybe there wouldn't be much gossip and speculation about Helen losing another man.

That evening at dinner, Trent told Helen and Sassy about the ongoing problems with Pete Kennedy and the watering situation. Helen showed little interest in ranching matters.

Then, he told them about meeting the single teacher and that he would be going to town again Friday to see her.

Helen smiled as she listened to Trent, thinking he had taken her advice seriously.

Sassy felt her heart plummet. She tried to tell herself she should have known Trent would find a woman more suitable than she could ever hope to be. She must be happy for him after all he had done to help her and her kin. She shouldn't let herself be jealous of this young woman. It was only right for Trent to marry and have a family. Her place was housekeeper, cook, and companion to Helen. Why should she have ever expected anything else? It was just a young girl's crush on an attractive older man; that was all, she tried hard to convince herself.

A few evenings later, Biggun joined them for supper, and during the meal he made a suggestion. "I've been thinking about the watering issue you're having with Pete and have an idea that might work," Biggun said.

All eyes turned to Biggun.

"What's on your mind?" Trent asked

"Why don't you have a few of the men, that's good with a hammer and saw, tear down the bunkhouse and rebuild it by the lake?" Biggun offered. Before anyone could speak, Biggun went on. "That would likely put some of the cowboys in that area on and off through the day, and they could keep an eye on things," he concluded.

Trent looked thoughtful as he considered Biggun's suggestion. Then he pounded the table with his fist, startling everyone. Trent laughed. "I think you hit on a damn good idea. I'll bet the fellows would like being that close to a place to go fishing."

"I agree, and a place to take a bath," Helen added with a chuckle, finally showing interest in something besides Ely being gone.

"Let's ride over tomorrow and see what it'll take to get the job done. We'll have to get some tents for the men until the bunkhouse is ready," Trent told Biggun.

Trent felt hopeful Biggun's idea would solve the issue with Pete. He had never thought fences or locked gates would keep anyone out if you had something they wanted, and it usually led to more trouble. Hopefully, the presence of the men would be a constant reminder to Pete about their agreement.

Two weeks passed and Helen had not heard one word from Ely. She became more subdued and spent most of the day in her room. When Sassy would go to ask her a question or just to check on her, she could tell that Helen had been crying.

Finally, Sassy could stand it no longer. She stayed up later than usual, hoping to talk to Trent without Helen knowing.

After Sassy had helped Helen retire for the night, she sat in the living room looking at a magazine until she was certain Helen was asleep. She knocked lightly on the office door that was already open.

Trent looked up. "What are you doing up so late?"

"I need to talk to you about Helen," she answered softly.

"Come in," he invited as he gestured toward a chair.

"Trent, I'm so worried about Helen. She's so down in the dumps about Ely going off without giving any reason, and she hasn't heard one word from him."

Trent ran his hand over his day's growth of whiskers. "I know. If we don't hear anything in another week, I'll hire someone to try to track him down. I don't want to see Helen go through what she did after Jack Thornton abandoned her."

Sassy let out a slow breath. "Me either," she said as she rose to leave.

"Sassy, I plan to invite Patsy Greenwell to come out to the ranch for the weekend. Would you fix up the other room upstairs?"

Sassy felt as though she couldn't breathe. She had known this would happen sooner or later, but she had hoped it would be much later. By him inviting Patsy to visit the ranch, Sassy knew he must be getting serious about her. She was certain now that she had never meant anything to him, except as an employee.

"Oh, yes, I'll give it a good cleaning. Is there anything special you would like for me to cook?" she asked, trying not to show how let down she felt.

Trent thought for a minute. "Yes, I remember Patsy saying she misses her mother's green tomato cobbler. I think one of the cooks canned some green tomatoes."

"I'll look. Goodnight," she murmured as she left the office.

Sassy did as Trent requested and thoroughly cleaned the other upstairs room. She made sure to use the best bed linens. There were plenty of canned green tomatoes to make the cobbler Trent requested. Sassy kept reminding herself to be happy for Trent.

The evening the teacher was to arrive, Sassy fixed fried chicken, cream gravy, mashed potatoes, corn on the cob, and flaky biscuits. When she was making the green tomato cobbler, the devil took hold of her. She deftly separated about a cup of the tomatoes and poured the rest carefully into the crust. Then, she added a bit of vinegar and no sugar to the cup of tomatoes and slyly poured them into one corner of the square baking pan. She slipped a toothpick into the crust so she could be sure the teacher got the tart tomatoes. Sassy knew she should be ashamed of herself for playing such a mean trick on the unsuspecting young woman, but she didn't really feel the least bit guilty about what she was going to do to the teacher. She let out a long sigh and thought, *this is likely another sin to add to my growing list.*

When Patsy arrived, Sassy was surprised to find she was quite friendly and very pretty. She could tell Helen liked the young woman. She saw Helen catch Trent's eye. Helen smiled and gave a quick affirmative nod of her head. Sassy felt a bit left out, but why would it matter what she thought. She wasn't a member of the family, only the hired help.

When it came time for dessert, Sassy dished the cobbler into bowls and topped it with whipped cream.

Patsy took in a deep whiff of the cobbler and smiled. "Green tomato cobbler, umm! One of my favorites," she exclaimed as she took a big bite. Instantly, her face turned bright red as she became choked and coughed most of the cobbler into her napkin. She wheezed, trying to catch her breath, and her eyes started watering.

Trent looked concerned. "Are you all right?"

At first, Patsy couldn't catch her breath enough to speak. After several attempts, she managed to croak, "It's very tart!"

"I don't know why it would be that tart. I put plenty of sugar in it," Sassy lied.

Trent took a bite and looked even more puzzled. "It tastes plenty sweet to me."

"Me too," Helen joined in.

Patsy looked thoroughly embarrassed. "I'm so sorry. Maybe it just went down the wrong way." Patsy attempted to put the matter to rest by taking another bite and forced herself to smile. After a few more small bites, she laid her spoon aside. "I think I'm too full to finish the cobbler," she said lamely.

"I'll finish it for you," Trent said as he reached for her bowl.

Sassy almost jumped out of her chair. "There's plenty, Trent. You don't have to eat anyone else's food," she told him as she grabbed his and Patsy's bowls.

The remainder of the weekend went by pleasantly enough. Sassy was glad when Sunday arrived. Patsy and the ranch women and children returned to town. She did happen to see Trent give Patsy a quick goodbye kiss. It was only a quick kiss, but it made Sassy want to cry.

Sassy took a long walk after lunch while Helen rested. She wrestled with her own feelings and decided the best thing she could do was to find a boyfriend to take her mind off Trent. There were several of the younger cowboys who had always been friendly and might like to have her as a girl-friend. Yes, that would be for the best, she told herself several times. The only problem was she didn't know how to go about letting one of them know she was interested in him. Maybe she should ask Helen for some suggestions, but that might make her even sadder. Maybe she should ask Trent how he knew a lady was interested in him.

A few evenings later, she noticed Trent standing on the front porch gazing into the distance. She wondered if he was longing to see Patsy.

As Sassy joined Trent on the porch, she saw he was staring at an ominous orange glow in the distance.

"Is that a prairie fire?" she asked in alarm.

"I'm afraid so," Trent answered, keeping his gaze steady.

"Should we pack to leave?"

"No, not unless the wind changes directions. I have riders out watching where it's headed. A rider should be coming in soon with a report," Trent answered.

"I wonder how it started?" Sassy asked.

"Likely a lightning strike from that fast-moving afternoon storm," Trent answered. "Here comes a rider now."

The man reined in near the porch. "It's still moving south. About the only thing we can figure that's in its way is Shorty's line shack. Two of the men have already gone to help him load up and get out of its way."

"Good. Tell Scooter and Amos to go out to relieve those two men."

"Will do," the man said as he headed toward the bunkhouse.

Trent remained on the porch, staring toward the orange glow.

"Don't worry, if it changes directions, we'll have plenty of notice," he said as he turned toward Sassy.

Trent walked slowly toward the porch swing and sat on one side. Sassy sat on the other side and gave the swing a slight push. They remained silent for several minutes.

"Trent, there's something I'd like to ask you about," she said tentatively.

"What's that?"

"I've been wondering how I would let a fellow know I might like to have him for a boyfriend?" she asked as she turned to look at Trent's face in the dim glow from the lamplight inside.

Trent cleared his throat and seemed to ponder her question.

"Well, how did you know Miss Patsy was interested in you?"

Trent laughed slightly. "Actually, I didn't. I was the one to make the first move, and she seemed receptive to the idea."

"Oh, so I should wait for the fellow to make the first move?"

"No, not necessarily. You can make it a point to talk to him. Find out some things he's interested in that you might have in common and so on."

"Oh, well, I don't know what things that might be. I don't think most men are interested in sewing or cooking or cleaning house," she answered, a bit disappointed.

"You like to go for walks by the creek. He might like to go for a walk with you and teach you how to fish."

"Yes, that might work."

They remained silent for several minutes.

"There's something else I'd like to ask about," she ventured.

"What else?"

"I overheard some of the ranch women talking about kissing and how there were different kinds of kissing. Could you show me what they mean by different kinds so I won't seem too backward to some fellow?"

Trent let out a low whistle. "I don't think I need to teach you about kissing. Don't you remember when we kissed at the hotel?"

"Yes, I remember, but this is different. It would just be a lesson, just like a lesson in fishing."

"Not exactly like a lesson in fishing. You'll catch on to kissing, but I guess you need to know a few things so you don't get into trouble," Trent ventured.

"What kind of trouble?"

Trent rubbed his hand over the stubble on his jaw and looked off into the distance. "Do you know what happens between a woman and a man to make a baby?"

Sassy felt her cheeks grow warm and hoped there wasn't enough light for Trent to see her blush. "Well, we did live in a small house, and sometimes I heard things during the night. I guess something about what my parents were doing caused another baby. I remember putting my pillow over my head to block out the sounds."

"Yes, that is likely right, and usually, it starts with kissing. Don't get me wrong, there's nothing wrong with kissing, as long as it doesn't go too far and lead to other things."

Sassy thought over what Trent had said. "Well, I need to know just how to not let things go too far, don't I?"

Trent turned so he was facing her. "Yes, I suppose you do," he said with a slight sigh. "Kisses between boyfriends and girlfriends or men and women usually start out with a brief kiss on the lips." He leaned forward and cupped her chin with his hand, turning her toward him. He leaned closer and kissed her briefly on the lips.

Sassy couldn't help herself. She liked the feel of his warm, strong mouth on hers. She wondered if she could ever find a fellow with that same kind of mouth.

"After a couple gets to know one another better, they usually kiss for a longer time," he said as he kissed her again, lingering and increasing the pressure of his lips against hers.

When he pulled away, Sassy wished the kiss had lingered on a bit longer, a lot longer.

Trent began to wonder if this had really been a very good idea after all. He found Sassy's response to his second kiss a little too enticing. Sadly, more exciting than any kisses he had shared with Patsy.

Trent's voice seemed huskier as he said, "When the man and woman are truly attracted to one another and are falling in love, they kiss like this," he said as he moved closer to Sassy, encircling her in his strong arms, pressing his chest firmly against her shapely bosom. His mouth played seductively over her warm lips as he urged her lips to part with his tongue. Before he could stop himself, the kiss had become far more intimate than he had intended. Then, he realized Sassy was responding whole-heartedly to his far more seductive kiss. Trent hated to admit he was wishing this kiss could lead to more, but he knew better. He remembered exactly what she had told him at the hotel when it came out that she knew what had happened between him and Flossy.

Sassy felt as though a swarm of butterflies had been let loose inside her body, and an unusual warmth spread through her. No one had to tell her these were womanly feelings. She wondered if she should pull away, as surely this was the kind of kissing that led to those other things Trent had talked about. She didn't want to be the one to break the kiss. This special kiss from Trent would have to last her a lifetime. She couldn't bear to think about him kissing Patsy in this same way.

Trent forced himself to abruptly push Sassy away, ending the heated kiss. The two just stared at one another, both breathing heavily.

"I shouldn't have let that happen," Trent said in a low tone. "That's the kind of kissing that leads to other things that might get you in trouble," Trent said just above a whisper.

Sassy dipped her head in embarrassment. "I don't blame you. I liked the way you were kissing me, but I understand what you meant by not letting things go too far and getting in trouble."

Trent let out a long breath. "Yes, that's right. If some fellow kisses you like that and you don't want him to, don't hesitate to push him away and tell him how you feel."

Sassy nodded her head in understanding. She quickly said goodnight and left the porch.

Trent remained in the swing, staring into the distance, not at the fire but in deep thought about the feelings that the last kiss had provoked. Why had he been fool enough to ever consent to teaching Sassy about kissing? It was Patsy he intended to make his wife. She was far more suitable. Patsy had grown up on a large ranch and understood the huge responsibilities he carried, and she already knew how to share in the experience. Patsy was only four years younger than he, educated, and she would make a proper wife. Sassy was a sweet girl but far too young. She had a minimal education and no clue what it took to run a ranch.

Trent rose and walked to the edge of the porch. Yes, he would ask Patsy to marry him. They would plan their wedding as soon as her folks could come for the festivities. He had not kissed Patsy in the way he had kissed Sassy, and he wondered if her kisses would provoke the strong feelings Sassy's kiss had caused. He needed to get Sassy out of his mind. Patsy was the right kind of woman he needed, he told himself again.

Trent felt like his life was in a constant battle. He battled the elements, like the wildfire he was watching swallow up acres of grazing land, storms that brought too much rain or not enough rain, and the cold winters that swept down and, at times, caused great losses of his livestock. Trent was almost certain he and Pete Kennedy would battle over the watering situation now that he owned the Schwab Ranch with its new sources of water. He battled the fluctuations in the prices he got for his livestock. And now, he was battling his own feelings. He knew what he should do about a wife. *Now get on with it,* he thought as he turned and walked through the still house to his bedroom.

A week earlier, Trent had hired a detective to track Ely. He had not heard anything, which concerned him greatly. Helen was becoming more and more depressed with each passing day, and he had seen some of her old cranky attitude returning. It would be especially hard on her to see him get married if Ely didn't return soon so they could be married first.

The next day, a rider brought a telegram from the tracker. Trent was relieved to learn the detective had followed Ely's trail to the border of Mexico. The man wanted to know if Trent wanted him to go on into Mexico.

Trent sent back a message, telling the detective to proceed as long as necessary.

Trent continued his trips to town to visit Patsy. After a few weeks, he got up his nerve to pop the question.

They were enjoying a leisurely dinner at one of the hotel restaurants. Trent reached across the table and took Patsy's hand. She looked up and smiled.

"Patsy, I know we haven't been seeing one another too long, but I hope you have come to care for me as I care for you," he paused. "I would like to ask you to consider becoming my wife," he continued with a hopeful smile.

Patsy looked a bit surprised but quickly recovered. "Oh, Trent, I do care for you and would love to become your wife."

Trent grinned. "I'll give it my damn best to make you a good husband and provide for you in every way."

Patsy laughed. "I have no doubt about you giving it your best effort."

Trent ran his finger over her ring finger. "I didn't buy you a ring because I didn't know the size or what you might like. We'll go tomorrow to pick out an engagement ring and our wedding bands, if that's all right."

"Yes, that will be just fine with me," Patsy agreed as she continued to smile.

"I do need to ask you one favor. We may need to hold off on the exact wedding date. I've sent a detective to trace Ely. I need to know if he really intends to come back to marry my sister," he said with a worried frown.

"Oh, surely, he does. That would be awful for Helen to go through again if he doesn't come back."

"Yes, it would. I think I might find Ely and—and, well, I don't know what I might do," Trent said angrily.

When Trent walked Patsy back to her room, he tried a more persuasive kiss, which Patsy responded to favorably, but then she quickly ended the kiss as she gently pushed him away. She smiled sweetly and whispered, "We can't get too carried away since it may be a while until our wedding. Besides, I want to write to my parents to see when they can come to see us married."

Trent was not discouraged. He knew she was right and felt certain she would be more loving once they were married. However, at the back of his mind, he still wondered if she would kindle the same strong desire Sassy had caused.

Chapter Twenty-Three

S assy worried over Helen constantly and tried every idea she could think of to cheer her up. She had thought Trent's announcement that he and Patsy were engaged might cheer Helen, but her excitement was short-lived.

Now, Ely had been gone over a month. Each day seemed to drag by, and still no word. Then, a rider came with another telegram. It said the detective had learned Ely had taken his stepson to Sonora, Texas, to bury him. The detective would continue to follow Ely.

Ely returned five days later. He looked haggard but wasted no time in going to find Helen and Trent. He told them about his stepson, Jess, from his first marriage. His wife had never permitted Ely to correct the spoiled boy. It had been obvious to Ely that the boy would wind up in trouble, but no matter what he said, his wife could not believe her son would go wrong. Ely told them the young man, now twenty-six years old, had been headed for trouble for several years. Jess and two other men had robbed a bank in New Mexico. The three had escaped from jail, killing the deputy, and headed for Mexico. Ely had tracked the three across the border, but two days before he arrived, they had tried to rob another bank and all three had been killed by the Mexican Federales. Ely had claimed his stepson's body, brought it back to Sonora, and buried him beside his mother.

Helen scolded him for not sending a telegram to let her know why he had left so suddenly.

Ely offered no excuses but asked for and received her forgiveness. He only said he wasn't sure what kind of trouble his stepson was in and didn't want to tell falsehoods. The man who had come to the ranch to tell him wasn't sure about many of the details either. Jess had been working for the man when he started running with the wrong crowd. The rancher had tried to keep Jess out of trouble but had failed. When Jess was put in jail, he asked the rancher to come for Ely.

Ely shook his head, "I'm glad his mother wasn't alive to know what Jess had done. It would have broken her heart," he said sadly.

Helen and Ely decided they would be married the following Sunday. They had waited long enough. Neither of them wanted anything else to prevent them from getting married.

Trent announced that he and Patsy would be married soon. It did not come as a great surprise, considering his frequent trips to Amarillo. Helen was delighted, thinking her brother had finally taken some of her advice, and she liked the young teacher.

When Sassy heard the news of Trent's approaching marriage, she forced a smile on her face and acted as though she was delighted, but inside, she felt like she was going to die of a broken heart. She had known it would happen, but it was still hard to believe he would be kissing another woman the way he had kissed her. She would never know the pleasures shared by a man and a woman with the one man she knew she could love. Night after night, she cried herself to sleep.

A brilliant blue sky with no threat of rain appeared on Helen and Ely's wedding day. The pastures were still filled with numerous varieties of wildflowers in stunning shades of blues, yellows, and reds. A gentle breeze blew from the north, giving just the right measure of coolness.

Guests started arriving a day early. Many went on to the creek and camped out overnight. The ranch families and ranch hands journeyed to the stream early Sunday morning. Sonny Tate held a worship service, which most guests attended.

Helen, Sassy, and Trent remained at the ranch house to get dressed for

the wedding and planned to arrive at 11:30 a.m., the time set for the ceremony. Ely had gone on with some of the others.

Sassy helped Helen into her lovely white dress with its rounded neckline trimmed in gathered lace and tiny glistening pearl buttons down the
front of the bodice to the waistline. The fitted sleeves flared out just below
the elbow with wide gathered lace matching the trim along the hemline of
the skirt. They decided to wait until just before they arrived to put on the
veil so it wouldn't blow in the wind and perhaps get damaged. Sassy had
copied Helen's wedding attire from a magazine they had bought in Amarillo and felt proud of her handwork. Helen made a radiant bride.

Sassy wore a lavender flowered print dress with a white collar and cuffs
also trimmed in lace. She had made a matching bow to tie her hair at the
nape of her neck but left two dangling curls framing her face. She looked
at herself in the mirror and could scarcely recognize the young woman
staring back at her. Her reflection revealed a lovely young woman with
shiny blonde hair, sparking sapphire-blue eyes, and rosy pink lips. She
wondered if any of the young men would take notice of her and ask her to
dance? The only dancing she had ever done was with the kitchen broom,
but she had been to plenty of dances when her ma and pa were alive.

Helen and Sassy waited in the living room for Trent to bring the buggy
around to the front of the house. When he drove up, Sassy pushed Helen's
wheelchair out to the edge of the porch. She had been so intent on not
letting anything brush against Helen's dress that when she looked up and
saw Trent walking up the steps, dressed in a fine-looking store-bought suit
and new shiny black boots, her heart seemed to start racing. He looked
stunningly handsome today. He gave the ladies a slow smile and then a
low whistle of approval.

"My, oh my, what a pretty pair of ladies I get to escort to the wedding,"
he teased. Trent thought they were both quite beautiful. He could hardly
wait to see the expression on Ely's face when he caught a glimpse of his
bride-to-be. He was certain plenty of the cowboys would be asking Sassy
for a dance. Trent instantly suppressed the pang of jealousy he felt at the
thought of other men holding her close. Her looks reminded him of a
caterpillar that had just emerged into a stunning butterfly.

As they neared the creek, Sassy placed the veil on Helen's head. They almost instantly heard loud applause and hoots of excitement from the waiting guests. As Trent pulled the buggy to a stop, Ely stepped forward and gently lifted his bride into his arms and placed her carefully in the wheelchair one of the ranch hands had grabbed from the buggy.

The pair just stared at one another in awe. Then Ely rolled the chair to the spot by the creek where they had picnicked during their courtship. Trent and Sassy took their places beside the bride and groom as the preacher began the ceremony.

Trent tried to concentrate on his sister's wedding ceremony but found it hard to keep from stealing glances at Sassy. He almost chuckled when he remembered finding what he assumed to be a boy trying to dig a grave. The transformation from then until today was remarkable. She was as lovely a young woman as he had ever seen. In her own way, she was even prettier than Flossy. Flossy had possessed a rare outward beauty, but Sassy possessed an exceptional inside and outside beauty that far outshined Flossy. Trent reminded himself he should be thinking about Patsy, not Sassy or Flossy.

Patsy had accepted his proposal. She hated to miss Helen's wedding but had already made plans to go visit her parents and announce her own upcoming wedding. Trent received a telegram saying she and her parents would arrive in two weeks. Patsy assured him she could plan a wedding in a week, and he would certainly leave that up to her.

"I now pronounce you husband and wife," the minister announced with enthusiasm as he beamed with pleasure at the wedding guests. "Ely, you may kiss your lovely bride."

Ely did not hesitate. He bent and kissed Helen as though the kiss was meant to last for a lifetime, and Trent truly expected it would.

Instantly, the women started setting platters and huge bowls of food out on one long table. The bride and groom were seated at a special table and served first. Five men started playing their fiddles and guitars, and the festivities were underway. As soon as some finished eating, they started to dance, as the children ran hither and yonder, playing games. Mothers spread blankets beneath the shade of the huge cottonwood, mesquite, and pecan trees that lined the edge of the creek and put their young ones down to nap or just to rest. Some of the women sat in small groups with their little ones, talking and laughing. Before long, some of the men had a game of horseshoes going while others visited and swapped stories of who caught the biggest fish and so on. Many led isolated lives, and rare occasions such as this were a time for socializing with their neighbors.

Trent finished eating, then ambled over to congratulate Helen and Ely once more, as he knew they would soon be leaving for the long drive to Amarillo. Tomorrow, they would board the train for Denver, Colorado. The two-week trip was a combination honeymoon and business trip.

After he saw them off, he turned to visit with their guests. He spotted Sassy dancing with one of the new ranch hands not much older than her. He was a good-looking kid, and the two seemed to be having a grand time. Well, maybe he should wait a bit to ask her for a dance, he thought, not wanting to interfere with her fun. She had been so downhearted since Two-Toes had returned without Nathan that it was good to see her laughing and having a good time.

Trent walked among the guests, greeting his friends and neighbors. He had been taught by his mother how to act as a host and knew she would expect him to be at his best on this occasion. He danced with several of the ladies he knew. Some were single, and others were married friends of the family. Neither made any difference, as the only one here he wanted to dance with was Sassy.

After about an hour, he looked around for Sassy but couldn't locate her among the guests. Maybe he should look around to be sure she was okay. For some inexplicable reason, he had felt a bit uneasy about her after the kissing lesson he had given to her. He hoped she really understood what he had been trying to tell her.

Biggun happened by on his way to get another drink.

"Have you seen Sassy lately?" Trent asked.

Biggun nodded his head in the direction of a well-worn path beside the stream.

"I saw her and one of the new cowboys walk off down the path a while ago," he answered with a big grin.

Trent followed the path that soon led out of sight of the guests.

"Stop, I said!" Sassy almost yelled at the young man as he continued to hold her much too close for her comfort and planted slobbery kisses on her face and neck. She twisted and turned, trying to avoid letting his mouth touch hers.

"Oh, come on, you know you want to kiss me!" the young man insisted as he continued his unwanted advances.

He was touching her in places she did not want to be touched. His behavior reminded her of her pa's friend and how he used to grope her in her private places. Only now, she was older and could certainly try to fend him off like Trent had said.

Sassy glared at the young man. "No, I don't. I don't even know you, so let me go!" she insisted as she tried to push him away and landed a swift kick on his shin, making him yelp with pain.

"I believe the lady said for you to stop," Trent growled as he grabbed the young man by the back of the neck with one big hand and squeezed so hard the kid let out a loud yelp of pain as he slowly sank to the ground.

When the young fellow saw who had interfered in his quest for the pretty young woman, he tried to stammer an apology.

"Get up, get on your horse, and don't let me ever see you on this ranch again!" Trent demanded as he threw a few bills at the lad's feet.

The young cowboy scrambled to his feet, grabbed the money, and took off at a full run toward where the horses were tethered.

Sassy could feel her cheeks burning and knew her face must be red, not from her struggle with the cowboy but from embarrassment at Trent being the one to come to her rescue.

She quickly straightened her clothing and worked up the courage to look at Trent.

"Thank you for helpin' me again. I was tryin' to push him away like you told me," she said hardly above a whisper, as she gazed into the eyes of the strong, robust man before her.

Trent extended his hand. He gave her a slow smile. "I was just coming to ask you for a dance," he said, trying to put her at ease. He knew the young man had not taken undue advantage of her but might have if he hadn't arrived when he did. That thought made a shudder run through him. He was half tempted to chase the fellow down and give him a good licking for what he had done. Instead, he led Sassy back toward the crowd and then swung her around with the other dancers as though nothing had happened.

Sassy felt secure in Trent's arms and enjoyed dancing near, but not too near, him. It would never do for him to hold her too close. If they danced as close as some of the couples were dancing, that would surely set the tongues to wagging, and Patsy might not like hearing about them dancing too close. She wondered if she could ever find a husband who would even remotely compare to Trent. It made her sad to know she could never be the kind of woman he would want, but as Biggun had said, they would always just be the hired help. Oh! How she wished she could be prettier, smarter, and have more money. Maybe then he would look on her more favorably, she reflected as they continued to dance. Suddenly, she realized they had been dancing for quite some time and likely should go dance with others before someone else noticed.

"I think I'll have some lemonade and go see Molly and Chet's new baby," she told Trent as the song ended.

He, too, had just realized they had been dancing for quite a while and politely nodded his head and strolled over to converse with a group of men.

They did not dance together again.

The party broke up about four o'clock, and most folks headed home. As Trent and Sassy drove back to the ranch house, he finally asked, "Would you like for me to stay in the bunkhouse while Helen and Ely are away?"

"Oh, no, I've already made arrangements to spend the nights with Mary and Sonny. You'll need time to work on the books, so that will work best."

Trent nodded his head, knowing what she said was true.

Chapter Twenty-Four

Sassy was already gone each evening by the time Trent reached the house. The house seemed too big with no one home but him. He hated the hollow echo his boots made as he walked through the empty house. He wished Sassy would stay for a while so they could sit in the swing on the big front porch and talk for a while. That shouldn't cause too much gossip. He hadn't seen her in the past four days to even suggest she wait for him to return home before she went to the Tates'. Well, considering what had happened the last time they had sat on the swing, maybe it was better this way, he thought as he rode toward the house.

He heard the distant roll of thunder and looked toward the north, where the sky was growing darker. Streaks of lightning were dancing across the prairie. He led his horse into the barn and tended to him as the thunder grew louder and the wind picked up considerably.

Just as he stepped out of the barn, he saw the greenish-black rolling clouds advancing quickly, and the streaks of lightning seemed more intense. The first big drops of rain started to fall. The wind had increased as a loud clap of thunder overhead seemed to shake the earth. He watched as a streak of lightning snaked its way out of the undulating clouds, striking the ground about a hundred yards from the barn. He quickened his steps toward the house; his shirt was already soaked. Then he felt the first stinging pelts of hail hitting his body with a ferocious bite, making him grimace.

As he ran up the back steps, Sassy ran out the back door, holding a dish towel over her head to protect her from the rain.

"You can't go out in this," he yelled over the sound of the wind and, now, pouring rain mixed with hail.

"But I have to go to the Tates'," she protested above the howling wind.

"You'll have to wait until this storm passes over. Go back in the house," he ordered as he took her elbow and propelled her toward the door.

Just as they entered the kitchen, a resounding crash of thunder shook the house, and they heard the crashing sound of the front door being blown open. Trent quickly ran to close and bolt the door. Before he could reach it, two windows in the living room were blown out, and glass sprayed through the air, scattering over the entire room. Two lamps toppled from their tables, crashing to the floor and adding to the shards of glass.

He turned to see Sassy standing in the doorway. Her expression was one of horrified disbelief. The thunder crashed again, shaking the house as brilliant streaks of lightning danced all around.

"Get back," he yelled just as a loud ripping sound tore across the roof.

Trent ran past her to his room and grabbed two quilts from the quilt rack and the pillows from his bed. He was back in an instant.

"Lie down against this inside wall," he ordered, shouting above the deafening roar of the storm.

Sassy did not question his demand as she lay down next to the wall. Trent stretched out beside her, gave her a pillow, and covered them with the two quilts. "Hold this over your head as tight as you can to protect yourself." He tucked the quilts tight around them and scooted so close he had her pinned against the wall.

Biggun and the other men had just finished their supper in the bunkhouse when the storm hit with a fury. At first, several of the ranch hands stood in the doorway, watching the oncoming ominous clouds and streaks of lightning flashing in the distance. As the storm grew nearer, one of the men started to close the door when it was suddenly wrenched from its hinges. He was blown backward into the men standing behind him. The storm sounded like the loud rumble of an approaching freight train. They all dove for cover under their bunks. More praying went on in that bunkhouse than had ever taken place before.

The rain and hail pummeled the building, knocking out windows along the north side and west end. The roof was ripped off as though it was made of paper, and rain soaked everything inside. Pieces of wood and glass flew through the air, slashing and pounding anything they touched. The bunks proved to be little protection against the fury of the storm.

All through the ranch headquarters buildings were ripped apart, torn from their foundations; huge posts were snatched from the ground, and beams were snapped like toothpicks. Within minutes, the entire headquarters was a pile of rubble strewn for half a mile or farther from where it had stood only minutes before.

The only sound was that of the receding rain and distant rolls of thunder as the storm moved farther away. An eerie silence fell over the area. As the clouds cleared, a full moon lit the strange site of unrecognizable total wreckage where houses, barns, and corrals had previously stood.

Biggun pushed and shoved, using his massive strength to free himself from the debris pinning him down. His face had been smashed into the ground, but he managed to turn his head enough to get some air flowing into his lungs. Little by little, boards and glass were flung aside. Something heavy was pinning his legs down. With considerable effort, he managed to squirm around enough to see one of the beams that had supported the bunkhouse roof was lying across his lower legs. He continued to pull, push, and twist his huge body until, at last, his legs were free. He lay gasping for breath after the great effort it had taken to free himself. He ached from the tips of his hair to the ends of his toenails. The way he felt reminded him of the summer when he and Trent were about fifteen and envisioned themselves as hot-shot bull riders. They spent more time flying through the air and landing hard on the ground, sometimes knocking the wind out of them, than they did on the back of the bull. Once, a bull had turned on him and had given him several good kicks and stomped on his left ankle before the cowboys had chased the enraged bull away from him. He'd been bruised from head to foot with four broken ribs, a dislocated right shoulder, and a broken left ankle. After that episode, Mr. Sanderson had put an end to his and Trent's illusions of pursuing bull-riding careers. Biggun chuckled softly as he remembered Mr. Sanderson saying it was to protect the bulls from two fools.

He heard a moan from somewhere nearby and then a faint, "Help, help me."

"Keep talking so I can find you under all of this mess," Biggun said to the voice as he pulled himself to a standing position and got his bearings.

Biggun began digging through the wreckage for men, and it seemed to go on and on. If a man was able to help, he did, but a few were hurt too badly to help. The third and fourth men they found were dead. Little by little, most of the cowboys that lived in the bunkhouse were accounted for, dead or alive, except for two.

They heard voices and movement coming from where Sonny Tate's house once stood. It and the three smaller houses for the married men were all gone. Biggun and those able went to help search for the families. When Biggun found two-year-old Clara Tate's limp body, it almost brought him to his knees. When Mary saw him holding her still child, her wail of sorrow filled the night air and sent a chill through every man.

Sonny tried to console his distraught wife as the others worked on, uncovering more of the living, several with injuries, and a seriously injured Sally Moore, mother of three and expecting another child in a few months.

"Stay close to your wife," Biggun told Sonny. "Those of us able-bodied can see to the rest," Biggun assured Sonny.

"Has anybody seen Trent?" Clarence Moore asked in alarm when he saw his wife's grave condition. "We've got to get some help out here. We need a doctor!" he said, still in shock.

Biggun paused in his work. "I ain't had a chance to go check on him and Sassy," he answered with apparent dread at what he might find beneath the wreckage of the main house. "You're right, though. I'll see if one of the hands can catch a horse, find some gear, and go after help."

Soon, he sent one man to town for help and another to the west ranch to see how they fared and if any of them could come to give them a hand.

Biggun and several men walked toward what once served as the main house. It, like the rest of the headquarters, lay in a heap of rubble higher than their heads. Debris was strewn as far as they could see by the moonlight now shining through the clearing clouds.

"Trent! Trent!" Biggun yelled several times but heard no reply.

"Sassy! Sassy!" he called, but no one answered. An odd silence filled the night.

"Let's start digging. Just be careful. They have to be under here somewhere, and we don't want to hurt them worse by stepping on top of them," Biggun cautioned. "We might as well try to separate what can be reused and what's just junk as we go," he suggested.

The men worked tirelessly on and on, calling for Trent and Sassy as they went, but they heard no answer. No moan of pain, nothing.

In the distance, they could still hear Mary Tate's grieving sobs for the loss of their little girl.

After what seemed like an eternity, one of the men called out, "I see a boot and leg!"

The men worked diligently to lift the heavy scraps of lumber and beams from Trent's lifeless-looking body.

Biggun knelt by his side and felt for a pulse. At last, he located the slow thump, indicating he was still alive. He breathed a deep sigh. "He's alive, but I think he may be bad hurt," Biggun told the others in a somber tone.

The men gently laid him on a piece of board and carried him near one of the three campfires that had been built from some of the wood that had not been soaked by the rain.

As Biggun and two of the men examined Trent for broken bones, he did not utter a sound. That made it harder for them to tell the severity of his injuries. They laid a blanket over him and left one of the men with a broken arm to sit beside him and keep watch for any sign of change in his condition.

The other men continued their search for Sassy. She was so covered in mud they could have missed seeing her if it hadn't been for the white dishcloth she still clung to. She, too, made no sound when she was moved near the fire. One of the women came and sat beside her. She gently tried to clean some of the mud from her face, hair, and arms.

"All we can do is wait for morning and help," Sonny Tate came to tell the men. "There are still two men missing from the bunkhouse. Two of the cowboys are walking out in the pasture, looking to see if they were blown away by the storm," he said with a tremor in his voice. His demeanor showed his worry. The possibility of losing four of their ranch hands was hard enough, but the loss of his own precious child weighed heavily on the man.

Sonny took his position as foreman seriously. With Trent apparently hurt so badly, he had to take charge. It was his duty, his responsibility. His consolation was in knowing he could depend on the hired hands to help him in any way needed. He also took comfort in knowing he could depend on Biggun for support.

About sun-up, ten hands from the west ranch came, bringing the chuck wagon filled with food and another wagon with tools of every description to start work on rebuilding the homestead. A short time later, two doctors, along with six men in wagons loaded with supplies, rolled into headquarters. By then, the bodies of the two missing men had been found and laid beside the other two men. Mary Tate still held the lifeless body of her child.

Trent had begun to show signs of life. He would moan and try to turn away when the doctor examined him.

"From what I can tell, Trent has a concussion, dislocated left shoulder, several broken ribs, and either a broken or badly sprained left ankle. I am most concerned about the concussion, but at least he's beginning to come around," one of the doctors told Sonny and Biggun.

"The young woman, Sassy, also has a concussion but is not responding," he said with a slight shake of his head. "She has a broken right arm, likely several broken ribs, and a broken right ankle. We need to get Trent, the young woman, Mrs. Moore, and three of the ranch hands that are the most severely injured to town as quickly as possible," the doctor said, and the other doctor agreed.

Within an hour, the two doctors and two more men driving wagons carrying the injured departed.

Four full-sized and one small casket were built out of scrap lumber by several somber-faced men. Graves were dug in the family cemetery. The four ranch hands and little Clara Tate were laid to rest. Sonny Tate bit back his tears of grief as he quoted several Scriptures and started to pray. Biggun stood beside Sonny and ended the prayer when Sonny could not go on. The sky was clear, the breeze was gentle, and a huge oak tree that had somehow survived the storm shaded their graves.

Chapter Twenty-Five

Trent awoke with a blinding headache. He squinted his eyes, attempting to clear his vision. All he could see was a white ceiling, white curtains, and a white wall. Damn, had he died and gone to heaven? He wondered as he tried to clear his head. It ached like he had been kicked by a bull or was coming around after a three-day drunk. Surely, heaven looked better than this, he reasoned, through the woozy haze of feelings that persisted. Something wasn't right, he reasoned. Heaven had streets paved with gold and mansions of splendor beyond human belief.

He heard hushed voices in the distance. He listened intently but couldn't understand what they were saying. He certainly hadn't heard a heavenly choir singing or any angels playing harps. From the way he hurt on the inside and the outside of his entire body, this might be the holding pen before you entered hell, he thought vaguely but really wasn't overly convinced that was the case.

"Hello," he rasped, hardly above a whisper. He realized he would have to do better than that to ever make the distant voices hear him. He tried again.

"Hello—Hello," he called a bit louder.

He heard approaching footsteps, and one curtain was pulled aside. He was relieved to recognize Nurse Becker, one of Doctor Walls' assistants. He was especially thankful to know he was still alive, on earth, and apparently in the hospital. But why was he here? What had happened to put him in the hospital? He tried to remember, but nothing came to mind to answer his questions.

Trent tried to lift his head but found the shooting pain it caused made him think better of that idea.

"No, don't try to get up! You stay still and let me get the doctor. He wanted to know the minute you woke. Now, stay still, and I'll get him," she said, a bit excited as she closed the curtain. Trent could hear her almost running retreating footsteps.

Within minutes, the curtain was yanked open again, and Doctor Walls, flanked by Nurse Becker, stood staring at him.

"I am certainly glad to see the whites of your eyes, Trent. You gave us all quite a scare. How do you feel?" the doctor asked as he approached his bedside and put the cold metal of his stethoscope on Trent's bare chest.

Before Trent could answer the doctor's question, it came to him that he lay nearly naked beneath the sheet. He almost blushed but remembered nurses were accustomed to seeing the male body as well as the female body in such a state of undress.

"I feel like I was caught in a stampede. What the hell happened? What am I doing here?" Suddenly, he wanted to know everything that had happened to put him in the hospital. He had been hurt plenty of times but had rarely ever been seen by a doctor.

Doctor Walls glanced up at Trent's face as he heard the strain in his voice. "Take it easy. Let me finish examining you, and then we'll talk."

Trent didn't much like that idea, but he didn't seem to have much of a choice in the matter. The doctor pushed and probed, asking questions as he went. After a while, he straightened and looked at Trent.

"Your ranch headquarters was hit by a tornado. I'm sorry to tell you everything was flattened," the doctor told him straight out.

Trent felt like he had been stomped by some mean-tempered bull and kicked in the gut when he heard what the doctor had to say.

"What about all the workers? Where is Sassy? Is she—is she—" He couldn't quite get the words out. She had to be alive. As he had lain beside her against the wall, he had prayed for their safety. He had asked God for forgiveness for his previous sins, including his transgression with Flossy, and had confessed he cared deeply for Sassy. Surely, God wouldn't have taken her from him. Helen needed her, and he needed her.

Doctor Walls reached out and gently laid a hand on Trent's arm. "Sassy is badly hurt, but I believe she'll pull through. She is a strong young woman, but it's going to take a long time for her to recover."

Trent wanted to shout with relief and joy, but instead, he briefly closed his eyes and said a silent, *Thank you, God.*

"I am afraid most of the news isn't good. Three men and Mrs. Moore are also in the hospital but are no longer in grave danger. Four men were killed in the storm, and little Clara Tate." The doctor slowly shook his head. "Poor Mary is mighty distraught over the loss of their youngest child. Sonny is holding up well, and he and Biggun are trying to restore some order to running the ranch."

"I need to get to the ranch," Trent stated as he attempted to rise and was once more knocked back to his pillow from the relentless pain in his head.

"Oh, no, you don't!" Doctor Walls stated emphatically. "If I catch you trying to get out of that bed until I say you can, so help me, I'll hog-tie you to the bed frame."

Trent remained still, breathing deeply until the worst of the pain passed. "Tell me about Sassy."

"She had a severe concussion but is coming around slowly. That is my main concern. Like you, she has some broken ribs, a broken right arm, and a broken right ankle. It's hard to tell yet if she has internal injuries," he said with a slight shake of his head.

"Will you tell me as soon as she's fully awake?"

Doctor Walls nodded. The doctor and Nurse Becker left, pulling the curtain closed behind them. Trent looked at his sterile, white surroundings and once more prayed for Sassy, for Mary and Sonny Tate, for Mrs. Moore and her unborn child, and for the four men who had lost their lives. He didn't even know who they were yet, but when he found out, he would have to contact their families with the sad news. A slight smile came to Trent's lips. He wasn't a particularly religious man, although he certainly believed in God and his almighty power. Strange, he thought, sometimes tragic things have to happen to make you remember who is really in charge. When everything was going well, he often forgot about God's ultimate power. Then he drifted into a peaceful sleep.

~

Patsy returned two days later. She came straight to the hospital as soon as she heard what had happened at the Flatland Ranch.

"Oh, Trent, darling, I'm so sorry I wasn't here when all of this happened," she said, obviously worried.

"There wasn't anything you could have done," he assured her.

Later that afternoon, Trent commented, "You've been sitting here for hours, which isn't necessary. I'm sure you have things you need to be doing besides just sitting here with me."

"I know, but I think you need company," she insisted.

The next day, she arrived with a book of poetry and read for hours. Finally, late in the afternoon, Trent held up his hand to signal her to stop. "Patsy, I think you are going to lose your voice if you keep reading," he said sympathetically. "I know you're trying to help the time pass faster, but that's enough for today. You need to go home, spend some time with your parents, get a good night's rest, and go back to school tomorrow," he strongly suggested.

Patsy tried to protest, but Trent held firm. Besides, he had heard enough poetry to last for many, many years.

Patsy returned Saturday morning but only stayed for a few hours. She explained that she had already volunteered to help with a bake sale to raise money for a community center. She explained about the upcoming activities the townsfolk would have available once one of the vacant buildings was refurbished. Her eyes sparkled in anticipation.

For days, Trent heard more about all of Patsy's activities and plans for the future. After a while, he felt it necessary to bring up the subject of the effect their approaching marriage would have on her involvement in town activities and plans. "Patsy, when we're married, you'll be living miles from town and won't be involved in any of these wonderful activities you keep talking about. Have you thought about that?"

Patsy gave him a pleading look for understanding. "Well, yes, I have. I was thinking I could still live in town and continue teaching, and you could come to town for several days at a time. You might find you like being in town. Then you could enjoy some of these things with me." Before Trent could answer, she rushed on. "Just last week, I heard the mayor saying Amarillo should be getting electricity in a year or two at the most. Just think how exciting and convenient that will be," she said, her eyes sparkling. "No more lighting lamps and actually being able to read by a bright light and walk down lighted streets at night."

Trent was shocked by her suggestion. "Patsy, I'm a rancher. That's a twenty-four hours a day, seven days a week job," he answered, a bit exasperated at such a suggestion, no matter how exciting town life might sound to her.

"You have Sonny, Biggun, and Ely, who could run the ranch while you're away."

"I know, and I do trust them, but I sure as hell never have been and never will be an absentee rancher. Overall, things just don't work that way. As soon as I get out of the hospital, I'll be headed back to the ranch," he insisted.

Patsy looked shocked. She had never heard Trent use profanity. She knew it was common among the ranch hands. Her father had never sworn in front of the women in the family. She took a deep breath to regain some calm. "Trent, you'll still be on crutches and need to rest. How will you manage at the ranch with no house, no conveniences?"

"I'll be fine. I need to be there to oversee the entire rebuilding and general running of the ranch. Damn, Patsy, that's my life!"

"Trent, I do care deeply for you, but I vowed, when I left the ranch I grew up on, that I'd never live on another one. It's just too lonely, too limiting."

"Patsy, I think you should have mentioned those feelings much earlier. It may be limiting at the Flatland, but I can't imagine you being lonely. Helen and Sassy will continue to live in the house with us, and there are the other ranch women," he pointed out.

"To be honest, Trent, I don't have that much in common with Helen, and Sassy is just the hired help," she said curtly.

Trent gave her a firm look. "If that's how you feel, I think we better call off our engagement," Trent answered.

"Let's not be too hasty in ending our engagement. Trent, I do care for you. Maybe we could still go out when you come to town and see if we can work something out." Patsy suggested, looking hopeful.

"I don't see much point to that. Either we care enough to marry and make a life together at the ranch, or we need to just go our separate ways," Trent answered ardently. Trent saw the unmistakable look of regret on Patsy's face.

Patsy rose and moved unhurriedly to the doorway. She paused and looked back at Trent as though she wanted to say more, but then she walked slowly out of his room.

Trent looked at the empty doorway and felt a slight pang of shame. Deep down, he had suspected the marriage would never take place. Now, he felt freedom like a final reprieve. When Patsy had returned, he had realized he could never love her with the deep passion a married couple should share. Thankfully, their relationship had terminated itself before they made the grave mistake of a lifetime.

Chapter Twenty-Six

SIX MONTHS LATER, OCTOBER 1901

Sassy's thoughts were reflecting on all that had happened during this past year. Last October was the first time she had ever met Trent and Helen. Only a year ago but, in a way, it seemed like years and years had passed.

"I can hardly wait to see what my brother is having built at the ranch," Helen told Sassy as they jolted along in the buggy. "Ely says the main house is darn near as big as the Felts' house but not as fancy. Trent is having rock hauled in to finish the outside of everything except the barn. Ely said the walls on the houses and bunkhouse are eighteen inches thick. I guess my brother thinks that might hold off another tornado." She laughed as she prattled on in excitement.

Sassy's recovery had been a long one, and just recently, she'd begun to feel her full strength had almost returned. Helen was so anxious to see what was going on at the ranch Sassy had finally consented to this trip.

Trent and Ely had insisted they remain in town as there was too much turmoil going on with the extensive building. The men had been living in tents until the new bunkhouse was recently finished.

"I don't think anything can hold off a tornado," Sassy answered, more to herself than to Helen.

"No, I expect you're right," Helen responded in a more somber tone. "It's a wonder more people weren't killed, including you and Trent. When we got back and drove out to the ranch, I could hardly believe what I was seeing. Most of the debris had been cleaned up, and reusable lumber was neatly stacked in piles, but it still looked so empty. In a way, it was hard to remember what it had looked like before the storm, and we had only been gone two weeks. I can't imagine the terror of living through such a storm."

Sassy gave a short laugh. "I can't imagine it either. The last thing I remember is Trent telling me to lie down beside the wall and him lying beside me. Then, he covered us with blankets and pillows. It sounded like a freight train was coming through the house. The next thing I remember is waking up in the hospital and you sitting beside my bed."

"It's probably for the best you don't remember being pinned under that pile of rubble for hours before they found you. I'm sure you would have been in lots of pain and scared half to death to boot."

"Likely so," Sassy agreed.

"Oh, look!" Helen exclaimed with enthusiasm as she pointed toward the huge structure coming into view. "My stars in heaven. I do believe Ely was right. That's one of the biggest houses I've ever seen in this part of the country," Helen almost shouted with excitement.

Sassy looked at the massive two-story structure and thought about how long it would take her to clean it. At times, she still felt a bit weak. She hated to ask for extra help, but she knew this would be beyond her ability for now or maybe ever. Ely had said it would be ready for them to move into in about three more weeks.

The house stretched lengthwise at least a hundred and thirty feet, with wide porches across the lower and upper floors. The porches were supported with ten huge cedar posts, and a cedar railing encompassed each porch. Six wide front steps were set in the center, with a circular ramp on each side of the steps. It was quite attractive. Sassy counted twelve windows across the front of the house's upper and lower floors. Large central doors led out to the lower and upper porches. It even had the fancy rounded turrets at the corners like the Felts' mansion. The center entryway on the bottom and top floor was rounded and extended out onto the porch about ten feet. Matching rectangular-shaped rocks surrounded the windows and doors to enhance their appearance.

"Isn't it grand?" Helen exclaimed with approval. "Just think of the wonderful parties we can throw and the number of overnight guests we can house. I believe Ely said there are twelve bedrooms in all, plus a huge living room, formal dining room, an office and a separate library that is also a sitting room, and an enormous kitchen. Oh, yes, there are two bathing rooms, one upstairs and another one downstairs. They even have flush toilets. Can you just imagine?"

Sassy sat in the buggy with her mouth slightly agape. No, she couldn't imagine living in such a fine house, and the thought of trying to take proper care of it and help Helen overwhelmed her.

"There you are," Ely greeted the ladies and gave Helen an affectionate kiss. "Come on, let me give you girls the grand tour."

He looked at Sassy's slightly pale complexion and noticed her worried expression. "Are you all right, Sassy?" he asked as he lifted Helen out of the buggy and into her chair.

"Yes, yes, I just wasn't expecting to see such a huge house." She laughed slightly. "I'll be working day and night to keep this place clean," she commented as she let Ely assist her from the buggy.

"Oh, I think Trent has all of that worked out. Don't worry about cleaning the house. Just enjoy seeing everything."

"Where is my brother?" Helen asked as Ely easily rolled her chair up one of the circular ramps to the porch.

"He's out checking some new cattle, but he'll be in before long."

Ely escorted the women through each room, pointing out the handsome woodwork framing the windows and doorways and the enormous beams across the ceilings. There were two rock fireplaces in the enormous living room, one in the dining room, and smaller ones in each of the other rooms. Ely showed Helen their massive bedroom, which was next to the downstairs bathing room.

Helen laughed with obvious delight. "We could hold a dance in this room," she said with a teasing smile for her husband.

Ely leaned over and whispered something in her ear. Helen giggled like a schoolgirl and swatted him on his arm. "You behave," she said with an impish smile.

Sassy walked on down the hallway to the next room, which appeared to be Trent's new office, with his enormous desk sitting near two large windows. The room next to it must be the library from the looks of the numerous built-in bookshelves. She recognized the wood as being mesquite, and it was finished with a slight shine on the surface. In a way, it seemed a shame to cover up that pretty wood with books, she thought as she ran her hand over the smooth surface.

Just as they were ready to tour the second floor, Trent arrived.

"Well, ladies, what do you think?" he asked with a broad grin that enhanced the laugh lines around his sparkling brown eyes.

"It's superb!" Helen exclaimed as she gestured toward their surroundings. "I never realized what good taste you have," she teased.

"I'm glad you're pleased, but the rest is up to you and Sassy," he said with a broad grin.

He noticed Sassy had not commented about the house. When he looked at her, she seemed to realize she was being included.

"The house is truly grand. I think Helen will have to be the one to pick out the furnishings. I can make the drapes once she picks the material."

Trent just smiled.

"Well, Ely, lead the way."

Sassy eyed the wide, winding stairway, wondering how they would manage to get Helen upstairs. They continued past the stairway and rounded a corner, and before them was a lift.

Both women gasped in surprise.

"I can't believe it, I...I just can't believe you had a lift put in for me," Helen cried out with joy as tears overflowed. She reached for Trent's hand.

After the upstairs tour, Ely and Helen returned to the downstairs. Upstairs were mostly bedrooms with two cozy sitting rooms and the upstairs bathing room.

Trent took Sassy's hand and pulled her out onto the porch. They walked to the railing to take in the view. The fall grass was not as vivid a green as in the springtime. The few trees that had survived the storm were beginning to shed their leaves. The open land held a strange beauty. You could see a rider coming from a far distance. The breadth of the sky, with its changing hues of color, was breathtaking as it showed off its own unique beauty.

As Sassy and Trent stood side by side, their arms scarcely touching, Trent reached for her hand and brought it to his lips. He kissed her fingers gently. Sassy turned and looked at him with a questioning gaze.

Trent spoke softly. "Sassy, when I started building this house, it was with the intent to marry and raise my family here. I plan to fulfill that dream."

"I know you and Patsy broke up for a while, but it's good you've made up. That's wonderful. I wish you great happiness." As she spoke, the words seemed to stick in her throat. She wondered how she had gotten them out, but she had.

Trent turned toward her and took her in his arms, pulling her firmly to him. Before she realized his intentions, he was kissing her. A kiss filled with passion and desire. The sort of kiss she believed he would soon be giving to another woman. It was the kiss she had dreamed of having just once more from Trent. She savored the taste of his mouth, the freshness that clung to him from spending countless hours outside, and the brush of his day's growth of whiskers against her tender skin. Why was he doing this if he was about to marry Patsy, she wondered. No matter the reason, she could not make herself pull away from him. This moment they shared was one of pure pleasure and almost unbearable torment. She would have this one last kiss to treasure for the rest of her life. Then she must let him go. She would have no choice but to stand by and endure watching him give his love to another woman.

Trent finally lifted his head and whispered, "Sassy, it's you I plan to spend the rest of my life with, here, in this house. We'll raise a passel of young'uns and love one another until we are old and fade away. The house will be finished in three weeks, and we'll be married here." He had not asked her to marry him but had told her what he had planned for them.

She looked at him, totally puzzled. "Aren't you marrying Patsy?"

Trent slowly shook his head from side to side. "No, Patsy didn't want to live at the ranch. She said once she left the ranch she grew up on, she'd vowed to never live on another. She had some crazy notion I could live in town part-time so she could go on enjoying her social life. I told her there was no way in hell I would be an absentee rancher and, although I have good men working for me, I'm the one who'll run this ranch. I finally realized she didn't love me enough to want to share my home, and I didn't love her either. It wasn't meant to be, and I'm glad. I knew I loved you, but I thought…I thought you were too young for me."

Sassy looked at him beseechingly. "Did you also think I was too ignorant and poor to become your wife?"

Trent gave her a solemn look. "I am ashamed to say those thoughts did cross my mind, but, at the same time, I knew I was falling in love with you. I thought Patsy would help me get over those feelings, but she didn't, and now I realize she never would have. Can you forgive me for being such a jackass?"

Sassy laughed. Before she could fully answer, he was kissing her again, leaving no doubt it was her he loved, and it was her he desired.

She felt elated and sad all at the same time. Joy filled her to think Trent Sanderson, a man who could have any woman, wanted her as his wife. It was true she had little education, came from a dirt-poor background, and knew nothing about running a house such as this. She could clean it as the housekeeper, but she felt at a loss as to knowing how to be the mistress of such a grand house. She feared that, in time, when the heat of passion had lessened, he would realize how lacking she was in trying to be a lady, the kind of wife he needed, and he would surely come to be ashamed of her. When that day came, knowing she would cause him such hurt and embarrassment at her lack of ability would surely break her heart.

She knew how cruel people could be. They would certainly wonder why Trent would have ever chosen her for his wife. The class of people he and Helen were accustomed to was foreign to her. She knew nothing of their ways and would surely appear foolish in their eyes.

No matter how much she loved Trent, it would never work. Somehow, she had to make him understand why she was about to refuse his proposal of marriage.

Sassy looked at Trent and she knew he could see and even sense her turmoil.

Despite the lump in her throat, she managed to speak softly. "Oh, Trent, you know how grateful I am to you and Helen for all you have done for me and my family, but I cannot become your wife. I know nothing about running such a grand house and being the kind of wife you need and deserve. You need a wife you can be proud of and know is capable of entertaining your many friends and people you'll do business with." She ducked her head slightly in embarrassment. "You know, sometimes I have trouble reading or writing and don't know much math either." She lifted her head and looked into the depths of his golden-brown eyes, which seemed darker than usual, and saw the somber expression on his face. She was afraid he was angry with her, but she continued, trying to make him understand the truth of their situation. "I'm afraid I'll make mistakes that will show how lacking I am, and then you'll be sorry you married me. You'll wish you had driven on and left me to bury my pa and never set foot in your house. You know everyone will wonder why you married so far beneath yourself," she said, pleading for his understanding.

Trent stood looking at the distressed expression on Sassy's face and heard the pleading in her voice for his understanding. He knew most of the things she had just said were true, but that did not change his feelings for her. He knew she was the woman he loved and wanted to spend the rest of his life with, only her.

"Sassy, do you love me?"

"You know I will always be grateful—"

Trent held up one hand to stop her. "Sassy, I didn't ask you if you were grateful. I asked you if you loved me," he repeated with more emphasis on each word.

She looked at him and nodded her head. "Yes, Trent, I do love you but—"

Once again, he held up his hand to stop her. "Either you love me enough to become my wife, or you don't. It has nothing to do with education, rich or poor, what people will say, or any of that nonsense. Now," he paused, still looking directly into her eyes, "once more, I am asking you, do you love me enough to become my wife?"

Sassy looked at Trent with wide eyes. In her mind, she felt certain she should refuse him, but in her heart, she knew she could not refuse him again.

"Yes, yes, I do! Oh, Trent, I want to be your wife, but I'm so afraid of what might happen to our love later if you're disappointed in me."

Trent finally smiled and took her in his arms again. He brushed a gentle kiss on her cheek and nuzzled his face in her lovely hair. He held her close and savored the joy she brought to him. He knew he had to ease her mind about her doubts. Come hell or high water, he had to make her understand he loved her and wanted no other woman as his wife, no matter her past or present circumstances.

"Sassy, stop worrying about your lack of education. Helen can help you learn all you want to know. There will be a library full of all kinds of books for you to use. She'll teach you about running this house. Our mother, who was an expert when it came to entertaining, taught Helen. Although it has been a long time since we've entertained much, I'm sure Helen will remember just how it's done," he said with confidence. "Just look at what a difference you have made in her life and my life. I'm the one who is just as grateful to you. Helen was making my life almost unbearable at times before you came. The night of the storm, I prayed for us to survive. I knew I wanted to spend the rest of my life loving you and having you love me." He kissed her sweetly on the lips and smiled. "Apparently, God heard me and gave Patsy the good sense to finally tell me she never intended to live on another ranch."

How could she argue with God? Sassy wondered as she took great pleasure in Trent's tender kisses.

Chapter Twenty-Seven

T he wide, expansive sky was a tropical blue dotted with a few white fluffy clouds. A light breeze blew from the north to cool the hundreds of guests who gathered at the new Flatland Ranch headquarters. There was a buzz of comments about the splendid, expansive house Trent had built for his bride-to-be. The finest and, for certain, the largest ranch house anyone had ever seen.

Most either forgot or chose to forget that this magnificent house was also to be shared with Helen and Ely.

"Just think, she went from being the housekeeper to the mistress of the mansion in just a matter of months," Pearl Moore whispered to Blanch Grimes. Both women were in their late fifties and plump; Pearl had more gray hair than Blanch and a slenderer face. Blanch looked at her longtime friend, nodded her head, and pursed her lips. "If you ask me, there might have been a bit more than just housekeeping going on around here," she whispered just loud enough to be heard by those nearby.

Pearl nodded her head in agreement. "If we see a baby come popping out in a few months, then we'll know for sure just why Trent would marry such a girl so soon after breaking up with that pretty teacher."

"Indeed!" Blanch agreed. "He's so handsome and rich. He could have had any young woman from a respectable family. I just don't understand what gets into men sometimes."

Buster Counts overheard every word the two women said and couldn't resist the temptation to put them in their place. They were just two old gossiping biddies, in his opinion. He leaned forward and whispered loud enough for everyone seated nearby to hear. "Maybe what got into him is something called love. I doubt either of you old crows can remember what that's like, if you ever knew," he said with a mocking smile.

Both women glared at him.

"Buster Counts, you mind your own business and stop eavesdropping! Besides, what does an old fuddy-duddy like you know about love?" Blanch scolded him.

"I know a damn sight more than either of you. I loved my Maggie from the day I first laid eyes on her until the day they put her in her grave, and I still love her! We spent many happy hours in one another's arms and—"

Pearl gasped at the thought of what he might be going to say next. "We don't want to hear any more about your love life. Just be quiet, you old horse's behind! They're about to start the wedding," she finished in a huff.

The two women turned toward where Trent and Sassy now stood at the top of the steps leading to the massive porch. Ely stood beside Trent, and Helen sat in her wheelchair beside Sassy.

Trent's smile and loving glint in his eyes reflected his admiration for his lovely bride. It seemed like ages since he had first found her and thought she was just a boy trying to do a man's job. Today, there was no mistaking she was a stunning young woman. Her blonde hair glistened in the sunlight as it fell to her shoulders in gentle waves, ending in soft curls. Sassy's blue eyes sparkled when she looked at Trent. Her cheeks glowed with a touch of pink, and her lips were a few shades darker. She wore a long, light pink dress with off-white lace trimming the rounded neckline on the fitted bodice. The dress had full sleeves and a gathered skirt. Both were enhanced with two rows of lace near their hem. She wore a matching wide-brimmed pink hat with lace trimming the edge and a large lace flower on the right side. Sassy was dazzling in Trent's eyes and those of most of the men attending the wedding.

The men thought Trent a lucky man to find such a beauty. The ranch hands also knew Sassy to be just as pleasing on the inside as on the outside. They cared not that she had been the housekeeper and cook and had attended to Helen. In their opinion, Trent couldn't have done better by marrying the teacher or some society woman either. In fact, in their opinion, after hearing about why he hadn't married the teacher, the consensus was that kind of woman wouldn't likely be suited to ranch life anyway.

"Dearly beloved, we are gathered here today in the presence of God and these witnesses to join Trenton Zachery Sanderson and Evangeline McCoy in holy matrimony. If anyone present knows a just cause why these two should not be joined, let him or her speak now or forever hold their peace."

A tall, slim, well-dressed man stood near the back of the crowd, taking in the proceedings, but he did not speak. As the ceremony continued, he turned, walked slowly to where he had left his horse, and rode away, scarcely being noticed by anyone present.

Long after dark, when most of the guests had departed, except for the Smyths and Daniel, who occupied the downstairs bedrooms, Trent and Sassy climbed the wide, curving stairway leading to the second floor. They walked with arms around each other down the hall to their massive bedroom.

Trent had ordered handcrafted furniture from Jacob Smyth, which had been delivered several days before the wedding by Jacob and Daniel. The rest of the family, Sally and the girls, arrived by train the day before the wedding. They were staying overnight and would all return to Wichita Falls the next day.

Trent had their room decorated with a huge four-poster bed with a wagon wheel carved into the massive headboard. There were two matching armoires, a chiffonier, and a dressing table for Sassy. Two matching wingback chairs with a small pedestal table between them were placed in front of the fireplace. In the corner turret, with windows facing northeast and rounding to the southwest, stood a writing desk. A rounded window seat with thick cushions surrounded the nook corner. Oh, what a marvelous place to write or read the many books from the library she had not read yet, Sassy thought as she took in her new surroundings. She was delighted that their bedroom was quite large but retained a feeling of coziness. Sassy was thrilled with Trent's choice of furniture and especially appreciated the fact it had been made by Jacob and Daniel.

Once the door to their sanctuary was closed, it felt as though they were far away in some secluded place meant only for newlyweds.

Trent took Sassy in his arms and kissed her with a cherished passion, showing his desire to possess her body and complete their union. Sassy felt a bit shy but knew now that he was her husband, his amorous advances were to be expected. She was a bit surprised to find herself readily joining him in each new experience.

Although she was inexperienced and had limited knowledge of men, she knew what to expect thanks to Helen's enlightening her as to the factual things that went on between married couples.

Helen had said some women didn't seem to enjoy the attention of their husbands, but she and Ely looked forward to the quiet of the evening when they could be alone and take pleasure in the privileges of marriage with no restraints or feelings of guilt.

Sassy had a strong inclination she and Trent would also look forward to the quiet of the evening when they, too, could take pleasure in expressing their love and fulfilling their desire for one another.

Once their cumbersome clothing had been gently but seductively removed, Sassy and Trent stood in the soft glow of the lamplight, taking in the allure and the fascination each felt toward the other. Words did not have to be spoken. Their mutual approval was evident in their heated gazes. As they came together, enticing, touching, exploring, and taking great delight in pleasing one another, their desires rose, and they became passionate lovers and began their journey as devoted husband and wife.

Chapter Twenty-Eight

TWO YEARS LATER, OCTOBER 1903

Numerous changes had taken place on the Flatland Ranch during the two years since Trent and Sassy were married.

Trent had managed to keep the peace with Pete Kennedy over his access to Flatland water, although, at times, tempers flared. On two occasions, Trent had intervened, just in time, to prevent battles that would have imitated the earlier range wars.

Helen had taken Sassy under her wing and taught her reading, penmanship, spelling, and math skills to an eighth-grade level, and Sassy continued to study on her own. Sassy discovered the room that held the beautiful mesquite wood bookshelves, now filled with books, was one of her favorite rooms in the house and where she spent hours poring over the vast array of information the books provided. If she didn't grasp the meaning of something, she would take the book to Helen for her to explain its meaning. Helen delighted in being Sassy's teacher and prided herself on Sassy's excellent progress.

Helen came to realize how much she enjoyed teaching and decided to take the state teachers' test. She passed every section with high marks. This led to a new plan Helen gave much thought.

Helen also taught Sassy the *dos and don'ts* of entertaining guests. Sassy was a quick learner and soon gained the reputation of being a gracious hostess. She also rode with Trent as he managed the ranch. She wanted to know the day-to-day details of running such a vast operation. Trent was amazed at her stamina and that she would willingly help with whatever chores the men were doing. She quickly gained further admiration of the cowboys and was treated with the respect due to the wife of their employer.

After Helen had her plan firmly formulated in her mind, she persuaded Trent and Ely to build a school. The families with school-age children could remain at the ranch, and she could teach their children. Her plan was accepted with enthusiasm.

The large one-room school building was finished in time for Helen to start teaching in mid-January 1904. A short time later, to Ely and Helen's delight, she discovered she was expecting a child, due in June.

Once the school was completed, Sassy brought Timothy and Martha to live at the ranch. To her delight, the big house with twelve bedrooms was slowly being filled.

Sassy felt great contentment most of the time. She rarely spoke Nathan's name aloud, but she still silently grieved for his loss and prayed constantly that someday, he would return to them.

On June 15, 1904, Helen delivered a healthy baby girl. Helen and Ely were not only enamored with one another but with their beautiful baby daughter they named Amanda.

Occasionally, Ely felt a pang of guilt when he remembered how, when he had first met Helen, he had decided to marry her for security and companionship, not love. Now, his love for her had grown far beyond what he could have ever imagined. At last, he had the family and the child of his own he had wanted for so many years.

After almost three years of marriage, Sassy was puzzled as to why she had not yet conceived. She tried not to fret over it each month when her cycle came, but recently, the disappointment each month had become more depressing. Her preoccupation with not conceiving had seemed to grow worse after the birth of her niece. Trent would try to reassure her it would happen when the time was right, but he, too, had begun to wonder about their failure to produce a child. He knew it certainly wasn't due to the lack of the intimate pleasures they shared.

The thought had crossed his mind that if they had not conceived a child in a few more months, they would take a trip to Dallas, where they had more advanced medical facilities, to see a specialist who dealt with such matters. He did not mention his plan to Sassy for fear she would become more upset over the situation.

On their third anniversary, Sassy confided in Trent she thought she might be pregnant as her cycle was three weeks late and her breasts had become very tender. Trent was delighted but warned her not to build her hopes too high just yet. By the end of November, Sassy was certain she must be carrying a child. She was never sick like many women, but she could feel an indescribable difference in her body. She and Trent paid a visit to Doctor Brown. He confirmed their suspicions. He predicted the baby would be born the following June.

Sassy and Trent were ecstatic over their long-awaited news and could hardly wait to share their excitement with Helen and Ely.

By the sixth month, she was huge and miserable. Her feet were swollen, and her back ached constantly. Doctor Brown decided she was likely carrying twins. At the end of her seventh month, Trent rented a house in town and hired two women to stay with her constantly. He rode to town every other day and left strict orders that, when she went into labor, the boy who worked at the nearby livery stable should come for him immediately, even if it was in the middle of the night.

Fortunately for the stable boy, he was sent to the ranch about mid-morning to let Trent know the time had come.

By the time Trent arrived, Sassy was in hard labor. Beads of sweat soaked her face and body. With each new contraction, she cried out in pain. Trent sat beside her, bathing her face and arms with a damp cloth. Trent spoke softly to Sassy, attempting to soothe her as much as possible. It tore at his heart to see his wife in such agony with each new contraction. Doctor Brown had examined her earlier and predicted it would be a while longer before she gave birth. Trent wondered just what *a while longer* meant as the hours dragged by. He felt frustrated and helpless as he watched his wife suffer in seemingly unbearable anguish as the contractions became harder and harder.

About eight o'clock in the evening, Doctor Brown reappeared. He examined her and smiled at Trent. "Almost there, my man. Sometimes, I think it is harder on the expectant fathers than the poor women who have to endure the pain," he said with a sympathetic smile.

Trent would have argued that point, but he was far more concerned about Sassy giving birth and being out of pain as quickly as possible. He knew she had to be exhausted after hours and hours of such severe pain.

Doctor Brown sat at the foot of the bed and told the two women what he wanted each of them to do.

Then he turned to Trent. "I know you're a big strong fellow, but I've seen men just as big as you faint during these times. If you start feeling queasy, you get out of here. I won't have time to stop to tend to you," he said with a quirky little smile.

But Trent wasn't about to leave his wife. He let her hold his arm and squeeze as hard as she liked as each new pain racked her tired body.

"Here we go," the doctor finally announced. He held up the first baby, smacked it firmly on its bottom, and handed the child to one of the women as the baby let out a strong cry of objection at such treatment. "A boy," the doctor announced. In a few seconds, he held up the second child, smacked it firmly on its bottom, and they heard an even stronger cry. "Another boy," he smiled at Trent. The doctor started to rise, then suddenly sat back down. "Well, well, well, look at this, we have another baby, and this one is a girl!" he exclaimed, sounding amazed himself. She let out a piercing yell all on her own.

Trent and Sassy looked at one another in utter amazement.

"Did he say two boys and a girl?" Sassy asked as though she thought she might have misunderstood.

Trent leaned forward and lovingly kissed her damp cheek. "That's exactly what he said," he told her, still in a state of shock over the sudden size of their family on May 09, 1905.

They fretted over the names for their three offspring but finally settled on Jordon, Jonathan, and Joanna.

As the children grew, it became apparent Jordon, the oldest by a minute or so, was the calmest and, apparently, felt it his duty to set a good example for his siblings by being cooperative in most situations. Jonathan was a bit high-strung, with occasional displays of temper when things didn't go to suit him. Joanna was what her father termed "a ring-tailed tooter." She left no doubt as to her pleasure or displeasure with any given situation. Trent indicated she took after her mother, who had earned her nickname, Sassy.

On one occasion, when their nanny decided each needed a dose of castor oil to cleanse their system to prevent winter colds, Jordon opened his mouth wide but immediately spit the nasty-tasting goo from his mouth and laughed as he smeared the mess he made with his little hands. Jonathan followed his brother's lead, spitting the oil from his mouth, but let out a yell of complaint and kicked his feet in protest to such treatment. Joanna spat, screamed, flailed her hands in the air, and kicked her feet with such vigor she almost toppled her highchair.

Later that year, in November, Helen and Ely became the proud parents of a second child, a boy. They named him Ely Sanderson Murry. They called him Sandy.

In December of that same year, Sassy miscarried and never became pregnant again.

There was a lively atmosphere in the big house with the sounds of five small children—the triplets and Helen's two children. In addition to the youngsters, nine-year-old Martha had moved to the ranch. Adding the nanny and four more adults, the house was occupied by eleven people. No matter Sassy's protest, Timothy had moved to the bunkhouse on his sixteenth birthday but visited often, especially about mealtime.

Through the next two years, the ranch prospered with only a few minor setbacks. Another wildfire, sparked by lightning from a fast-moving summer storm, burned over 100,000 acres, but no structures were destroyed, and the livestock had been quickly moved out of the path of the firestorm.

1908 was an extremely dry year. About a third of the livestock had to be sold to reserve the water needed for the remainder of the cattle and horses.

The children thrived, and, for the most part, life at the Flatland Ranch was satisfying and pleasant. Perhaps it was too near perfection to endure the test of time.

Chapter Twenty-Nine

I909 became the year that would change the Sanderson family forever. Two events occurred that challenged Trent and Sassy to the core of their survival and their love.

Angel, now a lovely young woman with a mass of chocolate brown hair and the same golden-brown eyes as Trent, had completed her formal schooling in 1906. The first year after Angel had finished school, several young men had courted her. Her aunt had declared that any one of them would have been a perfect catch. The second year, one man in particular had courted her, equally pleasing to her aunt. But after a year, the courtship had ended abruptly. The young man had been forced to marry another young woman, who was apparently in a family way. Angel had been heartbroken. She decided it was time for a change, so she returned to the ranch to assist Helen with teaching.

The number of families at the ranch with school-age children had increased to seven. During the drought, Trent tended to lay off the single men ahead of men with families to support.

Helen had a total of nineteen students from first through eighth grade. It would be a great help to have Angel take the fifth- through eighth-grade students, as their lessons took far more planning time. With Angel's help, Helen could spend more time with her own family.

The family had been caught by surprise when Angel wrote about her abrupt change of plans. They had felt certain she would have preferred to remain in the city where she was accustomed to having many friends, interesting places of entertainment to enjoy, and far better opportunities to meet eligible young men.

Everyone, except Trent, seemed pleased that Angel wanted to return to the ranch.

"The only thing I have to say is, if I catch her messing around with any of these half-civilized cowboys, I'll send her right back to the city. I'm not having her getting saddled with a man who can't care for her, and it's for damn sure no cowboy can afford to support her extravagant ways!" Trent thundered as he read her letter.

Sassy looked a bit shocked at her husband's adamant outburst.

"I suppose the rules will always be different for women than men," she casually commented.

"What's that supposed to mean?" Trent asked, still perturbed.

"Remember, you married a half-civilized girl," she said as she smiled sweetly at her dear husband.

Trent stared at her for several seconds and then started to laugh. "The difference is, my dear wife, I knew how to tame her, and I doubt Angel possesses one bit of that instinct when it comes to men. Besides, I could support you, and you wanted to learn so you would make me a proper wife, remember?" he challenged with affection at the recollection. "Most of these single cowboys are here today and gone tomorrow. I'm afraid the only thing they would see in Angel is a pretty face and a free meal ticket."

"Really! So, you think you have tamed me," she answered with an impish smile.

Trent crossed the room and lifted Sassy from where she sat, pulling her into a powerful embrace. He bent his head and claimed her lips with a searing kiss. Then he smiled. "Maybe I just taught you well," he said as he escorted her upstairs.

~

Sassy sat on one of the porch swings, enjoying the coolness of a late morning breeze as she mended some of the children's clothes. The five children of the household played nearby on the huge porch and in the vast yard. Trent had built a four-foot-high rock fence approximately sixty feet away from the house around the entire perimeter. It served two purposes. The first was to prevent a fire from reaching the house. He forbade one blade of grass, or tree, or any other plants to be grown inside the fence. In the dry summer months, any vegetation would make the house too vulnerable to fire. The second was to prevent the children from wandering too far afield.

Amanda looked up from where she sat, dressing her favorite doll, and gazed into the distance. "Somebody's coming."

"Probably another cowboy looking for work," Sassy answered, continuing her sewing.

"Not a cowboy, a buggy."

Sassy glanced toward the road but could not tell from that distance who might be coming to call.

"I guess we'll know soon who it is," she commented.

The buggy stopped outside the closed front gate. Sassy studied the driver and thought he looked vaguely familiar. She did not recognize the older woman or child who rode inside the open buggy.

Sassy descended the steps and crossed the yard. She continued to observe the two passengers but could not remember ever seeing either of them before.

"Good morning," she greeted them as she reached the gate.

"Good morning," the older woman answered and smiled in reply.

"Is this the home of Mr. Trent Sanderson?"

"Yes, it is. I'm Trent's wife, Sassy. Won't you come in for some refreshment after your long ride out here?"

"Thank you, ma'am," the woman answered.

The driver climbed down to assist the woman out of the buggy as the boy jumped to the ground, then took a few quick steps to the gate. The woman looked to be in her late fifties, with graying brown hair and soft gray eyes set in a pleasant, round face. The boy was a handsome child. He stood straight with his shoulders back. He had auburn-colored hair and was fair-complected. When he looked up and smiled, Sassy saw the same striking shade of green eyes she had seen once before but could not immediately recall where.

She extended her hand toward the boy, who immediately took it in a firm grip for a child of about seven or eight. "I'm Sassy Sanderson," she said with a warm smile to welcome their guests.

"I'm Zachery Trent Tatum, but everybody calls me Zack," the child proudly announced. "I've come to meet my daddy."

The woman put her hand on the boy's shoulder. "That was using very polite manners, Zack," she praised the child. "I'm Daisy Homes," the woman said as she, too, shook Sassy's hand.

Sassy felt as though the breath had been sucked from her body. She stared at the woman and then at the boy. She suddenly felt weak but managed to open the gate with a trembling hand. A premonition of impending doom filled her as she recognized the name Tatum. Now, Sassy remembered where she had seen that same shade of green eyes. Flossy Tatum, of course!

Sassy led the way up the steps and to the expansive porch. Then she remembered the man standing beside the carriage. She turned and motioned toward the barns. "Take your team to be watered and join us, or there is always coffee at the bunkhouse," she called to him.

When they reached the porch, Daisy suggested they sit in the shade and let Zack play with the other children since he had been confined to the buggy for hours.

Sassy brought lemonade and a plate piled high with cookies. The children sat in a circle to enjoy the refreshments as they talked and giggled.

"Mrs. Sanderson, I need to speak privately with you and your husband, or he may wish to hear what I have to say first," Daisy spoke softly at the first opportunity.

Sassy summoned Helen to come and supervise the children. She quickly introduced their visitors by their first names and told Helen they needed to speak privately with Trent.

Trent, Sassy, and Daisy entered Trent's office and closed the door.

"I am sure you remember Flossy Tatum working here for a short time several years ago," Daisy began as soon as they were seated.

Trent and Sassy exchanged a look, expressing their curiosity about this unexpected visit by a stranger. Both nodded their heads.

"Well, she came to Abilene, Kansas, after leaving here under what I believe was rather strained circumstances. I had a room for rent. My husband had passed, and I needed some extra income. Flossy rented the room, and soon, it became apparent she was expecting a child. She finally confided in me that the two of you had been intimate while she lived here," she nodded toward Trent and blushed slightly at discussing such a personal subject. "She said you had seduced her to your bed while just the two of you were here alone one night. Then, you wanted nothing further to do with her when she offered her affection, and then you sent her away." Daisy paused briefly and pursed her lips in disapproval. "She was heartbroken to be treated so uncaringly, as though she were a loose woman not worthy of your love," she said as she looked at Trent with obvious disapproval.

Trent stared at the woman, finding it hard to believe the fabricated story he had just heard.

He cleared his throat, stood, poured himself a whiskey, and turned to face the two women. One he loved with his entire being, the other a misinformed stranger.

"I seem to recall a bit different event than you have just described, ma'am," he said as he took a generous swallow of the soothing liquid. "I came in from work late, thinking all three of the women were in town for the night. Much to my surprise, I found Flossy lounging on the settee in the living room with a cozy fire glowing in the fireplace and only one lamp burning that cast a soft glow over her scantily clad body. Somehow, all these years, I have believed it was I who was seduced that night. After that one night, I did tell her it would never happen again. I meant it, and it didn't. It wasn't me that sent her away. My sister and Flossy never got along. It was Helen that sent her packing for not doing her job." It was obvious he was not pleased to have his personal life discussed by this stranger who had been badly misinformed.

He looked at Sassy, wishing he could read her thoughts. What must she think of him now? At the hotel, on their way home after searching for her two brothers, somehow, she had known about his brief encounter with

Flossy, and now look at the results of that one night of—? Trent wasn't sure what it had been; likely, lust was the best description. Once more, he had let Sassy down.

Daisy looked a bit dubious but did not try to dispute Trent's account of what had taken place between him and Flossy.

"Well, nonetheless, you have a fine son as a result of that night, and I have brought him to you," Daisy said, glad that part of their conversation was over. She didn't know which story was actually true, and it didn't really matter.

"A son," Trent repeated in obvious shock at such unexpected news. He felt as though he had been thrown from the back of a bull and hit the fence head-on! He looked at Sassy to see her reaction to this news. Her eyes were averted, and her expression was passive. A child with Flossy? He almost fell into his chair.

"Yes, a son. Your child by Flossy," Daisy answered.

Trent stared at Daisy for several moments as though she couldn't be right. Then he took a deep breath.

"Why bring him to me now?" Trent asked, obviously not pleased. The sudden appearance of the boy, of which he had no prior knowledge and with no advanced warning, had come as a bolt from the blue.

"Flossy took sick a few months ago. She finally realized she was not getting any better and asked me, if she should not recover, to bring the boy to his father. She would tell Zack his father was a rich rancher and that you would be proud to have him as your son, Mr. Trent. I have his birth records and information from the First Bank of Abilene, where she left the remainder of her money for her son. It is to be held in trust until he turns eighteen. She said it is now your responsibility to raise him since he is your son, too." Daisy tried to hand the papers to Trent, but when he did not reach out to accept them, she laid them on the edge of his massive desk.

"Where did she get money?"

"From you when you sent her away! I feel it must have been a tidy sum you paid to be rid of her. She never had to work. Oh, after Zack was born, she did start trimming hats for one of the better dress shops, but it was more to fill her time than for needing the money she made," Daisy replied, as though she thought he might be putting on an act in the presence of his wife.

"Once again, you are mistaken in your information. I never gave her anything but the wages she earned!" Trent declared, becoming more annoyed with the obvious lies Flossy had told.

"I only know what she told me, sir!" Daisy answered, expressing her own irritation.

Sassy sat listening to their exchange and knew she should tell Trent to ask Helen about the day Flossy suddenly left the ranch. When she did, she would also be admitting she had lied about what she had overheard and when she had returned to the kitchen. Perhaps it was time to let the truth come to light, she decided.

"Trent, let me get Helen. I believe she can explain what happened the day Flossy left," Sassy said softly as she rose to go get Helen.

Trent looked at Sassy with obvious questions but only nodded his head in consent. Then he stood and said, "I'll go with you and take a look at the boy." He looked out the window at the children playing on the porch. Trent cleared his throat. "He looks like his mother. How would I know for sure he's mine?" Trent walked swiftly to his office before Sassy could comment.

When Helen rolled her chair into the room, Trent repeated the story Flossy had told Daisy and what he had told her in return.

Helen did not blink or hesitate. "I did fire Flossy. Not for neglecting her duties, as I told you at that time, but because she was bragging about how you were going to marry her since she was expecting your child. I knew what kind of woman she was and couldn't bear the thought of you spending the rest of your life saddled with the likes of her," Helen stated with no qualms about what she had done to protect Trent. "Besides, how do we know for sure he is your child? She's the conniving kind that might go sleep with one of the hired hands and pass his child off as yours," Helen left no doubts about what she thought of Flossy.

Trent nodded his head in agreement with what Helen said.

"Yes, I paid her a handsome sum to pack her bag and leave that very day. I told her she better not ever come around here again, or I'd fix it so you wouldn't have anything to do with her, so she better stay away."

Trent looked at his sister, almost in disbelief at what she had done to protect him. He also wondered how Sassy knew he should ask Helen about what really happened that day. She must have heard more than she had told him. Why would she lie about what she knew? He wondered as he tried to make sense of the entire situation.

"If you look at his birth record, you'll see she was telling the truth. Just count the days from the night you spent together until his birth," Daisy said in defense of Flossy.

Then she turned her gaze on Helen. "Flossy died a month ago. That's why I am bringing her and your brother's child to him. She loved little Zack with her entire being, and she was a good mother," Daisy insisted.

Then she turned back to Trent. "She sent a man to tell you about his birth, but the day he arrived, you and the missus were being married. He felt it was not the proper time to tell you that you had a son by another woman. When he told Flossy you were married, she cried for days. You two should be ashamed for the way you treated the poor woman!" Daisy reprimanded Trent and Helen.

"I'm not one bit ashamed of what I did to save my brother from her clutches," Helen stated. Then she abruptly wheeled her chair around and rolled back outside.

Sassy quietly slipped back into the room, closing the door.

Once again, Sassy felt the pangs of guilt. Should she tell about following Flossy to Biggun's room and what he told her about their relationship? Why bring that up? If Zack was born when Daisy said, then she was already carrying Trent's child, so what purpose would it serve to tell more tales? To satisfy her own mind, she picked up the birth record and read Zachery Trent Tatum, September 20, 1901. Place of birth: Abilene, Kansas. The doctor's name on the birth record was William Bloom, M.D.

Sassy quickly added the months and knew it was likely true. The boy was tall for his age. But Trent was a tall man.

She had remained silent, listening, wondering, afraid of the truth. Could she love this child that belonged to Trent and Flossy? She knew she could never love him as she loved her own children. No, but she would try to love him because he was a part of Trent. They would provide a good home for the child. None of this was Zack's fault. She wondered if Trent could love Zack as much as he loved their children. He must, she thought. The past was the past, and somehow, they would deal with its consequences together.

"We'll take care of Zack and give him love and a good home," she heard her own voice quiver as she spoke the words. She hoped the words were true.

It was decided Daisy should stay a few days to give Zack time to adjust to his new family.

That night, when Trent and Sassy were alone in their own haven, he came to her, put his arms around her, and pulled her gently to him.

"Sassy, can you ever forgive me for what I've done? It seems the more I love you and want to protect you from any hurt or harm, I hurt you even more," he spoke softly as he breathed in the fresh scent of her.

If her love for him died because of his failures, life would hold little meaning for him. He would have his children to love and care for, but the rest of his life would forever be like the miles and miles of empty prairie—dull, barren, unfulfilled. The thought of such an existence terrified him. What if her next words were words of disgust or even hate? If she sent him away, they would merely exist under the same roof. For the first time in a very long time, perhaps since the night he prayed for them to survive the tornado, he prayed for his beloved wife and for God to forgive him.

Sassy stood for a long while with Trent's familiar arms holding her. He was a strong man, a passionate man, and an ardent lover. She had never doubted his love for her, but now would he think of Flossy each time he looked at Zack? Would he remember the night they had spent together fulfilling their lustful passions? She couldn't keep from wondering. That thought made her want to weep. Had she lost some of her feelings of love, her fervent belief in his love for her, and her complete trust in her husband today? Sassy continued to think about her new doubts.

"Trent, I need some time to sort out my feelings. I can't answer your question yet. I, too, am guilty in this matter. I lied to you about what I overheard the day Helen fired Flossy. I have known all along she claimed to be carrying your child and how she would make you marry her. I should have told you long ago, but I didn't. I was glad when she was gone. I was already falling in love with you and was afraid I would have to endure knowing you belonged to her. I'm sorry, too, Trent. I finally told Helen what I knew and that I had lied to you." Sassy gave a short laugh. "Helen told me to keep quiet and then said something about what tangled webs we weave through our lies, and she was right."

Trent slowly let his arms fall to his sides. "Do you want me to move to another room?" he asked softly, but she could hear the hurt reflected in his question.

She hesitated, then answered. "We can share the same bed, but not as husband and wife just yet."

Trent let out a long breath. "I'm truly sorry, Sassy, for all the times I have let you down. You had the notion you didn't deserve me because I was better educated and wealthy, but I am the one who doesn't deserve you. The lie you told was also to protect me, just like what Helen did was for the same purpose. It might not have been right, but it was because both of you cared, and that certainly gains my forgiveness if any is needed."

Sassy looked at him as a tear rolled down her cheek. "Thank you, Trent," she whispered softly and turned away.

For nine long nights, they lay side by side, not touching, scarcely talking as they had always done. Sassy realized this could not go on any longer. She had to accept the situation and tell Trent she had also forgiven him. After all, it wasn't as though he had ever been unfaithful to her, and she felt fairly certain he never loved Flossy. If he had, why would he have refused her after that one night when she was apparently willing to continue their affair?

On the tenth night, when they lay in their bed with what seemed like a mile between them, she turned to face Trent, reached out, and laid her hand on Trent's chest over his beating heart.

He did not speak but placed his hand on top of hers and gently caressed it.

"Trent, I forgive any transgressions you have made. I cannot go on without knowing you still love me and desire me as your wife. I love you beyond life itself and certainly want us to live together as a husband and wife should live. There is one thing I must ask you. Do you think of the night you spent with Flossy when you look at Zack?"

"No!"

Trent did not speak further but pulled her to him and kissed her with the eagerness of a young lover. Their passion rekindled, reuniting them and restoring them to the satisfying life they had shared.

The subject of Zack's birth mother was rarely mentioned.

Trent's love for Zack grew. He was a lovable child and fit well into their family.

Sassy tried to love Zack. She treated him well and knew she could never purposely hurt the boy. But every time she looked at Zack, she saw Flossy. His mother had been a beautiful woman, and Zack was a handsome and adoring child. No matter how hard she tried, Sassy could not love him as she thought she should. She prayed for the love to come. Sadly, it never fully came to fill her heart as she desired. Sassy felt downhearted that she could not love Trent's other child. It weighed heavily on her heart.

Chapter Thirty

In June, Angel arrived in a flurry of excitement. She brought gifts from the city for the children, including Zack. She had just learned about him a few days before her departure. She also brought gifts for the adults, including Biggun. Angel had always viewed him as a favorite uncle.

Angel was more beautiful than ever. Now, she was a mature woman, not just a teenage girl. The ranch hands followed her every move with adoring glances and leers of lust. Trent kept a close watch on each man who came within shouting distance of his youngest sister.

"My, oh my, he's like a bear protecting its cub when it comes to Angel," Helen laughed as she looked out the window one afternoon. "All of those cowboys better content themselves with trips to town Saturday nights because my brother isn't going to let one of them close to his little sister, who isn't his little sister anymore." She chuckled with amusement.

"Well, Angel may get tired of his overbearing interference and do as she pleases if she finds one of those men attractive enough," Sassy replied as she joined Helen at the window.

"That's what I'm afraid of, and then there will be hell to pay when Trent finds out. She doesn't belong stuck out here, miles from town. I don't know why she wanted to come home to stay after living in the city most of her life."

"Maybe she missed her family more than you or Trent realize," Sassy suggested.

"I suppose," Helen agreed. "She'll likely tire before long of being isolated from all the things she's accustomed to enjoying and go back to Philadelphia. I certainly wouldn't blame her. If she does stay, it will be nice to have her help when school starts." Helen sighed.

One morning in late July, Sassy and Trent sat on the front porch enjoying their morning coffee as the early rays of dawn spread their golden light.

Trent looked toward the road and, in the distance, could make out the figure of a lone rider.

"Looks like another cowboy headed this way looking for work," he commented as the figure drew nearer.

"Do you have work for another one?" Sassy asked as she, too, watched the approaching rider. "He must have been riding most of the night," she remarked, feeling sorry for the man who must be tired and hungry.

"I believe Sonny said they need some help at the west headquarters, so I'll send him on over there unless one of the other men wants to move."

"From the looks of his clothes, he does seem a bit down on his luck," Sassy ventured as the man stopped outside the gate.

The rider dismounted and walked to the bottom of the steps as he gazed at the couple on the porch. Trent rose to greet the man. Before he could say anything, the stranger started up the steps. Trent stood with his feet slightly apart, giving the impression the stranger was about to intrude where he didn't belong.

The man stopped about halfway up the steps. He pushed his hat back as he tilted his head so he could peer around Trent to get a good look at Sassy. Then he gave her a grin of recognition. "Good morning, sister," he said with a big grin.

Sassy felt as though she had been struck by lightning. The morning had brightened, and she could plainly see the man's handsome features and felt as though she were looking at a younger version of her pa. She put her hands to her mouth and let out a cry of sheer joy. She quickly rose and came to stand beside Trent.

"Nathan, Nathan, is that really you?" she asked in disbelief.

"In the flesh," he answered with that cocky grin and devilish glint in his smoky-blue eyes.

Sassy almost jumped down the steps and into his arms. They hugged and laughed with sheer joy as she covered his face with kisses. Tears of relief and happiness ran down her cheeks. All she could manage to do was repeat his name over and over as though she still couldn't believe it was really her lost brother come home.

"Oh, Nathan, I've prayed every day for this day to come, and now, it's really here, it's really here!" she almost shouted.

"Yes, sister, it's really here," he assured her as they continued to hug one another. It was as though their bliss might erase the lost years and put his past to rest, he thought, but he knew it would take far more than a few hugs to put his troubled past to rest.

Trent watched the pair and was thankful his wife's years of worry and deep sadness were finally over. Her family was complete. Their family was complete.

By late afternoon, word had spread about the miraculous return of Sassy's lost brother. A pig and cow had been butchered and were roasting on the spit. The kitchen was in a whirl of activity as they prepared the rest of the feast. Word had been sent to the west headquarters for the ranch hands to come join in the celebration.

Trent watched Sassy. She seemed to be floating on air as she took Nathan all around the ranch, introducing him to his niece and nephews, the rest of the family, the hired hands, and talking nonstop. Timothy and Martha were almost as excited as Sassy about their brother's return. Biggun went to town for some supplies and sent a telegram to Daniel to let him know about Nathan's unexpected return.

Trent was happy for his wife and hoped the euphoria would last. However, as Trent observed Nathan, he could see hardness in the young man that he had never seen in anyone his age. He had seen it in some of the older cowboys that had led rough lives. Nathan was likely about seventeen or maybe eighteen by now. Trent was anxious for some time alone with him to find out exactly where he had been and to learn the kind of life that had been forced on him. That bit of information would let him know what to expect in the future once the newness of his return had worn off.

~

Nathan was given a few days to rest and enjoy being reunited with his family. Daniel arrived two days later, and the celebration continued.

The next Monday morning, at breakfast, after several days of celebrating and visiting, Trent told Sassy it was time for Nathan to start working just like everyone else at the ranch. She was not especially pleased with his decision but knew it was only fair. Timothy worked every day alongside the other men, and Martha helped in the house with the cleaning and other household chores.

"I'll wake him in a bit and tell him to come find you," Sassy reluctantly agreed.

"Good morning," Nathan greeted them as he entered the dining room.

"Oh, good morning. I was about to come wake you. Trent needs you to start working today," she said pleasantly, as though he would be doing them a favor.

"That so. Well, I had in mind to ride into town and spend a few days kicking up my heels before settling down to a job. Besides, I might look around in town for a job. I've been stuck way out on a ranch most of my life and would like to see how other folks live," he said with a mirthful chuckle.

"That's fine, Nathan," Trent answered before Sassy could protest such an idea. "But if you come back here, you're expected to put in a full day's work just like everyone else. You'll live in the bunkhouse with the other men since you aren't still in school."

Nathan let out a snort of laughter. "I ain't never been in school since I left the orphans' home. That old bas—brute I worked for never sent any of us to school. Now, I ain't good enough to live in your big fancy house, either," he accused with a sneer.

Sassy caught her breath. They had been so busy savoring his return that she had not thought to ask about the kind of life that had been forced on him while he was still so young.

Trent instantly regretted he hadn't pushed for that talk he had wanted to have with the young man. He had a foreboding feeling they were about to hear a very brutal story.

"Where were you, Nathan?" Sassy asked. "We searched all along where the train had put children off for adoption, and Two-Toes even went back to that one place." She turned to Trent, "What was the man's name?"

Before Trent could answer, Nathan supplied the name.

"B. B. Branson, the Triple B Ranch," he answered with obvious revulsion and a look of absolute hatred on his face.

"Yes, that was it. Biggun and Two-Toes, he's an Indian who had been a scout for the army for many years, went there. But Branson told them you had run away while he and two of his ranch hands were buying supplies. Two-Toes didn't believe him and went back. He spent a week or more searching for you but never found you. He was a sad man when he came back without you. He said he had only failed to find two men and you in his many years of being a tracker, but it hurt him deeply when he couldn't find you. Where were they hiding you?" Sassy asked, obviously puzzled.

"Injin, that was what I heard Branson calling somebody, but I didn't know who he was talking about. I heard Biggun talking, but I didn't know Injin. I was there that day, lying in the hayloft. Jessie was pinning me down, holding a knife to my throat. That sorry little sh—well, he would have killed me if I'd made the slightest noise. I guess Branson was afraid they might come back, so he sent me off to a line shack for a couple of weeks. They wouldn't even let me go outside to pee. Then, I guess he decided no one was coming back, so my life in hell went on and on, ever damn day until the day I killed that sorry old bastard and rode off!" He finished with a wicked, uncaring laugh as he glared at Trent and his sister.

Sassy gasped at the horror of what Nathan had just told them but more at the thought of him killing a man, even an apparently horrible man. If only he had tried to find a way to escape without killing anyone, she thought in despair.

Trent stared at Nathan. "I don't believe your sister or anyone else needs to hear that kind of talk except me."

Trent rose to leave the table, expecting Nathan to follow him to his office.

Nathan remained seated. "You ain't no priest I need to confess my sins to, and it ain't none of your damned business anyway," Nathan snarled at Trent.

"I am married to your sister, and I will protect her from you or anyone else who tries to hurt her. Make no mistake about that. You can talk to me or not, but while you are here, don't you ever tell her anything else that will upset her. She has worried over you for eight long years. We tried our best to find you, just like the others. I'm sad to say we failed, but you have no reason to take out your bitterness on your sister. Take it out on me. I was the one who persuaded her to put you children in the orphans' home, thinking it was for the best."

Trent clearly saw Nathan's rage as he glared at Trent with his piercing blue eyes.

Nathan rose and threw his napkin on his plate as he kicked his chair backward. It crashed into the wall with a loud bang. "Go to the devil, Trent Sanderson!" he scoffed, not holding back his bitterness. He brushed past Trent and was gone.

Sassy burst into tears.

Chapter Thirty-One

Six days later, Trent rode to town on business.

He happened to run into Marshal Wade Nelson coming out of the bank. He was a formidable man in his mid-forties with coal-black hair and black eyes that seemed to pierce right through to a man's core.

Marshal Nelson extended his hand as he greeted Trent. "Trent, I have your brother-in-law in the lock-up. He's one mean SOB," Wade said with a shake of his head. "He got rip-snortin' drunk, tore up the Golden Nugget to the tune of about three hundred dollars, and abused two of the women pretty bad before me and Deputy Long could corner him. You can bail him out and pay his damages or let him rot in jail. That's likely the best place for his sort," the marshal concluded as he spat a stream of tobacco juice in the street.

Trent ran his hand over his chin as he considered the best way to handle the matter.

"He's just come back to see his family. My wife has grieved over him for eight years, and if she finds out about this, it will break her heart again. I don't know if I can handle him or not, unless I knock him in the head, but I'm willing to give it a try," Trent said with a short laugh. "Apparently, he's been living in pretty much of a hell hole and don't likely know how to act around civilized folks," Trent said, trying to explain the reason for Nathan's dreadful behavior. "I don't believe he knows how to care about anyone but himself. That seems to be the way he survived all these years."

"Well, that's a sad thing to happen to a kid, but if he comes back to town, he better have learned some manners first. You know I don't put up with that kind of nonsense out of nobody." The marshal was adamant in his answer.

"I know," Trent answered. "I'll come get him when I start back to the ranch."

On the ride back to the ranch, Trent laid down the law to Nathan. "You are in a different place and with different people than you've been around, so you better learn how to behave accordingly. I won't have your sister being upset any further by your behavior. I don't give a damn if you like me or hate me, but you will treat me as your employer and brother-in-law, with due respect."

"Respect," Nathan half jeered. "I hardly know the meaning of that word. The kind of respect I'm used to was a kick in the teeth if I didn't do whatever the old man or Jessie demanded. I watched Jessie get swept away by the current when the creek flooded and laughed in his face when he begged me to save his sorry ass." Nathan half laughed. "He got what he deserved, and now, he's likely burnin' in hell for all his meanness. He was meaner than a rattlesnake and enjoyed every lowdown thing he done," Nathan stated with a deep-seated bitterness.

Trent momentarily reined in at the creek to let the horses drink.

"Why did you kill Branson? Surely not just to get away," Trent asked, since Nathan seemed in a talkative mood. He hoped if he could piece together what all had happened to Nathan, then maybe he could figure out a way to help the boy deal with and overcome his seemingly pathetic past. Trent glanced at Nathan before he spoke and thought: *No, he isn't a boy. He's a hardened, bitter young man.*

"He was cursing me and pulled a knife on me when I told him I was too damn sick to get out of bed to work. I picked up my pistol and shot the sorry bastard right in the face to shut him up. I felt just as happy to see him die as I did the day Jessie got washed away by the flood. Then, I drug myself to the barn, saddled the best horse there, and rode off knowin' it would be hours before anybody would find him. I should've stuck around. They would of likely give me a big party for gettin' rid of the sorry old buzzard." Nathan laughed. It was the most wicked, malicious, uncaring laugh Trent had ever witnessed.

"Why hadn't you left earlier if you carried a gun?" Trent asked, a bit puzzled by Nathan's story.

"He was a cagey old cuss. He'd pit us against each other, so if I'd tried, somebody would've stopped me," he sneered. Then, he actually looked sad. "The only person there I could've trusted to help me got stabbed by one of Brandon's snitches. Toby only lived a few hours. 'Tweren't nothin' I could do to help him. So, after that, I was all on my own," he paused. "All of us was took from the orphans' train and never had a chance in hell after that." He looked at Trent and gave his devil-may-care laugh, "Now, ain't that a hell of a story?"

Trent felt bad for what Nathan had gone through but needed to convince him things were very different now and this was his chance at a far better life. "Nathan, it's for sure you drew a sorry lot in life. But now is your chance to turn things around."

"Yeah, like I'm really gonna become a gentleman rancher like you, with a sweet little wife and family," he mocked.

Trent studied the young man for quite a spell. He could plainly see the hate and resentment reflected in everything about him. His face, his voice, and his movements told the story of years of pent-up hatred.

At last, Trent spoke. "What would it take to make you happy, make you feel like you have a chance at a better life?"

Nathan looked at Trent and sized up the situation that might just work to his advantage. "Well, how about twenty-five thousand dollars for a start?"

"What would you do with that kind of money?"

Nathan removed his hat. He ran his hand through his matted blond hair and over the whiskers that had grown during his stay in jail. "Well, I think I'd head out west, buy a piece of property, and raise fine horses," he said in a more serious tone than he really felt. He knew that wasn't likely what he'd do at all. He'd have a high old-time drinking, chasing women, and gambling until every last cent was gone. Then, he could come back with some hard-luck story and tap the well for more. He almost laughed out loud, but knew better than to tip his hand.

Trent studied him some more. His gut feeling was that Nathan was lying through his teeth.

"I'll tell you what I'll do. You work for six months, behave like you should, cause your sister or nobody else any trouble, and I'll stake you to that twenty-five thousand dollars," Trent said as he continued to study Nathan's reaction.

Nathan grinned, "Well, well, brother-in-law. You surprise me, but you just cost yourself twenty-five thousand dollars," he said with a self-satisfied laugh, thinking what a fool Trent really was to believe that story.

Trent straightened in the saddle and lightly spurred his horse. "Don't misjudge my generosity. That is all you will ever get, so don't think you can come back broke and wheedle more out of me. You won't even get a job on the Flatland Ranch," he said with a bigger smile to let Nathan know exactly what he expected him to do.

Nathan did move to the bunkhouse, and, much to Trent's surprise, he was a top-notch cowboy. His stamina for long hours of hard work was unsurpassed. He would have dinner with the family most evenings and managed to act civil. Trent did notice he often managed to sit next to Angel, and the two seemed to enjoy one another's company. Trent saw to it that was as far as their contact went. He still didn't trust Nathan. Trent thought Angel might be too innocent to recognize the kind of man he really was.

Chapter Thirty-Two

School started in mid-September, with Helen teaching the first through fourth grades and Angel teaching fifth through eighth grades. Nineteen students belonged to the ranch families, and Zack made twenty students to start school.

Zack was a good student, and Helen often praised him to Sassy. Sassy liked the boy. He was polite and never gave her or Trent any trouble, yet she still did not feel the love she had hoped would come in time. When she looked at Zack, she saw Flossy. At times, she would study the boy, trying to recognize some of Trent's features, but for the life of her, all she saw was his strong resemblance to his mother. It made her sad to not feel the love she knew she should feel for Trent's child.

Once word had gotten around that there was a school at the ranch, more married men were willing to go to work for Trent. He liked having the married hands as they were more settled and more likely to stay on.

The family was still somewhat amazed that Angel had remained at the ranch. However, she seemed to have adjusted quite well to the quieter life with occasional trips into Amarillo for shopping. There, she would attend some special event or party where she could have her pick of eligible young men from the best families. Thus far, the only problem seemed to be she apparently didn't want to pick any of those men for a prospective husband.

Nathan was a handsome young man with sun-streaked blond hair and a summer tan that enhanced the color of his smoky-blue eyes that often twinkled with mischief as he mildly teased and flirted with Angel. He could turn on the charm when it suited him. Apparently, it suited him, especially when he was out of sight of the family.

Helen debated about mentioning the situation to Trent but hesitated. She had not seen any inappropriate overtures from Nathan toward Angel. She would just continue to keep her eye on their relationship and say nothing unless their friendship seemed to become more than just friendship.

One Saturday afternoon in October, Angel took a meandering walk that eventually led her to the creek where they swam in the summer. She sat beneath a shade tree, enjoying the light, cool breeze as she read poetry from one of her favorite books she had brought with her.

After a time, she became so relaxed that she began to feel drowsy. She leaned her head against the broad tree trunk, closed her eyes, and soon dozed lightly.

Warmth seemed to surround her. Unyielding lips were firmly pressed against her slightly open mouth. Startled, her eyes sprang open as she met the ardent gaze of cold blue eyes that seemed to darken with burning desire. His lips pressed firmer as his tongue darted into her mouth, caressing her tongue and sending waves of shock throughout her body. He roughly groped her full breasts and tried to ram his hand down the front of her dress. Several eager young men had courted her when she lived in Philadelphia, but none had ever kissed or touched her in such a forward manner.

In the past, she had flirted with many men and done some heavy spooning, but none of that compared to the brazen, unwanted attention this man was forcing on her. She tried to push him away for behaving in such a forward manner, but the harder she tried to thwart his advances, the more adamant he became.

"Stop fighting me, or I'll slap you," he growled as he lifted her skirt.

"Stop! Stop!" she pleaded as she tried to push his groping hands away.

"Shut up!" he snarled as he yanked her away from the tree, shoving her so she was lying flat on the ground. "I'm gonna have you one way or the other," he groaned as he pushed her skirt and petticoats over her head to pin her arms so she couldn't fight him. He looked with sheer lust at her shapely legs as he yanked fiercely at her bloomers.

She flailed her legs, trying to kick him. Utter panic set in when she realized he was struggling to unfasten his pants.

He quickly slapped her legs so hard the throbbing sting made her cry out in pain. She tried again to kick him, but he hit her even harder, making her legs go limp in excruciating agony.

"No!" she begged. How could he do this to her, she wondered as she endured the torture he inflicted.

She let out a cry of pain and shame when he took her with brutal force. Seconds later, she endured his cry of pleasure. Tears stung her eyes, knowing she had been ruined for any decent man.

She lay still, wondering what he would do next. It didn't take long to find out how low of a man he really was.

He rolled off her and yanked her skirt and petticoats down from covering her face. He stood and stared down at her tear-streaked face.

"Don't think you'll run home to tell your brother what happened 'cause if you do, you'll be sorry," he threatened, showing no remorse for what he had just done.

She looked up, not seeing his face clearly, for the sun behind him cast it in shadow. "Trent will kill you," she hissed.

"Well, now, it would be a real shame for somethin' bad to happen to one of those sweet little nieces or nephews you seem to dote on," he said with a wicked chuckle.

Angel gasped at the horrifying thought of what a man like him might do to one of the children.

He laughed when he saw the look of shock in her eyes. "Yes sir, not long ago, late one night, I walked right up the front steps of the big house, up the stairs to the second floor, turned left, opened the door to the nursery, walked over to the little girl's crib, and just watched her sleep," he paused to see her reaction.

Angel sucked in her breath and unknowingly put her hand over her heart.

"Yes, sirree, it would be a real shame, so you better keep your mouth shut!" he said as he turned and walked unhurriedly toward his horse.

Angel covered her face with her hands and wished to die, but she knew she would never tell anyone about what had happened beside the creek. His secret was safe with her.

Ten days later, Angel became concerned when her monthly cycle did not occur. She prayed she would start soon. The days dragged by with no monthly sickness. As much as she had always detested it before, now it would be a welcome sign. She could go on as usual and not tell anyone what had happened. Her constant fear was of the threat he had made toward the children. What if he did something to one of them after all, even if she didn't tell her ugly secret? Then she would blame herself for not telling Trent. What if she did tell Trent and, somehow, he found out. She knew beyond a doubt Trent would fly into a murderous rage and kill the man, no matter who he was. That would cause such havoc she couldn't even begin to imagine the far-reaching consequences.

Angel rarely went out for walks anymore. When she did venture out, she stayed close to headquarters for fear he might catch her alone again and repeat what he had done before. Her sleep was fitful, although she always placed a chair in front of her door and propped it so it would fall over if anyone opened the door. Even that gave her little comfort.

November came, and there was no monthly cycle again. Angel was certain she was carrying a child but knew she could not confide in anyone. She was grateful she rarely felt nauseated and never enough to throw up like she had heard many pregnant women did. If she suddenly decided to go back east, they would expect her to return to Philadelphia. That would never do. Her aunt would soon know her plight. If she went anywhere else, they might be too suspicious. Angel constantly fretted over the situation and knew she had to soon devise some plausible plan to leave the ranch.

Eventually, she remembered a girl from school who came from a rather poor family. They had never been close friends, but her classmate was always friendly. *She might be willing to help me if I give her some money,* she thought. Angel was willing to give her everything she owned if she would help her out of this unbearable situation.

Angel immediately wrote a pleading letter to Mary Bostwick of Pier Point, South Carolina. She offered a generous amount of money for lodgings and suggested a plausible story for Mary and her family about her friend from Texas whose husband had been killed in a cattle stampede. She portrayed herself as a young woman distraught since she had just discovered they were expecting their first child and needed desperately to get away from the awful reminders of her loss. Her reason for not going to her aunt or other school friends was that they, too, would be a constant reminder of her loss since they had all met her husband when they traveled to Texas for their wedding. She desperately needed a change, a quiet place to wait for the birth of her child. Angel had already decided, once the child was born, she would go to some big city and give it up for adoption. Angel could not imagine wanting to raise a child conceived in such a despicable manner. She sealed the envelope with a prayer that Mary would give her the help she so desperately needed. Then she waited anxiously for Mary's reply.

She could leave just after Christmas. If she left before, Trent would suspect something, but if she delayed any longer, her condition might start to become obvious. She would tell her family Mary had just recently been widowed, as her husband had drowned in a boating accident just after she had learned she was expecting their first child. The poor young woman desperately needed her dear friend Angel to come and console her during this difficult time. Yes, this would be the perfect solution, she decided with self-satisfaction at her fabricated stories.

Chapter Thirty-Three

T rent had caught a cold when a sudden icy blast of wind blew in, carrying with it drenching, frigid rain. He had been working on a distant part of the ranch and was freezing by the time he got home.

Sassy had insisted he stay inside for a few days and not take a chance on getting worse, with Thanksgiving only a few days away. They were expecting Daniel and the Smyth family to spend the holiday with them this year.

Trent was working in his office when Biggun came in with several letters he had picked up while in town for supplies.

Trent slit each envelope with the pearl-handled letter opener that had belonged to his father. He withdrew a letter and began to read it when he suddenly realized it was addressed to Angel. His eyes were riveted to the words, and he could not force himself to return the letter to the envelope unread. A slight pang of guilt nagged at his conscience as he continued to read. Then his ire rose and rose to a full-blown fury. Bile seemed to bubble up and fill his throat and mouth with an acrid taste. When he finished the disturbing letter, he rose and stalked down the hallway in search of Angel.

He found her in the kitchen helping the cook prepare to bake pecan pies.

"Angel!" He almost shouted, making the two women jump.

He held up the letter and gave a quick jerk of his head in the direction of his office. "Come with me!"

Angel felt her stomach tighten, and a foreboding dread warned her that Trent had found her out.

She walked meekly behind him, trying desperately to think how to defend herself while refusing to tell him who was the father of her baby. She couldn't take the chance to tell her dear brother the father's name, and that would drive him crazy. He would have no choice but to let her leave to avoid a huge scandal that would not only ruin her reputation but would also reflect poorly on the entire family. That was her only leverage in this matter, and she intended to use it and anything else she could think of to her advantage. He could threaten all sorts of things, but he really couldn't force her to say anything, she decided as she entered his office and closed the door.

"Explain this!" he yelled as he waved the letter before her.

"If you let me read what it says, perhaps I can explain whatever it is you don't seem to understand," she said as though it were some innocent matter that needed clarification.

Trent flung the letter in her direction, and it fell to the floor at her feet.

"Don't you dare act so innocent with me! It's obvious from that letter you are no longer innocent or a virgin, as you should be until you're married," he bellowed, as his face grew red with rage.

Angel leaned forward and placed both hands on the desk. They were staring eye-to-eye across the massive piece of furniture but close enough to feel the other's heated breath. "No, dear brother, I am no longer innocent or a virgin. I suppose I took after you when it came to controlling my lustful desires," she hissed in a mocking tone. Inside, she was quivering and hated herself for saying such a hurtful thing, but she knew she must.

Trent slapped her face with a stinging blow. "Don't you dare ever talk to me in that tone of voice again. You have disgraced yourself and this family!" he shouted loud enough that anyone nearby could have heard him, even with the door closed.

Angel rubbed her stinging cheek with a quivering hand. "I will never tell you who the father is, even if you beat me to death. All you can do is let me go visit Mary and give the baby away at birth," she stated almost too calmly.

"Mary doesn't want you. Even your money can't buy a poor girl's respect," he said through gritted teeth as he sat heavily in his chair.

"Sit down," he demanded.

Angel sat with her rigid back not touching the plush chair.

"Now, tell me who got you in this condition."

"No! I won't tell you or anyone else," she vowed stubbornly.

"You will marry the man! If you thought enough of him to let him bed you before marriage, then you will marry the man!" Trent stated emphatically.

Angel laughed. "Oh, he didn't bed me, as you put it. He took me down by the creek in broad daylight!" Angel fought to maintain her haughty demeanor. She knew she had to play the part to protect the children.

"How dare you act like a common trollop! Give me the man's name, now!" Trent demanded, still outraged.

"No, I will not!"

Trent sat for several long moments with the fingers of his open hands pressed together at the tips as he thought about the damned mess his younger sister had created. He was finding it hard to believe her willful resistance to telling him the name of the man involved.

Finally, he spoke. "Well, then, I will find a man to marry you. A paid husband you will be stuck with for the rest of your miserable life," he threatened.

"I will refuse to marry anyone I don't choose," she insisted.

"Then, you better choose in a hurry whether he is the father or not. You will not go away to have this child and give it to strangers. You will marry immediately. Now, dear sister, who is your choice?"

Angel looked at him with as much defiance as she could muster, knowing she had to bluff her way through this agonizing conversation. Then it came to her. She only had to choose the most unlikely candidate, and maybe Trent would back off. "I choose Biggun!"

Trent looked shocked, as though she had struck him.

"No! You won't do this to him. He is a friend and a damn decent man. I won't let you ruin his life!" Trent glared at her.

"It's Biggun or no one," she said coldly.

Trent slowly stood, placed his hands on his hips, took several steps, and turned to face Angel. "I believe I'll go have a talk with Billy Green."

Angel shot to her feet. "No, no, you wouldn't dare try to make me marry that ugly, foul-smelling, ignorant cowboy!" she protested as her eyes grew huge, and she looked like a colt about to bolt.

"Well then, perhaps the handsome Nathan McCoy would be more to your liking. He is at least good-looking to go along with foul-smelling, ignorant cowboy."

A moment of panic seized Angel. Perhaps he was just fishing for a name and watching her for a reaction as he threw out different names.

"Leave me alone! Just let me go away. I'll just tell the family I'm going to see my friend, Mary. No one will ever find out the truth."

Trent walked around the desk and leaned down within inches of her face. "If I ever find out the truth, he will most assuredly be a dead man!"

"Why? He didn't force me. Like I said, maybe I take after you, dear brother. After all, you fathered a bastard!" she haughtily accused as she stared back at her brother.

Angel rushed out of the office. She ran up the stairs to the safety of her room. She slammed the door, fell across her bed, and buried her face in her pillow to cry and cry for hurting her brother.

After Thanksgiving lunch, Angel put on her coat and walked out to the back porch for a breath of fresh air. Her nerves were on edge. She needed to get away from the hullabaloo inside. Too many questions were being asked about her upcoming trip after Christmas. She was afraid one slip of the tongue might give something away to raise their suspicions. Trent had finally grudgingly agreed to go along with her story about going to see a former classmate expecting her first child. The distraught woman had recently lost her husband. Angel didn't want to take a chance on giving anything away to make the others question her story.

"Well, well, you've pulled this off without a hitch," came Nathan's jeering remark as he joined her. "Going back east to help a dear friend is so noble!" he scoffed.

"I've done what you said and not told anyone about what happened at the creek. Now leave me alone!" she snapped and turned her back to continue her walk.

"Good girl. I ride by the creek ever so often, hoping to find you snoozing under the tree, but—"

"Shut up, you fool. I'm warning you, if Trent ever finds out it was you, it won't matter that he's married to your sister, he will kill you!" she warned him, but said it while smiling in case someone was looking out the window.

Nathan's look changed to somber. "Just let him try. I've already killed two men and won't hesitate to kill a third, even my sister's husband!"

Angel looked at him in shock.

Nathan laughed at the fright he saw reflected in her eyes and on her pretty face. "Oh yes, my dear lover, you are carrying the child of one mean son of a—"

His words were cut short when unexpectedly Trent grabbed him from behind, slamming him against the wall the house.

"You!" he yelled. "I will kill your sorry, rotten hide for what you've done to my sister," Trent shouted as he banged Nathan's head against the rock wall.

Instantly, Trent felt the tip of a knife blade at his throat and saw the cold, murderous look on Nathan's face.

Jessie's face flashed through Nathan's mind. He could almost feel the point of Jessie's knife at his own throat. How easy it would be to just give it a little shove and see Trent Sanderson die, he thought with no feelings of guilt.

Nathan let out a mirthful, sneering laugh. "Yeah, I'm the one that done it to her, and she liked it!"

"That's a lie! You know you forced yourself on me. I tried to fight you off, but I couldn't!" Angel sobbed.

"It don't matter anyhow 'cause I'm gonna kill your high and mighty brother!" Nathan vowed.

"Please, stop, both of you! Trent, please, please let him go. I don't want a scandal. Please, just let him go!" Angel begged.

Nathan laughed. "Yeah, Trent. If people find out and I get arrested, who do you think a jury would believe? The poor, missing, mistreated boy or the spoiled rich girl?"

Trent's eyes flickered.

Nathan was certain he had seen a spark of doubt in the man's eyes. The two men seemed to tighten their grip on each other.

Angel let out a scream that brought several people running to the back porch, but they stopped short when they saw Trent and Nathan locked in a stand-off and the point of Nathan's knife at Trent's throat.

"I have a pistol in my pocket, and it is pointed right at your gut," Trent snarled as he pressed the barrel against Nathan's stomach. "We may well kill each other this day, but it will give me great satisfaction to know you'll burn in hell for eternity," Trent threatened through clenched teeth.

Nathan gave a snorting laugh. "We'll see whose damn sorry-ass soul gets there first!"

"No, you won't!"

They all heard Sassy's slightly quivering voice. The few words she spoke carried such strength that both men realized they were spoken with authority.

"Nathan, I have a gun pointed straight at your head. I won't hesitate to pull the trigger if you put one mark on my husband. Drop that knife. Now!" There was no doubt where her loyalties lay, and her words were no idle threat.

Nathan stood stark still, weighing his options. Was it worth his life to kill the mighty Trent Sanderson? Yes, the great Trent Sanderson, the man who rescued his brothers and younger sister but failed him. The man who married his older sister and gave them all an easy life while he lived in hell for eight long years. No, he had lots of living to do. Besides, someday, his chance to even the score just might come again. At least he had inflicted some pain on the Sandersons by what he had done to Angel, and he reveled in that knowledge. Nathan let the knife drop. It hit the stone porch with a loud clatter.

"Go to hell!" Nathan shouted. "All of you go to hell." He let his heated gaze, full of hatred, penetrate each one as he turned and slowly walked toward the barn to get his horse.

"Please, let him go!" Angel pleaded. "I—I can't go through the disgrace his trial would bring. Please let him go!" Angel begged.

Trent slowly nodded his head.

Sassy handed the gun she held to Ely. He and Biggun followed Nathan to make certain Nathan left the ranch. In fact, they escorted him into town, bought a ticket on the next westbound train, and personally escorted him aboard.

Sassy walked to her husband with tears of relief glistening in her blue eyes that still intrigued him after all these years. She put her arms around him and rested her cheek against his chest, listening with contentment to the strong beat of his heart. Trent rested his chin on the top of her head and held her close. They did not need to exchange words. The tenderness they shared as they clung to one another said far more than words.

Chapter Thirty-Four

During the years after Nathan left the ranch, Sassy often wondered what had become of her brother. At times, she still shed a few tears over his loss. After Angel told them about Nathan's threat against the children if she told them what he had done, Sassy knew she didn't want him to return. She would be too afraid to have him at the ranch even if he begged for forgiveness. She wondered if he might be in prison or dead, knowing his temperament and disregard for others. Despite everything that had happened, feelings of guilt for the way he turned out still plagued her.

Angel's plight also bothered her. Poor Angel had been an innocent victim caught up in Nathan's lust, rage, and hate. She had traveled east to a city where she was unknown and entered a Catholic home for unwed mothers. After much anguish over her situation, she finally gave her baby girl up for adoption. When she was able to travel, she went back to live with her aunt in Philadelphia, where she re-entered society. A year later, she married a previous suitor, and Sassy felt certain from the tone of her letters it had become a satisfying marriage filled with love.

She often wondered if Nathan had gone to the war like Timothy and many of the ranch hands had done. Six of the cowboys went, and two did not come back after the war. One of those killed left a widow with several children. Thankfully, Timothy came home physically uninjured, but she could sense a change in him. Some of the men were greatly affected by the awful experiences they had endured. They did not speak of it but were supportive of one another, and, in time, most learned to deal with the terrible memories.

Everyone left at the ranch worked even harder to make up for those off fighting for their country. A few drifters worked on and off, and the ranch survived.

Chapter Thirty-Five

Sassy tried to be content raising her own three children and Zack. To her own sorrow, she still could not love Zack. She had prayed and tried to convince herself that she loved the boy, but deep in her heart, she knew she did not possess the feelings she should have felt for Trent's child by Flossy. This puzzled her since he was a caring child, always respectful and obedient. He adored his father and younger half-siblings. Sassy had to admit that every time she looked at Zack, she still saw the likeness of his mother and could not let go of the jealous feelings she had toward Flossy, the woman who had wooed Trent to her bed and bore his firstborn child.

Trent loved every one of his children equally. When he looked at Zack, he did not immediately think of Flossy and how she had seduced him. He could not totally blame her for what had happened. He was a grown man and knew the possible consequences. It was just one of those unfortunate circumstances that occurred in life, and he certainly would never blame Zack or hold the circumstances of his birth against the boy.

The ranch prospered through the years. Harsh summers with little rain made it hard at times to maintain their large herds of cattle. Trent implemented a supplementary feed program by designating several areas on the ranch near the flowing creeks for raising feed crops to supplement the sparse grass in dry years.

Now, the family enjoyed the convenience and comfort of owning an automobile for more frequent trips to town. Both families often enjoyed Sunday trips to attend church. Trent had also purchased several farm trucks to help lighten the workload for the ranch hands. That addition had speeded up the time it took to do the chores for the cowboys and filled in the gaps while so many of the men were fighting in the war.

One truck was assigned strictly to Biggun. Trent laughed every time he saw Biggun driving. He drove it more like he was herding cattle with a horse than just driving from one part of the ranch to another.

Sonny Tate had resigned as foreman. Mary had never fully recovered from the loss of their daughter during the tornado. Sonny had taken a job near Abilene so Mary could be near her family. There was no hesitation on Trent's part in appointing Biggun as foreman. That came as no surprise to any of the workers, and no one objected. Biggun had already earned their respect.

One afternoon in early November, the northern sky grew darker by the hour. The brutally cold north wind blew in like a blustering schoolyard bully.

"Trent, that blue norther's gonna be here by bedtime. I think I'll carry a load of hay out to the east pasture," Biggun said as he pulled on his heavy coat.

"Yeah, there may be a sheet of ice everywhere by morning, the way it looks. Take Zack with you. He can help unload the hay."

Zack heard his name and came running.

"Help Biggun take the hay to the east pasture," Trent said as he reached out and gave him a playful slap on the shoulder. During the past year, Zack had shot up and was as tall as his pa. "Get your hat," Trent reminded him.

Zack grinned at his pa. "Sure thing!"

Trent watched the two walking toward the farm truck. In another year,

Zack could outgrow him and be as tall as Biggun the way he was shooting up, he thought as a smile touched his lips. He was a damn good kid, Trent mused. He had to remind himself that Zack wasn't a kid anymore, but at seventeen, he was now a young man.

Jordon and Jonathan had turned thirteen, and Jordon took far more interest in the routine management of the ranch than his brother. Jonathan was more inclined to help Helen with the bookkeeping. That was fine as both were an important part of the ranch remaining successful. Trent viewed Joanna as a combination of her mother and Aunt Helen. She could certainly be sassy at times and did not hesitate to let anyone know her likes or dislikes of any particular matter, including him.

Zack was smart and a hard worker. He wanted to know everything possible about ranching. That pleased Trent as someday he would inherit part of this ranch just like his children by Sassy, Trent mused.

"When are you going to start letting me drive your truck? I've driven the other trucks lots of times," Zack half-teased Biggun.

"When you're as tall as me, I'll let you drive my truck," Biggun answered as he always did.

"What if I don't grow that tall?"

"I guess you won't get to drive my truck," Biggun teased as they bounced along in the truck.

"Watch out!" Zack almost yelled when he saw the truck headed toward a big rock.

"Now, don't go telling me how to drive, Mr. Smarty Pants," Biggun grumbled.

"Sorry, sir," Zack answered, feeling bad for his outburst.

By the time they unloaded the hay, it was almost dark. The overcast sky was bringing nighttime early. The howling north wind was making the temperature drop fast.

When they started to get in the truck, Biggun took Zack by the arm and pointed toward the driver's seat.

"Today! Now?" Zack asked in surprise.

"Guess we might as well get started in case you turn out to be a runt," Biggun laughed.

Zack pointed the truck toward headquarters.

"Turn on the lights," Biggun said.

They rarely drove the trucks after dark. Zack looked down to find the light switch.

"Watch out!" Biggun yelled just as the truck suddenly tilted to one side, momentarily hanging in mid-air at a precarious angle, before rolling to one side with a great crashing sound. The truck took several bounces before settling on the passenger's side. Glass spewed in every direction as the metal crunched.

Zack landed on top of Biggun. Both had the breath knocked out of them. Neither man could utter a sound. Then, Biggun let out a deep, rumbling moan as he caught his breath, wincing in pain.

"Zack," he wheezed, "are you hurt?"

"I don't think so," Zack answered as he started to move.

Biggun took in another deep breath. "Be careful. My arm is pinned under the top of the door," he said through gritted teeth.

"Oh, geez, I'm sorry, Biggun. Pa's going to have my hide when he finds out what happened," Zack answered with worry.

"Don't worry about that now. Just see if you can climb out and go get help."

Zack looked about to see how to go about getting out without hurting Biggun more. "You've got a bad cut on your forehead. It's bleeding bad," Zack said with concern. "I'll take my shirt off. Can you hold it to your head with your other hand to stop the bleeding?" Zack asked as he slipped off his coat and started unbuttoning his thick flannel shirt.

"Don't do that, it's too cold. You'll need all the warmth you can get going for help," Biggun gritted between moans.

"I'll still have my coat. I'll be running, so I'll be warm enough," Zack answered.

With as little twisting and turning as possible, Zack managed to get out of the long-sleeved shirt. Just as he turned to hand it to Biggun, he heard the man take in a sharp breath.

"Sorry, I was trying not to make the truck move," Zack said, worried.

"It's okay. Is that blood on your shoulder?" Biggun asked as he stared through the twilight at the dark red spot on Zack's shoulder.

"No, it's a birthmark," Zack answered. "It looks like a pear."

Biggun said nothing. He could not speak for the lump that filled his throat.

Biggun watched Zack climb out of the truck and start running. He felt tears sting his eyes as he lay in the oncoming darkness and shivered when the north wind gusted so hard the truck shook, sending shooting pain up his arm into his shoulder. The tears were not for the pain in his arm and shoulder but for the ache in his heart. When his good hand and arm would tire holding Zack's shirt to his head, he would let it rest on his broad chest. In the fading rays of light, he could see the shirt was soaked with his blood.

Biggun drifted in and out of consciousness. He saw Flossy in the twilight, smiling at him, opening her arms, and beckoning him to come to her. He felt overwhelming joy, knowing it was him she truly wanted. He would reach for her, and then she was gone, leaving only the dark shadows and a sadness he could not shake off. He shivered in the cold darkness and drifted far away.

Biggun did not hear the rattling of the farm truck as it came to a stop, nor did he hear Trent the first few times he called his name.

Eventually, he heard a far-away voice calling his name. This time, it was not Flossy beckoning to him.

"Biggun, Biggun! Can you hear me?" he heard Trent calling.

"I'm here," he managed to answer.

"We're going to set the truck up, so just hang on," Trent yelled.

"I'm ready," Biggun mumbled.

Within minutes, the truck was upright. Men were carrying Biggun to the cab of another truck. Trent held a flask to his mouth and told him to drink. Biggun expected whiskey but found warm chicken broth instead. The men climbed in the back as Trent slid behind the steering wheel.

"Where's Zack?" Biggun asked, still feeling weak.

"He wanted to come back, but I told him I knew about where you were. Sassy insisted he stay home and eat some hot soup to warm him up. He told me what happened, and I'm sure he thought I'd be plenty mad. I told him the most important thing was to get you home and tended to, and then we'd have a talk about what happened."

"Don't blame the boy. I was the one that let him drive," Biggun groaned as the truck bounced over a deep rut.

The two men were quiet for several minutes. Then Biggun broke the silence. "Trent, I discovered something about Zack that you need to know," Biggun said.

"Don't wear yourself out talking. You've lost a lot of blood. You can tell me later," Trent said.

"No, I need to tell you now, just in case somethin' happens to me."

Trent gave a nervous laugh. "I don't think you're about to die. You're just weak from losing blood."

"Listen to me anyway. Zack has my mark," Biggun said almost reverently.

"What are you talking about?" Trent asked as he glanced toward Biggun and saw the serious look on his face.

"Zack has the same pear-shaped birthmark on his shoulder that I have," Biggun said and tried to see Trent's face in the dim light.

Trent felt as though Biggun had hit him in the gut. Suddenly, he couldn't breathe; he felt light-headed as he gripped the steering wheel. He recalled seeing that strange birthmark on Biggun's shoulder years ago when they used to swim in the creek. Zack had always worn an undershirt when he went swimming so his fair skin wouldn't burn. Trent supposed no one had ever seen or noticed the birthmark Zack carried.

"How can that be? We have his birth certificate and—"

"All I know is Flossy came to me for comfort when you refused to have anything else to do with her after that one night. At first, I didn't intend for things to go as far as they did, but then I thought she was falling in love with me. Well, we became lovers. I wanted to marry her. Then, the next thing I knew, she was gone. I never heard from her again. I believed she had a good reason to think Zack was your child, but when I saw that birthmark today, I knew he was my son," he said as he let out a long breath.

Trent stared ahead, just trying to breathe. Finally, he cleared his throat.

"I don't doubt what you're saying, but I want to see that birthmark for myself."

"That's fine. What are we going to tell Zack?"

"Nothing for now. I'll hire an investigator to go find out more about his date of birth. There are ways to change birth dates."

When Trent told Sassy about what Biggun had discovered, she felt a great weight lifted from her soul. She felt vindicated for not loving Zack as Trent's child. She didn't say it aloud but thought Flossy was so desperate to catch Trent she would do whatever it took to snare him. She wanted to be a rich man's wife and her son to be a rich man's son. Well, thanks to Helen and an accident, it hadn't worked.

A few weeks later, Jack Harris, the private investigator, stood in Trent's office as Trent, Sassy, Helen, Ely, and Biggun sat around the big desk. He opened his briefcase and spread several pages of official-looking documents on the desk.

"This turned out to be a rather simple case. The story you heard about Flossy Tatum from her friend, Daisy Homes, was true except for the actual birth date of her son, Zack. It wasn't hard to track down the doctor who delivered Zack." He picked up one of the pieces of paper. "Doctor William Bloom is his name. Before the interview went very far, I realized the good doctor is an alcoholic. The right amount of booze and money loosened his tongue. He confessed to falsifying Zack's birth certificate. It seems Flossy paid him a sizable amount of money for the slip of his pen in filling out the birth record. His actual date of birth was twenty days later than his birth certificate shows. You folks can draw your own conclusions as to the rest of this story," Mr. Harris said kindly.

He picked up one of the documents and handed it to Trent. "This is the corrected birth certificate."

Trent stared at the birth record and handed it to Biggun.

After a few questions were answered, Mr. Harris excused himself from the meeting.

Everyone sat in silence for several moments. Trent cleared his throat.

"I suppose Biggun and I need to have a talk with Zack," he said as he rose from his big leather chair.

"What will you tell him?" Sassy asked.

Trent detected a note of anxiety in her voice.

"The truth," Trent answered emphatically. "Now's the time for him and Biggun to be together. I think it's only fair that he knows I am not his birth father and that he'll never inherit part of the Flatland Ranch." When Trent and Biggun reached the office door, Trent turned and looked at Helen and then at Sassy. "I think more than enough lies have been told around here," he stated as he and Biggun left.

The two men found Zack working one of the young colts in the first corral. They motioned for him to join them at the fence, out of earshot of the other men. The two explained the circumstances of Zack's birth and true parentage.

As the two men talked, it was obvious Zack was becoming agitated. The rejection his mother must have felt from Trent hit him full force. When they finished telling him the truth about his mother and who his actual father turned out to be, Zack looked from one to the other with contempt. Then he set his gaze on Trent.

"You threw my mother away when you were through with her, and now, you're doing the same to me," he said bitterly. "So, now, I'm just the hired help's son," he flung at them, his resentment flaring as he shouted at the two men.

Biggun felt his heart plummet when he saw and heard Zack's reaction. The same sadness he had felt when he learned Flossy didn't love him filled him again. He had hoped Zack would be proud to be his son. But why would he want to be just the son of the hired help? He tried to reason. Apparently, Zack was like his mother; she didn't want to be the wife of the hired help.

Before either man could answer, Zack vaulted over the fence and took long strides to one of the farm trucks. His back was rigid, and he never looked back. He sped away from them, leaving a plume of dirt swirling in his wake.

Zack cursed the two men as he pounded his fist against the steering wheel. "Well, Mr. Trent Sanderson, you may think I'll never own part of this ranch, but you could be very wrong," he shouted in anger. "I don't intend getting stuck just being the hired help's son," he seethed in rage and disappointment. He drove faster, letting his fury rule him. After a few miles, he slowed the truck and let it roll to a stop. Then he smiled. *I know exactly how I'll do it,* he thought as though he were talking to Trent. *I'll do what Sassy did. In a few years, I could marry your dear niece, Amanda, or marry your own daughter, Joanna. She might be a better choice,* he smirked. "Now, what will you think of that, Mr. Sanderson, you SOB!" Zack scoffed, knowing he still had a chance to own part of the Flatland and live in the big house with the rest of the Sanderson family. He didn't care about love. In his opinion, all it had gotten his mother was a broken heart. His entire life had been one big lie. His own mother had lied about who was his real father in hopes he would have a better life. Should he pity her or despise her for what she had done? That would take some deep soul searching through another day.

Zack had always had strong doubts about Sassy ever loving him as her stepson. She tried to pretend she cared, but he knew better.

Zack didn't need love; he needed status and respect as a somebody. "By damn, I'll make it happen one way or the other," he swore as he pounded the steering wheel again with his fist. "If it takes lies, then I'll lie through my teeth to get what I want. A few sweet lies to either of the girls should do the trick," he vowed as he turned the truck around and headed back to headquarters.

Chapter Thirty-Six

FIVE YEARS LATER, 1923

Zack caught sight of Joanna just as he was riding away from the homestead. "Hey, Joanna," he called. "Are you ready for the street dance tomorrow night?"

Joanna gave Zack a friendly wave and one of her bright smiles. "Sure am. Got a pretty, new dress to wear."

Zack let out a wolf whistle as he rode out the gate, grinning to himself. *Yeah, and I'll have a heck of a time keeping all those randy cowboys treating you with respect instead of trying to get you off in the dark.*

For the past five years, Zack had been carefully molding his plan to marry into the Sanderson family and become a somebody like his mother had tried so desperately to do. He wasn't going to spend his life just being a hired hand like Biggun had done. To his way of thinking, Biggun had missed a golden opportunity by not courting Helen after her fiancé threw her over. Trent would have likely welcomed his longtime friend with open arms. Oh well, apparently, Biggun wasn't as ambitious as his mother had been. Flossy had planted the seeds of desire to be a somebody for as long as he could remember.

Zack had spent his time working harder than anybody else to prove he would be worthy enough to marry into the family. He had not only worked long hours but had also learned as much as possible about the ranching business and beyond. Last year, they had struck oil on the ranch, and the money kept rolling in. Zack expanded his plan by learning as much as he could about the oil business. He likely knew more about the Flatland Ranch than Sandy, Jonathan, or Jordon. Sandy never cared about ranching and had already started planning a military career. Jordon liked the day-to-day running of the ranch, and Jonathan was far more interested in helping Helen with the ranch accounts. That was fine with Zack, as he figured he was likely smarter than the three of them put together.

Zack pulled up to the front gate in Helen and Ely's new Lincoln L Touring Car. It was a beauty-long body, painted dark green with a black top. Zack felt like he was a somebody when Ely told him to use the car when he escorted the girls to the local barn dances or the street dances in town.

Zack had worked hard to gain the trust of the two fathers. Now, it was getting close to time to make his move. When Amanda and Joanna were together, it was easier to judge which one of the girls he could tolerate best as a wife. If his first choice didn't work out, then he would settle for number two. Both girls were pretty, and each had a pleasant personality most of the time.

Amanda was a year older than Joanna and had a more settled disposition. Her dark hair was almost black like her father's, and she had deep blue eyes. Her features were soft, like her mother's. She was tall for a girl, about five foot eight inches. That was no problem since he was over six feet tall. They made good dance partners.

Joanna was high-spirited, slender, and well developed where it counted. Her hair was flaxen blonde from the summer sun, and her eyes reminded him of the light blue forget-me-not flowers growing in one of the flower beds near the house. She was also a flirt, which kept Zack's attention, protecting her from getting mixed up with the wrong men.

As the girls approached, Zack stood holding the car door open for them. "Now, aren't you two about the prettiest gals in Texas," he teased.

Joanna twirled around to show off her new pink dress with its full skirt, perfect for dancing. Well brought up young women no longer were expected to wear their dresses long, but the hemline was only a few inches above their ankles. "Does that mean you've already met all the girls in Texas?" Joanna quipped.

Amanda laughed as she slid to the middle of the front seat. "From the looks of the girls around here vying for his attention, it probably wouldn't take him long if he decided to."

"I'm glad you noticed my popularity. You should be grateful to have me as your escort," Zack answered.

"Oh, I don't know, some of the other cowboys are pretty good-looking," Joanna taunted.

"Oh, yeah, could it be Bronco Bob with snuff dripped on his shirt and his odiferous smell?" Amanda laughed, and the other two joined in.

"Just remember to stay in the main dance area so I can find you. No sneaking around back of any building with some fast-talking guy," Zack said with a chuckle, but the girls knew he meant it. At the second dance he had taken them to, he had spied Joanna headed out to a car with some guy. When he caught up to them just before they got in the car, he threatened to send the fellow home with a broken jaw. Then he turned his ire on Joanna. "Do you want me to drag you home by the hair of your head and let you tell your parents what you were up to?" he hissed through gritted teeth. Of course, Joanna had promised it would never happen again. Zack would make damn sure it didn't, in case she was the one he decided to marry. The following dances had gone fine, but Zack was always on the lookout for trouble. He knew all too well how people lied, especially lustful guys, to get what they wanted.

Zack glanced at his watch and saw there was likely time for only a couple of dances before the dance would end. He glanced around and saw Amanda being escorted to the edge of the street. "Amanda," he called as he headed toward her. "Have you seen Joanna lately?"

Amanda pointed, and Zack caught sight of her not far away. "How about we dance these last songs," he suggested as he reached out his hand. Amanda slid her hand into his as he swung her into the crowd of dancers. "You look mighty pretty tonight. Is that a new dress you have on?" he asked.

Amanda looked at him with disgust. "Really now! Do you know how many times I've heard those same words tonight?"

Zack felt a bit embarrassed. Did all men use the same lines to flatter the girls? He questioned. He grinned to cover his mistake. "How many?"

Amanda rolled her eyes. "At least six or seven."

"Wow! I really didn't mean it as a line to flatter you."

Amanda smiled as her dark eyes twinkled. "Try to be more original next time," she kidded.

Zack stared at her for a few seconds, then he grinned. "There may not be a next time after that goof." They both laughed as he drew her near for the final dance, a waltz. He looked down at her lovely face. "If we were alone, I think I might kiss you," he whispered.

Amanda smiled. "I think if we were alone, I would let you," she answered sweetly.

During the summer, Amanda was a bit surprised at how much she looked forward to dancing with Zack. With Zack, she didn't feel she needed to pretend she believed that line he had used or that she was interested in what he was saying. She was interested in what Zack had to say. It was a bit frightening, but she realized she had developed a crush on Zack. She had known him since childhood, but lately, she had noticed how hard he worked. He seemed very smart. He knew all about the ranch and the oil business. On top of that, his keen green eyes and auburn hair made his looks unique and very alluring. He was tall and thin but had developed plenty of muscles because of the ranch work he did for hours almost daily. She often found herself daydreaming about Zack and trying to figure out ways to get his attention without being too obvious.

Joanna thought Zack was, without a doubt, the cutest guy around and openly vied for his attention. She wasn't shy about going after what she wanted, and then, maybe when she was a little older, they would really, really fall in love and get married. This summer, she had decided Zack was exactly who she wanted for her number one boyfriend. She suspected her cousin liked Zack a lot. The way she saw it was to let the best girl win, and she had no qualms about running over anyone who got in her way.

A few days later, Joanna saw Zack headed toward one of the corrals to get his horse.

"Hey, Zack, where you headed this afternoon?" she called from the back steps.

"Going to check fences," he answered.

"There's nothing to do here," she pointed toward the house. "Can I ride with you?" she pleaded sweetly.

"It's going to get mighty hot, and I can't bring you back," he said.

"I promise I won't complain," she said with one of her charming smiles.

"Ok, go tell your mom where you're going. I'll saddle your horse."

Joanna was almost to the corral when Zack came out leading their horses. "Good," he said. "I see you got a hat and canteen," he grinned. She was also wearing rather form-fitting riding britches and a pretty, pink checked blouse. Pink seemed to be her favorite color, and it made her complexion glow.

They rode and chatted. Zack would dismount occasionally to check a fence and tighten wires. About two hours into their ride, they reached one of the small lakes on the property.

"Oh, that water looks cool and inviting!" Joanna exclaimed.

"If you don't mind getting your clothes wet, we can go for a swim," Zack suggested. He was ready to cool off.

Joanna gave him a coquettish grin. "Who says I have to get my clothes wet? Just turn your back for a few minutes."

Zack turned his back and took off his shirt. He heard a splash and Joanna laughing. "It's wonderful. Come on in," she coaxed.

Zack saw her pile of clothes on the ground and hoped her undergarments were not underneath. He waded into the cool water and did a shallow dive, coming up near Joanna. Before he could say anything, she splashed him in the face, and the war was on.

Growing up with two brothers and a boy cousin, Joanna had learned at an early age to hold her own. She didn't back away from water fights, snowball fights, or doing her best to outshoot the boys. At least half of the time, she had been the instigator of mischief. That had always amused Zack, and now she was bombarding him with huge onslaughts of water. He dove under the water and quickly swam behind her. He came up before she figured out where he had gone and wound his arms tightly around her, rendering her powerless.

"Let's hear it, Joanna."

"Hear what?" she laughed and tried to wriggle out of his hold.

Zack instantly caught his breath, thinking this tactic might have been a mistake. "I surrender my flag!" he reminded her. As children, they had each carried their personal flag into battle. Most were made from worn-out towels or part of an old quilt. The overall winner was determined by who captured the most flags. Often, it turned out to be Joanna.

"Oh, no! If I give you a token, can I keep my flag?" she carried on with the game.

"Um, it better be a really special token," Zack taunted.

Joanna instantly turned in his arms, threw her arms around his neck, and kissed him. Before he could react, she kissed him again with a long, seductive kiss as she pressed her scantily clad body against his firm chest.

The kiss was very tempting, enticing Zack to want to carry things further, but he knew he could never let that happen. If he decided on Joanna, he wanted to be welcomed into her family. If they kept on and he got her pregnant, he would never be allowed to fit in. He would be the outcast son-in-law, a nobody.

Zack pulled Joanna's arms from around his neck and swam back several feet.

"Joanna, you're very attractive and a seductive young woman," he said in a husky tone. "You need to be more cautious about how you behave around men."

"Be more cautious," she repeated. She gave him a puzzled look as though she didn't understand what he meant.

"Yeah, tone it down, Joanna."

"It's just you, Zack, that I don't want to be so ladylike around," she answered. "Haven't you figured it out? I'm crazy about you," she readily admitted.

"No, I hadn't realized you had feelings for me. But even so, we can't get carried away. If I got you in trouble, your folks would hate me," he paused. "You don't want that to happen. Our lives would be miserable," he finished in a serious mood.

"Don't you know how to do it and not get me in trouble? How can we be sure we're really suited for one another unless we, you know?" Joanna asked, a bit uncertain.

"Joanna, most people get married before they fool around. And no, I don't know how to do it and be certain you won't get pregnant," Zack answered, a bit exasperated, and he didn't want this conversation to continue.

"It's time to go," he said a bit sharply.

A few days later, Zack saw Amanda walking with the Patton children toward one of the pens to see a new foal.

"Hey, Amanda, what are you doing with all these little Pattons?" he teased.

"They wanted to go see the new foal," she answered.

"Where's Timmy," Zack asked. "He's the horse lover," he stated.

"Timmy got a high fever during the night. Sue couldn't get it down. She and Hank have taken him to town to the doctor."

Zack let out a low whistle. "Sorry to hear that," he said.

"Where are you headed?" Amanda asked, wishing she could go with him.

"West, looking for some strays."

"Looks like you might run into a little rain," Amanda commented.

Zack gazed to the west. "That's ok, may cool me off," he chuckled. "See you later," he waved to the group as he rode off.

He kept a close watch on the approaching rain and decided it was moving fast, so it wouldn't last long. He saw no need to get out his slicker. He had ridden a couple of miles when he felt the first cool drops of rain.

Ah, that feels good on this hot afternoon, he thought. He rode on, enjoying the refreshing rain. Seconds later, he heard the earsplitting clap of thunder and, at the same time, saw a brilliant flash of lightning strike the ground no more than twenty feet away. His horse reared, twirling in fright, and Zack was dashed to the hard-packed ground. Zack lay motionless and unaware as the chilly drops of rain pelted him.

Sometime later, he opened his eyes. The rain was gone. The sky was almost clear except for the dazzling colors of double rainbows. Zack felt so strongly that he could reach up and touch the vivid colors of the one nearest him that he lifted his hand. Then he realized that had been a misguided thought. Zack didn't want to move. He wanted to drink in every magnificent detail of the two rainbows. One so brilliant, the other a bit faded. *What is the significance of the two rainbows?* He tried to reason out their intent. Sassy and Helen had often read Bible stories to him and the other kids. He knew the story of Noah and the meaning of one rainbow, but what about two. *There must be some vital point to the two rainbows.* His head ached, and tiredness overtook him. He closed his eyes.

"Zack, Zack, can you hear me?" he heard Biggun's voice from far away. "Zack, open your eyes, son," he heard the big man plead as he gently shook his shoulder. *That sounded strange. Biggun never called him son.*

It was a struggle, but Zack managed with great effort to open his eyes. He looked at the face of an uneasy man. "Hi, Biggun. What you doing here?"

"When your horse showed up without you, we got worried. Thought we better come see what happened. Some of the fellows are out searching, too," Biggun explained. "How long you been lying here?" Biggun asked with real concern since Zack hadn't tried to move.

"Not sure," Zack answered.

"Can you move, son?"

There it was again, son. "You never called me son before," Zack said gently as he began to move toward a sitting position.

Biggun looked self-conscious as he ducked his head. "No, I reckon not," he admitted.

"Well, I kind of like it, Pa," Zack grinned as he reached for Biggun's hand to help him up. The two men stood just looking at one another and then embraced as though they had just met after a long absence.

Zack sat under a tree near the bunkhouse, enjoying the cool evening after the brief rain. His thoughts kept returning to the double rainbows, and finally, he believed he had figured out the meaning for him. For five years, he had been planning to marry Amanda or Joanna so he could be a rich somebody. He smiled to himself. Today, as he lay looking up at the rainbows, several things had happened. He had gained insight and realized he didn't need to marry money to be somebody. He was already a somebody. He didn't want to spend the rest of his life living a lie like his mother had done. She found no happiness in life because she couldn't or wouldn't let go of the lies. When he had learned the truth, it had been hard to accept that Trent was not his father, a rich man and half-owner of a huge, successful ranch. Now, he realized the truth. His real father was a fine, hard-working, honorable man. Honor, that was what he really wanted. It had been in front of him for years. Trent was an honorable man, and so was Biggun. Why had it taken him so long to see it?

Something else had happened today, and he was going to take care of it tonight. He would be honest, and if things worked out, he would be forever grateful to God.

Zack stood, stretched his sore muscles, and walked toward the front of the big house. Another thought dawned on him. *It took nearly getting struck by lightning to knock some sense into me.*

He couldn't help but laugh at his own foolishness and seeing life as it really was.

When he reached the top step, he could hear several voices coming from the living room. Zack knocked, out of courtesy, and opened the door.

Seated in the living room were Trent, Helen, and Jordon.

"Come in," Trent invited. "Glad to see you looking better than when Biggun brought you home."

"Thanks, Trent."

Zack cleared his throat. "I'd like to talk to Amanda, out on the porch," he said to the three.

Jordon called out to his cousin. "Amanda, Zack's here to see you, on the front porch," he finished in a tongue-in-cheek manner.

When Amanda came into the room, Joanna was right behind her.

"Joanna," Trent said, "he only asked for Amanda."

Joanna looked a bit surprised, but then her dad's words sunk in.

When Amanda saw Zack standing beside the door, she couldn't suppress her smile. Their eyes met; Zack gently took her hand, drew her outside, and closed the door.

Trent awoke later that night and lay for a while looking at the brilliant moonlight shining through the windows. He rose quietly, in hopes he wouldn't disturb Sassy. He walked to the window seat and sat so he could see the magnificent vista. The full moon shone so brightly it almost looked like daylight.

"What are you doing?" Sassy asked softly as she walked toward him.

"I'm looking at God's awesome creations," he answered. Trent pulled Sassy to him and sat her on his lap. "Just look at that bright moon and millions and millions of stars and our land. I am a blessed man, and I'm especially grateful for you, Sassy," he whispered as he hugged the woman he loved more than he had the words to tell her.

"Yes, Trent, we do have so much to be thankful for. I love you, my dear husband," she smiled, and their lips met in a kiss of endearment.

About the Author

Judy McGonagill is a native Texan and loves the rich history of the Lone Star State. Judy grew up in a small town where church and school were the focus of the community. She has been married to her beloved husband for many years and has two adult sons. She is a retired teacher with an interest in history and enjoys writing historical novels.

www.ingramcontent.com/pod-product-compliance
Lightning Source LLC
Chambersburg PA
CBHW020540020726
47494CB00006B/1854